P9-DCC-381

HAZARDOUS DUTY

ALSO BY W.E.B. GRIFFIN

HONOR BOUND

HONOR BOUND
BLOOD AND HONOR
SECRET HONOR
DEATH AND HONOR
(and William E. Butterworth IV)
THE HONOR OF SPIES
(and William E. Butterworth IV)
VICTORY AND HONOR
(and William E. Butterworth IV)
EMPIRE AND HONOR
(and William E. Butterworth IV)

BROTHERHOOD OF WAR

BOOK I: THE LIEUTENANTS
BOOK II: THE CAPTAINS
BOOK III: THE MAJORS
BOOK IV: THE COLONELS
BOOK V: THE BERETS
BOOK VI: THE GENERALS
BOOK VII: THE NEW BREED
BOOK VIII: THE AVIATORS
BOOK IX: SPECIAL OPS

THE CORPS

BOOK I: SEMPER FI
BOOK II: CALL TO ARMS
BOOK III: COUNTERATTACK
BOOK IV: BATTLEGROUND
BOOK V: LINE OF FIRE
BOOK VI: CLOSE COMBAT
BOOK VII: BEHIND THE LINES
BOOK VIII: IN DANGER'S PATH
BOOK IX: UNDER FIRE
BOOK X: RETREAT, HELL!

BADGE OF HONOR

BOOK I: MEN IN BLUE
BOOK II: SPECIAL OPERATIONS
BOOK III: THE VICTIM
BOOK IV: THE WITNESS
BOOK V: THE ASSASSIN
BOOK VI: THE MURDERERS
BOOK VII: THE INVESTIGATORS
BOOK VIII: FINAL JUSTICE
BOOK IX: THE TRAFFICKERS
(and William E. Butterworth IV)
BOOK X: THE VIGILANTES
(and William E. Butterworth IV)
BOOK XI: THE LAST WITNESS
(and William E. Butterworth IV)

MEN AT WAR

BOOK I: THE LAST HEROES
BOOK II: THE SECRET WARRIORS
BOOK III: THE SOLDIER SPIES
BOOK IV: THE FIGHTING AGENTS
BOOK V: THE SABOTEURS
(and William E. Butterworth IV)
BOOK VI: THE DOUBLE AGENTS
(and William E. Butterworth IV)
BOOK VII: THE SPYMASTERS
(and William E. Butterworth IV)

PRESIDENTIAL AGENT

BOOK I: BY ORDER OF THE PRESIDENT
BOOK II: THE HOSTAGE
BOOK III: THE HUNTERS
BOOK IV: THE SHOOTERS
BOOK V: BLACK OPS
BOOK VI: THE OUTLAWS
(and William E. Butterworth IV)
BOOK VII: COVERT WARRIORS
(and William E. Butterworth IV)

HAZARDOUS DUTY

W.E.B. GRIFFIN

AND WILLIAM E. BUTTERWORTH IV

G. P. PUTNAM'S SONS
NEW YORK

PUTNAM

G. P. PUTNAM'S SONS
Publishers Since 1838
Published by the Penguin Group
Penguin Group (USA) LLC
375 Hudson Street
New York, New York 10014

USA · Canada · UK · Ireland · Australia
New Zealand · India · South Africa · China

penguin.com
A Penguin Random House Company

Library of Congress Cataloging-in-Publication Data

Griffin, W.E.B.
Hazardous duty / W.E.B Griffin and William E. Butterworth IV.
p. cm.—(A presidential agent novel; 8)
ISBN 978-0-399-16067-7
1. Castillo, Charley (Fictitious character)—Fiction. 2. United States. Army. Delta Force—Fiction. 3. Undercover operations—Fiction. 4. International relations—Fiction. I. Butterworth, William E. (William Edmund). II. Title.
PS3557. R489137H39 2013 2013029657
813'.54—dc23

Printed in the United States of America
1 3 5 7 9 10 8 6 4 2

26 July 1777

The necessity of procuring good intelligence is apparent and need not be further urged.

George Washington
General and Commander in Chief
The Continental Army

FOR THE LATE

William E. Colby
An OSS Jedburgh First Lieutenant
who became director of the Central Intelligence Agency.

Aaron Bank
An OSS Jedburgh First Lieutenant
who became a colonel and the father of Special Forces.

William R. Corson
A legendary Marine intelligence officer
whom the KGB hated more than any other U.S. intelligence officer—
and not only because he wrote the definitive work on them.

René J. Défourneaux
A U.S. Army OSS Second Lieutenant attached to the British SOE
who jumped into occupied France alone
and later became a legendary U.S. Army intelligence officer.

FOR THE LIVING

Billy Waugh
A legendary Special Forces Command Sergeant Major
who retired and then went on to hunt down the infamous Carlos the Jackal.
Billy could have terminated Osama bin Laden in the early 1990s
but could not get permission to do so.
After fifty years in the business, Billy is still going after the bad guys.

Johnny Reitzel
An Army Special Operations officer
who could have terminated the head terrorist
of the seized cruise ship *Achille Lauro* but could not
get permission to do so.

Ralph Peters
An Army intelligence officer
who has written the best analysis of our war against terrorists
and of our enemy that I have ever seen.

AND FOR THE NEW BREED

Marc L
A senior intelligence officer, despite his youth,
who reminds me of Bill Colby more and more each day.

Frank L
A legendary Defense Intelligence Agency officer
who retired and now follows in Billy Waugh's footsteps.

OUR NATION OWES THESE PATRIOTS
A DEBT BEYOND REPAYMENT.

I

[ONE]

The James S. Brady Press Briefing Room
The White House
1600 Pennsylvania Avenue, N.W.
Washington, D.C.
1315 5 June 2007

"I will take one last question," President Joshua Ezekiel Clendennen announced from behind the podium. He pointed. "Mr. Danton, there in the back."

President Clendennen, a pudgy, pale-skinned fifty-two-year-old Alabaman who kept his tiny ears hidden under a full head of silver hair, was, kindly, not very tall. If he had not been standing on a small platform behind the podium it would have hidden him from the White House Press Corps.

As Roscoe J. Danton—a tall, starting-to-get-a-little-plump thirty-eight-year-old—rose to his feet he thought, *The sonofabitch got me!*

Roscoe J. Danton, of the *Washington Times-Post* Writers Syndicate, as his byline read, was, depending on to whom one might talk, either near the bottom of the list of first-tier Washington journalists, or at the very top of the second tier.

Roscoe was surprised—even startled—that the President had honored him by selecting him to pose the last question of the press conference. For one thing, his hand had not been one of those raised in the sea of hands begging, like so many third-graders having urgent need of permission to visit the restroom, for the President's attention.

Moreover, Danton had good reason to believe that the President could not be counted among his legion of fans. He had often heard the President refer to him as "that pissant," which Roscoe had learned from *The Oxford Un-Abridged Dictionary of the English Language* was Alabama-speak for, *one who is irritating or contemptible out of proportion to his or her significance.*

The first thing Roscoe thought when called upon was that he had fallen asleep, and the President, seeing this, had seen it as an opportunity to embarrass him. Clendennen liked to embarrass people, and did so often.

Roscoe thought it was entirely possible that he had dozed off. He was not in the briefing room to make notes on what the President would say but rather because it was one of the very few places in Washington where Miss Eleanor Dillworth could not follow him.

Miss Dillworth, who brought to her stalking techniques her twenty-seven years' experience in the Clandestine Service of the Central Intelligence Agency, had been lurking in a dark corner of the bar in the Old Ebbitt Grill on Fifteenth Street, N.W.—around the corner from the White House—at noon when Roscoe had entered for his breakfast Bloody Mary.

He managed to make it to the White House press conference safely, thus sparing himself from being presented with yet another cornucopia of unpleasant revelations vis-à-vis the CIA Miss Dillworth wanted to bring to the attention of the American people via Roscoe's columns, which were published in more than three hundred newspapers in the United States and around the world.

Miss Dillworth, Roscoe had learned some months ago when he first met her, was a disgruntled former employee who had been relieved of her position as CIA station chief in Vienna, Austria—and later fired—for bungling the defection of two very senior officers of the SVR—the Russian Service for the Protection of the Constitutional System, renamed from KGB.

Since meeting Miss Dillworth, and becoming close—he often thought "much too uncomfortably close"—to others involved in the incident, Roscoe had come to the conclusion that the facts were not quite as she presented them and that she royally deserved getting the boot from the CIA.

But, surprising Roscoe not at all—there was a former Mrs. Roscoe Danton who was also highly intelligent, strong-willed, and found it impossible to accept that she could ever do anything wrong even if the facts clearly proved otherwise—Miss Dillworth was determined to wreak havoc on the CIA and had selected Roscoe as her instrument to do so.

"Well, Mr. Danton?" the President asked, flashing his famous benign smile.

Danton's brain went on autopilot. He heard his words as they came out of his mouth.

"I was wondering, Mr. President, how goes your unrelenting war on drugs and piracy?"

That ought to fix you, you bastard!

You know as well as I do that you're losing it.

"Unmitigated disaster" is a gross understatement.

The President's benign smile widened as he replied.

"I'm glad you asked that, Roscoe," the President replied. "I didn't have a chance to get into that earlier in the press conference."

I recognize that "gotcha" smile!

And I wouldn't be getting it unless he somehow got me again. But how?

I'll be goddamned!

That had to be the one question he didn't want to "get into earlier."

Or ever.

"Just as soon as this press conference is over," the President went on, "I'm going to meet with members of my Cabinet, and other senior officials, to deal with those wars. I'll be the first to admit they haven't been going well, and frankly, I think it's time for everyone to start thinking out of the box."

That's my cue to ask for a follow-up question.

And whatever the question is—such as "How high is the moon?"—the answer will be whatever he already plans to say.

He's playing me like a violin.

"Follow-up, Mr. President?" Roscoe asked.

"Roscoe," the President said in a gently chiding tone, "we've known one another more than long enough for you to know that I always say what I mean and always mean what I say. I said 'one last question' and that's what I meant."

"Thank you, Mr. President," Robin Hoboken, the presidential press secretary, said. President Clendennen disappeared for a moment as he stepped off the stool behind the podium and then reappeared a moment later marching purposefully out of the room.

Mr. Hoboken was new on the job. His predecessor, Press Secretary Clemens McCarthy, had died in a spectacular explosion. The White House Yukon sport utility vehicle in which he was riding had collided as it approached Andrews Air Force Base with a huge tank of butane mounted on a sixteen-wheeler tractor trailer. The resultant fireball had incinerated McCarthy and Secret Service Agent Mark Douglas, and closed down the Beltway for two days.

Roscoe had heard a story that it was no tragic accident, that both men had been agents of the SVR and disposed of by a CIA dinosaur. The story would have been incredible on its face except that Roscoe had very good reason to believe the same CIA dinosaur had disposed of a treasonous CIA agent by sticking an ice pick in his ear in the CIA parking lot in Langley, Virginia, and also that Miss Eleanor Dillworth believed deep in her soul that the same dinosaur had expressed his displeasure with her and the Russian SVR *rezident* in Vienna by leaving the garroted corpse of the latter sitting in a taxi outside the U.S. embassy in Vienna with her official calling card on his chest.

Robin Hoboken was a pleasant, Ivy League–type young man who didn't look like he could be an SVR agent, but neither had Clemens McCarthy or Mark Douglas. For that matter, the dinosaur in question didn't look like someone who had more notches on his gun, figuratively speaking, for disposing of SVR agents than Clint Eastwood ever had in the bloodiest of his spaghetti western motion pictures.

Roscoe believed, however, that Mr. Hoboken couldn't help but be carrying the weight of an odd family. What kind of people would name an innocent baby boy Robin? That was even worse than Mr. Cash trying to hang "Sue" on his son Johnny.

Roscoe went to the front of the room and patiently waited for his turn at the ear of Mr. Hoboken. Finally, it came:

"Is that all you've got for me on this 'out of the box' thinking the President mentioned?"

"I'm not sure I understand the question, Mr. Danton."

"Did the leader of the free world give you anything else about his out-of-the-box thinking about his unrelenting wars against the drug trade and piracy, to be slipped to me when no one else was looking?"

"Of course not!" Robin Hoboken said. "Anything else, Mr. Danton?"

"Does the term 'dinosaur' have any meaning for you?"

Robin thought it over, then shook his head and said, "No. It doesn't. Should it?"

"I heard a story that some dinosaurs are still alive," Roscoe said.

"I don't think that's possible."

"Check into it for me, will you, and send me an e-mail?"

"All right."

You and I both know, Robin, that you're going to "forget to do that" the moment you leave this room.

Pity. If you asked around you might have learned that within the intelligence community, dinosaurs are those politically incorrect clandestine service old-timers who believe that the only good Communist is a dead Communist.

That would have given you something to worry about: "Why did that pissant Danton ask me about dinosaurs?"

"Thanks, Robin."

Then they went their separate ways, which in the case of Mr. Danton meant that he walked back to the Old Ebbitt Grill, checked to make sure Miss Dillworth was no longer there, and then went in for his breakfast Bloody Mary.

[TWO]

The Cabinet Room
The White House
1600 Pennsylvania Avenue, N.W.
Washington, D.C.
1330 5 June 2007

The Cabinet Room, which is off the Oval Office, looked practically deserted when the President, following Supervisory Secret Service Agent Robert J. Mulligan, walked in. Everyone in it could have easily been seated comfortably in the Oval Office.

President Clendennen preferred to hold meetings of the type he was about to convene in the Cabinet Room, even if there were just a few—say, four or five—people involved.

This afternoon, there were nine senior officers sitting at the long mahogany table—a gift of former President Richard Nixon, although this was rarely mentioned—waiting for the President. They were Secretary of State Natalie Cohen, who was in a chair to the right of the President's chair. The chair on the right of that was empty. Vice President Charles W. Montvale sat next to the empty chair, which most of the people at the table thought of as "Belinda-Sue's throne."

Sitting across the table from them were Frederick P. Palmer, United States attorney general, Director of National Intelligence Truman C. Ellsworth, CIA Director A. Franklin Lammelle, Secretary of Defense Frederick K. Beiderman, FBI Director Mark Schmidt, and General Allan B. Naylor, commander in chief of the U.S. Central Command.

They were a diverse group of very intelligent—one might even say brilliant—and powerful people who really agreed on only one thing vis-à-vis President Joshua Ezekiel Clendennen.

Secretary Cohen—she was of course a diplomat—had admitted in a very private conversation with the CIA director that she had been forced to the conclusion that the President had "some mental problems." CIA Director Lammelle, who was not a diplomat, had replied that he had concluded, based on the same criteria, that the Commander in Chief was "absolutely bonkers, as mad as the legendary March hare."

The opinions of the others were somewhere between these two extremes, but all were agreed the President's mental health was a serious problem.

There is, of course, provision in the law for the removal from office of a President who is physically incapable of performing his duties, and this is understood to include mental illness, although those words do not appear. No one likes to admit that a President might become, to use Mr. Lammelle's phraseology, absolutely bonkers.

Each of the people in the Cabinet Room was familiar with previous problems of Presidents who left, or should have left, office before their successor was sworn in on Inauguration Day. Obviously, these included Richard M. Nixon, who ultimately resigned, and William Jefferson Clinton, who had to face an impeachment trial in the Senate but managed to hold on to his job.

And there were other cases of Presidents whose physical condition raised serious questions about their ability to properly discharge their duties.

Woodrow Wilson, for example, was one of these. Many people believed that after suffering a massive debilitating stroke in 1919 he should have resigned and allowed the Vice President to assume his duties. Instead, he stayed on in the White House and allowed his wife, the former Edith Bolling Galt, to determine which visitors he saw, and which he did not, and which papers were presented to him for his approval, and which were not, leading his detractors to refer to his wife as the "first unelected President."

Whenever anyone at the Cabinet table thought of biting the bullet and getting rid of Joshua Ezekiel Clendennen by making his psychological problems public, the face of First Lady Mrs. Belinda-Sue Clendennen popped into their minds.

From the moment—and perhaps even before—her husband had acceded to the presidency following the sudden demise of his predecessor from a ruptured aortal aneurysm, Belinda-Sue had had her eyes on the vice presidency and perhaps—even probably—the presidency itself.

The first clue to this came when Belinda-Sue sat down on her throne at her husband's very first Cabinet meeting as President. As soon as she could get the secretary of State alone, she opened a conversation dealing with the political history of the Argentine Republic, especially that of its president, Juan Domingo Perón.

"Do you know that President Perón appointed his wife," Belinda-Sue began, "not the blonde, Evita, the other one, the redheaded one, Isabel, to be vice president?"

"Circumstances in Argentina are somewhat different than they are here, Mrs. Clendennen."

"You can call me Belinda-Sue, honey," Mrs. Clendennen said. "And I'll call you Natalie."

The secretary had smiled wanly but had not replied.

Mrs. Clendennen's ambitions regarding the vice presidency had had to be put on hold when her husband was forced to appoint

Charles W. Montvale to that office. His only other option was to face impeachment charges in the Congress for a number of offenses. One of these, for example, was described by the attorney general as so egregious that its "illegality boggled the mind."

But she had by no means abandoned them, which everyone in the Cabinet Room had to consider very carefully when they thought about getting President Clendennen out of the White House.

So long as her husband was President, there was the possibility that Vice President Montvale would suffer a rupture of his aorta, or get run over by a truck, thus making the office of vice president vacant once again. If something like that happened, God forbid, Belinda-Sue wanted to be available.

The people in the Cabinet Room today had decided—not in a formal meeting, but in an interlocking series of private conversations between no more than three of them at a time—that the best, and probably only, way to deal with the situation was to do nothing and hope for the best.

The President's aorta was reported to be in absolutely no danger of rupturing, and it was highly unlikely that he would get run over by a bus, but hope, someone said, springs eternal in the human breast.

Eventually the President's term of office would expire. In the meantime, they would just have to live with him and with Belinda-Sue attempting—with only slight success—to decide who got to see her husband, and who did not, and what documents of state were—and were not—presented to him for his signature.

In the meantime, they would pretend the President was sane, and that the First Lady was indeed the twenty-first-century embodiment of Martha Washington, which was, she had confided to her friend Natalie, how she often thought of herself.

Everyone stood as the President walked from the door to the Oval Office to his chair.

"Good afternoon," he said, flashing his benign smile. "Please be seated."

Everyone sat down and looked at him expectantly.

"Inasmuch as the First Lady had to go to Mississippi to deal with a family medical problem and won't be with us, we might as well get started," the President said.

"I hope it's nothing serious, Mr. President," Secretary of Defense Frederick K. Beiderman said solicitously.

Freddy, CIA Director A. Franklin Lammelle thought, *you know as well as I do that means that Belinda-Sue's mother has once again escaped from the Ocean Springs Baptist Assisted Living facility and is now holed up somewhere they can't find her with three Mason jars full of Mississippi's finest 140-proof white lightning.*

"Nothing serious," the President said. "A recurring problem."

Usually recurring about once a month, Lammelle thought.

Well, at least Belinda-Sue won't be here to offer her solutions to the nation's problems.

"I have been thinking . . ." President Clendennen began.

Oh, shit! We're in trouble!

". . . about our war on the drug trade and piracy."

Double shit! In spades!

"And I have concluded we should start thinking out of the box," he went on. "And, doing that, I have come up with an idea that I want your wholehearted cooperation in implementing."

How bad can this get?

"Specifically, I think we should involve Lieutenant Colonel Castillo."

What did he say?

Lammelle looked at Secretary of State Cohen, whose eyes were rolling.

That's involuntary. Natalie plays the game of life with a poker face Las Vegas gamblers would kill for.

"Now, that may surprise some of you, but surprise is what you get when you start thinking out of the box," the President went on. "And this will surprise you even more, but after thinking about it at length, I've concluded that my predecessor had a pretty good idea when he first involved Colonel Castillo in affairs of state.

"When that diplomat was kidnapped in Argentina, my predecessor wanted a knowledgeable, objective observer to see how the situation was being handled, and to report his observations and recommendations directly to him.

"He bungled the carrying out of the idea, as we all know, but the idea was sound. If he had given Colonel Castillo the proper supervision, everything would have worked out fine. I won't repeat that mistake. I'm very good at supervising people. Hands-on is how I think of it.

"How soon can we get him in here?"

No one replied.

"General Naylor?"

"Mr. President, Colonel Castillo is retired."

"What's that got to do with anything? He can be recalled to active duty."

"Yes, sir, Mr. President, in 'extraordinary circumstances' Colonel Castillo could be recalled to hazardous active duty."

"General, would you call Mexican drug cartels shooting up the streets of Laredo and El Paso—my God, the next thing you know they'll be doing that in Biloxi—ordinary circumstances? Not to mention Somali pirates holding three of our tankers for ransom? Call Colonel Castillo to active duty and get him in here. Where is he?"

"I don't really know, Mr. President," General Naylor confessed.

"What about you, Mr. Ellsworth?" the President asked. "Does my director of National Intelligence know where Colonel Castillo is?"

"I have some unconfirmed reports that he's either in Budapest or Argentina, Mr. President," Truman C. Ellsworth replied. "I'll look into it further for you, Mr. President."

"Huh," the President snorted. "You'll do better than that. You will personally go to Budapest to see if he's there and, if so, order him to report to me immediately. And while you're doing that, General Naylor will go to Argentina for the same purpose. And while they're doing that, if my CIA director acquires unconfirmed intelligence that Colonel Castillo is in Timbuktu, Mr. Lammelle will go there for the same purpose. And while all that is going on, you, Secretary Beiderman, will handle the administrative details of recalling Colonel Castillo from retirement."

Ellsworth, Naylor, and Beiderman all said, "Yes, sir," on top of one another.

"And the rest of you will take whatever action in this regard that pops into your fertile imaginations," the President went on. "I'm sure you all heard what I said about wanting your wholehearted cooperation in that matter."

He let that sink in for a moment, and then dismissed them by saying, "That will be all. Thank you for coming."

Then he stood and walked to the door to the Oval Office, which Supervisory Secret Service Agent Robert J. Mulligan opened for him as he approached, and went through it.

[THREE]
The Portico
The White House
1600 Pennsylvania Avenue, N.W.
Washington, D.C.
1405 5 June 2007

The vehicles that had brought everybody to the White House were lined up on the drive waiting for them when they came out.

With the exception of the silver Jaguar Vanden Plas in which Truman C. Ellsworth, at his own expense, moved around Washington, they were all black—or very dark blue, almost black—GMC Yukons. But their drivers and assistant drivers—read bodyguards—reflected the agency whose chief they were moving around.

Ellsworth's driver and bodyguard were from the CIA's Internal Security Staff, as were those of CIA Director Lammelle. The CIA was forbidden by law from operating within the United States, which seemed to imply they couldn't go about armed. If anyone noticed that Ellsworth's and Lammelle's drivers and their assistants had previously been officers of the CIA Clandestine Service, no one said anything.

Vice President Montvale's driver and assistant were special agents of the Secret Service. In addition, wherever Montvale went, so did Supervisory Secret Service Special Agent Thomas McGuire.

Secretary Cohen's driver was a member of the State Department's Diplomatic Security Service. In lieu of an assistant, Charlene Stevens, a blonde, Rubenesque former Secret Service agent who headed Secretary Cohen's security detail, always rode with her in her Yukon.

Defense Secretary Beiderman's driver and his assistant were agents of the Office of Naval Intelligence. Beiderman was a former naval officer.

General Naylor was traveling in a Yukon assigned to the fleet of the chief of staff, U.S. Army. Its driver and his assistant were special agents of the Counterintelligence Corps and no one mentioned that before they had been assigned to protect the chief of staff and a very few other very senior officers, they had been members of the Ultra Secret Black Fox section of the Special Operations Command.

"Give me a call sometime, Frank, please," Secretary Cohen said, as she prepared to get into the backseat of her Yukon.

"Absolutely," Lammelle replied, and then directed his attention to General Naylor. "It looks a little crowded in there, General," he said, nodding toward Naylor's waiting Yukon. "Why don't you let me take you out to Andrews? It's on my way."

There were already five people in the Yukon Naylor had been provided by Brigadier General Homer S. Dutton, junior deputy assistant chief of staff to the chief of staff, when the task of transporting the Central Command commander in chief from Andrews Air Force Base to the White House and back again had been laid on him.

While General Dutton's precise role in the Pentagon hierarchy might pose problems for the layman, it was actually quite clear to Pentagon *cognoscenti* and even to some officials—such as Mr. Lammelle—who dealt often with the Pentagon.

At the top of the pyramid was the chief of staff himself, a four-star general. To assist him in the discharge of his duties, the chief of staff had a chief of staff, also a four-star general, who was chief of staff to the chief of staff. This luminary also had an assistant, known as the assistant chief of staff to the chief of staff. He was a lieutenant general, a three-star general. To assist him in carrying out his many duties, he had two deputies. These were a major general (two stars) who was the senior deputy assistant chief of staff to the chief of staff, and a brigadier general (one star) who was the junior deputy assistant chief of staff to the chief of staff. This was General Dutton.

It had been General Dutton who had sent an urgent radio message earlier in the day to General Naylor, who had then been aboard his airplane bound for Fort Lewis, Washington, informing him that the Commander in Chief wished to see him at 1330 in the Cabinet Room at the White House.

Lammelle recognized three of the people in Naylor's Yukon. One was Naylor's senior aide-de-camp, Colonel J. D. Brewer, who was always with Naylor. A second was one of his junior aides-de-camp, Captain Charles D. Seward III, who performed the traditional duties of an aide-de-camp, in other words anything that spared the general's time for more important matters. Taking care of the luggage, for example. He was also usually very close to the general.

The third officer Lammelle recognized was the commanding officer of Headquarters & Headquarters Company, United States Central Command & Combined Base MacDill. Combined Base MacDill was formerly designated MacDill Air Force Base. The name had been changed to reflect its role vis-à-vis Central Command, which included naval, Marine Corps, and Army elements.

This officer was responsible for feeding and housing the military personnel and their dependents assigned to any of these, and for the base fire department and the schools. In civilian parlance, he would have been the mayor.

Most officers would regard the assignment as desirable. It would give them a chance to shine before the many senior officers of Central Command. It was jokingly but accurately said there were enough Army, Air Force, and Marine generals and Navy admirals in Central Command to form a reinforced platoon of infantry.

The incumbent, Lieutenant Colonel Allan B. Naylor, Junior, had confided in Frank Lammelle that he hated it. His father, who had had no role in his son's selection for the assignment and shared his opinion that it was not a particularly desirable assignment for a newly promoted lieutenant colonel of cavalry, nevertheless saw a silver lining in his son's black cloud.

Because all he had to do was keep the schools running and the fire department ready to do its job, et cetera, and didn't need permission from anyone to leave his office, he would be free to accompany his father on many of his travels, which would expose him to command at the very highest levels, which would prove of great value to him when general's stars gleamed from his own epaulets.

There was no question in General Naylor's mind that his son would become a general officer. That was what Naylors did. They went to West Point, served in the cavalry, became general officers, and then retired to the family farm in Virginia.

The problem with this scenario, Allan, Junior, had confided in Lammelle, was that the fire department and the schools and the garbage collection services did not run themselves, the result of which was he had two full-time jobs, "as the goddamn mayor and the goddamn unofficial aide-de-camp."

"Thank you," General Naylor said simply in response to Mr. Lammelle's offer of a ride to Andrews Air Force Base. He then went to "his" Yukon, told them what was going on, and then got in the backseat of Lammelle's Yukon.

As the vehicle turned onto Pennsylvania Avenue, Mr. Lammelle took what looked very much like a BlackBerry from his pocket, punched one of its buttons, and put the device to his ear.

"Well," he said, "what thinks the Queen of Foggy Bottom?"

General Naylor's face showed that he thought it inappropriate for the CIA director to refer to the secretary of State in such disrespectful terms.

"I don't know," Lammelle went on. "I'll ask him." He looked at Naylor and said, "Natalie wants to know what you think of what just happened."

General Naylor's face showed that he thought it inappropriate for the CIA director to refer to the secretary of State by her first name. He threw up both hands in a gesture that was both an expression of this and signified he had nothing to say.

"The most important general in the world," Lammelle said, "has taken the question under consideration, but has nothing to say at this time."

Andy McClarren, of Wolf News, who had been the most watched news personality on television for ten years and counting, had so described Naylor. He argued that while the chief of staff *administered* the Army, he had few troops actually under his command. Naylor's Central Command, on the other hand, was made up not only of the Army elements thereof, but also of Air Force and Navy components, placing him in direct command of more soldiers, sailors, and airmen, plus more artillery, tanks, aircraft, and warships, than any other officer anywhere in the world.

The description was accurate, but General Naylor was uncomfortable with it.

"One more question, Natalie," Lammelle said, "and then I'll let you go. Do we tell Truman Ellsworth that Charley is not in Budapest and save him that tiring trip?"

"How do you know that Charley's not in Budapest?" Naylor asked.

"Charley's in Argentina," Lammelle said.

"How do you know that?" Naylor asked, and then before Lammelle could reply, said, accusingly, "The President asked you if you knew where he was."

"No, he asked you and Ellsworth," Lammelle said. "If he had asked Natalie or me, we probably would have told him."

"'*Probably*'?" Naylor parroted indignantly. "That's outrageous! He's the President of the United States!"

The exchange illustrated the cultural differences between the worlds of General Naylor and DCI Lammelle. Naylor was a product of West Point—as five previous generations of his ancestors had been—and tried very hard to live his life according to the West Point Code of Honor, which holds that one must not lie, cheat, or steal, nor tolerate those who did.

Lammelle had been in the intelligence business all his life. He had learned as a young Army Counterintelligence Corps sergeant—and later as a CIC officer—that lying, stealing, and cheating was often the only way one could get things done. And when he'd joined the CIA's Clandestine Service and had risen to the top of that organization, he had learned that the higher one rose the more one had to lie, steal, cheat, and closely associate oneself with world-class lowlifes who were fantastically skilled liars, cheats, and thieves to get things done.

"So what are you going to do, Allan?"

"Comply with my orders, of course."

"You mean you're going to go to Argentina, try to find Charley, and if you can, tell him to report to the President?"

"Those are my orders."

"Not getting into the subject at all of all the questions that are going to be asked—by, among others, the vibrant voice of Wolf News, Andy McClarren, who seems fascinated with anything you do—about why the C in C Central Command is flying off to Argentina, and presuming you can find Charley—and I'm not going to tell you where in Argentina he is—have you considered what Charley's reaction to this is going to be?"

Naylor glared at him.

"The possibility, for example, that Charley will say, 'With all possible respect, sir, tell our nutcake President to take a flying fuck at a rolling doughnut'?"

Naylor didn't reply.

"I think that's a credible scenario, Allan. I don't think that Charley has forgotten that the last time the Commander in Chief sent someone looking for him, the idea was to load him and his lady love on an Aeroflot airplane and ship them to Russia."

After a long moment, Naylor asked, "What would you do, Frank?"

"I don't have a clue how I'm going to handle this latest idiocy," Lammelle said. "So I'm in no position to suggest what you should do. Except, maybe . . . Why don't you see what McNab thinks?"

"What makes you think I'd ask him about anything?" Naylor said. "We can't even make him privy to the Cabinet meeting. Everything that happens at a Cabinet meeting is Top Secret, Presidential."

"No fooling?" Lammelle asked sarcastically. "I guess I should have known that."

Naylor's face whitened, but he didn't say anything.

He didn't say anything at all during the rest of the way to Andrews Air Force Base, except, "Thank you for the ride," when he got out of Lammelle's Yukon.

[FOUR]

Pope Air Force Base, North Carolina

1510 5 June 2007

As the C-37A—the military designation of the Gulfstream Aerospace Corporation's Gulfstream V—made its approach to the airfield, which abuts Fort Bragg, an olive drab Dodge SUV drove onto the tarmac beside Base Operations and stopped under a sign reading *Absolutely No Parking At Any Time.*

Two men got out of the vehicle. One of them was a barrel-chested, very short, totally bald civilian wearing a T-shirt on which was painted in red the legend "Chief Snake Eater." The second was a small, muscular, ruddy-faced man sporting a flowing red mustache. He wore aviator sunglasses and a camouflage-patterned Battle Dress Uniform.

An Air Force senior master sergeant came quickly out of Base Operations, his mouth open as if to say something—for example, "Can't you see the sign, stupid?"—and as quickly he closed his mouth and went back in the building.

There was a red plate above the bumper of the SUV with three silver stars on it, indicating that it carried a lieutenant general. Lieutenant generals, like diplomats in any country but their own, can park just about wherever they want to, and this is especially true on an air force base where the commanding general has but one star to dazzle his underlings.

Moreover, the senior master sergeant recognized the man wearing the camo BDUs as Lieutenant General Bruce J. McNab, commanding general, United States Special Operations Command. He recognized the civilian, he had seen him many times before, often in the company of General McNab, but he couldn't put a name on him. Very few people outside the upper echelons of the Special Operations community could.

The civilian's name was Victor D'Alessandro. He was a civilian employee of the Department of the Army, a GS-15, which regulations stated entitled him to be considered an "assimilated colonel" when it came to providing quarters and so forth. He had retired from thirty years and three days of Army service as a chief warrant officer, grade V (CWO-5), which had paid him essentially the same pay and allowances as a lieutenant colonel. And before becoming a warrant officer, junior grade (WOJG, pronounced Woe-Jug), Mr. D'Alessandro had been a sergeant major.

The C-37A/Gulfstream V taxied up to the visiting aircraft tarmac a minute or so later. The upper portion of its fuselage was painted in a gleaming white, and the lower portion pale blue. There was no reference to either the U.S. Air Force or the U.S. Army in its markings, although it carried the star-and-bar insignia of a military aircraft on its engine nacelles. UNITED STATES OF AMERICA was lettered on the fuselage above the six windows. There was an American flag painted on the vertical stabilizer.

When the aircraft had stopped, the stair door behind the cockpit windows unfolded even before the whine of its engines died. A tall, erect lieutenant colonel of Cavalry who was in his thirties came nimbly down them, marched up to General McNab, saluted crisply, and announced, "General Naylor's compliments, General. The general asks that you attend him aboard the aircraft."

General McNab returned the salute.

"I hear and obey, Colonel Naylor," McNab said, and walked toward the Gulfstream.

"Hey, Vic," Lieutenant Colonel Naylor said, and extended his hand.

"How they hanging, Junior?" Vic D'Alessandro replied, and then wrapped his arms around him affectionately.

"One beside the other," Naylor said, and waved D'Alessandro toward the airplane.

When he entered the Gulfstream, General McNab saw that General Naylor was sitting in what he thought of as "first class," the foremost section of the passenger compartment, which held two chairs and a table.

He marched down the aisle, came to attention, saluted, and barked, "Lieutenant General McNab, Bruce J., accepting General Naylor's kind invitation."

Naylor was aware that McNab was being a wiseass again—what custom dictated that he should have said was "General McNab reporting as ordered"—and that saying what he had was to remind Naylor that he did not have the authority to order McNab to do anything.

He decided to let it ride.

He returned the salute, waved McNab into the other chair at the table, and said, "Thank you for meeting me, General."

And then when he saw Vic D'Alessandro coming down the aisle toward them, Naylor added, "I was hoping for a private word with you."

"Well, if you insist, I'll send Vic away," McNab said. "But if you'll let him stay, that'll save me the trouble of having to tell him later everything that happened here. I tell my executive secretary everything. Otherwise, you'll understand, he couldn't do his job."

Naylor thought: *McNab is entirely capable of having D'Alessandro on his organization chart as his executive secretary. He would find that amusing.*

Naylor extended his hand.

"How are you, Mr. D'Alessandro?"

"I'm fine, thank you, sir."

"Getting right to the point," Naylor said. "I've just come from the White House."

"I know," McNab interrupted. "Frank Lammelle told me what happened there and said you'd be stopping by. Would it save time if we cut to the chase?"

"Lammelle told you?" Naylor asked coldly.

"He called me on my trusty CaseyBerry," McNab said. "No. Correction. He called *Vic* on *Vic's* trusty CaseyBerry, and told Vic when he found me to tell me you'd just broken ground at Andrews and were headed here. When I got the message, I called Frank and he told me why you were coming to see me. So can we cut to the chase?"

The "CaseyBerry" to which McNab referred was a cellular telephone resembling the BlackBerry. Officially, its name was Casey XP-13, which stood for Experimental Prototype, Version 13. It had a number of characteristics the BlackBerry did not have.

BlackBerrys communicate with "cell tower" antennae scattered widely across the United States and other places on earth. The CaseyBerrys communicated with satellites scattered twenty-seven thousand miles above the earth. CaseyBerrys automatically encrypted and decrypted whatever they transmitted (voice or images) in a code that even the vast National Security Agency batteries of computers at Fort Meade could not break.

This was because the designer and builder of the NSA codebreaking systems, Aloysius F. Casey, Ph.D., also designed the CaseyBerry XP-series communication devices.

Shortly after the First Desert War, Dr. Casey, the chairman of the board of the AFC Corporation, flew to Fort Bragg, N.C., in one of the firm's Learjets. He had an appointment arranged by his U.S. Senator with the then newly appointed deputy commander of the John F. Kennedy Special Warfare Center, Brigadier General Bruce J. McNab. McNab had returned from the war with his third Distinguished Service Cross, a Brigadier General's Star, and the young second lieutenant who had been his personal pilot and whom he had named to be his first aide-de-camp.

McNab, suspecting that Dr. Casey was trying to sell the Army something, ordered his young aide-de-camp, whose name was C. G. Castillo, to get rid of Casey.

"I don't care how, Charley, just keep that politically well-connected salesman away from me."

Thirty minutes after meeting Dr. Casey, and after taking him on a helicopter tour of Smoke Bomb Hill, Blood Alley, and other Fort

Bragg–area tourist attractions in which he thought Casey might be interested, Lieutenant Castillo telephoned General McNab and told him he thought the general really ought to talk to Dr. Casey.

"You better be right about this, Charley," McNab replied. "Okay, bring him to lunch."

Castillo was right about Dr. Casey. At lunch, Casey told them that during the Vietnam War he had been the commo sergeant on a Special Forces "A" Team. He told them that when he came home to Boston, instead of going to work for the post office or getting a job as a bus driver, as "somebody like me" was expected to do, he went to the Massachusetts Institute of Technology in Cambridge and applied for admittance.

"I told them I didn't have a high school diploma, but I'd been in the American Amateur Relay League since I was ten, and that I hadn't met anybody in the Army who knew as much about the propagation of radio waves as I did, and I wanted to learn more. So they asked me a couple of questions . . . Correction, they questioned me for a couple of hours, and decided to give me a chance.

"I wouldn't have had the balls to ask MIT to take a chance on a poor Irish kid from South Boston if I hadn't been a Green Beanie, so now it's payback time."

"I gather you made it at MIT?" General McNab asked, much more cordially now that he recognized Dr. Casey as a fellow Green Beanie.

"I got my bachelor's and my high school diploma the first year, my master's the next, and my Ph.D. in my third. I spent another year there teaching—that was payback I figured I owed—and while I was doing that, I started the company."

"What do you mean, Dr. Casey, that it's 'payback time'?" Lieutenant Castillo asked.

"I told you once, Hotshot, to call me Aloysius," Dr. Casey replied. "Don't piss me off by making me tell you again."

At this point, Dr. Casey, as was his wont, went off on a tangent.

"General, Hotshot here, who doesn't look like he's old enough to vote, is sporting wings *and* a Combat Infantry Badge. He's got both?"

"And a Silver Star, two Purple Hearts, and a Distinguished Flying Cross," General McNab replied.

"I'll be goddamned," Casey said, and then came back on course.

"What I mean is that I'm going to pay back what I got from Special Forces by giving you the best commo going."

"That's very kind of you," McNab said. "But I'm sure you remember Special Forces gets its commo gear from the Signal Corps. Even if we had any money, and we don't, we couldn't buy—"

"You're not listening. I didn't say I wanted to *sell* you commo gear. I said I was going to *give* you commo gear. Payback is what I said."

"That kind of equipment would entail a great deal of money," McNab said.

"Yeah, well, my tax people tell me I can write it off as research and development. I'll call what I give you prototypes or something."

"And how soon were you planning to start doing something like this, Dr. Casey?"

"You can call me Aloysius, too," Casey replied. "What I'd like to do is take Hotshot here out to Vegas this afternoon. I'll show him what I have that I think Special Forces could use, and he could tell me what Special Forces needs and I'll start working on that."

"Why don't you call me Bruce, Aloysius?" General McNab said.

"I couldn't do that, for Christ's sake, you're a fucking general."

"You have a point there, Aloysius," General McNab said, and then turned to Lieutenant Castillo. "Go pack your bag, Charley, you're going to Las Vegas."

"And what did the director of Central Intelligence tell you, General, on your trusty CaseyBerry?" General Naylor asked.

General Naylor had seen CaseyBerrys function often enough to be familiar with their capabilities. He knew, too, that while Mr. Lammelle and General McNab, and McNab's executive secretary, and Secretary Cohen—and others—had one, he didn't.

This annoyed him greatly, and his annoyance spilled over into lost temper, as it often did when he was dealing with General McNab.

"Perhaps why I don't have a CaseyBerry?"

"Yes, sir. He touched on that subject."

"And what did he say?"

"If memory serves, sir, and mine usually does, he said something like, quote, *Thank God, Naylor doesn't have a CaseyBerry. If he did, he would have known where Charley is, and would have told our Loony Tune Commander in Chief, and we would really be up the creek on this.* End quote. That is just about verbatim, sir."

"He actually referred to the President in those terms?"

"Well, he knew that no one who would hear him would disagree with his characterization of President Clendennen."

"And what do you think Mr. Lammelle meant when he said if the President knew where Castillo is, we would be . . ."

"'Really up the creek on this'?"

"Yes."

"DCI Lammelle feels, sir, and I agree with him, that disabusing the President of his notion to re-involve Castillo in the drug wars and involving him in the piracy problem is not going to be possible. So what he suggests, and Secretary Cohen concurs, is that we give the appearance of going along with it, until the President tires of it, whereupon he will come up with another nutty idea and forget this one."

"Go on."

"DCI Lammelle suggested that if you, he, Natalie Cohen, and I gave Colonel Castillo our word that he would not be loaded on an Aeroflot airplane and shipped to Siberia, he might be induced to appear to have answered the President's call to hazardous duty.

"He would go to Mexico and, after reconnoitering the situation there, offer a solution to the drug problem that the President would feel was unsatisfactory."

"Which would be?"

"I'm sure the general is aware of the scurrilous rumor circulating that the unofficial motto of Special Forces is 'Kill everybody and let God sort it out.'"

"I've heard that," Naylor said.

He thought that over for a long moment and then said, "That just might work."

"We have a problem there, I'm afraid," McNab said.

"Why? As long as the President thinks his orders are being obeyed, he'll be less prone to order any additional action. If he can be stalled, so to speak, for sufficient time—"

"The problem is once again, sir, Lieutenant Colonel Castillo, Retired."

"How so?"

"I spoke to him about an hour ago—"

"Amazing device, that CaseyBerry, isn't it?" General Naylor interrupted.

"Yes, sir, it is. I outlined the parameters of the situation to Colonel Castillo, sir, and asked him how he would react to the suggestion that he accept a recall to active hazardous duty for a period not to exceed ninety days."

"And what did he say?"

"He broke the connection without saying anything, sir."

"He hung up on you?"

McNab nodded and then said, "I gave him ninety seconds in the belief that would be sufficient time for him to recover from his fit of hysterical laughter, and called back. Sweaty took the call—"

"'Sweaty'?" Naylor parroted. "Oh, the Russian woman."

"Yes, sir. Former Lieutenant Colonel Svetlana Alekseeva of the SVR. Now known as Susanna Barlow. Colonel Castillo's fiancée."

"His what? He's going to marry her?" Naylor asked incredulously.

"Yes, sir. Just as soon as they can somehow get the government of the Russian Federation to declare her former husband, SVR Polkovnik Evgeny Alekseev to be deceased. Colonel Castillo is a gentleman, and gentlemen feel an obligation to marry women carrying their unborn children."

"She's pregnant?"

"Yes, sir, I understand that to be the case."

"McNab, I have the feeling you're mocking me," Naylor said furiously.

"As you well know, since our plebe year at Hudson High, just being in the same room with you has induced an uncontrollable urge in me to mock you, even when you're not in your Self-Righteous Mode, as you are now. But if you can bring yourself to call me Bruce, I will stop doing so now and we can see about solving the problem at hand as two old soldiers and classmates should do."

Naylor glared at him for a long moment, and finally said, "Please do." And then, after another pause, added, "Bruce."

"Allan, I would not have violated Charley's privacy by telling you that Sweaty's in the family way, except that it's obviously a fact bearing on our problem."

"Understood. Thank you," Naylor replied, and again added "Bruce" after a pause.

"When Sweaty came on the line, I gathered that she was less than enthusiastic about Charley doing what the President wants him to do. She said if I ever brought the subject up again, she would castrate me with a rusty *otxokee mecto nanara*."

"With a what?"

"Latrine shovel."

"Have you any suggestions on how we can solve our problem?" Naylor asked.

"As a matter of fact . . . Natalie says the last thing we can afford to happen is for C. Harry Whelan, Junior, or Andy McClarren to wonder what the hell you're doing in Argentina and start asking questions—"

"I've been ordered to go down there," Naylor interrupted.

". . . so you can't go down there."

"What's the alternative?"

"You want it step by step, or all at once?"

"All at once."

"We're all agreed on this, Allan. Frank, Natalie, and me."

"Understood. Let's hear it."

"Frank's Gulfstream comes here and picks up Vic D'Alessandro—"

"I think I see where you're headed," Naylor said.

"Stop interrupting me, for Christ's sake, Allan!"

"Sorry."

"And picks up Vic D'Alessandro, who is Charley's oldest friend in Special Operations except for me. When Charley was flying me around in Desert One, Master Sergeant D'Alessandro was on the Gatling gun in the back."

"I wasn't aware of that."

"I guess if you're the most important general in the world, nobody can tell you to shut up."

"Sorry," Naylor said, and then, "I mean it. I'm sorry, Bruce, please go on."

"And Charley's oldest friend," McNab went on.

Naylor opened his mouth to ask what was meant by that, but with a massive effort didn't speak.

McNab pointed at Lieutenant Colonel Allan B. Naylor.

"They've been buddies since they were in short pants in that school in Fulda . . ."

"Saint Johan's," Lieutenant Colonel Naylor furnished.

"Unfortunately, Colonel, you're apparently a chip off the old blockhead," McNab said. "Shut up. When I want input from you, I'll tell you."

"Yes, sir. Sorry, sir."

"That was when Charley was only Karl Wilhelm von und zu Gossinger. Later, when he had also become that famous Texican—one Carlos Guillermo Castillo—Junior here followed him to West Point. Most recently, he was involved—on the fringes, to be sure, but involved—in Charley's brief but successful incursion in the People's Democratic Republic of Venezuela.

"Vic and Junior are, Natalie, Frank, and I feel, the ideal people to tell Charley all sides of the story. The three of us also feel that it is only fair to offer Charley the advice of fellow Outlaws we feel he might wish to bring with him, should he decide to go on active duty. People he trusts almost as much as he trusts Sweaty, who therefore may be able to overcome Sweaty's rather firm position.

"To accomplish that, Frank's Gulfstream will fly Vic and Junior to scenic Tocumen International Airport in the Republic of Panama, where they will board—on the CIA's dime, by the way—yet another Gulfstream, this one owned by Panamanian Executive Aircraft, a wholly owned subsidiary of the LCBF Corporation.

"It will then fly to Argentina piloted by Colonel Jacob Torine, USAF, Retired, who was Castillo's de facto chief of staff in the glory days of the Office of Organizational Analysis and later in the era of the often-maligned-by-the-President Merry Outlaws.

"His co-pilot will be Major Richard Miller, USA, Retired. On one hand, Major Miller is much like Colonel Naylor. He, too, marches in the Long Gray Line, and his father, too, is a general officer. On the other, before he got himself shot down and pretty badly banged up in Afghanistan, Miller was one hell of a Special Operations pilot and not only with the 160th Special Operations Aviation Regiment.

"All of these people will confer with Castillo and his charming fiancée, and then we will hear whatever it is he has to say.

"That's our best shot at this problem. The final decision, of course, is up to you, Allan. If you want to go to Argentina and deal with Charley yourself, no one can—or should—try to stop you."

Tapping the fingertips of both hands together, General Naylor considered the question for a full thirty seconds, and then said, "Bruce, please call Mr. Lammelle and ask him to send his airplane."

McNab nodded and then looked at Vic D'Alessandro, who gestured with his CaseyBerry.

"ETA here is fifteen minutes, General," D'Alessandro reported.

II

[ONE]

The House on the Hill
Las Vegas, Nevada
1605 5 June 2007

The eavesdropping on the communications of the world by the National Security Agency at Fort Meade, Maryland, is a rather simple procedure: They record everything said over the telephone, over the radio—and sometimes heard by cleverly placed "bugs"—by those in whom the several intelligence agencies of the United States are interested and then run it through a computer that filters out the garbage and after cracking any cryptography involved transfers the good stuff to another tape that is then distributed to the appropriate intelligence agency for analysis.

The idea is simple, the technology required is not.

Before the AFC Corporation took over the supplying of the technology—hardware and software—the NSA was relatively as deaf and useful as a stone pole. Afterward, of course, it was not.

Before the AFC Corporation took the NSA contract, Dr. Aloysius Casey— by far the majority stockholder in AFC, and both its chief engineer and chairman of its board of directors—could not be honestly said to have been putting victuals on his table with food stamps.

After the contracts went into force, though, he *really* prospered.

To the point where he had confided to his friend Charley Castillo—to whom he no longer referred to as "Hotshot"—that he had more money than he knew what to do with. He confided this to Castillo not only as a friend, but also because he knew that Castillo, too, had more money than he knew what to do with.

One of the things Casey had done with his wealth was of course to provide prototype equipment free of charge to the Special Forces community, but this—especially after Casey's platoon of tax lawyers taught him how to charge this off as "research and development"—didn't make much of a dent in the bottom line.

He had spent a hell of a lot of money building the House on the Hill for Mary-Catherine, whom he had married immediately after returning from the war in Vietnam. Their first home had been a basement room in her parents' row house in South Boston. She had supported him emotionally—his and her parents thought he was either nuts or smoking funny cigarettes—when he went to MIT. And supported them financially by stuffing bags for long hours in a Stop & Shop Supermarket.

They had four years together in the House on the Hill, and then cancer got Mary-Catherine. Got her very quickly, which was the only good thing that could be said about that.

A year after Mary-Catherine left him alone—they'd never been able to have kids—in the House on the Hill, the demise of both the Office of Organizational Analysis and the Merry Outlaws, which was a brief reincarnation of the former, caused two of its members to be without work.

Casey had come to know both of them, and felt a kinship with both.

One of these was First Lieutenant Edmund "Peg-Leg" Lorimer,

MI, USA, Retired, who had worn the Green Beret as an "A" Team commo sergeant—which logically really resonated with Casey—before getting a battlefield commission. He had been an officer just long enough to make first lieutenant when he was wounded in—and ultimately lost—his left leg just above the knee.

The other was Gunnery Sergeant Lester Bradley, USMC, Retired, who was twenty-one but looked much younger. He had been part of Castillo's operation from the very beginning, even before they had been first formalized as the Office of Organizational Analysis.

Then a corporal in the Marine Guard detachment at the American embassy in Buenos Aires, Bradley had been sent—as the man who could best be spared—to drive an embassy truck carrying two fifty-five-gallon barrels of helicopter fuel to Uruguay. He was pressed into service in support of a hastily organized raid Castillo had undertaken to snatch Dr. John Paul Lorimer, a renegade American, for forcible repatriation to the United States.

Dr. Lorimer and Lieutenant Lorimer, it should be pointed out, were in no way related.

Castillo had handed Bradley an M-14 rifle and ordered him to do what he could to protect the fuel while he and other Special Operations operators—plus an FBI agent also pressed into service from his duties in the Uruguayan embassy looking for dirty money—conducted the raid.

The raid had promptly started to go sour, and might have failed—probably would have failed—had not Bradley taken out two of the bad guys with head shots, fired offhand from one hundred yards from his M-14 rifle and the FBI agent, taking his pistol out of its holster for the first time ever except on the FBI Academy's pistol range at Quantico, used it to take out two more of them.

When he returned to the United States, then-Major Castillo had reported to the President—President Clendennen's predecessor—that, since they obviously couldn't be returned to their embassy duties, he had brought Corporal Bradley and FBI Special Agent David W. Yung home with him. He also reported that Dr. Lorimer had been killed by what they had learned were agents of the SVR as he was opening his safe. The safe had a little over sixteen million dollars' worth of bearer bonds in it the SVR thought was theirs, Castillo told the President, and he had brought that home, too.

The President had a solution that dealt with what should be done with Castillo, others on the raid (including Bradley and Yung), and the money. He issued a Top Secret Presidential Finding establishing the Office of Organizational Analysis, named Castillo its chief, assigned Bradley, Yung, and everybody involved in the raid to it, and funded it with $500,000 from his Confidential Fund.

"In the meantime, Charley," the President went on, "understanding I'm not telling you to do this, if you should happen to find sixteen million in bearer bonds somewhere on the sidewalk, you might consider using that for the expenses of OOA until I can come up with some more money for you."

Special Agent Yung, who was an expert in the laundering of funds, established an account for the Lorimer Charitable & Benevolent Fund in the Riggs National Bank in Washington, and deposited sixteen million dollars in bearer bonds into it.

That was the beginning of what would become the LCBF Corporation, which was formed after, shortly before his untimely death, the President found it necessary to disband the OOA and order its members to disappear from the face of the earth.

When that happened, neither Lieutenant Lorimer nor Sergeant

Bradley had anywhere to go. Neither had any family to speak of, and they had been retired from the service. Neither could Bradley continue to be Castillo's shadow. Among other reasons for that was a redheaded Russian called Sweaty, who while she really liked Lester, did not want to have him around for breakfast, lunch, and dinner seven days a week.

Aloysius Casey offered both men a job working for the AFC Corporation laboratories in Las Vegas. He was working on a new project for the gaming industry, a computer-driven system that would, when completed, discreetly scan the faces of guests as they entered the lobby and instantly come up with their biographies, credit ratings, and the balances in their bank accounts. This would be of great interest to the gaming industry, and one of the titans of that industry, who had become a pal of Aloysius, told him that they would pay through the nose for it if he could make it work.

Aloysius, not sure if he believed it, told Peg-Leg and Lester that he thought they would be useful to him as he perfected the new system. He also said that, until they got settled, they could stay with him in the House on the Hill.

"There's certainly plenty of room," he said.

In addition to the twenty-three rooms in which Aloysius was—with the exception of the Mexican couple who took care of him—rattling around alone, there were four "guest cottages," each consisting of a bedroom, a living room, a game room complete with nickel slot machines—their motherboards rigged to pay out more than they took in—and a complete kitchen.

Lester moved into one of these cottages next to the putting green, and Peg-Leg into the one nearest the pool, which he used often for therapeutic reasons connected with the damaged muscles of his leg.

From the beginning, things went well—except for the incident with the motorcycle. One day when Lester was in the lobby of Mount Vesuvius Resort & Gaming Palace watching people come in, so he could determine the best location to place the scanning cameras, he had an idle moment and dropped a quarter into a slot machine, just so he could see how it worked without anybody seeing him watching.

There then suddenly came a bleating of trumpets, the flashing of lights, the screaming of sirens, and a recorded voice repeatedly bellowing, "There is a winner!"

Lester had won the Grand Prize offered by that slot machine—an absolute top-of-the-line Harley-Davidson that was sitting on a pedestal just inside the lobby. Aloysius suspected a glitch in the slot machine's motherboard, as that particular motorcycle had been sitting there for as long as he could remember and no one had ever won it.

The thought of Lester riding that monster up and down the Strip and then up and down the mountain every day brought forth in Aloysius what he thought of as a manifestation of the Special Operators creed that one Special Operator always covers another Special Operator's back, but was probably more of a manifestation of previously unsuspected paternal instincts.

He conferred first with Peg-Leg, who then told Lester that while he was happy with Lester's good fortune, his peg leg would keep him from ever getting on the motorcycle with him.

In his next tactical move, he conferred over the CaseyBerry system with David W. Yung, now the chief financial officer of the LCBF Corporation, and who was managing Lester's investment portfolio, and got him to agree to tell Lester that the purchase of an automobile of any kind would interfere with the growth of the portfolio.

The CIA had promptly paid to the LCBF Corporation the $120

million it had been offering to anyone who could deliver a Top Secret Russian Tupolev Tu-934A aircraft to them when Colonel Jake Torine and Lieutenant Colonel Charley Castillo had brought one back with them from the Venezuelan incursion known as Operation March Hare.

The Executive Compensation Committee of the LCBF Corporation—David Yung and Edgar Delchamps—had determined that Lester was one of those entitled to one of the one-million-dollar (after taxes) bonuses to be paid to active participants in Operation March Hare.

Aloysius did not want Lester to consider that he was in a financial position to walk into the Las Vegas showroom of Bentley Motor Cars and write them a $245,000 check for their best red convertible if he wanted to.

A red convertible did figure in the final step of Aloysius's covering of Lester's back, however—a Ford Mustang. One was sitting, gleaming, top down, in the lobby of the Mount Vesuvius, when Lester came in to claim his prize.

So was the general manager of the Mount Vesuvius, who was beside himself with remorse for having to tell Lester that his prize had been recalled by the Harley-Davidson people for unspecified mechanical problems and that it would be a month, six weeks, perhaps even longer, before a replacement could be made available.

"Perhaps, sir," the manager asked, "you might be interested in the Mustang as your prize in lieu of the Harley-Davidson with mechanical problems you can't get for a month, six weeks, perhaps even longer anyway?"

Ten minutes later, Lester drove the red Mustang down the Strip and then up the mountain to the House on the Hill, where he showed it to Aloysius and Peg-Leg, who both agreed with him that the red Mustang was one hell of a set of wheels.

The general manager of the Mount Vesuvius had been so obliging because he had standing orders from the man who owned the Mount Vesuvius, three other of the more glitzy Las Vegas hotels, and three more in Atlantic City, New Jersey, and Biloxi, Mississippi, to do for Aloysius Casey whatever he wanted done.

This gentleman, whose code name was "Hotelier," was one of five members of a group of men known to very senior officers of the intelligence community as "Those People in Las Vegas."

The others were a well-known, perhaps even famous, investment banker, whose code name understandably was "Banker." Another, who had made an enormous fortune in the data processing business, was a Naval Academy graduate whose code name was "Annapolis." A fourth, who had once confessed to a reporter from *Forbes* magazine that he didn't really know how many radio and television stations he owned, had the code name "Radio & TV Stations." The fifth important member of Those People in Las Vegas was Dr. Aloysius Casey, whose code name was "Irish."

What Those People did was secretly fund covert intelligence operations of the various "Alphabet Agencies" when the agencies could not either get the funds to do so from Congress or even dare to ask for such funds. Those People didn't want credit for what they were doing, and for that reason—and also because what they were doing was, while inarguably patriotic, almost certainly illegal—used code names.

Dr. Casey's role in Those People was unique. He had been asked to join, and been happy to do so, shortly after he moved about half of the AFC's manufacturing capability and its most important research and development laboratory to Las Vegas.

Hotelier had learned that the redheaded middle-aged woman with the Boston accent who religiously—and for precisely one hour—dropped quarters into the slots in one of his places of business every morning after Mass was married to the chairman of the board of the AFC Corporation and drove a Chevrolet Suburban with Special Forces stickers on both its rear window and windshield.

He reasoned that Dr. Casey, as a Special Forces veteran, might be willing to make substantial financial contributions to the patriotic activities of Those People. And Dr. Casey, when approached, had been happy to do so.

Hotelier didn't ask any questions about—and Dr. Casey did not volunteer any information about—Dr. Casey's current and ongoing involvement with the intelligence or Special Operations communities.

It never entered Hotelier's mind, either—or the minds of the other Those People—that Casey regarded them as no more than well-meaning amateurs whose money sometimes came in handy.

This came to a head when Casey learned that some of Those People had concluded that President Clendennen's somewhat cold-blooded solution to a serious problem made sense.

The problem was that not all of an incredibly lethal biological warfare substance known as Congo-X had been destroyed when President Clendennen's predecessor, shortly before his untimely death, had ordered the obliteration of a twenty-square-mile area in the former Belgian Congo on which was situated the laboratory that invented Congo-X and the manufactory, operated by former East Germans.

The President had ordered the use of every explosive weapon, except nuclear, in the American arsenal to be used for this purpose. It hadn't worked. There wasn't a tree left standing in the target area, but the Russians soon provided proof they still had some Congo-X.

They proposed, in the spirit of international love and brotherhood, that they would turn over all they had and swear on all they held dear never again to make any.

In exchange, all they asked for was the return to the motherland of two SVR officers, Colonel Dmitri Berezovsky and Lieutenant Colonel Svetlana Alekseeva, who had defected from their posts as the SVR *rezident*s in Berlin and Copenhagen, respectively, and promptly told the American intelligence officer who had arranged their defection all about Congo-X. The Russians wanted him, too. His name was Lieutenant Colonel Carlos G. Castillo.

President Clendennen thought this seemed like a reasonably fair deal and ordered that the swap be made. Some of Those People thought the President had made the right decision.

Before the people sent to find Castillo and the two Russians and to load them onto an Aeroflot aircraft could do so, Castillo learned that the Congo-X that the Russians had sent to the Army's Medical Research Laboratory at Fort Detrick, Maryland, had been flown to the Western Hemisphere aboard a Tupolev Tu-934A, which was then sitting on the tarmac of an airfield on Venezuela's La Orchila Island with the last liter of Congo-X aboard.

About a week later, the Tupolev landed at Andrews Air Force Base flown by Jake Torine and Charley Castillo. On board, in addition to the last liter of Congo-X, were some people, including General Vladimir Sirinov of the SVR, whom President Putin had personally put in charge of the operation, and Mr. Roscoe J. Danton, of the *Washington Times-Post* Writers Syndicate.

While they were waiting for the CIA to write the check for the $120 million bounty they had offered for a Tupolev Tu-934A, the Merry Outlaws, as President Clendennen disparagingly had dubbed them, went to the Venetian Hotel in Las Vegas to talk to Those People about their agreeing with President Clendennen's decision to throw Charley, Sweaty, and her brother Dmitri on an Aeroflot airplane.

With an effort, Charley rejected Edgar Delchamps's suggestion—which had Sweaty's enthusiastic support—on how to deal with Those People. This was to "throw them all in the great white shark aquarium at the Mandalay Bay Hotel and Casino and let Neptune sort them out."

At the confrontation, Annapolis gave Charley his word of honor that he had been dead set against President Clendennen's solution from the start and would not have permitted it to happen. As a former member of the Corps of Cadets at the U.S. Military Academy, Castillo knew that he could accept without question the word of honor of a former member of the Brigade of Midshipmen at the U.S. Naval Academy.

Radio & TV Stations surprised everyone by backing up his statement that he had told Those People that they would load Charley on a Moscow-bound Aeroflot aircraft only over his dead body by revealing not only that he had been an Army helicopter pilot during the Vietnam War—it would be a toss-up between Radio & TV Stations and Lester Bradley as to which looked less like a warrior—but that Charley's father, shortly before he was killed, had rescued him from certain death at great risk to his own life.

But the biggest surprise of the confrontation had been that between Hotelier and Edgar Delchamps.

"Actually," Hotelier said, "I thought Clendennen was right."

That, Castillo and Casey decided instantly, meant Hotelier wasn't going to live long enough to go swimming with the great white sharks in the Mandalay Bay aquarium. Delchamps was going to throw him out the window right there in the fortieth-floor Venetian penthouse.

"How's that?" Edgar asked softly.

"Odds are my business," Hotelier replied. "What would you say the odds were that Colonel Castillo was going to get away with his Venezuelan incursion?"

"Hundred to one against?" Delchamps asked.

"I'd have taken the bet at two hundred to one against," Hotelier said. "And that being the case, I started wondering how—or who—could get the Congo-X and Castillo and the others away from the Russians."

"Once they got Charley, Sweaty, and Dmitri on the nonstop to Moscow, that would be close to impossible. Even taking a shot at it would take a hell of a lot of money."

"I have a hell of a lot of money," Hotelier said.

Delchamps had looked at Hotelier for a long moment and then turned to Castillo.

"Ace, I trust this guy," he said. "And since you trust these two, I guess only the others go swimming with those big fishes as we discussed."

"If I may make a suggestion?" Hotelier had asked.

"Why not?" Delchamps had replied.

"As hard as you might find this to believe," Hotelier said, "some of the guests in my places of business try to cheat. When we catch them doing so, we reason with them, point out they have made a bad decision, and tell them what's going to happen if they ever again make such a bad decision or even think about doing so.

"If we—you and I, Mr. Delchamps—went to the gentlemen we're talking about and reasoned with them, I'm sure they would recognize how gross an error they have made, and would be willing to offer their solemn assurance they would never do so again. If we did this, we would not be shutting off, so to speak, the money spigot."

"Yeah," Delchamps said. "Why don't you call me Edgar?"

Despite the satisfactory resolution of the Confrontation, Aloysius still felt he had let down Castillo—had not covered his back—as he should have and resolved never to let that happen again.

To accomplish this he designed, built, tested, and then installed in the House on the Hill a miniature version of the interception system he had designed, built, tested, and installed for the NSA at Fort Meade.

The system he had installed at Fort Meade had several acres of computers to perform its tasks, but the one Casey installed at home was not designed to intercept messages of all kinds but only those going through the CaseyBerry Communications System; it fit in a small case about the size of two shoe boxes stacked one upon the other, which he kept in what had been Mary-Catherine's wardrobe.

The best way to explain its capabilities is by example:

For example, when the system heard Mr. Lammelle ask, "Well, what thinks the Queen of Foggy Bottom?" it automatically went into Record/Alert mode as the words "Queen," "Foggy," and "Bottom," in any combination, were in the filter database.

It turned on the Secondary Recording function, which went to the Primary Recording system, which operated all the time in a Run & Erase mode, and copied from it everything that had been recorded from a point in time ten seconds before the system had been triggered by hearing "Queen" and transferred it to the Secondary Recording function.

It added a date and time block, identified the parties to the call as

Mr. Lammelle and Secretary Cohen, and found and stored their locations. But so far it didn't do a thing to Mr. Casey's CaseyBerry.

When, however, DCI Lammelle inquired of the secretary of State whether or not they should tell Truman Ellsworth that Charley was not in Budapest, "Charley," or variations thereof, being the number one search filter, Mr. Casey's CaseyBerry burst into life.

It vibrated, buzzed, and tinkled pleasantly to get his attention, and when he pushed ACTIVATE BUTTON #3, flashed on its screen the names of the parties to the call, their locations, and Charley's location. When he pushed ACTIVATE BUTTON #4, it played back the entire conversation.

In a similar manner, Mr. Casey was made privy to Mr. Lammelle's second call to Secretary Cohen; Mr. Lammelle's call to General McNab in which he told McNab to expect General Naylor to stop by; General McNab's call to Charley; General McNab's second call to Charley, during which Sweaty threatened to castrate General McNab with an *otxokee mecto nanara* (including the translation of this phrase from the Russian language); Lammelle's call to Colonel Torine, ordering the charter of a Panamanian Executive Aircraft Gulfstream on the CIA's dime to be held ready to fly to Argentina; and finally Lammelle's call to Mr. D'Alessandro telling him when the DCI's Gulfstream was expected to arrive at Pope Air Force Base.

At that point, Mr. Casey pushed another button, which connected him with Hotelier.

"Listen to this," he said, "and tell me what you think."

He punched a button that transmitted all of the intercepts to Hotelier's CaseyBerry, whereupon Hotelier listened to them.

"I would hazard the guess Clendennen has somehow gotten out of his straitjacket," Hotelier said.

"I'm worried that Lester will hear about this and rush down there to protect Charley," Casey said.

"Aloysius, as you have so often told me, acquiring as much intelligence as one can has to be the first step before taking any action. Now, who in Washington has the best access to what our President is up to at any given moment?"

"Roscoe Danton."

Casey pushed a button and learned that Mr. Danton was in The Round Robin Bar of the Willard Hotel in Washington, D.C.

"And who do we have in Washington who can best extract this information from Mr. Danton?"

"Delchamps? Or maybe Yung?"

"Precisely. One or the other, preferably both."

"Thank you. I'll keep you in the loop."

"Please do."

Casey pushed the appropriate buttons and learned that Mr. Yung was in his office in the Riggs National Bank building and Mr. Delchamps was across the Potomac River at Lorimer Manor, an assisted living facility at 7200 West Boulevard Drive in Alexandria, Virginia.

He pushed the button that would connect him with the latter.

[TWO]
The Round Robin Bar
The Willard Hotel
1401 Pennsylvania Avenue, N.W.
Washington, D.C.
1730 5 June 2007

When David W. Yung and Edgar Delchamps walked in, Roscoe J. Danton was sitting at the bar about to sip at his third serving—at $27.50 per serving—of Macallan's twenty-four-year-old scotch whisky. The intoxicant was being provided to him by the lobbyist for the American Association of Motorized Wheelchair Manufacturers, who was delighted to provide a journalist such as Mr. Danton with anything at all he wished to drink.

If he did so, the lobbyist reasoned, it was possible—not likely, but possible—that Mr. Danton's columns might not echo the scurrilous stories going around that the furnishing of products of the AAM-WCM, which cost an average of $4,550, absolutely free of charge to mobility-restricted Social Security recipients was near the top of the list of outrageous rapes of the Social Security system.

"Well, there he is," Mr. Yung said.

"How are you, ol' buddy?" Mr. Delchamps added.

Mr. Danton turned from the bar to see who was talking to him. As he did so, Mr. Delchamps offered his hand. In a reflex action, Mr. Danton took it.

"Your car is here, Roscoe," Mr. Yung said.

"Parked illegally, so we'll have to hurry," Delchamps said. "Say goodbye to the nice man, Roscoe, and come along."

Intending to say, "I'm not going anywhere with you," he got only as far as "I'm not . . ." before an excruciating pain began in his hand and worked its way quickly up his arm to his neck.

Mr. Delchamps had grasped Mr. Danton's hand with an ancient grip he had learned from an agent of the Chos-n'g-l, the North Korean Department of State Security, whom he had turned during his active career in the Clandestine Service of the CIA.

No lasting damage was done to the gripee's body, the agent had taught him, but as long as pressure was applied, gripees tended to be very cooperative.

Waiting in the NO STANDING ZONE outside the street door of The Round Robin was a black, window-darkened Yukon Denali SUV bearing the special license plates issued by the Commonwealth of Virginia to the physically handicapped. On the door was lettered in gold LORIMER MANOR HANDICAPPED TRANSPORT # 2.

The rear door was open. Through it one could see the driver, who looked like an actress sent over from Central Casting in response to a call for "an elegant grandmother type in her seventies," and, sitting on his haunches in the captain's chair beside her, a dog, a 125-pound Bouvier des Flandres.

Mr. Yung quickly climbed in, and then Mr. Delchamps, still clutching Mr. Danton's hand, assisted him in getting in, then got in himself.

"Where we going?" the driver inquired.

"We might as well go home," Delchamps said. "This might take some time."

Home to Mr. Delchamps was Lorimer Manor, a large house—it could be fairly called a mansion—on an acre of manicured lawn on

West Boulevard Drive in Alexandria. There was a tasteful brass sign on the lawn:

> **LORIMER MANOR**
>
> **ASSISTED LIVING**
>
> **NO SOLICITING**

Lorimer Manor was also home to eleven other people—including the elegant grandmother in her seventies driving the Yukon—who were all also retired from the Clandestine Service of the CIA.

It had been originally purchased by the Lorimer Charitable & Benevolent Fund—using the funds from Dr. Lorimer's safe, hence the name—in the early days of the Office of Organizational Analysis as a safe house.

On the demise of that organization, the question of what to do with the property was initially solved by Mr. Delchamps, who said he needed a place to live, and would rent it from the LCBF Corporation temporarily.

Word spread quickly among the Retired Clandestine Community—known disparagingly by many newcomers to the CIA as "the Dinosaurs"—that ol' Edgar Delchamps was holed up comfortably in a big house in Alexandria. Perhaps there would be room for one more of them?

The place was shortly full up, and there was a waiting list. It was of particular interest to females who had retired from the Clandestine Service. They were uncomfortable living, for example, in the Silver Springs Methodist Retirement Home for Christian Ladies, and places of that nature.

Mr. David W. Yung—he was good at this sort of thing—had quickly set up a nonprofit corporation to handle the administration of the facility. A housekeeper—herself a retired Special Operations cryptographer married to a retired member of Delta Force—was engaged, rates were set, a board of directors established, and so on, and soon Lorimer Manor was off and running, so to speak.

As part of the deal, two rooms in Lorimer Manor were always kept in readiness for Merry Outlaws who happened to be in our nation's capital and needed a discreet place to rest their heads.

Mr. Delchamps led Mr. Danton into Lorimer Manor's recreation room, which was essentially a bar offering as large a selection of intoxicants as the one in the Willard he had just left.

The centerpiece decoration of the bar was two dinosaurs, facing each other. One of them had a pink ribbon around its neck.

"Sit, Roscoe," Edgar ordered. "And tell Two-Gun and me everything you know about how our President's latest aberration affects our leader."

Mr. Delchamps's reference to Mr. Yung as "Two-Gun" unnerved him. He had no idea why the Merry Outlaws so referred to Mr. Yung, but the mental image of Mr. Yung with a pistol in each hand, blazing away at the bad guys, à la Mr. Bruce Willis in many of his motion pictures, was menacing.

The explanation was simple. In the very first days, Mr. Yung and Mr. Delchamps had gone from Montevideo, Uruguay, to Buenos

Aires. Both had pistols. In the case of Mr. Yung, this was perfectly legal, as Mr. Yung was then still officially a legal attaché of the U.S. embassy in Montevideo, which position afforded him diplomatic status. Diplomatic status, in turn, permitted him to go about armed and to park wherever he wanted to.

Mr. Delchamps, who did not have diplomatic status, not only had to pay to park his car like ordinary people, but would have been arrested had he attempted to pass through Argentine customs with his preferred lethal weapon—a Colt Officer's Model 1911A1 .45 ACP semiautomatic pistol—tucked in the back of his trousers. The solution was simple. He handed the .45 to Mr. Yung, who passed through customs carrying both. He had thereafter been known to his fellow Merry Outlaws as "Two-Gun Yung," which had a certain onomatopoetic ring to it.

Thus Mr. Danton, reasonably, was unnerved by the moniker. As was he unnerved after having been kidnapped from The Round Robin Bar.

But what really unnerved him was being reminded that both Delchamps and Yung regarded him as one of their own—as, in other words, a fellow Merry Outlaw.

Roscoe was willing to admit they had their reasons. One was that he had permitted dreams of journalistic glory to overwhelm his common sense. Specifically, armed with a borrowed Uzi machine pistol, he had jumped aboard the Black Hawk helicopter that Castillo had bought from a corrupt Mexican police official just before it had taken off in the Venezuelan incursion known as Operation March Hare.

And, Roscoe was willing to admit, he had taken "the King's Shilling." Actually, it was "the Merry Outlaws' Million Dollars After Taxes." Mr. Delchamps and Mr. Yung had decided that since Roscoe had gone to the Venezuelan airbase on La Orchila Island carrying an Uzi, he was as much entitled to the bonus as anybody else who had gone on the operation.

When the money was offered, Roscoe had thought only a fool would refuse a million dollars after taxes. He had since often wondered if that had been the right decision.

"Edgar," Roscoe said, with all the sincerity he could muster, "with Almighty God as my witness, I have no idea what you're talking about."

"My sainted mother, Roscoe," Delchamps said, "taught me that religion is the last refuge of the scoundrel."

"Have Roscoe play the intercepts," Two-Gun said. "If that doesn't trigger his memory, we'll let him play with the dogs."

Edgar could see from the recreation room windows the dogs to which Two-Gun referred. There were eight or nine Bouviers des Flandres in the backyard of Lorimer Manor. One of them was playing tug-of-war with the garden hose. The gardener had one end still in his hands as the Bouvier dragged him around the garden on his stomach. The rest of the Bouviers, like a herd of buffalo, bounded after them, competing for the gardener's back, onto which they leapt and rode like a sled until one of their siblings knocked them off and took their place.

"Roscoe, take out your CaseyBerry and push button number nine, which will cause some intercepts to play. When you have listened carefully, tell us what you think."

While Roscoe was doing so, Edgar went behind the bar and prepared three drinks of twelve-year-old Macallan single malt whisky. He then signed Roscoe's name to the honor system bar tab. He slid one glass to Two-Gun, but when Roscoe reached for what he thought was intended for him, Edgar waved his index finger at him negatively and said, "First, analysis, then booze."

"Depending, of course," Two-Gun amplified, "on the quality of your analysis."

As Roscoe listened to the intercepts, the elegant grandmother type in her seventies came into the recreation room with a tray of hors d'oeuvres.

"If you give me one of those," she said, pointing to his drink, "I will give you access to these." She held up the tray.

"Deal," Delchamps said, and made her a drink.

By the time he was finished, Roscoe had finished listening. He began to deliver his preliminary analysis: "I would hazard the guess that Jake Torine and Dick Miller are going to Argentina."

"The question then becomes, 'Why are they going to Argentina on Frank Lammelle's dime?'" Two-Gun said.

"It . . . This is so wild I hate to even suggest it," Roscoe said. "But it may have something to do with the President's announcement at his press conference that he was convening a Cabinet meeting right after the press conference to implement his out-of-the-box thinking vis-à-vis the Somali pirates and the Mexican drug problem. Maybe he had Charley—"

"That's the best you can do, Roscoe?" Edgar interrupted.

"I swear to G— Yes, it is."

Two-Gun said, "It's really too far off the wall that Clendennen would want to involve Charley—"

"You've got to stop thinking like an FBI agent, David," Edgar interrupted him. "And start thinking out of *your* little box. This is so far off the wall that I think there's probably something to Roscoe's analysis."

He slid the glass of twelve-year-old Macallan to Danton.

Danton took a sip, then said, "Thank you."

"You're welcome."

"But as much as I hate to leave such pleasant company, I'm going to have to run along," Roscoe said.

"And you're going to have to start thinking out of your journalist's little box, Roscoe. You're one of us now. And when one Merry Outlaw appears to be in the really deep doo-doo, other Merry Outlaws rush to help—they do not go into hiding. Got it?"

"Got it."

"Good. Just so we're all on the same page."

"What do we do now?" Roscoe asked.

There was an ordinary telephone—a base plugged into the wall with a cord and a handset—sitting below the two dinosaurs behind the bar. Delchamps went to it and dialed a number from memory.

"Good afternoon, Mr. Director, sir. This is one of your retired employees, sir, Edgar Delchamps. How are you this afternoon, sir?"

"What can I do for you, Edgar?" DCI Lammelle asked.

Twenty-plus years previously, on his first assignment as an officer of the CIA Clandestine Service, Lammelle had been sent to Athens, Greece, to work for the station chief there, Mr. Edgar Delchamps.

His orders had been to "shine shoes, make beds, and do whatever else Delchamps tells you to do. And be goddamned grateful for the chance to see him at work."

"Well, Louise and I have been sitting around Lorimer Manor—you remember Louise, don't you, Mr. Lammelle?"

Two assignments after Greece, Lammelle had been sent to Lima, Peru, where Louise Chambers had been the CIA station chief. His orders then had been "to wash dishes, make beds, and do whatever else Miss Chambers tells you to do. And be goddamned grateful for the chance to see her at work."

"Yes, of course," Lammelle said.

"Well, as I was saying, Mr. DCI, sir, Louise and I have been sitting around Lorimer Manor having a little taste, watching the grass grow, and wondering if anything interesting was happening at our former place of employment. So we thought we'd give you a call for Auld Lange Sync and ask."

"I can't think of a thing, Edgar, but it's nice to hear your voice."

"And it's always a pleasure to hear yours, sir. I guess you don't consider chartering a Gulfstream from Panamanian Executive Aircraft to fly to Argentina as interesting as Louise and I do."

"How the hell did you hear about that?" Mr. Lammelle inquired, and then hung up.

Fifteen seconds later, Mr. Delchamps's CaseyBerry buzzed.

Delchamps said, "I'll put this on loudspeaker," and then punched the appropriate buttons.

Mr. Lammelle's voice on the CaseyBerry loudspeaker picked up the conversation where he had left it: "Casey told you, right?"

"A good Clandestine Service officer, even a retired one, never reveals his sources. I thought I taught you that," Delchamps said.

When Lammelle didn't reply, Delchamps went on. "Well, if you're not willing to share this with us, Mr. DCI, sir—and by this I mean everything, of course—then I guess ol' Roscoe Danton, who just happens to be sitting here with Louise and me, is going to have to ask Mr. Blue Jay Hoboken, President Clendennen's—"

"His name is Robin, not Blue Jay," Lammelle interrupted without thinking.

"Whatever. I've never been much of an ornithologist. We'll just have Mr. Danton ask Mr. Robin Redbreast Hoboken what transpired at the President's Cabinet meeting that might have an effect on Charley Castillo. You remember Colonel Castillo, don't you, Mr. DCI, sir?"

"Oh, shit!" DCI Lammelle said, and then, biting the bullet of recognition that he had no other choice, reported all he knew.

When he had finished, and there was no reply from Delchamps, Lammelle said, "Okay, Edgar, now it's your turn. What do you know that I don't?"

"Not a thing."

"What are you thinking?"

"I think we have to wait until we learn what happens in Argentina. I can't believe Charley would go along with a recall to extended hazardous duty, but he's surprised me before."

"That's all?"

"Why don't you call Panamanian Executive Aircraft and have them bill the LCBF Corporation for the charter? Why did you volunteer to have the Agency pay for it, anyway?"

"Because I didn't think Jake would fly his airplane down there pro bono. Why does LCBF want to pay for it? Isn't that robbing Peter to pay Paul?"

"LCBF isn't going to pay for it. Casey got Those People to advance us a million dollars for our expenses in this."

"So Casey is where you got your information?"

"No. I just got it from the CIA. Nice to talk to you, Mr. Director, sir. Let's take lunch sometime when your busy schedule permits."

"Edgar, I'm asking as nice as I know how. Please don't do anything rash."

"Have I ever done anything rash as long as you've known me?"

Lammelle grunted.

"I will pass on to you anything I hear, Edgar, if you do the same. Deal?"

"Deal."

[THREE]
Aeropuerto Internacional Teniente Luis Candelaria
San Carlos de Bariloche, Río Negro Province, Argentina
0045 6 June 2007

The Gulfstream 550 touched smoothly down after a five-hour-and-twenty-six-minute flight—mostly at forty-five thousand feet and averaging 475 knots—from Panama City, Panama.

The co-pilot, who had made the landing, was a thirty-six-year-old, six-foot-two, 220-pound, very black native of Philadelphia, Pennsylvania. When he had taxied the Gulfstream to the visiting aircraft tarmac and started to shut it down, he turned to the pilot, a forty-seven-year-old, six-foot-one, 170-pound, pale-skinned silver-haired native of Culpepper, Virginia.

"Candelaria was the first guy to fly over—I guess, really *through*—the Andes," the co-pilot, Major H. Richard Miller, Junior, USA, Retired, announced. "Very large set of gonads."

"Who was? And he did what?" Colonel Jacob D. Torine, USAF, Retired, asked.

"Lieutenant Luis Candelaria," Miller clarified. "On April thirteenth, 1918, he took off from Zapala, Argentina, in an eighty-horse

Sounier Morano *Parasol*, and two hours thirty later put it down the other side of the mountains in Cunco, Chile. He was Argentina's first military aviator."

"Thank you for sharing that with me, Dick. I always like to begin my day with little nuggets of aviation history."

"You're welcome."

"And you are going to tell me, right, why you chose to enrich my life with that particular nugget at this moment in time and space?"

"Because that's where we are," Miller said. "Aeropuerto Internacional Teniente Luis Candelaria." He pointed to a sign on the terminal building that said so. "The first time I came in here I saw that and figured I'd landed at the wrong airport—the Garmin screen said it was lining me up to land at Bariloche International—so I looked it up."

"Experienced Air Force pilots such as myself never fully trust computerized navigation systems. I thought I'd taught you that."

Miller didn't reply, and instead pointed out the window. "There's Pevsner's chopper, Liam Duffy, and the local authorities, but I don't see either a brass band or our leader."

A glistening black Bell 429XP helicopter sat on the grass just off the tarmac. Beside it were two official trucks and eight men in an assortment of uniforms.

"I was afraid of that," Torine said. "McNab told me that when he told Charley we were coming down here to talk about what the President wants him to do, Charley said unless Clendennen wanted to help him commit hari-kiri, he wasn't interested in doing anything for him. When McNab said we were coming anyway, Charley said we would be wasting our time. And then he said, 'Nice to talk to you, sir,' and hung up."

"So," Miller interrupted, "when Charley got word we were an

hour out, he came here in that 429, loaded Sweaty and Max into that adorable little three-million-dollar Cessna Mustang Sweaty gave him for his birthday, and the two of them took off . . ."

Torine took up the thought: ". . . and right about now he is making his approach to Santiago, Chile, or Punta del Este, Uruguay, or some other exotic South American dorf—"

"Where they will register in a nice hotel as Señor and Señora José Gonzales of Ecuador," Miller finished the scenario.

"I see that our great minds are still marching down the same path," Torine said. "So what do we do when we learn Charley is not available to be convinced he should trust the Commander in Chief and answer his call to extended hazardous active duty? And incidentally, what's that '*hazardous* duty' all about?"

"Hazardous duty pays an extra two hundred a month, and the President thinks that will entice Charley to accept the offer."

"I forgot that. He must know how desperately Charley needs another two hundred a month. So, what do we do when we can't find Charley?"

"We will get on our CaseyBerrys and have Junior tell his daddy and have Vic D'Alessandro tell General McNab. They are accustomed to being screamed at by them."

"Colonel Naylor doesn't like it when you call him 'Junior,'" Torine said.

"I know. Payback. When we were at the Point, he encouraged my roommate to call me that. He knew I didn't like it."

"And what did he call you at West Point?"

"'Sir.' Junior was a year behind Charley and me."

Torine pushed himself out of the pilot's chair.

"Let's go get the bad news," he said.

Comandante Liam Duffy of the Argentine Gendarmería Nacional was waiting at the foot of the stair door. He warmly embraced both Torine and Miller.

"So tell me," Miller said, "what's my favorite Argentine-Irish cop doing out here in the boonies so far from the crime and fleshpots of Buenos Aires?"

"You mean in addition to greasing your way through Immigration and Customs?" Duffy replied in English that made him sound as if he had been born and raised in South Boston.

"Yeah."

"I hoped you would ask," Duffy said. "I am making sworn on the Holy Bible statements to His Eminence Archbishop Valentin and his chief of staff, Archimandrite Boris, of the ROCOR—which I'm sure you know is the Russian Orthodox Church Abroad—vis-à-vis Sweaty's late husband—"

"What the hell is that all about?" Miller asked.

"Even a heathen like you should know that the Holy Scripture—specifically First Corinthians chapter seven, verse nine—clearly says that it's better to marry than to burn."

"What the hell are you talking about, Liam?"

"I'd love to clear things up, but they're holding dinner for us."

"'Us' including Charley, Liam?" Torine asked.

"Of course. He's the one burning to get married. I wouldn't do what I'm doing for anyone else. Get in the helicopter. We'll take care of the luggage."

"Who's driving?" Miller asked.

"I am," a pleasant-appearing man about Miller's age said. "Colonel Castillo said that you would probably ask. Former Major Kiril

Koshkov, onetime chief instructor pilot, Spetsnaz Aviation School, at your service, Colonel Junior Miller."

Torine laughed and put out his hand.

"Jake Torine, Major. Pleased to meet you."

"An honor, Colonel," Koshkov said. "Would you like to ride in the left seat?"

"Thank you," Torine said. "Junior, why don't you get in the back with Vic and the other Junior?"

Two minutes later, they were airborne, and flying up the east shore of Lake Nahuel Huapi.

As a young officer, Torine had read a book—*Grey Wolf: The Escape of Adolf Hitler*, by two Englishmen, Simon Dunstan and Gerrard Williams—that posited that Adolf and Eva Braun had not committed suicide in the Führerbunker but rather had made it to Argentina, where they had lived on Estancia San Ramon, east of Bariloche, until the early 1960s.

That was right about where they were now.

He had dismissed the book as bullshit then and continued to do so until his first visit to Aleksandr Pevsner's La Casa en Bosque—where they were headed now—several years before. The house was well named. It had been built on 1,500 hectares of heavily wooded land on the western shore of Lake Nahuel Huapi.

The moment he walked into the mansion, Torine had had the feeling he'd either been there before, or seen photographs of the foyer. This was damned unlikely, as Aleksandr Pevsner's desire for privacy was legendary, and there was no chance he would have allowed a photographer from *Better Homes and Gardens* or *Country Living* or *Architectural Digest* anywhere near the place.

But the "I know this place" feeling didn't go away, and the next day Torine mentioned it to Charley Castillo.

"Really?" Castillo had asked, smiling, and then he went into the false top of his laptop where he kept various things he didn't want people to see and came out with a somewhat battered photograph.

It showed two men, Reichsmarschall Hermann Göring and a Wehrmacht colonel, standing with their hands folded in front of them in the foyer of La Casa en Bosque.

"The man with Göring is Oberst Hermann Wilhelm von und zu Gossinger," Castillo said. "My grandfather."

Confused, Torine had blurted, "But how could that have been taken here?"

"That was taken at Göring's Karin Hall estate in Prussia," Castillo said. "Shortly after Grandpa managed to get on the last plane out of Stalingrad."

"What is this place, Charley? A clone of Karin Hall?"

"It certainly looks like it. All I know is that Pevsner bought this place from an American woman when he got out of Russia. After I showed him this photo, he told Howard Kennedy—"

"The ex–FBI agent who worked for Pevsner?" Torine interrupted. "The one someone slowly beat to death with an angle iron in the Conrad Hotel and gambling joint in Punta del Este? That Howard Kennedy?"

Castillo had nodded.

"Aleksandr explained to me that both Mr. Kennedy's death and the painful manner thereof was necessary *pour l'encouragement des autres* not to think they could get away with setting the boss up to be whacked.

"Anyway, Kennedy couldn't find the American woman who sold

him this place and he looked very hard. As you well know, when Aleksandr tells somebody to do something and they don't do it, or screw it up, his tantrums make the famous tantrums of General McNab in such circumstances look like a small, disappointed frown.

"But Aleksandr did manage to get the plans for Karin Hall from a dishonest German civil servant, and they looked like a Xerox copy of the plans from which this place was built. Or vice versa."

"You think Göring was going to try to come here?" Torine asked.

"I don't know, Jake," Castillo had said, "and I don't think anyone ever will."

The Bell 429 made a sudden turn to the left, still close to the water, and both Jake Torine and Dick Miller decided it was some kind of evasive maneuver, and both wondered what they were evading.

Three minutes after that, Koshkov turned on the landing lights, and ten seconds after that floodlights came on in what a moment before had been total blackness, and a moment after that a sign illuminated, giving the wind direction and speed.

And forty-five seconds after that the 429 touched down. As soon as it had, the floodlights and the sign went off, replaced by less intense lighting illuminating the helipad.

Janos Kodály, Aleksandr Pevsner's hulking Hungarian bodyguard, was standing at the front fender of a Land Rover. Behind the Land Rover was a Mercedes SUV, beside which stood four men with Uzi submachine guns hanging from their shoulders.

It was a five-minute ride through the hardwood forest to the mansion, where Janos led them through the huge foyer to the library. There the females of the family were waiting for them.

One was the mistress of the manor, Aleksandr Pevsner's wife, Anna. The second was their fifteen-year-old daughter, Elena, who, like her mother, was a fair-skinned blonde. The third was Laura Berezovsky, now Laura Barlow, wife of Tom Barlow, formerly SVR Polkovnik Dmitri Berezovsky. The fourth was their fourteen-year-old daughter, Sof'ya, now Sophie Barlow. The fifth was former SVR Podpolkovnik Svetlana Alekseeva, now in possession of Argentine documents identifying her as Susanna Barlow. Susanna and Tom Barlow were brother and sister. The Barlows and the Pevsners were cousins, through Aleksandr Pevsner's mother.

They were all wearing black dresses, buttoned to the neck and reaching nearly to their ankles. The dresses concealed the curvatures of their bodies. Each had a golden cross hanging from her neck. Simple gold wedding rings on Anna's and Laura's hands were the only jewelry visible on any of them.

On the flight from Panama City, Lieutenant Colonel Naylor, who had never met either, asked Vic D'Alessandro what Mesdames Pevsner and Berezovsky looked like.

"Typical Russian females. You know, a hundred and sixty pounds, shoulders like a football player, stainless steel teeth . . ." D'Alessandro had replied, and then when he got the shocked look he was seeking from Colonel Naylor, said, "Think Lauren Bacall in her youth, dressed by Lord and Taylor, and bejeweled by the private customer service of Cartier. Truly elegant ladies. And the girls, their daughters, Elena and Sophie, look like what their mothers must have looked like when they were fourteen. Four attractive, very nice females."

Lieutenant Colonel Naylor knew what former Lieutenant Colonel Svetlana Alekseeva looked like. Sweaty—her Christian name had quickly morphed into this once she became associated with Lieutenant Colonel Castillo and his associates—was a striking redheaded beauty given to colorful clothing that did the opposite of concealing the lithe curvature and other attractive aspects of her body.

Today, the women's hair, which usually hung below their shoulders, was drawn tightly against their skulls and into buns. They wore no detectable makeup, not even lipstick.

"Hey, Sweaty, where's your *otxokee mecto nanara*?" Vic D'Alessandro asked, as he kissed her cheek.

She waited until he had exchanged kisses with Laura, Sophie, and Anna before saying, "You will find out soon enough, if, when you get in the dining room, you—any of you—do or say anything at all that offends His Eminence the Archbishop or His Grace the Archimandrite in any way."

"Not a problem, Sweaty. Liam Duffy told us about the archbishop and Mandrake the Magician. So we will just stay away from them until Charley's free."

"*Archimandrite*, you idiot!" she flared. "He's the next thing to a bishop. A holy man."

"As I was saying, Sweaty, where can we hide until these holy men are finished with Charley, or vice versa?"

"If the archbishop did not wish to talk to you, you wouldn't be here," she again flared. "Or Janos and I would have greeted you with swinging *otxokee mecto nanaras* when you tried to get off your airplane."

"What do these fellows want to talk to us about?" Torine asked.

"Not 'these fellows,' Jake," Sweaty said. "I expected better from you. They are an archbishop and an archimandrite and deserve your respect."

"Jake," Anna said, "His Grace and the archimandrite are here in connection with Charley and Svetlana's marriage problem. This is serious."

"Okay," Torine said.

"Now, when Janos takes you into the dining room, what you do is bow and reach down and touch the floor with your right hand . . ."

Sweaty demonstrated.

". . . then you place your right hand over your left hand, palms upward . . ."

Sweaty demonstrated this.

". . . then you say, 'Bless, Your Eminence.' In Russian."

"I don't speak Russian," Naylor said.

"Repeat after me. Благослови, ваша светлость," Sweaty ordered.

"Благослови, ваша светлость," Naylor repeated.

"Again," Sweaty ordered.

"Благослови, ваша светлость," Naylor said again.

"Now you know how to say 'Bless, Your Eminence' in Russian," Sweaty said. "When you say it in the dining room, the archbishop will reply, 'May the Lord bless you,' and make the Sign of the Cross, and place his right hand on your hands. Then you kiss his hand. That's it, unless His Eminence decides to introduce you to the archimandrite. If he does, then you go through the routine for him."

"Got it," Naylor said.

"You better have it. If you fuc— don't get it right and His Eminence or His Grace is offended, I'll chop you into small pieces with my *otxokee mecto nanara*."

"I don't suppose there's any way I can opt out of this charming ritual?" Dick Miller asked.

"Not and live, there isn't," Sweaty said. Then she ordered, "Janos, take them to His Eminence."

Janos opened the door to the dining room and announced, in Russian, "Your Eminence, Your Grace, the Americans are here."

"Please ask them to come in," a voice replied in Russian.

Janos signaled for the Americans and Liam Duffy to enter the dining room.

There were six men in the room, all dressed in black. One of them was Aleksandr Pevsner, a tall, dark-haired man who appeared to be in his late thirties; his eyes were large, and blue, and extraordinarily bright. Another was Lieutenant Colonel Carlos G. Castillo, who was a shade over six feet tall, weighed 190 pounds, and also was in his late thirties. The third was Tom Barlow, who looked so much like Castillo they could pass for brothers. The fourth was Nicolai Tarasov, a forty-odd-year-old short, stocky, and bald Russian. His mother and Aleksandr Pevsner's mother were sisters. These four wore dark blue, nearly black, single-breasted suits, white shirts, and red-striped neckties. They were all cleanly shaven and looked (at least everyone but bald cousin Nicolai did) to be freshly barbered.

The fifth and sixth men in the room looked as if they hadn't been close to a barber in a decade or more. Their black beards dropped down over their chests. They, too, were dressed in black, but it was not a single-breasted business suit.

The material of the archimandrite's garment, the hem of which nearly touched the floor, was velvet, heavily embroidered with white-gold thread. Near the bottom were two representations of winged cherubs surrounded by a leafless tree, also embroidered in gold or white-gold, or maybe platinum, thread.

Draped over his shoulders was a foot-wide—for lack of a better term—black velvet shawl with a white-gold fringe at its ends. Running all the way around it was a white-gold-embroidered border an inch and a half wide into which had been sewn at six-inch intervals gemstones, most of which seemed to be emeralds. The shawl also had representations of cherubs, various versions of the Holy Cross, and some other decorative features. A large golden crucifix hung from a golden chain around his neck, and on his head was a foot-tall white-silk-covered headdress with a tail—like that of French Foreign Legionaires in the desert, D'Alessandro thought—reaching down past his shoulders.

The archbishop was similarly attired, except that he had even more white-gold embroidery and a larger golden crucifix.

Taking a chance that the latter might be His Eminence Archbishop Valentin, Vic D'Alessandro dropped to his knees, touched the floor, put his right hand over his left hand, palms upward, and said, "Благослови, ваша светлость."

"May God bless you, my son," His Grace the archbishop said, in American English.

When Archimandrite Boris saw the surprised look on Vic's face, and as he waited for Torine, Miller, and Naylor to play their parts in the ritual as Sweaty had taught them to do, he smiled and said, "Both His Eminence and I were born and raised in Chicago."

[ONE]

La Casa en el Bosque
San Carlos de Bariloche
Río Negro Province, Argentina
0115 6 June 2007

Colonel Jacob Torine was accustomed to being around very senior people, some of whom had worn exotic clothing—among other assignments, he had served as the senior aircraft commander of Air Force One—so while he was impressed with Archbishop Valentin, he wasn't dazzled.

As soon as the introductions had been made, he said, "It is very gracious of Your Eminence to hold dinner for us."

"Not at all," the archbishop replied. "While we were waiting, we've been at these magnificent hors d'oeuvres and heeding the advice of Saint Timothy, who admonished us, you may recall . . ."

"'Drink no longer water, but use a little wine for thy stomach's sake,'" Torine picked up. "In the King James Bible, First Timothy, chapter five, verse twenty-three. One of my favorite bits of Holy Scripture."

"That would suggest you're a Christian, Colonel," Archbishop Valentin said, "which is one of the questions I planned to pose."

"I think I am, Your Grace," Torine replied. "My wife is not so sure. Which brings us, of course, to the First Epistle to the Corinthians. . . ."

"'Let Your Women Keep Silent,'" the Archbishop quoted, chuckling. "On the basis of your knowledge of Holy Scripture, Colonel, I will regard you as a Christian. I'll get to the other gentlemen in a moment, but right now, why don't we all have a glass of the very excellent Saint Felicien Cabernet Sauvignon that Aleksandr has so graciously provided."

He raised his hand and a man in a starched white jacket appeared with a tray holding bottles of wine and glasses.

When the wine had been poured, Archimandrite Boris raised his glass.

"I would like to thank you all for coming here to help His Eminence and myself, even understanding that wasn't your primary purpose in coming."

When there was no response to that, the archimandrite went on: "Will someone tell us what that primary purpose is?"

When there was no response to that, the archimandrite nodded toward Naylor.

"Perhaps you would be willing, my son, to do so."

Naylor opened his mouth. But before a word came out, the archimandrite asked, "Are you a Christian, my son?"

"When I was a kid, I was confirmed—Colonel Castillo and I were—in the Evangelische Church in Germany. Saint Johan's, in Hersfeld. And then I became an Episcopalian when I was at West Point. My parents are Episcopalian."

"That's very interesting, but my question was 'Are you a Christian?'"

"Yes, sir."

"And what is it that brings you here, that so infuriates Mrs. Alekseeva?"

Naylor looked at Castillo, obviously asking for his permission to answer. Castillo nodded.

"I am to relay to Colonel Castillo the request of the President of the United States that he enter upon extended hazardous active duty in connection with the Mexican drug and Somali pirates problems."

"And why would you say this so infuriates Mrs. Alekseeva?"

Naylor again wordlessly asked for—and got—Castillo's permission to reply.

"Probably because the last time Colonel Castillo worked for the President, the President tried very hard to kidnap Colonel Castillo—and Mrs. Alekseeva and her brother—with the intention to load them on a plane and ship them off to the SVR in Russia."

"So they've told me. So why are you in effect doing so?"

"Obeying orders, Your Grace."

"Obeying orders from whom?"

"My father."

"Heeding the scriptural admonition to 'Honor thy father and mother . . .' et cetera?"

"It's more that my father is a general and I'm a lieutenant colonel, Your Grace."

"And do you think the President will again try to turn Colonel Castillo over to the kind ministrations of the SVR?"

"It wouldn't surprise me, Your Grace."

Castillo snorted.

The archimandrite asked, "Yet you're here to tell him what President Clendennen wants him to do?"

"And to tell him I think he'd be a damned fool to do it."

The archbishop joined in: "Your father is aware of what might happen to Colonel Castillo if Colonel Castillo accedes to President Clendennen's request?"

"Yes, Your Eminence, he is."

"Then why . . . ?"

"Because he's a soldier, sir. Soldiers do what they are ordered to do."

"Soldiers, I would suggest," the archbishop said, "like priests, are *expected* to do what they have been ordered to do. Sometimes, a priest—and, I would suggest, a soldier—gets an order he knows it would be wrong to execute."

"Yes, sir. That's true, Your Eminence."

"Posing for him the problem of doing what he's ordered to do knowing it's wrong, or disobeying the order, while knowing disobedience is wrong."

"Then, Your Eminence," Naylor said, "he must decide which is the greater evil: disobedience, or complying with an order he knows is wrong."

"Or choosing the middle path," the archbishop said. "Which apparently you have done. Complying with your orders, but making it clear that Colonel Castillo would be a 'damned fool' for doing what your father and the President want him to do."

"Sorry about the language, Your Eminence," Naylor said.

"That wasn't blasphemy, my son, simply colorful language spoken in the company of men. But, while fascinating as this conversation is, I think we should turn to why the archimandrite and I are here, and your role in that. That is, I'm afraid, going to take some time."

"We are at your pleasure, Your Eminence," Jake Torine said.

"My pleasure was the exchange between Colonel Naylor and myself. This is duty, and as we just discussed, duty sometimes—perhaps even often—is not a matter of pleasure.

"And so I am here to deal with a matter between Patriarch Alexius the Second and myself. Do any of you know who His Beatitude is?"

"Isn't he sort of the Pope of the Russian Orthodox Church, Your Eminence?" Torine asked.

"His Beatitude is the Patriarch of Moscow and all Russia," the archbishop said. "A position analogous to the Roman Catholic Pope. But having told you that, I suspect that you don't know much more than you did previously.

"Let me ask this question, then, of all of you. How much Russian history do you know? Specifically, how much do you know about the Oprichnina?"

"Not much about either, Your Eminence," Torine confessed.

The others shook their heads, joining in the confession of ignorance.

"Sweaty . . . Svetlana has told me about the Oprichnina, Your Eminence," Castillo said.

"In addition to his other duties, the archimandrite is in charge of our seminaries," the archbishop said. "In that function he has reluctantly become far more of an academic than I am. Boris, could you give our friends a quick history lesson—Oprichnina 101, so to speak?"

"If that is your desire, Your Eminence," the archimandrite said. He took a long moment to collect his thoughts, and then began.

"I suppose I should begin with Ivan the Fourth, sometimes known as 'Ivan the Terrible.'"

Both Castillo and Naylor had first heard of Ivan the Terrible when they were eleven and students at Saint Johan's School in Bad Hersfeld. He had stuck in their memory because they had learned he had amused himself by throwing dogs and men off the Kremlin's walls because he liked to watch them crawl around on broken legs.

"Ivan the Terrible—Ivan the Fourth—was born in 1530," the archimandrite went on. "There was then no Czar. Most of the power was in the hands of the Grand Duke of Muscovy, Ivan's father, Vasily the Third. His power came from the private armies of the nobility, the boyars, who placed them at Vasily the Third's service, providing they approved of what he was doing.

"Vasily the Third died in 1533, when Ivan was three years old. The boy became the Grand Duke of Muscovy. The boyars 'advised,' through a series of committees, the Grand Duke what Grand Ducal decrees he should issue.

"As soon as he reached puberty, and very probably before, the boyars began to abuse Ivan sexually, more to remind him how powerful they were than for pleasure, although at least some of them enjoyed what they were doing.

"In the belief that he was firmly in their control, they allowed him to assume power in his own right—in other words, without the advice of the committees—in 1544, when he was fourteen.

"During the next three years, Ivan developed a close relationship with the church, specifically with Philip the Second, Metropolitan of Moscow. The Metropolitan discovered Holy Scripture that suggested God wanted Ivan to be Czar, and in January 1547, the Metropolitan presided over the coronation of Czar Ivan the Fourth. Ivan was then seventeen years old.

"Ivan, who had figured out that if he had the church on his side, he would also have the support of the peasants and serfs, who were very religious, then began to favor the boyars he felt sure he could control, and undercutting the power of the others.

"Phrased less kindly, as soon as he became Czar, he began feeding those boyars who questioned his divine right to rule to pits of starving dogs. Then he seized their property and divided it between himself, the church, and the boyars, who did think he had God on his side. It is important to remember here that boyar property included the serfs who lived on the land, and that the various private armies involved were made up of serf conscripts.

"The church—Philip the Second, it must be admitted—was involved in this un-holy scheme of things up to his ears. In payment for telling the faithful that Ivan was standing at the right hand of God, and making the point that challenging Ivan was tantamount to challenging God, the church grew wealthy.

"Ivan also began to form an officer corps from the merchant class. Their loyalty was to him personally, and he bought it by paying them generously. What had been two or three dozen private armies under the control of that many boyars became one army answering only to Ivan.

"This went on for about eighteen years, until 1565, when he decided he had arranged things as well as he could. Then he went into action. First, he moved his family out of Moscow to one of his country estates. When he was sure that he and they were safe in the hands of his officer corps, he wrote a letter to Metropolitan Philip the Second. The Czar said he was going to abdicate and, to that end, had already moved out of Moscow. He posted copies of the letter on walls and, importantly, in every church.

"The people, the letter said, could now run Russia to suit themselves, starting by picking a new Czar, to whom they could look for protection. This upset everybody. The people didn't want a new Czar who was not chosen by God. The boyars knew that picking one of their own to be the new Czar was going to result in a bloodbath. The officer corps knew that the privileges they had been granted were almost certainly not to be continued under a new Czar, and that the boyars would want their serfs back.

"The Czar was begged not to abdicate, to come home to Moscow. After letting them worry for a while, during which time they had a preview of what life without Czar Ivan would be like, he announced his terms for not abdicating.

"There would be something new in Russian, the *Oprichnina*—'Separate Estate'—which would consist of one thousand households, some of the highest nobility of the boyars, some of lower-ranking boyars, some of senior military officers, a few of members of the merchant class, and even a few families of extraordinarily successful peasants.

"They all had demonstrated a commendable degree of loyalty to the Czar. The Oprichnina would physically include certain districts of Russia and certain cities, and the revenue from these places would be used to support the Oprichnina and of course the Czar, who would live among them.

"The old establishment would remain in place. The boyars not included in the Oprichnina would retain their titles and privileges; the council—the *Duma*—would continue to operate, its decisions subject of course to the Czar's approval. But the communication would be one way. Except in extraordinary circumstances, no one not an Oprichniki would be permitted to communicate with the Oprichnina.

"The Czar's offer was accepted. God's man was back in charge. The boyars had their titles. The church was now supported by the state, so most of the priests and bishops were happy. Just about everybody was happy but Philip the Second, Metropolitan of Moscow, who let it be known that he thought the idea of the Oprichnina was un-Christian.

"The Czar understood that he could not tolerate doubt or criticism. And so Ivan set out for Tver, where the Metropolitan lived. On the way, he heard a rumor that the people and the administration in Russia's second-largest city, Great Novgorod, were unhappy with having to support Oprichnina.

"Just as soon as he had watched Metropolitan Philip being choked to death in Tver, the Czar went to Great Novgorod, where, over the course of five weeks, the army of the Oprichnina, often helped personally by Ivan himself, raped every female they could find, massacred every man they could find, and destroyed every farmhouse, warehouse, barn, monastery, church, every crop in the fields, every horse, cow, and chicken."

He paused, then said, "And so was born what we now call the SVR."

"Excuse me?" Jake Torine asked. "I got lost just now."

"Over the years, it has been known by different names, of course," the archimandrite explained. "It actually didn't have a name of its own, other than the Oprichnina, a state within a state, until Czar

Nicholas the First. After Nicholas put down the Decembrist Revolution in 1825, he reorganized the trusted elements of the Oprichnina into what he called the Third Section.

"That reincarnation of the Oprichnina lasted until 1917, when the Bolsheviks renamed it the All-Russian Extraordinary Commission for the Suppression of Counterrevolution and Sabotage—acronym Cheka."

"That sounds as if you're saying that the Czar's secret police just changed sides, became Communists," D'Alessandro said.

It was his first comment during the long history lesson.

"My son, you're saying two things, you realize," the archbishop said. "That the Oprichnina changed sides is one. That the Oprichnina became Communist is another. They never change sides. They may have worked for different masters, but they never become anything other than what they were, members of the Oprichnina."

"Excuse me, Your Eminence," D'Alessandro said, "but I've always been taught that the Russian secret police, by whatever name, were always Communist. Wasn't the first head of the Cheka—Dzerzhinsky—a lifelong Communist? I've always heard he spent most of his life in one Czarist jail or another before the Communist revolution. That's not so?"

"The Dziarzhynava family was of the original one thousand families in Ivan's Oprichnina," the archbishop said. "Felix Edmundovich Dzerzhinsky, the first head of the Cheka, was born on the family's estate in western Belarus. The estate was never confiscated by the Bolsheviks or the Mensheviks or the Communists after they took power. The family owns it to this day."

The archimandrite picked the narrative up.

"The Czar's Imperial Prisons were controlled by the Third Section. How well one fared in them—or whether one was actually in a prison, or was just on the roster—depended on how well one was regarded by the Oprichnina. The fact that the history books paint the tale of this heroic revolutionary languishing, starved and beaten, for years in a Czarist prison cell doesn't make it true."

The archbishop took his turn by asking, "And didn't you think it was a little odd that Lenin appointed Dzerzhinsky to head the Cheka and kept him there when there were so many deserving and reasonably talented Communists close to him?"

D'Alessandro put up both hands in an admission of confusion.

"The Cheka," the archimandrite went on, "was reorganized after the counterrevolution of 1922 as the GPU, later the OGPU. A man named Yaakov Peters was named to head it. By Felix Edmundovich Dzerzhinsky, who was minister of the interior, which controlled the OGPU.

"Dzerzhinsky died of a heart attack in 1926. After that there were constant reorganizations and renaming. In 1934, the OGPU became the NKVD—People's Commissariat for State Security. In 1943, the NKGB was split off from the NKVD. And in 1946, after the Great War, it became the MGB, Ministry of State Security."

"What you're saying, Your Grace," D'Alessandro said, "is that this state within a state . . ."

"The Oprichnina," the archimandrite furnished.

". . . the *Oprichnina* was in charge of everything? Only the names changed and the Oprichnina walked through the raindrops of the purges they had over there at least once a year?"

"My son," the archbishop said, "you're again putting together things that don't belong together. Yes, the Oprichnina remained—*remains*—in charge. No, not all the Oprichniki managed to live through all the purges. Enough did, of course, in order to maintain the Oprichnina and learn from the mistakes made."

"Excuse me, Your Eminence," Torine asked. "Are you saying the Oprichnina exists today?"

"Of course it does. Russia is under an Oprichnik."

"Putin?" D'Alessandro blurted.

"Who else," the archbishop replied, "but Vladimir Vladimirovich Putin?"

"And that Mr. Pevsner, Swe . . . Svetlana, and Colonel Berezovsky were—are—Oprichniki?"

Nicolai Tarasov raised his pudgy hand above his bald head.

When Torine looked at him, Tarasov said, smiling, "Yes, me, too. I confess. If there were membership cards, I would be a card-carrying Oprichnik."

"How do you get to be an Oprichnik?" D'Alessandro asked. "Like the Mafia makes 'made men'? First you whack somebody, then there's a ceremony where you cut your fingers to mingle blood, and then take an oath of silence?"

"One is born into the Oprichnik," the archbishop said. "Or, in the case of women, marries into it. Only very rarely can a man become an Oprichnik by marrying into it. There is no oath of silence, such as the Mafia oath of Omertà, because one is not necessary. It is in the interest of every Oprichnik to keep what he or she knows about the state within the state from becoming public knowledge."

"May I have your permission, Your Eminence, to make a comment?" Aleksandr Pevsner asked. It was the first time he'd said anything.

The archbishop nodded.

"But please, my son, try to not get far off the subject," he said.

"The Oprichnina has not endured for more than four hundred years without difficulty," Pevsner said. "From time to time, it has been necessary to purify its membership—"

"Purify it? How was that done, Mr. Pevsner?" Jake Torine asked.

"I recently found it necessary to purify my personal staff of a man—an American—who betrayed the trust I placed in him."

"Howard Kennedy?" Torine asked.

Pevsner did not respond directly, but instead said, "As I was saying, we have found it necessary to purify our ranks from time to time and also to place under our protection certain individuals who have rendered one or more of us—and thus the Oprichnina—a great service.

"This was the case with our Charley. Before he met Svetlana and Dmitri, I very seriously considered eliminating him as a threat. God in His never-failing wisdom stayed my hand, and Charley lived to save my life at the risk of his own. Knowing that others, in particular Vladimir Vladimirovich, still wanted our Charley out of the way, I sent word to Vladimir Vladimirovich that I considered our Charley my brother.

"Ordinarily, that would have been enough to protect our Charley, as a friend of the Oprichnina, but Vladimir Vladimirovich apparently decided that our Charley posed a threat he could not countenance and/or that I no longer had the authority to categorize Charley as a protected friend of the Oprichnina.

"He sent Dmitri and Svetlana to eliminate our Charley in Marburg, Germany. That operation turned out disastrously for Vladimir Vladimirovich, as you all know. Not only did Dmitri and Svetlana decide not to eliminate our Charley, but enlisted his aid in helping them to defect.

"Vladimir Vladimirovich had SVR agents waiting in Vienna to arrest Dmitri and Svetlana. Instead, our Charley flew them to Argentina and ultimately brought them here."

"Can I jump in here, Your Eminence?" Vic D'Alessandro asked.

"I was afraid this would happen," the archbishop asked. "But yes, my son, you may. Try to be brief."

"Thank you," D'Alessandro said.

"Dmitri—"

"Please call me Tom, Vic."

"Okay. *Tom*, why did you defect? From all I've ever heard, all the intelligence services in Russia live very well, and I'm guessing that you Oprichniks lived pretty high on the hog. So why did you defect?"

"Because we came to the conclusion that sooner or later, Mr. Putin was going to get around to purifying us. We knew too much. We had family members—Aleksandr and Nicolai—who had, Vladimir Vladimirovich could reasonably argue, already defected."

"I don't think Vladimir Vladimirovich, if he could get his hands on us, would have actually fed us to starving dogs or thrown us off the Kremlin wall," Aleksandr Pevsner said, "but keeping us on drugs in a mental hospital for the rest of our lives seemed a distinct possibility."

"What did he have . . . does he have . . . against you?"

"You didn't tell them, Charley?" Pevsner asked.

Castillo shook his head.

"Would you have told them if they asked?" Pevsner asked.

"If they had a good reason for wanting to know, I would have."

"You really have the makings of a good Oprichnik," Pevsner said. "Well, now there is that reason, so I will tell them.

"In the former Union of Soviet Socialist Republics, I was a *polkovnik*—colonel—in both the Soviet Air Force and the SVR. I was in charge of Aeroflot operations worldwide, both in a business sense and in the security aspect. These duties required me to travel all over the world, and to make the appropriate contacts. My cousin Nicolai was my deputy in both roles.

"When the USSR collapsed, the SVR—which is to say Vladimir Vladimirovich—learned the new government had the odd notion that the assets of the SVR should be turned over to the new democratic government."

"What assets?" Torine asked.

"Would you believe tons of gold, Jake?" Castillo asked.

"Jesus Christ!" Torine said.

"Now *that* was blasphemous," the archbishop said.

"I'm sorry, Your Eminence," Torine said.

"You need Our Savior's forgiveness, not mine."

"Plus some tons of platinum," Castillo said, chuckling. "Not to mention a lot of cash."

Pevsner, his tone making it clear that he didn't appreciate contributions from others while he was explaining things, then went on:

"As I was saying. When Vladimir Vladimirovich was faced with the problem of not wanting to turn over the SVR's assets to the new democratic government, he turned to me. Nicolai and me. He correctly suspected that we would know how to get these assets out of Russia to places where they would be safe from the clutching hands of the new government.

"At about this time, Nicolai and I realized there were some aspects of capitalism we had not previously understood. As Ayn Rand so wisely put it—she was Russian, I presume you know—'No man is entitled to the fruits of another man's labor.'

"So Nicolai and I told Vladimir Vladimirovich we would be happy to accommodate him for a small fee. Five percent of the value of what we placed safely outside the former Soviet Union."

"Jake," Castillo said, "you've always been good at doing math in your head. Try this: In 1991, when the USSR collapsed, gold was about $375 an ounce. How much is five percent of two thousand pounds of gold, there being sixteen ounces of gold in each pound?"

"My Go— goodness," Torine said.

"'Goodness' being a euphemism for God," the archbishop said, "there are those, myself included, who consider the phrase blasphemous."

"Again, I'm sorry, Your Eminence," Torine said, then looked at Castillo. "And you said 'tons of gold'? Plural?"

"So now you know," Castillo said, "where ol' Aleksandr got the money to buy Karin Hall, and all those cruise ships, and the Grand Cozumel Beach and Golf Resort, et cetera, et cetera."

"We started out with a couple of old transports from surplus Air Force stock," Pevsner said. "We flew surplus Soviet arms out of Russia, and luxury goods—Mercedes-Benz automobiles, Louis Vuitton luggage, that sort of thing—in.

"Mingled with the arms on the flights out of Moscow were fifty-five-gallon barrels of fuel. You would be surprised how much gold one can get into a fifty-five-gallon drum. That, unfortunately, is how I earned the reputation of being an arms dealer; but regretfully that was necessary as a cover. No one was going to believe I prospered so quickly providing antique samovars and Black Sea caviar to the world market.

"But turning to Vladimir Vladimirovich, who is really the subject of this meeting . . ."

"I'm so glad you remembered, my son," the archbishop said.

"As long as I have known Vladimir Vladimirovich, which has been for all of our lives, I always suspected—probably because of his father; the apple never falls far from the tree—that he was more of a Communist than a Christian, which means that he was far more interested in lining his pockets than promoting the general welfare of the Oprichnina."

"That characterization, I would suggest," the archbishop said, "qualifies as a rare exception to the scriptural admonition to 'judge not,' et cetera."

"I gather you are a Christian, Mr. Pevsner?" Naylor asked.

"Of course I'm a Christian," Pevsner said indignantly. "I'm surprised our Charley didn't make that quite clear to you."

"It must have slipped his mind," Naylor said.

"Where was I?" Pevsner asked.

"You were saying that Mr. Putin was very much like his father," D'Alessandro said.

"He is."

"The story I've always heard is that his father was a foreman in a locomotive factory who became Stalin's cook."

"That's what the official biographies say. Actually, he was Stalin's cook as much as Felix Edmundovich Dzerzhinsky was a tortured prisoner of the Czar until he was twenty-six. Vladimir Putin the elder was a general in the KGB, who served, among other such duties, as political commissar during the siege of Stalingrad."

Pevsner paused long enough to let that sink in, then said, "With the gracious permission of His Eminence, I will continue."

"Keep it short, my son," the archbishop said.

"Where to begin?" Pevsner asked rhetorically, and then answered his own question. "At the beginning . . .

"During the revolution of 1917, a substantial portion of Third Section, the Czar's secret police, was co-opted by the Bolsheviks of Vladimir Ilyich Lenin and renamed the Cheka—"

"'A substantial portion'?" D'Alessandro interrupted.

"If they had taken it over completely, Vic," Pevsner said, "none of us would be here today, and there would be no Oprichnina."

"And with no Oprichnina, God alone knows what would have been the fate of the church," the archbishop added.

"Who didn't get co-opted?" D'Alessandro asked.

"My family, obviously, and the Alekseev family, and perhaps fifty or sixty others," Pevsner said. "May I continue?"

"Alek," Castillo said, "all Vic is trying to do is make sure he and everybody else understands what you're trying to tell them."

"Be that as it may, friend Charley, if I am continually interrupted, I'll never finish."

"Sorry, Alek," D'Alessandro said.

"The Cheka," Pevsner went on, "arrested the Imperial Family—Czar Nicholas the Second, Czarina Alexandra, their five children—Czarevich Alexei, and Grand Duchesses Olga, Tatiana, Maria, and Anastasia—and a half dozen of the intimate friends and servants and took them to Yekaterinburg, which is some nine hundred miles east of Moscow.

"There, on July seventeenth, 1918, at the personal order of Vladimir Ilyich Lenin, they were murdered and their bodies buried in unmarked graves in a forest.

"The Bolsheviks then turned to destroying the church."

"Their greatest mistake, in my humble judgment," the archbishop said. "Wouldn't you agree, Father Boris?"

"Absolutely, Your Eminence," the archimandrite said.

"They murdered clergy, confiscated church property, burned seminaries, turned churches and cathedrals into warehouses . . . that sort of thing. Shipped millions of Christian people to Siberia. But the church was stronger than they thought it would be."

"In large part because of the faithful within the Oprichnina, it must be admitted," the archbishop furnished.

His face showing that while he appreciated the archbishop's kind words, he still didn't appreciate being interrupted, Pevsner picked up his history lesson.

"One of the first things to happen was the formation of the Russian Orthodox Church Outside Russia—ROCOR."

"The archimandrite and I have the honor of humbly serving the ROCOR," the archbishop said.

"And it is my honor to humbly serve His Eminence, who heads ROCOR," the archimandrite said.

"ROCOR remained part of the Russian Orthodox Church," the archbishop went on, "that is to say, under the authority of the Moscow Patriarchate, until 1927—"

"I was about to get to that, Your Eminence," Pevsner said.

His face showing that he disliked being interrupted, His Eminence continued: ". . . when the godless Bolsheviks finally broke the will of Metropolitan Sergius, who headed the church. They had had him in a Moscow prison cell for about five years at the time, which probably had a good deal to do with what he did: He pledged loyalty to the Communist regime.

"That was too much for one of my predecessors, who informed

Sergius that while we still regarded Sergius as an archbishop, we no longer could consider ourselves under the patriarchal authority of someone who had pledged loyalty to the Communists."

He paused and then said, "You may continue, Aleksandr, my son."

"In 1991, the year the Soviet Union imploded," Pevsner went on, "it was announced that the unmarked graves of the Royal Family had been found. Since Vladimir Vladimirovich Putin was involved, I suspected that he had known all along where they were.

"So, what was he up to? The answer was simple: He wanted to replace Stalin. And—no one has ever suggested that Vladimir Vladimirovich is not a very clever man—he knew the way to become the new Czar of all the Russias was to follow the philosophy of Ivan the Terrible—get the church on his side—rather than the failed philosophy of Lenin and Stalin to destroy the church.

"He was also smart enough to know that he couldn't do this the way Ivan did, by throwing money at the church. For one thing, he flatly denied knowing anything about the assets of the SVR.

"Nicolai and I, I should point out, had already moved many of these assets to the Cayman Islands, Macao, and, of course, here to Argentina. If Vladimir Vladimirovich had started to give the church money, the Patriarch in Moscow was certain to have asked where he'd gotten it.

"So, what he needed to do was prove his devotion to the church. First, he found the long-lost unmarked graves of the Royal Family, hired DNA experts to determine they were indeed the royal bones, and then decided that the martyred Czar and his family should have the Christian burial those terrible Communists had so long denied them.

"This took place—with Vladimir Vladimirovich playing a significant and very visible role in the ceremonies—on July eighteenth, 1998, sixty years to the day from their murder in Yekaterinburg.

"The reinterment of the mortal remains of the Royal Family," the archimandrite chimed in, "was in the Saints Peter and Paul Cathedral inside the Saints Peter and Paul Fortress in Saint Petersburg, which the Communist authorities had renamed during their reign as Leningrad."

"Thank you, Your Grace," Pevsner said with as much sincerity as he could muster, and then went on much more pleasantly as he suddenly remembered something about that. "It was well known within the Oprichnina that Vladimir Vladimirovich had been one of the more strident voices demanding of the new government of Russia that they change Leningrad back into Saint Petersburg to reflect its Christian heritage."

"There is some good in even the worst of sinners," His Eminence pronounced.

"After the funeral, Vladimir Vladimirovich's reputation was that of a staunch and faithful supporter of the church," Pevsner went on. "And about that time, he began to start inviting Nicolai and me back to the motherland for conferences. I wasn't suspicious of this until one time when I told him I could fit it into my schedule, but Nicolai was tied up. He said he'd rather wait until we could come together.

"After that, neither Nicolai nor I could ever seem to find a time to travel to the motherland either together or alone."

"But we did get word to Dmitri and Svetlana," Nicolai furnished, "that it might be a good idea for them to visit us—"

"Together," Pevsner interrupted.

". . . for an extended period."

"That was after Vladimir Vladimirovich sent word to us that he'd thought it over and come to the conclusion that five percent was excessive for the service we had rendered."

"But that we could make things right," Nicolai furnished, "if we deposited half of what we had earned to an account of the SVR in a bank in Johannesburg, South Africa."

"Well, when Vladimir Vladimirovich realized that Nicolai and I were neither going to accept his kind invitation to visit the motherland, or—having become capitalists, where a deal is a deal—send half of what we had honestly earned to Joburg, he decided to demonstrate that the SVR was something still to be feared."

"You don't *know* that, Alek," Nicolai interrupted.

"I also don't *know* if the sun will rise tomorrow morning, but based on what's happened in the past, I'll bet it does."

"What do you suspect Vladimir Vladimirovich of doing, Aleksandr, my son?" His Eminence asked, just a little impatiently.

"There were several people around the world who had, in one way or another, gotten in the SVR's way," Pevsner explained. "Vladimir Vladimirovich decided that eliminating them all, at the same time, would send the message 'Fear the SVR' or 'Fear Vladimir Vladimirovich Putin' both around the world and within Russia.

"One of those he eliminated, for example, was Kurt Kuhl, who owned several pastry shops—called the Kuhlhaus—in Vienna, Prague, and Budapest. Vladimir Vladimirovich had good reason to believe that Herr Kuhl was a CIA asset who over the years had facilitated the defection of a number of SVR personnel, and agents controlled by the SVR.

"The bodies of Herr Kuhl and his wife were found behind the Johann Strauss statue in the Stadtpark in Vienna. They had been murdered with metal garrotes of the type the former Hungarian secret police, the Államvédelmi Hatóság, were fond of using. It isn't much of a secret that those members of the Államvédelmi Hatóság who hadn't been hung by their countrymen when Hungary severed its connection with the Soviet Union often found employment with the SVR, so Vladimir Vladimirovich could send that message, too, to other CIA assets. 'We know about you, and are going to eliminate you.'

"Another problem for Vladimir Vladimirovich was right here," Pevsner continued, gesturing toward Liam Duffy. "The SVR had a very profitable business going shipping cocaine and heroin from Paraguay and elsewhere through Argentina to Europe and the United States. The profits were used to fund SVR operations all over South America. When, rarely, the movements were detected, palms were greased, the drugs went back into the pipeline, and the shippers either never went to trial, or if they did were either freed or slapped on the wrist.

"Then my friend Liam was assigned the duty—the Gendarmería Nacional was—and things changed. Liam is a devout Roman Catholic who took his oath of office seriously. When his people intercepted a drug shipment, they burned the drugs and ran the shippers before courts which were not for sale.

"Worse than that, so far as Vladimir Vladimirovich was concerned, was that Liam began to hold—what's that charming phrase?—*drumhead courts-martial* at the arrest scene, which saved the government the cost of trials and the expense of feeding the drug people during long periods of incarceration."

"Holy Scripture teaches us," the archbishop said disapprovingly, to 'judge not, lest thee be judged.'"

"I considered that prayerfully, Your Eminence," Duffy said, "and decided I could successfully argue my case before Saint Peter."

"Vladimir Vladimirovich sent people to eliminate my friend Liam," Pevsner continued, "and his family, and the attempt was made on Christmas Eve. All of the assassinations, or attempted assassinations, took place on Christmas Eve. In Liam's case, the attempt failed.

"And finally, there was a reporter, Günther Freidler, who worked for Charley's *Tages Zeitung* newspaper chain."

"Excuse me?" the archbishop asked, and then parroted, "'Charley's newspaper chain'?"

"My brother Charley has two personas, Your Eminence," Pevsner explained. "One of them is Lieutenant Colonel Castillo, U.S. Army, Retired, and the other is Herr Karl Wilhelm von und zu Gossinger, who is by far the principal stockholder of Gossinger Beteiligungsgesellschaft, which owns, among other things, the *Tages Zeitung* newspaper chain." He paused, and then added, "If Your Eminence was concerned that my brother Charley's interest in marrying my cousin Svetlana is based on her affluence, I respectfully suggest it is not a factor."

"I don't understand," the archbishop said.

"I'm a bastard, Your Eminence," Castillo said. "Born out of wedlock to an eighteen-year-old German girl, following her seventy-two-hour dalliance with an eighteen-year-old American chopper jockey."

"'Chopper jockey'?" the archbishop parroted.

"Helicopter pilot," Castillo clarified. "Whom she never saw or heard from again."

"There are men like that, unfortunately," His Eminence said. "I hope you can find it in your heart to forgive him."

"I have managed to convince myself, Your Eminence, that my father never knew he had . . . left my mother in the family way."

"I can't let that ride, Charley," Naylor said.

Castillo shrugged.

The archbishop made a *go on* gesture to Naylor.

"Charley's mother didn't know what had happened to Charley's father until she was literally on her deathbed," Naylor said.

"How do you know that?" the archbishop said.

"I was there," Naylor said. "My father was deeply involved. What happened was that Charley's mother, knowing she was about to die and Charley would be an orphan—his grandfather and uncle had died in a car accident on the autobahn the year before; she thought he was really going to be alone—asked my father to find Charley's father."

"Asked your father?" the archbishop said.

"Yes, sir. My father was an officer in the 14th Armored Cavalry, then patrolling the border between East and West Germany. The border line had cut Charley's family's property just about in half. Charley's mother and my mom were friends.

"So my father started looking for Charley's father. He wasn't hard to find. He was buried in the National Cemetery in San Antonio, Texas. A representation of the Medal of Honor was chiseled into his headstone.

"Once the Army learned that the twelve-year-old German boy about to be an orphan was the son of an American officer who had posthumously received our nation's highest award for valor—at nineteen—the Army instantly shifted into high gear to take care of him. They knew that when his mother died, he would inherit just about all of Gossinger Beteiligungsgesellschaft, G.m.b.H., and were concerned that Charley's inheritance would fall into the hands of Charley's father's family and be squandered.

"While a platoon of senior Army lawyers began looking into trust funds and anything else that would protect him, my father was sent to San Antonio to see if he could find Charley's family, and to see what problems they were going to pose for Charley.

"He found Charley's grandmother and showed her a picture of Charley."

"And my *abuela*," Castillo said softly, visibly fighting his emotions, "took one look at the picture, said I had my father's eyes, and two hours after that, she and General Naylor—he was then a major—were in my grandfather's Learjet en route to New York, where they caught the five-fifteen Pan American flight to Frankfurt.

"When they showed up at the house, I didn't want to let them in. My mother was in great pain, looked like a skeleton, and I didn't want anyone to see her looking like that, and in a cloud of cognac fumes.

"*Abuela* pushed past me, found my mother's bedroom, and said . . ."

He lost his voice, and it took a very long moment before he was able to continue: ". . . and said, 'I'm Jorge's mother, my dear. I'm here to take care of you and the boy.'

"And my mother looked up at the ceiling and said, 'Thank you, God.'"

"Two weeks after that, I got on another Pan American flight with my grandfather, carrying my new American passport as Carlos Guillermo Castillo, and flew to the States. My *abuela* stayed with my mother, who didn't want me to see her in her last days. Two weeks after I got to San Antonio, she died. And I began my new life as a

Texican, which is how Americans of Mexican background are described."

"Your ancestors emigrated from Mexico to the United States, my son?" the archbishop asked.

"Your Eminence is familiar with the Alamo?" Castillo asked.

"Of course."

"The Alamo today is owned by the Alamo Foundation, membership in which is limited to direct descendants of those men—some of Spanish blood—who died at the Alamo at the side of Davy Crockett, Jim Bowie, and Daniel Boone trying to keep the Mexicans out of what later became Texas. My grandmother served for many years as president of the Alamo Foundation. No, sir, I do not consider myself to be descended from Mexicans who immigrated to the United States. I am a Texican."

"And a Hessian, apparently," the archbishop said. "Fascinating!"

"If I may?" Pevsner asked.

The archbishop nodded his permission.

"Vladimir Vladimirovich sent another team of ex–Államvédelmi Hatóság to Germany with a dual mission. First, they were to eliminate Günther Friedler in a particularly nasty way—"

"Why?" the archbishop asked.

"'Particularly nasty way'?" Archimandrite Boris repeated.

"Why?" Pevsner said. "Because he had been asking too many questions about the SVR 'fish farm' in the Congo where the former East German people were developing, even starting to produce, that very nasty biological warfare substance the Americans called 'Congo-X.'"

"An abomination before God!" the archbishop said.

"You know about that?" Castillo asked.

"The church, my son, has its sources of information."

"Oddly enough, Your Eminence," Castillo said, "that's exactly how Colonel Hamilton, who heads our biological warfare laboratory, described that stuff, as 'an abomination before God.'"

"And so it is," the archbishop pronounced.

"Was," Pevsner said. "Before Charley. Now there's no more of it, whatever it's called."

"God will bless Colonel Castillo for his efforts in that regard," the archbishop announced.

"As I was saying," Pevsner said, "Vladimir Vladimirovich's assassins eliminated Herr Friedler in a particularly nasty way—they tried to make it appear he had died as a result of a spat between homosexuals—for his journalistic enterprise. But Vladimir Vladimirovich didn't stop there. He wanted to send *another* message to the journalistic community that writing about the fish farm was dangerous, and the way he decided to do it was to assassinate the senior staff of the Tages Zeitung organization during Friedler's funeral."

"The senior staff being?" the archbishop asked.

"Eric Kocian, Your Eminence, publisher of the Budapest edition; the senior editor; Otto Görner, the managing director of Gossinger Beteiligungsgesellschaft; and the owner thereof, Herr Gossinger. I don't really think he knew our Charley had two personas."

"You are underestimating Vladimir Vladimirovich, Aleksandr," Nicolai Tarasov said. "That's dangerous. I'm quite sure he knew all about our friend Charley."

"Then we are agreed to disagree," Pevsner said. "I think we can agree, however, that Vladimir Vladimirovich regarded the elimination of Kocian, Görner, and my brother Charley as too important to be left to the Államvédelmi Hatóság, despite their well-deserved reputation for efficiency in such tasks, and therefore ordered Dmitri to assume command—after Friedler was in his casket—of the operation, to make sure Kocian, Görner, and my brother Charley were eliminated."

"Your Eminence," Nicolai said, "while I regret having to differ with my cousin Aleksandr again, I must. My feeling has always been that Vladimir Vladimirovich had no intention of shipping Dmitri and Svetlana to Russia when they were arrested in Vienna—having them in Russia would have posed a number of problems for him. Having them eliminated in Vienna, perhaps while trying to escape from the Austrian authorities, on the other hand, would have permitted Vladimir Vladimirovich to place the public blame for all the assassinations on Dmitri and Svetlana, and thus off himself, so far as the Germans were concerned. The SVR would know what had happened, that Vladimir Vladimirovich had eliminated his potentially most dangerous opponent—*opponents*, Dmitri *and* Svetlana. He would be ahead on both accounts."

"Dmitri, my son," the archbishop said, "what do you think?"

"Knowing Vladimir Vladimirovich as well as I do, Your Eminence, what Nicolai suggests may well be the case. I just don't know."

"I think that Nicolai and I can agree that the Marburg affair was a total disaster for Vladimir Vladimirovich," Pevsner said. "None of the intended targets was eliminated; Dmitri and Svetlana, instead of being arrested in Vienna, were flown to safety here. Where they told my brother Charley about the fish farm, which resulted in the President of the United States doing his best to eliminate that 'abomination before God.'"

"And the SVR *rezident* in Vienna, Kirill Demidov, who eliminated the Kuhls—or had them eliminated—with a Hungarian secret police garrote, was found sitting dead with such a device around his own neck in a taxicab outside the American embassy," D'Alessandro said.

"You sound as if you approve, my son," the archbishop said.

"Your Eminence, I'm not Russian Orthodox, I'm a Roman Catholic, but so far as I'm concerned you're a priest and I can't lie to a priest. I thought the sonofabitch got what he deserved. Maybe taking out the old man was justified—he knew the game he was in—but Frau Kuhl? I knew her. She was a sweet old lady. I'd have garroted the sonofabitch myself if I could have gotten at him."

"Colonel Castillo, what do you know about this murder?"

"Not much more than Mr. D'Alessandro, Your Eminence."

"Really?" His Eminence replied, his tone suggesting he did not accept what Castillo had said as the truth, the whole truth, and nothing but. When he went on, "But do you know who murdered this man?" the same tone was in his voice, as if he did not expect an honest answer.

There was a perceptible pause before Charley replied.

"I have a good idea, Your Eminence."

"And whom do you suspect?"

"That's none of your business, sir," Castillo said.

"Charley," Pevsner said warningly, "you can't talk—"

"To put a point on it, did you order the murder of this man?" the archbishop interrupted.

"Weren't you listening when I just told you I don't *know* much about it?" Castillo said, now visibly angry, and then the anger took over. "What would you like me to do, Your Eminence, lay my hand on a Bible and swear that I did not order the execution of Demidov?

"It has been my sad experience," Castillo snapped, "that the worst of liars are willing to utter the most outrageous untruths with one hand on the Holy Bible and the other on their mother's tombstone or the heads of their children."

Castillo stood up.

"Go fuck yourself, Your Eminence," he said. "I've had enough of this whole affair, the history lesson, telling you a hell of a lot that's none of your business, and especially you, you self-righteous sonofabitch. I thought I was willing to do damned near anything to get you to give Sweaty permission to marry me. But you just stepped over that legendary line drawn in the sand and that no longer seems to be the case.

"Let's go, guys. This session of the Russian Inquisition is over."

The archbishop laughed heartily, which was the last reaction Castillo—or anyone else—expected of him.

"I now understand why Svetlana was swept off her feet by you, my son," he said. "Aleksandr, would you ask the ladies to join us?"

"Excuse me?" Pevsner said, his utter confusion evident in his voice and demeanor.

"Go out into the foyer, Aleksandr, and bring the women in here," the archbishop ordered.

Pevsner did so.

"Svetlana, my child," the archbishop then said. "If you will stand there"—he pointed—"and Carlos, my son, if you will stand beside her, and if the other ladies will find places at the table, we can deal with the situation before us."

"Svetlana," he ordered, "place your hand in Carlos's hand."

He stood up, put his hand on the gold crucifix hanging around his neck, and held it out in front of him at shoulder height.

"Let us pray," he boomed. "May God the Father, God the Son, and God the Holy Ghost bestow his manifold blessings on the union of Svetlana and Carlos in the holy state of matrimony in which they are soon to enter. Amen."

He lowered the crucifix and let it fall against his chest.

"The archimandrite and I would be honored to officiate at the ceremony, if that is your desire," the archbishop said. "And now I suggest we have our dinner. No, first I think champagne is called for. And then dinner. During which Archimandrite Boris will continue his history lecture—Oprichnina 101—during which I'm sure he will satisfy Carlos's questions why I felt it necessary to conduct the Russian Inquisition."

[TWO]

"Oh, my Charley," Svetlana whispered in Castillo's ear. "I was so afraid you were going to do something to offend His Eminence, show a lack of respect, or get into an argument with him, or say something at which he would take offense."

"By now, sweetheart, you should know me better than that."

"If you two can spare the time for him . . ." His Eminence said.

Just a little thickly, Charley decided. *He's about half plastered. First all that wine, and then the champagne, and now more of the grape. . . .*

". . . the Archimandrite Boris will continue with Oprichnina 101."

"I beg Your Eminence's pardon," Charley said.

"Not at all," the archbishop said.

The archimandrite stood up and, as he collected his thoughts, took a healthy swallow from his wineglass. He swayed just perceptibly as he did so.

I guess the protocol here, Castillo thought, perhaps a bit cynically, *is that if the archimandrite falls down during his lecture, the rest of us will pretend not to notice.*

"As I touched on briefly before," the archimandrite began, "the Russian Orthodox Church Abroad, Russkaya Pravoslavnaya Tserkov' Zagranitsey, sometimes known as the Orthodox Church outside Russia, acronym ROCOR, is a semiautonomous part of the Russian Orthodox Church.

"ROCOR was formed soon after the Russian Revolution of 1917, when the anti-Christian policy of the Bolsheviks became painfully evident. It separated itself from the Russian Patriarchate in 1927, when the Moscow Metropolitan—in effect the Pope—offered its loyalty to the Bolsheviks.

"His Eminence serves Russkaya Pravoslavnaya Tserkov' Zagranitsey as its spiritual head, and I humbly serve His Eminence.

"His Eminence is the spiritual leader of thirteen hierarchs—each headed by a bishop; what the Roman Catholics and the Anglicans would call dioceses—and controls our monasteries and nunneries in the United States, Canada, Australia, New Zealand, Western Europe, and South America.

"Metropolitan Alexy of Leningrad ascended the patriarchal throne of the Russian Orthodox Church in 1990 as Alexius the Second, after the Soviet Union imploded. Became the Russian Orthodox Pope, if you like.

"There were calls after that from the faithful for ROCOR to place itself under the new Patriarch. While, on its face, this was a splendid idea, there were those opposed to it."

"Including," Nicolai Tarasov said, "the Tarasovs, the Pevsners, the Berezovskys, and our cousin Svetlana."

"Why?" Jake Torine asked.

"They felt there was too much SVR influence on the Patriarch," the archbishop said. "I decided that it was my Christian duty to give the Patriarch the benefit of the doubt, and last month . . ."

"On May twenty-seventh, a day which, like Pearl Harbor, will live in infamy," Tarasov said, "you signed the 'Act of Canonical Communion with the Moscow Patriarchate.' "

"Nicolai," Laura Berezovsky said to her uncle, "you can't talk like that to His Eminence!"

"Why not? Svetlana's Charley called him a 'self-righteous sonofabitch.' "

"He did what?" Svetlana demanded incredulously.

She glared at Castillo. "Did you?"

"That was after Charley told him to go fuck himself," Vic D'Alessandro confirmed, wonderingly. "I never thought I'd hear anyone tell an archbishop to go fuck himself, not even a Russian one."

Castillo, stonefaced, shrugged.

"Children, children," the archbishop said placatingly. "We all make small mistakes from time to time. Mine was in not listening to Aleksandr and Nicolai when they told me of their suspicions about SVR influence on the throne of the Moscow Patriarch.

"And then I immediately compounded the error by what I thought at the time was an offering of, so to speak, an ecumenical olive branch. I notified His Holiness the Metropolitan that, barring any objections from him, it was my intention to authorize the marriage of one of his flock now living outside Russia. I speak, of course, of Svetlana."

"And what did this guy say?" D'Alessandro asked.

If behavior in the past is any key to the future, Charley thought, *one more glass of wine and Vic will start singing "O sole mio" and then, weeping, confess to breaking his mother's heart when he joined the Army instead of becoming a priest.*

"Not 'this guy,' my son," the archbishop said, "but His Eminence, the Patriarch of Moscow."

"Got it," Vic replied. "So what did he say?"

"Boris, my son," the archbishop said, "will you tell our friends how the Church feels about marriage and divorce?"

"The Church," the archimandrite began, "disapproves of divorce. Divorced individuals are usually allowed to remarry only after they have satisfied a severe penance imposed on them by their bishop. Second-marriage wedding ceremonies are more penitential than joyful. On the other hand, widows are permitted to remarry and their second marriage is considered just as valid as the first."

"It was on the basis of this," His Eminence broke in, "that I could see no reason to deny Svetlana permission to remarry as a widow. Her intended, Aleksandr told me, and she confirmed, was un-churched, canonically speaking a heathen, but that could be dealt with. Aleksandr, Dmitri, and Nicolai were all willing to serve as Charley's godfathers.

"I informed His Holiness the Patriarch of my reasoning. He immediately replied that I apparently wasn't aware of all the facts, in particular that the reason Svetlana was a widow was because she had either arranged for the murder of her husband, the late Polkovnik Evgeny Alekseev, or killed him herself. His Holiness also said that Svetlana's intended, one Colonel Carlos G. Castillo, had a well-deserved reputation as one of the CIA's best assassins and had most recently shown his skill at that by garroting a fine Christian KSB officer, one Podpolkovnik Kirill Demidov, and leaving his body in a taxi outside the American embassy in Vienna."

Vic D'Alessandro said: "So that's why you were pushing Charley so hard about what he knew about Demidov getting whacked. The . . . what do you call him? The *Patriarch* was accusing him of being the whacker."

"I would suggest, my son, that the Patriarch made that accusation because someone had told him that vile accusation. I recall your comment that you couldn't lie to a priest. Neither should anyone professing to adhere to our faith."

Jake Torine said, quoting, "'It has been my sad experience that the worst of liars are willing to utter the most outrageous untruths with one hand on the Holy Bible and the other on their mother's tombstone or the heads of their children.'"

The archbishop nodded.

"Carlos, my son, I understand why you thought I was making reference to you when I said that, but I really wasn't."

"I deeply apologize for what I said, Your Eminence," Castillo said.

"What exactly *did* you say?" Sweaty demanded. "I can't believe that you actually called His Eminence a sonofabitch and told him to go—"

"I'm sure, my child, I would remember if Carlos said anything like that to me," the archbishop said, and changed the subject. "So when I heard from the Patriarch about what terrible people you and your Carlos were, Archimandrite Boris and I came down here to see what Aleksandr, Nicolai, and you had to say. And to speak to Carlos, and, if I could find them, to any friends of his.

"And then those friends, without warning, suddenly appeared," the archbishop said. "And here we are, with the problem solved."

The archbishop helped himself to a little more wine, and then said, "What I'm curious about now is your mission here, Colonel

Torine. While we eat, could you tell me about that, or does Carlos think that's none of my business?"

"I'd like to hear that, too," Svetlana said.

"Go ahead, Jake," Castillo said. "You're going to have to tell Sweaty sooner or later, and with His Eminence here, you're probably safe from her *otxokee mecto nanara*."

About three minutes into his explanation, Jake looked at the archbishop and stopped.

The archbishop's head was bent over. His eyes were closed, and he was snoring softly.

"What do I do?" Torine asked.

"Eat your dinner, my son," the archimandrite said. "If His Eminence wakes, resume. If he doesn't, you can tell us at breakfast."

The archbishop was still soundly asleep in his chair when the dessert—strawberries in a cream and cognac sauce—was served and consumed.

After that, everyone but Archimandrite Boris quietly left the room and went to bed.

IV

[ONE]

La Casa en el Bosque
San Carlos de Bariloche
Río Negro Province, Argentina
0600 7 June 2007

Sweaty woke up, sat up, and shook Charley's shoulder.

When he looked up at her, she ordered, "You better go, and quietly, down the corridor to your room."

"Like a thief in the night?" Charley responded.

"I don't want His Eminence to suspect we're sleeping together," she said.

"His Eminence either suspects we have been sharing this prenuptial couch for some time or is about to proclaim 'Hallelujah! A second immaculate conception.'"

"God will punish you for your blasphemy," Sweaty announced, and, when that triggered something else on her mind, went on: "And don't try to tell me you didn't tell His Eminence to go fu—"

"You heard what he said, my love," Charley argued.

"His Eminence said he 'would remember if you said something like that.' Not that you didn't say it. He remembers it all right!"

"Try to remember that you're a bride-to-be and an expectant mother, and no longer an SVR *podpolkovnik*, my love."

At that point, Sweaty literally kicked him out of the bed.

Then, with Max, his 120-pound Bouvier des Flandres, trailing along after him, he went down the corridor to "his room."

Charley had "his room" in La Casa en el Bosque from his first visit, which was to say long before Sweaty. Originally, it had then been "the Blue Room," the one from which he had just been expelled. After Sweaty, in consideration of "what the girls"—Alek's and Dmitri's daughters—would think of illicit cohabitation, the Blue Room had become Svetlana's room, and the not-nearly-as-nice room he walked into now, his.

"The trouble with getting kicked out of bed at oh-six hundred, Max," Charley said as the dog met his eyes and turned his head, "is that I can never get back to sleep. Is it that way with you?"

There was no question in Charley's mind that Max understood everything he said to him.

Without realizing that he was doing so, he had spoken in Hungarian. Max had been born and raised in Budapest, where he had lived with Eric Kocian, publisher of the Budapest edition of the *Tages Zeitung*.

Max cocked his head the other way, and then moved it again in what might well have been a nod, signaling that he, too, had trouble getting back to sleep after having been kicked out of bed.

Eric Kocian had been an eighteen-year-old *unteroffizier*—corporal—in the Wehrmacht at Stalingrad. Wounded, he had sought shelter in the basement of a ruined building, where he found a seriously wounded *oberst*—colonel—who he knew would die unless he immediately received medical attention.

At considerable risk to his own life, Kocian had carried the officer, Oberst Hermann Wilhelm von und zu Gossinger, through heavy fire to an aid station. While doing so, he was again wounded.

At the aid station, doctors decided that the Herr Oberst be loaded onto a Junkers JU-88 for shipment out of Stalingrad. And done so immediately, as the Russians were about to take the airfield, after which there would be no more evacuation flights.

At the airstrip, Oberst von und zu Gossinger refused to allow himself to be loaded aboard "the Aunty Ju" unless Unteroffizier Kocian was allowed to go with him. There was literally no time to argue, and the young *unteroffizier*, dripping blood from his last wound, was hoisted aboard.

The aircraft—the last to leave Stalingrad—took off.

Surprising the medics, Oberst von und zu Gossinger lived and had recovered to the point where he was on active duty when the surrender came. Having found his name on an SS "Exterminate" list, his American captors quickly released him from the POW camp in which he and Kocian—now his orderly—were confined.

The *oberst* returned to the rubble of his home and business in Fulda, and Kocian went to Vienna, where he learned his family had been killed in an air raid. Kocian then went to Fulda.

It became a legend within the Gossinger Beteiligungsgesellschaft, G.m.b.H., organization that the type for the first postwar edition of any of the *Tages Zeitung* newspapers had been set on a Mergenthaler Linotype machine "the Colonel" and "Billy Kocian" had themselves assembled from parts salvaged from machines destroyed in the war.

Billy Kocian began to resurrect other *Tages Zeitung* newspapers—starting in Vienna—as the Colonel gave his attention to resurrecting the Gossinger Beteiligungsgesellschaft, G.m.b.H., empire in other areas.

After deciding he had all the Viennese *gemütlichkeit* he could stomach, Kocian moved to Budapest as soon as the Communists were gone, where he devoted his time to needling the Soviet Union and bureaucrats of all stripes on the pages of the *Budapester Tages Zeitung*, holding the editors of the seven other *Tages Zeitung* newspapers to his own high standards, and playing with his Bouvier des Flandres dog, Max.

Max was really Max IV, the fourth of his line. Billy had acquired Max I after checking into—and finding credible—the legend that a Bouvier des Flandres had bitten off one of Adolf Hitler's testicles while Der Führer was serving in Belgium during the First World War.

Max II and Max III had appeared when their predecessors had, for one reason or another, gone to that great fireplug in the sky. Max IV was something special. It was quickly said that Billy Kocian was so enamored of Max IV that the animal could have anything it wanted.

What Max IV wanted became painfully obvious when the dog scandalized the guests of the luxurious and very proper Danubius Hotel Gellért—where he and Billy lived in a penthouse apartment overlooking the Danube—by pursuing a German shepherd bitch through the dining room, the lobby, and down into the Roman baths below the hotel, where he worked his lustful way on her for more than two hours.

As soon as he could, Billy procured suitable female companionship for Max. She was a ninety-something-pound Bouvier, one he named Madchen.

The Max–Madchen honeymoon lasted until Madchen realized

she was in the family way and sensed that Max IV was responsible. Thereafter, she made her desire to painfully terminate his life by castration quite clear whenever Max IV came within twenty feet of her.

So, what to do? Billy dearly loved Max IV, but he had come to love Madchen, too, and couldn't find it in his heart to banish her, after what Max IV had done to her.

The answer came quickly: give Max IV to Karlchen.

Karlchen was the Colonel's grandson.

Karlchen had played with Max I as an infant; they had loved each other at first sight. When Max II had come along, same thing. It was only because of Karlchen's mother's awful sickness, her arguments that with the Colonel and her brother gone, and her being sick, she couldn't care for the dog, that he hadn't given Max II to Karlchen right then, to take his mind off things.

But Billy had taken Max II to Rhine-Main airfield to see Karlchen off to the United States just before his mother died. When Billy saw how the boy, crying, had wrapped his arms around the dog, he decided that Max II should go with him.

That had resulted in a front-page headline by the bastards at the *Frankfurter Rundshau*: "Tages Zeitung Publishing Empire Chief Jailed for Punching Pan-American Airlines Station Chief Who Refused Passage for Fifty-Kilo Dog."

Things were different when Madchen banished Max IV from the canine connubial bed. Karlchen was now not only a man, but in the Colonel's footsteps, an *oberstleutnant* in the American Army himself. He denied being an intelligence officer, but Billy had been around armies long enough to know better than that. Run-of-the-mill lieutenant colonels don't fly themselves around the world in Gulfstream III airplanes.

The next time Karlchen—now known as Charley—appeared in Budapest, Uncle Billy explained the Max IV–Madchen problem to him. Charley had understood.

"Let's see what he does when I tell him to get on the airplane. I'm not going to force him to go."

He stood inside the door of the Gulfstream.

"Hey, Max," he called in Hungarian. "You want to go to Argentina with me?"

Max looked at Billy for a moment, then trotted to the airplane and took the stair-door steps three at a time.

Billy Kocian went back to the penthouse in the Danubius Hotel Gellért and shared three bottles of the local grape—known as Bull's Blood—with Sándor Tor. Tor, after doing hitches in the Wehrmacht, the French Foreign Legion, and the Budapest Police Department, was now chief of security for Gossinger Beteiligungsgesellschaft, G.m.b.H., and Billy's best friend.

During their conversation, Billy told Sándor that he now knew what his father must have felt like "when, wagging my tail like Max just now, I left home to go in the goddamn Wehrmacht."

"Let me get a quick shower and then I'll get dressed, and we'll go for a walk," Castillo now said to Max IV. "I just can't go back to sleep."

Max leapt with amazing agility and grace for his size onto the bed, put his head between his paws, and closed his eyes, as if saying, "Okay, you have your shower and I'll take a little nap while I'm waiting."

Charley came out of the bathroom and asked, "Ready?"

Max got gracefully off the bed, walked to the French doors, and waited for Charley to open it. When he had, Max went through it, walked to a five-foot-tall marble statue of Saint Igor II of Kiev, who had been Grand Prince of Kiev before becoming a monk, which stood in the center of the patio, and raised his right rear leg.

"You know what'll happen if Sweaty sees you pissing on her favorite saint again."

Max ignored him, finished his business at hand, and then walked to the opening in the patio wall leading to the walkway and waited for Charley to join him.

The walkway led toward the shore of Lake Nahuel Huapi. When Charley went through the opening, lights along the path automatically came on.

Nothing of La Casa en el Bosque or its outbuildings was visible from the lake, or from the Llao Llao Hotel, which was across the lake, but the reverse was not true. At four places along the nearly half-mile shoreline there were, just about entirely concealed by huge pine and hardwood trees, four patio-like areas from which just about all of the lake, and the hotel, was visible.

To a soldier's eye, and Charley was a soldier, the patios appeared to have been designed and installed by someone familiar with the finer points of observation posts and machine-gun emplacements. While he had never seen a machine gun or a mortar tube in any of them, he would not have been surprised if such could be installed in minutes.

He didn't know if the patios and the neat little buildings that might be holding machine guns and mortars had been there when Aleksandr Pevsner had bought the place—that it was a clone of Hermann Göring's Karin Hall was very interesting—or whether Aleksandr Pevsner had put them in.

Just that they were there, and manned around the clock.

And being a soldier, Charley knew that when he and Max got to the patio now, they had arrived as the corporal of the guard, so to speak, was about to post the new guard.

There were five men on the patio, four sturdy, good-looking men with Uzi submachine guns hanging from their shoulders and a huge man, a Hungarian by the name of Janos Kodály, who had been in the Államvédelmi Hatóság before becoming Aleksandr Pevsner's bodyguard, and was now in charge of his security.

They all came to attention—Castillo was not surprised, as he knew the four men were all ex-Spetsnaz, the Russian equivalent of Special Forces, and what to do when an officer appeared was a Pavlovian reaction for them—when Charley and Max walked onto the patio.

"Стоять вольно," Charley ordered in Russian, and the men stood "at ease" in response to Charley's Pavlovian reaction. Then he switched to Hungarian and said, "Janos, aren't you a little long in the tooth to be playing Corporal of the Guard at this hour?"

Two of the ex-Spetsnaz apparently spoke—or at least understood—Hungarian, because they smiled.

Janos didn't reply directly, instead saying, "My Colonel, there is a thermos of tea."

"Great," Charley said.

When he was five, Charley's great-aunt Erzsebet Cséfalzvik, his grandfather's sister, had decided to teach him how to speak Hungarian. His response had been amazing. Within a week, he was chattering away fluently with the old woman, which greatly annoyed his mother, who did not speak Hungarian.

By the time he left for the United States, Aunt Erzsebet had died, but he had heard some of her story, and later learned the rest.

She was considerably older than her brother. As a very young woman she had married a Hungarian nobleman whom she had met while he was a student at Philipps University in Marburg an der Lahn. That explained why Karlchen's mother had sometimes derisively referred to her as "the Countess."

There was some kind of bad blood between her and the Gossingers—Charley later learned his great-grandfather had been violently opposed to her marriage—and she never returned to Germany until after World War II. Then she showed up at her brother's house in Fulda, destitute and starving. She had been evicted from "the estates" by the Communists, and had nowhere else, no one else, to turn to.

She earned her keep when Charley's grandmother died soon after his mother was born. Aunt Erzsebet had raised his mother.

As long as she lived, the old woman regaled Karlchen with tales of life in Hungary during "the Good Times." He regarded them as being something like the story of King Arthur in Camelot, nice, but unbelievable.

When he was six, Karlchen was enrolled in Saint Johan's School, which was experimenting with the notion that a good way to teach a foreign language to the young was to start when they were young. Karlchen was enrolled in the English program, and was old enough to understand this had caused problems between his mother and his grandfather. Something to do with his mysteriously missing father.

Two weeks into that program, Charley's teacher asked him, "I didn't think you spoke any English at all."

"I didn't."

"And all of a sudden you do?"

"I guess I got that from Allan," he had truthfully replied, in English, making reference to his new buddy, an American boy by the name of Allan Naylor. "I started to talk to him, and pretty soon it got easy."

By the time Karlchen went to the United States as Carlos Guillermo Castillo, he spoke Hungarian, Russian, French, Slovak, and Italian, in addition, of course, to German and English.

And he was also smart enough to know that his unusual facility with languages caused people to look upon him as some sort of freak, so he kept his mouth shut about it.

When two weeks of conversation with his newfound cousin Fernando Lopez had him speaking Spanish as well as Fernando, whose mother tongue it was, he kept that under his hat until his newfound *abuela* commented on it.

He started to lie to her, to tell her he had studied Spanish in Saint Johan's School, but when he saw his grandmother's eyes on him, he realized he couldn't lie to her, and told her the truth.

His *abuela* told him that she thought it would be a good idea if he didn't tell people about that gift from God; they probably wouldn't understand.

Later, when the Army sent him as a young lieutenant to the Language School at Monterey for the basic course in Cantonese Chinese, he was rated as having "native fluency" in Mandarin Chinese, Japanese, and Vietnamese, when given those tests.

At this point another mentor, this one Brigadier General Bruce J. McNab, offered advice much like that offered by his grandmother.

"What we are going to do, Hotshot, is lose this report from the Language School. If those chair warmers in Washington learn about this, God only knows what they'll come up with for you to do. They took a superb officer, Lieutenant General Vernon E. Walters, who has the same affliction you do—he hears a language and then can speak it—out of uniform and made the poor bastard ambassador to the goddamned United Nations."

There had been one final contact with Karlchen's first language instructor. In 1990, the newly independent government of Hungary had returned to their rightful owners all properties of the Hungarian nobility that had been seized on one pretense or another—or simply seized—by Admiral Miklós Horthy, the Hungarian regent; the Nazis, who replaced the admiral; and the Communists, who replaced the Nazis.

This included the estates of the late Grafin—Countess—Erzsebet of Cséfalzvik. In her last will and testament, the countess had left all of her property of whatever kind and wherever located to her beloved grandnephew, Karl Wilhelm von und zu Gossinger, and decreed that the Cséfalzvik titles would pass on her death to her aforesaid beloved grandnephew.

Billy Kocian took over the administration of the estates, which included Castle Cséfalzvik, now a hotel, the farmlands, the vineyards, and considered then decided against moving into the Cséfalzvik mansion in Budapest. Instead, he rented it to a Saudi Arabian prince who was fascinated with Hungarian women and was willing and more than able to pay whatever asked to rent a suitable place to entertain them.

Billy Kocian also told Karlchen that if he was waiting for him to address him as His Grace, Duke Karl I of Cséfalzvik, it would be wise not to hold his breath.

[TWO]
La Casa en el Bosque
San Carlos de Bariloche
Río Negro Province, Argentina
0930 7 June 2007

Following Morning Prayer in the chapel, breakfast was served in the Breakfast Room of La Casa, which overlooked the mansion's formal gardens.

Charley had attended Morning Prayer because he knew if he didn't Sweaty would deny him the privileges of their prenuptial couch and also because he liked the ceremony itself. Much of the service was sung—men only, including about a dozen ex-Spetsnaz—and their voices had a haunting beauty.

His Eminence was in fine voice, and showed no signs of suffering from all the wine of the previous evening.

The breakfast that followed was literally a movable feast. Just as soon as His Eminence had expressed his gratitude to the Deity for the bounty they were about to receive, white-jacketed servants began rolling in that bounty on carts. There was champagne and cognac (Argentine, and labeled as such because the Argentines could see no reason to give the French exclusive rights to those appellations for sparkling wine or distilled white wine); salmon (Chilean, from a bona fide fish farm Aleksandr Pevsner owned there); caviar (Uruguayan, which Aleksandr Pevsner decreed as just about as good as that from the sturgeon in the Black Sea); the expected locally sourced eggs, breads, ham, trout, and fruit; and the not expected—Aleksandr

Pevsner's favorite breakfast food, American pancakes, served with what he called "that marvelous tree juice," or maple syrup.

Sweaty beamed when His Eminence called to her to sit beside him at the long table. "And you, Carlos, my son, on my other side."

And her smile grew even broader when His Eminence said, "I think the time has come to discuss plans for the wedding."

It disappeared a moment later when His Eminence went on, "Starting with when. How long do you think your intended will be gone?"

"Gone where, Your Eminence?" Svetlana asked.

"Wherever this 'extended hazardous active duty' Colonel Naylor told us about takes him. How long would you say that's going to take him?"

Svetlana was struck dumb.

"Carlos," His Eminence went on, "is really fortunate in that very few brides-to-be have the sort of experience you do. Most would not understand how important answering the call of duty is."

"Your Eminence," Charley said, "I never like to take risks without a good reason, and I don't see any good reason to take this one."

"But I would suggest your friends do," His Eminence reasoned, "otherwise they wouldn't be here."

His Eminence leaned over and looked past Svetlana to Jake Torine, who was sitting farther down the table.

"Colonel, why do you think Colonel Castillo should take this assignment?"

"Your Eminence," Charley said politely, and then very quickly realized (a) that his temper was rising, (b) had in fact risen, and (c) that he had every right to be pissed—*Who the hell are you to be deciding what I should or should not do?*—went on, somewhat less politely, "I don't give a damn what Jake thinks. It's my ass on the line here, not his. Or, for that matter, yours."

"Carlos!" Sweaty said, horrified.

The archbishop was unruffled.

"Perhaps you would be good enough, my son, to tell me why you are so opposed to doing your duty?"

"Generally, because it's not my duty, and specifically because I don't want to wind up in the basement of that beautiful building on Lubyanka Square."

The beautiful building to which he referred had been built in Moscow in 1900 as luxury apartments renting for two or three times the norm. The Trump Towers or the One57 building of its time, so to speak. In 1919, the capitalist tenants were evicted by Felix Dzerzhinsky so that the building could be put to use for the benefit of the workers and peasants. The Cheka moved in, and the storage areas in the basement were converted to cells. The building has been occupied ever since by successor organizations to the Cheka.

His Eminence apparently knew about Lubyanka, but was again unruffled.

"And you believe, my son, that would be inevitable?"

"I don't play Russian roulette, either," Charley said.

Vic D'Alessandro laughed, then raised his hand and asked, "Permission to speak, Colonel, sir?"

"If you think this is funny, go fuck yourself," Charley replied.

"I'll take that as 'Permission granted,' " D'Alessandro said. "Thank you, sir."

Charley gave him the finger.

"Your Eminence," Svetlana said, "I hope you can find it in your heart to forgive my Carlos. He tends to forget his manners when he's a little upset."

The archbishop graciously gestured that he was prepared to forgive Svetlana's Carlos, and then that D'Alessandro should continue.

"Your Eminence, I have known Colonel Castillo since he was a second lieutenant maybe five months out of West Point," D'Alessandro said. "When I met him he already had the Distinguished Flying Cross and his first Purple Heart—"

"Jesus Christ!" Charley said.

"If you love God, you should not blaspheme, my son," the archbishop said. "Please continue, Mr. D'Alessandro."

"And in the next couple of weeks," D'Alessandro went on, "he had the Silver Star, another Purple Heart, and an assignment as aide-de-camp to an up-and-coming new brigadier general.

"At that point, we began to call him, and he thought of himself, as 'Hotshot.'"

"What's that got to do with anything?" Charley demanded. "And I never thought of myself as 'Hotshot.'"

D'Alessandro laughed, shook his head, and then went on, "And what Hotshot decided then was that he had the Army figured out. Just so long as he kept getting medals, he wouldn't have to do what ordinary soldiers spent most of their time doing."

"I don't think I understand," the archbishop said.

"Napoleon said, 'An army travels on its stomach,'" D'Alessandro said. "He was wrong. The army travels on paper."

The archbishop shook his head, signaling he still didn't understand.

"Soldiers, Your Eminence, especially officers, spend a great deal of time making reports of unimportant things that no one ever reads. For all of his career, Charley skillfully managed to avoid doing so. But that's over."

"What the hell are you talking about?" Castillo asked.

"Solving your problem with the President."

"By writing reports?" Castillo asked. "Reports about what?"

"On the way down here, Frank Lammelle sent me this," D'Alessandro said, as he took out his CaseyBerry. "He recorded it while the President was telling everybody about his latest brilliant idea. Pay attention."

He played the recording.

"Well," D'Alessandro then asked Castillo, "what did you get out of that?"

His Eminence answered the question.

"Paraphrasing what the President said, he wants to involve Colonel Castillo as a knowledgeable, objective observer of the piracy and drug problems to see how those situations are being handled, and to report his observations and recommendations directly to him. What's the problem there? That sounds reasonable. It doesn't even seem hazardous."

"He also asked, 'How soon can we get him in here?'" Castillo said. "That sounds hazardous to me."

"Cutting to the chase, Charley," D'Alessandro said, "all you have to do is stall until the President gets tired of this nutty idea and moves on to the next one."

"If 'stall' means ignore him, I've already figured that out myself," Castillo said.

"Ignoring him won't work. I said, 'stall.'"

"How do I do that?"

"Tomorrow, Allan sends an Urgent message through the proper channels to POTUS—"

"POTUS?" His Eminence parroted.

"President of the United States, Your Eminence," D'Alessandro explained. "And we send it through the military attaché at the embassy in Buenos Aires; that should slow it down three or four hours, maybe longer."

"I don't understand," the archbishop said. "It sounds as if you intentionally wish to slow down what you just said was an urgent message."

"Precisely," D'Alessandro said. "An Urgent message, big 'U,' is the second-highest priority message. Operational Immediate is the highest. That's reserved for 'White House Nuked' and things like that.

"So, what happens here is that Allan sends a message to the people who sent him down here. I mean the secretary of State, the CIA director, the director of National Intelligence, and of course, his daddy.

"The message says something like, 'Located Castillo. Hope to establish contact with him within twenty-four hours.'

"That message goes from the embassy to the State Department. It will have to be encrypted in Buenos Aires and then decrypted at the State Department, and then forwarded to the Defense Department, the director of National Intelligence, and of course his daddy.

"That process will buy us probably three or four hours.

"Finally, Allan's daddy—or maybe Natalie Cohen, that makes more sense—gets on the telephone to the White House and hopes the President is not available. But eventually the President will get the message and learn that his orders are being carried out.

"And then, twenty-four hours after the first message we send another, 'Meeting with Castillo delayed for twenty-four hours.' And we start that process all over. Getting the picture, Hotshot?"

"Vic," Castillo said, "you know I never agreed with everyone who said you were a nice guy but a little slow and with no imagination."

"I'm curious," the archbishop said. "If you really had to communicate as quickly as possible with the President, or Colonel Naylor's father in a hurry, urgently, how would you do that?"

D'Alessandro held out his CaseyBerry.

"If I push this button," he said, "I'm connected with the White House switchboard. It will tell the operator I'm calling from Fort Bragg. If I push this button, the telephone on General Naylor's desk will ring. The caller ID function will tell him I'm calling from Las Vegas, confirming General Naylor's belief that I spend my time gambling and chasing scantily clad women."

"Fascinating," the archbishop said.

"But speaking of Vegas—with your kind permission, Colonel Castillo, sir, I'm going to call Aloysius and ask him to send Peg-Leg and your faithful bodyguard down here, just as soon as they can go wheels up in Aloysius's Gulfstream."

"Why Peg-Leg?" Castillo asked.

"Peg-Leg?" His Eminence repeated. "Bodyguard?"

"First Lieutenant Edmund Lorimer, Retired," D'Alessandro answered most of both questions at once, "after losing his leg—hence the somewhat cruel if apt appellation—became expert in what might be called obfuscatory paper shuffling.

"I think we have to go with the worst scenario—that our beloved Commander in Chief will cling to this nutty idea of his for a long time—Peg-Leg can prepare the reports of your progress we're going to have to send him from various tourist destinations around the world."

"Yeah," Castillo agreed.

"Bodyguard?" His Eminence asked. "You have a bodyguard, Carlos?"

Aleksandr Pevsner answered that question.

"To whom, Your Eminence, I owe my life," he said. "He looks like he belongs in high school, but he's very good at what he does."

"Think the opposite of Aleksandr's Janos, Your Eminence," Sweaty chimed in. "Lester looks like a choirboy, and he is not going to stay in Las Vegas if Peg-Leg comes down here."

The archbishop's curiosity was not satisfied.

"'Tourist destinations'?" he asked.

"Mogadishu, Somalia, comes immediately to mind," D'Alessandro said. "Because of the pirates. And of course Mexico because of the drug problem Charley's going to solve there. And a grand tour of Europe, probably starting with Budapest. But I would suggest that we start with Mexico, until the colonel is up to speed again. And then probably Fort Bragg, while he forms his team. Or maybe Fort Rucker, Charley. That would give you a chance to see your son."

"His *son*?" His Eminence asked. "I was asked if Carlos had ever been married and told he had not."

"There is one little problem with this scenario," Charley said.

"Your hitherto undisclosed marriage, you mean?" His Eminence asked. "That opens a number of windows through which we must look before you can be married."

"It's not a problem, Your Eminence," Sweaty said. "My Carlos has never been married."

"The problem is," Castillo said, "that I'm not going along with this tour of the world. I'm not going anywhere. Sweaty's right: it would be committing suicide."

"Don't be silly, my darling," Sweaty said. "Of course you are. You heard what His Eminence said about how important answering the call of duty is. You're going, and I'm going with you."

"'And Ruth said,'" the archimandrite quoted approvingly, "'Entreat me not to leave thee, or to return from following after thee: for whither thou goest, I will go. . . .'"

"First Ruth, sixteen," the archbishop amplified.

"Vic, call Aloysius," Sweaty ordered.

A moment later, Vic D'Alessandro said, "Hey, Aloysius, how's things in Sin City?"

As that conversation began, His Eminence said, "Carlos, my son, tell me about your son."

Charley said, "Jake, hand me that bottle of cognac."

[THREE]
Embassy of the United States
Avenida Colombia 4300
Buenos Aires, Argentina
1705 7 June 2007

Former Major Kiril Koshkov, the onetime chief instructor pilot of the Spetsnaz Aviation School, flew Lieutenant Colonel Allan Naylor, Junior, to Buenos Aires' Jorge Newbery International Airport in the Cessna Mustang twin-engine jet that Sweaty had given Charley for his birthday.

There they were met by a Mercedes SUV driven by another former member of Spetsnaz. He had been sent from Aleksandr Pevsner's home in Pilar—"the World Capital of Polo," forty kilometers from downtown—to take them to the embassy.

This took place during the Buenos Aires rush hour—actually *hours*, as the period started at half past four and did not slack off until eight, or thereabouts. They arrived at five past five. When Colonel Naylor presented himself at the embassy gate and said he wanted to see the Defense attaché, the Argentine Rent-A-Cop on duty announced that that official was gone for the day and he would have to return tomorrow.

Allan considered that information, and then decided that while a certain delay was what they were after, delaying fourteen hours was a bit too much of a good thing.

"In that case, I wish to speak to the duty officer," Colonel Naylor announced.

To get through to the duty officer, Allan first had to deal with a Marine sergeant of the Embassy Guard, but finally an Air Force captain appeared. The captain was extremely reluctant to contact the Defense attaché at his residence without very good reason.

"What's your business with the colonel, Colonel?"

Colonel Naylor had been around the military service all his life, and he knew that if he did tell the captain that he wished to send a highly classified message, the captain would almost certainly not have the authority to permit him to do so without checking with his superior, and that superior would not be the Defense attaché himself, but rather an officer, probably a major, immediately superior to the captain. And then the whole sequence would start again with the major's superior, probably a lieutenant colonel. Et cetera.

Thus causing too much of a delay.

"Captain," Naylor said, "you are not cleared for any knowledge of the nature of my business. Contact the Defense attaché immediately and inform him that an officer acting VOCICCENCOM demands to see him personally and now. That is an order, not a suggestion."

The captain wasn't sure he recognized what the acronym stood for, but did recognize an order when he heard one, and said, "Yes, sir. If the colonel will have a seat there, I will telephone Colonel Freedman."

The captain pointed to a row of attached vinyl-upholstered chrome chairs against the wall.

Naylor did so. After five or six minutes he looked up at the wall and saw large photographs of President Joshua Ezekiel Clendennen, Vice President Charles W. Montvale, and Secretary of State Natalie Cohen smiling down at him.

He took out his CaseyBerry and punched a button.

"Yeah, Junior?" CIA Director A. Franklin Lammelle's voice answered, after bouncing off a satellite floating twenty-seven thousand miles above the earth's surface.

"Sir! Sir!" the Marine Guard sergeant called excitedly from behind the bulletproof glass of his station. "You can't do that!"

"In the embassy, waiting for the attaché," Naylor said.

"Good man! I'll alert Natalie."

Naylor put the CaseyBerry back in his shirt pocket.

"I can't do what, Sergeant?"

"Use a cell phone in here."

"This one worked just fine."

"Sir, you're not allowed to have a cell phone in here!"

"Why not?"

"You're not a member of the embassy staff. I'll have to ask you for your cell phone."

"No."

"Sir, I'll have to insist."

"Sergeant, the last I heard, sergeants can't insist that lieutenant colonels do anything; it's the other way around."

"Sir, I'll have to insist."

"You already said that. The only way you're going to get my cell phone, Sergeant, is to pry it from my cold dead fingers."

As the sergeant considered that option, the situation was put on hold when the door to the plaza outside burst open and a spectacularly dressed officer entered.

"What the hell is going on here?" he demanded.

Naylor decided there was likely to be just one officer in the embassy who would be wearing the mess dress uniform of a full colonel of the USAF, and consequently this man had to be Colonel Freedman, the Defense attaché.

"Colonel, he has a cell phone and won't give it up!" the Marine sergeant announced righteously.

"Who the hell are you?" Colonel Freedman demanded.

"Lieutenant Colonel Allan B. Naylor, Junior, sir. Are you the Defense attaché, sir?"

Naylor saw in Colonel Freedman's eyes that the Air Force officer was aware that there was an Allan B. Naylor, Senior, and of the latter's place in the military hierarchy.

"I'm Anthony Freedman, the Defense attaché. What can I do for you, Colonel?"

Freedman put out his hand and Naylor took it.

"Sir, I need the embassy's communications facilities to send a Top Secret Message to Washington."

Freedman considered that, nodded, and said, "Well, we can take care of that for you, Colonel. But just to dot all the 'i's . . . may I see your ID and your orders?"

Naylor handed him his identity card. Freedman examined it, handed it back, and then asked, "And your orders, Colonel?"

"I'm acting VOCICCENCOM, sir," Naylor said.

That was the acronym—pronounced "Voe-Sik-Sen-Com"—for Verbal Order, Commander in Chief, Central Command. While it was in common usage around Central Command, and the Pentagon, the Office of the Defense Attaché in Buenos Aires is pretty near the foot of the military hierarchal totem pole and it was obvious from the look on Colonel Freedman's face that he had no idea what it meant.

And equally obvious that he wasn't going to admit that he didn't to an Army lieutenant colonel.

"Yes, of course you are. But in the absence of written orders, Colonel, how can I *know* that?"

"Sir, may I suggest you call CICCENCOM at Combined Base MacDill for verification?"

CICCENCOM, pronounced Sik-Sen-Com, is the acronym for Commander in Chief, Central Command.

"Right," Colonel Freedman said. "Sergeant, call what he said."

"The extension is six-six-one," Naylor said.

"Yes, sir."

Two minutes later the sergeant reported, "Sir, they say the Sik-Sen-Sen . . . *Sik-Sen-Com* . . . is not available."

"Try extension seven-seven-one, Sergeant," Naylor suggested. "That's the DEPCICCENCOM."

DEPCICCENCOM, pronounced Dep-Sik-Sen-Com, is the acronym for Deputy Commander in Chief, Central Command.

Two minutes later, the sergeant reported, "I have General Albert McFadden on the line, sir. He wants to know who's calling and how you got his personal number."

Colonel Freedman's face, as he reached for the telephone, which the sergeant was passing through an opening in the bulletproof glass, showed that he knew very well who the four-star Air Force general he was about to talk to was.

"Sir, this is Colonel Anthony Freedman, the Defense attaché . . .

"I was given this number by Lieutenant Colonel Naylor, who says you can verify he's here acting . . . What the hell was it, Naylor?"

"VOCICCENCOM, sir."

"Vok-Ick . . . Vodka-Ick . . .

"Yes, sir, General, *Voe-Sik-Sen-Com*. That's it, sir.

"No, sir. Now that I think about it, I can't imagine why a fine officer like Colonel Naylor would say something like that if it wasn't the case."

Colonel Freedman held out the phone to Naylor.

"The general wants to talk to you, Colonel."

Naylor took the phone.

"Good afternoon, sir.

"Not a problem, sir. I spoke to the sheriff and the district attorney and they both assured me no one will be arrested just so long as we use chips and there's no cash on the tables.

"Sir, I can only suggest the chaplain got carried away when he said we're all going to go to jail.

"I really hope to be there, sir, but there's no telling how long this job will take.

"Yes, sir. Thank you, sir. My regards to Mrs. McFadden."

Naylor handed the telephone back through the opening in the bulletproof glass. Then he saw the look on Colonel Freedman's face and took pity on him.

"General McFadden's wife," he explained, "is raising money for the Parent–Teacher's Association by running Las Vegas Night at the VFW Hall in Tampa. In addition to my other duties, I'm the de facto president of the school board. The chaplain, who thinks gambling is a sin, even for a good cause, has been giving us trouble, and the general was a little worried. I was able to put his concerns to rest."

"Yes, of course you were," Colonel Freedman said. "Now, about this Top Secret Message you want to transmit?"

"I'd prefer to get into that, sir, in a secure environment, sir."

"Yes, of course you would. I can't imagine what I was thinking," Colonel Freedman said. "Sergeant, unlock the door."

"Colonel, he's still got his cell phone."

"What cell phone?"

"The one in his pocket, sir. The one he said I'd have to pry from his cold dead fingers."

"Just push the button and unlock the damned door, damn it!"

There was a buzz, and the door to the interior of the building swung open. Freedman led Naylor to an elevator, which took them to the top story of the building. The commo center was behind two locked steel doors that were about in the middle of the corridor.

There was an American man on duty, visibly surprised to see the Defense attaché there after duty hours and wearing his spectacular mess dress uniform.

"The colonel has a message to send—"

"Encrypt and send," Naylor corrected him. "And if you don't mind, I'll operate the equipment myself. Just get me on the State Department circuit."

Naylor sat down at the table, and as he waited for the technician to connect him with the State Department took a sheet of paper from his pocket and laid it next to the encryption device keyboard.

When he became aware that Colonel Freedman was trying desperately to sneak a look at the message, Naylor considered laying his hand on it, or turning it over, but in the end handed it to the Defense attaché.

"You're onto State," the technician announced.

Naylor waited until Freedman had finished reading, then laid the sheet of paper next to the keyboard again, tripped the ENCRYPT/TRANSMIT lever, and began to type. It didn't take long.

```
TOP SECRET

URGENT

DUPLICATION FORBIDDEN

TO: POTUS

SUBJECT: CGC

VIA SECRETARY OF STATE
```

MAKE AVAILABLE (EYES ONLY) TO:

DIRECTOR, CIA

SECRETARY OF DEFENSE

DIRECTOR OF NATIONAL INTELLIGENCE

C IN C CENTRAL COMMAND

SITREP #1

US EMBASSY BUENOS AIRES 2020 ZULU 7 JUNE 2007

1-TELEPHONE CONTACT ESTABLISHED WITH CGC 0600 ZULU 7 JUNE

2-FACE TO FACE MEETING PROBABLE WITHIN TWENTY-FOUR TO THIRTY-SIX HOURS AT TO BE DETERMINED LOCATION

3-UNDERSIGNED AND VDA BELIEVE CGC AMENABLE TO CALL TO EXTENDED HAZARDOUS DUTY IF HIS PHYSICAL CONDITION PERMITS.

NAYLOR, LTC

TOP SECRET

"That doesn't make a lot of sense to me," Colonel Freedman said, as Naylor waited for the machine to report the message had been received and decoded.

"I suppose not," Naylor said.

The message wasn't supposed to make a lot of sense to anyone except the President. Actually, it was intended to pacify the President, by deceiving him into thinking his orders to get Castillo on extended hazardous duty were being executed.

"Who is CGC? A person, presumably."

"Sir, you're not cleared for that information."

Freedman was annoyed but tried hard not to let it show.

"I understand," he said. "I'm not asking for classified information I shouldn't have—"

"It's a question of Need to Know, sir."

"What I'm curious about, Colonel, and I don't think it gets into a classified area, is why send the message at all? I mean, we had General McFadden on the phone. Presumably he knows what this is all about and—"

"I could have just given him the essence of it, paraphrased a bit?"

"Exactly."

"Two reasons, sir. Because this is going to the President, and when you're dealing with POTUS you go by the book. And also because General McFadden does not know what this is all about, just that I am acting pursuant to a VOCICCENCOM."

"I can understand that."

"And now I have to get out of here, sir. I have something else to do that can't wait."

"I understand. I'll walk you out."

"I really appreciate your assistance, sir."

"Not at all. Glad that I could be of service."

When Naylor had passed through the door of the embassy, the Marine sergeant asked, "Sir, what the hell was that all about?"

"You're not cleared for information at that level, Sergeant," Colonel Freedman replied. "And you should know better than to ask."

Major Kiril Koshkov was waiting with the Mercedes SUV when Lieutenant Colonel Naylor came through the gate in the embassy fence.

Colonel Freedman watched until Naylor got in the Mercedes and it drove off. Then he looked at his watch and said, "Damn, I'm going to be late," and hurried to his embassy car (actually a black GMC Yukon armored with ballistic steel) and told the driver to take him to the embassy of the Republic of Botswana.

The Botswanese really knew how to throw a cocktail party.

Aleksandr Pevsner's Mercedes SUV took Naylor and Koshkov back to the airport, where they fired up Castillo's Mustang and flew back to Bariloche.

[FOUR]
Office of the Director
The Central Intelligence Agency
Langley, Virginia
1910 7 June 2007

As A. Franklin Lammelle, the CIA director, removed a dart from the right ear of the photograph of Vladimir Putin he used as a target and was in the process of removing a second from Mr. Putin's nose, his CaseyBerry buzzed.

He shoved the dart back into Putin's left nostril, took the Casey-Berry from his shirt pocket, looked to see who was calling, and then inquired, "And how may the CIA be of service to the Queen of Foggy Bottom?"

Natalie Cohen, the United States secretary of State, got right to the point.

"I have an URGENT from Buenos Aires," she said.

"Junior called to say he was at the embassy," Lammelle replied.

"What do I do with it?"

"Unless memory fails, Madam Secretary, we were agreed that you would now dispatch a member of your security staff to make the other addressees familiar with it. 'Eyes Only' means you can't send them a copy as it is one of those quote Duplication Forbidden end quote documents."

"You're an 'other addressee,' Frank."

"Well, you can skip me. I know what it says. I wrote it."

"And Truman Ellsworth is in Budapest, looking for Castillo. What do I do about him?"

"I've given that some thought, as a matter of fact. When you see the President, you can tell him where ol' Truman is. One more proof that his faithful staff is carrying out his orders."

"Faithfully carrying out his orders is not what we're doing, Frank, and you know it."

"Consider the alternative, Natalie."

She didn't respond to that directly. "And what do I do with General Naylor?"

"If the President convenes another meeting, you can show the message to General Naylor when he shows up."

"And what do I do if I call the White House and he is available?"

"The last I heard was that Senator Foghorn and the other Good Ol' Boys have already shown up at the White House for a little white lightning and two-bit-limit poker. I don't think he will be available tonight."

"And what if he decides to take Senator Fog . . . *Forman* into his confidence about this?"

"I think that's unlikely; he knows what a loud mouth Forman has. But we'll just have to wait and see."

"I'm very nervous about this whole thing."

"Well, so am I. That's why I'm paid the big bucks. You have to have nerves of steel to be the DCI."

"Oh, God!" she said, and broke the connection.

He immediately called her back.

"What?"

"Our 'keep me posted' deal is still in place, right?"

"That's why I'm paid the big bucks, Frank. Your word has to be good when you're sec State."

[FIVE]
1920 7 June 2007

"Mrs. Clendennen's personal extension."

"This is Natalie Cohen. Is the First Lady available?"

"One moment, please."

"Hey, sweetie! How are you?"

"I'm sorry to disturb you, Mrs. Clendennen—"

"Natalie, honey, I keep telling you and telling you that you can call me Belinda-Sue."

"Belinda-Sue, that's very kind of you."

"Don't be silly. We girls have to stick together, particularly since there are so few of us around here. What can I do for you, honey?"

"Well, I know the President would like to hear they've found Lieutenant Colonel Castillo, but when I called just now, they said he was in conference, and I wondered if you thought I should insist on talking to him, or whether telling him can wait until the morning."

"Just between us, honey, what he's doing is playing pinochle in Lincoln's bedroom with the boys from Buildings, Bridges, and Monuments."

"Excuse me? With whom?"

"When Zeke was in the House, he was co-chairman—with Senator Forman—of the Joint Select Committee on Buildings, Bridges, and Monuments. You know, when one of them loses an election and has to go home, they name a building or a bridge after him. Or put up a statue, a monument they call it, if his hometown allows it. Zeke said it's the only really bipartisan committee in Congress. No arguments, no gridlock. Everybody gets one of the three."

"Oh, yes, I'd forgotten," the secretary said.

"Just between us girls, honey, he's likely to be a little hungover tomorrow, so keep that in mind when you come in the morning."

"You think it would be best if I came to the White House in the morning?"

"I'll call the chief of staff to put you on the list as Number One. That's the eight-thirty slot."

"Thank you, Belinda-Sue."

"My pleasure, honey," the First Lady said. And then went on,

"Say, I just thought, the next time he gets together with those bums, I'll give you a ring, and you can come over and we'll hoist a few belts ourselves. What's gander for the goose, as they say."

"That would be very nice, Belinda-Sue," the secretary said.

[SIX]
The Oval Office
The White House
1600 Pennsylvania Avenue, N.W.
Washington, D.C.
0825 8 June 2007

President Joshua Ezekiel Clendennen, followed by Supervisory Secret Service Agent Robert J. Mulligan, walked into the Oval Office. The President's secretary and Presidental Spokesman Robin Hoboken, who stood waiting, watched as Mulligan pulled out the chair behind the presidential desk and the President sat down.

Mulligan went to the wall beside the windows looking out into the Rose Garden and leaned on it.

The President jabbed his finger in the direction of the coffee service on a side table, indicating he could use a cup, and said, "And put a little Hair of the Dog in it."

"Yes, Mr. President," his secretary said.

"No," the President said, pointing at Hoboken. "Let Whatsisname here do that. I need a confidential word with him. You go file something or something."

"Yes, Mr. President," his secretary said, and left the office.

Robin Hoboken went to the side table and poured a cup of coffee three-quarters full. Then he went to a bookcase and took from behind a book a large white medicine bottle labeled "Take Two Ounces Orally at First Sign of Catarrh Attack."

He added two ounces of the palliative to the President's coffee cup and then presented the cup and its saucer to the President.

The President picked up the cup with both hands and took a healthy swallow.

He did not say "Thank you."

"Mr. President," Robin Hoboken said, "your eight-thirty is Senator Forman. Is there anything I should know?"

"Wrong," the President said. "For two reasons. One, Mulligan had to carry ol' Foggy out of here last night and load him in his car, and the only place the senator's going to be at eight-thirty is in bed. Two, the First Lady got me out of bed by telling me the secretary of State called her last night to tell her we've got a message saying they found Colonel Castillo, and Mrs. Clendennen told her to deliver it this morning."

"Yes, Mr. President."

"I want you here for that. Don't say anything, just listen. Sometimes, when I'm suffering from a catarrh attack—and this one's a doozy—my memory isn't what it used to be."

"I understand, Mr. President."

"I think I'll have another little touch of that catarrh elixir, Robin," the President said. "Why don't you pour a little in a fresh coffee cup before you get ol' Natalie in here? That way she wouldn't see the bottle."

"Of course, Mr. President."

"Let her in, Mulligan," the President ordered.

"Good morning, Mr. President," Secretary of State Cohen said as she walked into the Oval Office.

"What's so important that you told the First Lady you wanted to see me first thing this morning?"

"Actually, Mr. President, I wanted to see you—or at least talk to you—last night. When I spoke with Mrs. Clendennen she set up this appointment for me."

"Well, what have you got?"

Cohen handed him the message.

He read it.

"What's it mean?" he asked.

"Apparently Colonel Naylor has found Colonel Castillo."

"Correct me if I'm wrong, but isn't he a lieutenant colonel?"

"You're correct, Mr. President. Castillo is a lieutenant colonel, retired."

"And LTC means lieutenant colonel, too, right? I thought I told General Naylor to go down there and look for *Lieutenant* Colonel Castillo. So how come *LTC* Naylor went?"

"That was my decision, sir. I felt that someone in the press would find out if General Naylor went down there—"

"Somebody like Roscoe J. Danton?"

"Yes, Mr. President. Somebody like Mr. Danton."

"Good thinking, Madam Secretary. The less anybody knows about this the better, and if Danton, that sonofabitch, got wind of it . . ."

"That was my thinking, Mr. President."

". . . it would be all over Wolf News and in every goddamned newspaper in the country," the President finished.

"Yes, sir," the secretary of State said.

"It says on here No Duplication, but it also says Make Available to Lammelle, Ellsworth, and Whatsisname, the secretary of Defense. God, the Military Mind! How are you going to do that?"

"After I spoke with the First Lady, Mr. President, I showed the message to Secretary Beiderman and DCI Lammelle. And when I leave here, I will send a State Department security officer to Tampa to show it to General Naylor. And with your permission, sir, I will get in contact with Mr. Ellsworth, telling him to return. You will recall you sent him to Budapest. When he comes back, I'll show the message to him."

"And what we do now is wait until we see how this face-to-face meeting with *Lieutenant* Colonel Castillo comes off, right?"

"Yes, Mr. President. As I read the message, that may take place late this afternoon or early tomorrow morning. We should know the results within an hour or two after that."

"And you'll bring me the results as quickly as you brought this message, right?"

"Yes, sir. Of course."

"Well, that's it, then. Thank you, Madam Secretary. Mulligan, show the secretary to her car."

Ten seconds after the door closed on Mulligan and Cohen, the President asked, "Robin, how the hell did that stupid woman ever get to be secretary of State?"

"I don't know, Mr. President," Robin Hoboken confessed.

"All she had to do was get on the goddamn telephone to General Naylor and read the goddamn message to him. What she's going to do is send one of her security people down to Tampa with the message. She may even fly him down there in an Air Force jet, just so he can say, 'Take a quick look at this, General Naylor.' How much is that going to cost the poor taxpayer?"

Robin Hoboken confessed, "I don't know exactly, Mr. President. But you can bet a pretty penny."

"I am surrounded by idiots and cretins, Robin."

" 'Cretins,' sir?"

"A cretin is a high-level moron. You didn't know that?"

"No, sir, I didn't. But I will from here on."

"On the other hand, there's always a silver lining, as Belinda-Sue is always saying."

"Silver lining, sir?"

"I've been thinking out of the box again, Robin."

"You have, sir?"

"The more I think of this idea of mine of having Castillo look into the piracy and drug problems, the more I like it. Even if Castillo doesn't come up with something useful—and he even might; strange things happen—if the word gets out that what I've done is tell a brilliant intelligence officer to look into the problem and make recommendations, I don't think that would adversely affect my reelection campaign, do you?"

"You're going to go on TV, sir? Or hold a press conference and make an announcement?"

"If I held a press conference, not only would it make me look immodest but some bastard would ask me questions I don't want to answer. Christ, you should know that, you're the presidential spokesman and nobody believes anything you say either.

"What I'm doing is going to have to reach the American people via the press who are going to discover what I'm doing."

"How are you going to arrange that?"

"Roscoe J. Danton," the President said.

"He hates you, sir."

"Yeah, I know. And everybody knows he hates me. That's why people will believe him."

The President looked impatiently around the room.

"Where the hell is Mulligan? He's never around when I need him. How the hell long does it take to load one pint-sized female into her car?"

"Mr. President," Robin Hoboken replied thoughtfully, "I would estimate about four minutes—no longer than five, unless Special Agent Mulligan encountered an unexpected problem."

"Tell me, my fine-feathered friend, when you spent all those years at the Missouri School of Journalism, or later when you were covering women's lacrosse for *Time* magazine, did the subject of rhetorical questions ever come up?"

Mr. Hoboken opened his mouth so that he could reply in the affirmative and define "rhetorical question" for the President's edification. But before a sound slipped out Supervisory Special Agent Mulligan came into the Oval Office.

"Saddle up, Mulligan, it's Round-Up time," the President said.

[ONE]
The Watergate Apartments
2639 I Street, N.W.
Washington, D.C.
0935 8 June 2007

In the parking garage, Roscoe J. Danton stepped off the elevator and, his heart full of pleasant anticipation for what was shortly to follow, walked briskly toward his automobile.

First, just as soon as he unlocked the door and got in, his nostrils would be assailed by the smell of the fine leather in his new 2007 Jaguar XJR, a present to himself the day after he deposited his million-dollar-after-taxes bonus from the LCBF Corporation. Next, he would have the pleasure of driving this automotive masterpiece on a beautiful spring day across town to the Old Ebbitt Grill, where he would partake of his regular breakfast of Chesapeake Bay eggs Benedict (succulent lumps of blue crab meat in place of the usual leathery Canadian bacon served by lesser establishments) washed down with one—or perhaps two—Bloody Marys.

None of this was to happen.

Just as he was putting the key in the door of his automobile, a familiar voice spoke to him.

"Good morning, Mr. Danton. And how are you, sir, on this fine spring morning?"

Roscoe turned and saw Supervisory Special Agent Robert J. Mulligan of the Secret Service, head of President Clendennen's security detail.

"What can I do for you, Mulligan?" Roscoe asked.

"Actually, sir, this is a question of what Mr. Robin Hoboken can do for you."

"Like what, for instance?"

"Mr. Hoboken did not elect to share that with me, Mr. Danton," the massive Irishman said. "He sent me to offer you a ride to the White House, where he is waiting for you, sir."

"Please tell Mr. Hoboken that while I appreciate his courtesy, unfortunately my schedule is such . . ."

Several things then occurred with astonishing rapidity.

Mr. Mulligan raised his hand above his head.

A GMC Yukon Denali with darkened windows suddenly appeared. Two muscular men erupted from it, grabbed Roscoe's arms, lifted him off the ground, carried him to the Yukon, and deposited him in the backseat.

Supervisory Special Agent Mulligan got in the front seat and the Yukon started off.

"What the hell is going on here?" Roscoe demanded.

"Actually, Mr. Danton, it's the President who wants to see you. I didn't want to say that where there was a chance I might be overheard."

[TWO]
The Oval Office
The White House
1600 Pennsylvania Avenue, N.W.
Washington, D.C.
1005 8 June 2007

"Good morning, Roscoe," President Clendennen said cordially. "I really appreciate your coming here on such short notice." Then he ordered, "Put Mr. Danton down, fellas, get him a cup of coffee, and then get the hell out."

The Secret Service agents carried Roscoe to an armchair and dropped him into it. Supervisory Special Agent Mulligan held open the door as they left, then closed it after them, and crossed his arms as he leaned on it.

"I hope you didn't have to interrupt anything important to come here, Roscoe," the President said. "The thing is, Robin and I had what we think is a splendid idea, and we wanted to share it with you as soon as possible."

Hoboken said: "I'm sure you remember asking me, Roscoe, if the President—you referred to him as 'the leader of the free world'—had given me 'anything else about his out-of-the-box thinking about his unrelenting wars against the drug trade and piracy, to be slipped to you when no one else was looking.'"

"Clearly," Roscoe admitted.

"Well, Roscoe," the President said, "no one's looking now. Mulligan makes sure of that."

"Now this is sort of delicate, Roscoe," Hoboken said. "By that I mean if anything came out—by that I mean, if anything came out *prematurely*—in the interest of national security, the President would have to—by that I mean, *I would have to,* speaking for the President, as we don't want to involve him at all—deny any knowledge of it at all. You understand that, of course."

"I don't know what the hell you're talking about," Danton confessed.

"What he means, Roscoe," the President said, "is that this is just between us. Okay?"

"What is just between us, Mr. President?" Danton asked.

"My out-of-the-box thinking that you asked him about."

"And what exactly is that?"

"What would you say if I told you that I have decided to enlist the services of Lieutenant Colonel Castillo in my war against the Mexicans and the Somalians."

"Your war against the Mexicans and the Somalians?"

"What the President *meant* to say, Roscoe," Hoboken interjected, "is the Mexican *drug cartels* and the Somalian *pirates.* President Clendennen has absolutely nothing against the Mexican or Somalian *people.* Quite the opposite—"

"Roscoe knows that, for Christ's sake," the President said. "So, what do you think, Roscoe?"

"What do I think about what?"

"About getting Colonel Castillo's opinion of the Mexican and Somalian problems."

"What the President meant to say—" Robin Hoboken began.

"Roscoe knows what I meant," the President interrupted. "Well, Roscoe?"

"I would say you have two problems, Mr. President," Roscoe said.

"The first is to find Colonel Castillo, and then to get him to agree to do what you want him to do."

"A representative of General Naylor is going to meet with Castillo either late today or early tomorrow," the President said. "He will relay to him my request that he enter upon temporary active duty to do what I want him to do."

"That's very interesting, Mr. President."

"And as I'm sure you know, Roscoe, I'm the Commander in Chief, and Castillo is a retired officer so that 'request' is more in the nature of an order than a 'pretty please.'"

"I suppose that's true, Mr. President."

"Now here's where you fit in, Roscoe," the President said.

"The President likes you, Roscoe," Robin Hoboken said. "You must know that. He wouldn't think of fitting anyone else in the White House Press Corps in. He told me that when I went to him and told him you had asked me if he had anything about his out-of-the-box thinking he wanted me to slip to you when no one else was looking. He said, correct me if I'm wrong, Mr. President, 'It has to be old Roscoe who fits in, or nobody.'"

"That's what I said," the President confirmed. "And I'm sure you understand that when I said 'old Roscoe' it was a figure of speech. I don't know exactly how old you are, Roscoe, but you certainly look younger than that. What I should have said was, 'It has to be *young* Roscoe who fits in, or nobody.'"

"Fits in where, Mr. President?" Roscoe asked.

"You tell young Roscoe, Robin," the President said.

"You probably have been wondering, Roscoe, what you may do for your President, not what your President can do for you, but if so, you're wrong. This is a case where we're going to tell you what the

President is going to do for you, and later, what you can do for President Clendennen."

"Which is?"

"I'm going to arrange for you to be with Colonel Castillo on this mission," the President said. "Wherever it takes him, Mexico, Somalia, wherever."

"I don't think that Colonel Castillo would be agreeable to that, Mr. President," Roscoe said.

"And while you're with him you can keep the Commander in Chief and me up-to-date on how things are going," Robin Hoboken added.

"I don't think Colonel Castillo would be agreeable to me going along with him, Mr. President, and—"

"He was agreeable to you going along with him when he nearly got us into a war with Venezuela by invading their island and stealing that Russian airplane, so why not now? Besides, I'm not going to suggest he take you along; I'm going to tell him."

"'Whither Colonel Castillo goeth, thou wilt go,' so to speak," Robin contributed.

". . . and," Roscoe continued after a moment, "I know he won't want me making reports on how, or what, he's doing."

"He doesn't have to know about that," the President said. "As a matter of fact, it would be better if he didn't. Keep that part of this under your hat."

Roscoe gathered his courage.

"Mr. President, I'm honored and flattered—"

"Why don't you wait until the Commander in Chief tells you what he's going to do for you before you thank him?" Robin asked, just a little sharply. "That way you would know what you're thanking him for."

"Robin and I are going to make sure, Roscoe," the President said, "that as an expression of our appreciation for your cooperation in this matter, no one else will have the story. If I'm not mistaken, I think they call that a 'scoop.'

"When it comes out—and it will—that my out-of-the-box thinking has caused significant advances in my unending war against the Mexicans and the Somalians—"

"The President meant to say, of course," Robin interjected, "his war against the Mexican *drug cartels* and the Somalian *pirates*. As I said a moment ago, the President has nothing but the highest regard for the people of Somalia and Mexico."

"Roscoe knows that, for Christ's sake," the President said, somewhat snappily. "Why do you have to keep telling him?"

"I thought, Mr. President, that it was better to repeat it, in case it had slipped Roscoe's mind."

"Do you know what a cretin is, Roscoe?"

"Yes, sir. A high-level moron."

"And I'll bet that someone like you knows what a rhetorical question is. Right?"

"I think so, Mr. President."

"Sometime when you have a spare moment, Roscoe, you might tell Robin."

"Yes, sir. I'll be happy to."

"As I was saying, Roscoe, when it comes out that we're making significant advances against the drug cartels and the pirates, the press will wonder how that happened. They will ask questions, and I will tell them. A week *after* I tell you you can write the story about my out-of-the-box thinking. And you write the story. Now, is that a scoop, or isn't it?"

"Yes, sir. That would be a scoop," Roscoe replied. He found his courage again. "Mr. President, I can't go along with this."

"You know what would happen, Roscoe, if you refused an offer like this from your Commander in Chief?"

"No, sir."

"A couple of things come immediately to mind," the President said. "Like, for example, I ask your pal C. Harry Whelan to come see me, the way I asked you. And I tell ol' C. Harry that I first thought of you to provide this service to your Commander in Chief, but then I heard something that really shocked me about you."

"What would that be, Mr. President?"

"I wouldn't make any wild accusations, of course, but I would tell ol' C. Harry that I heard that the IRS was looking into the one million dollars you recently deposited into your account at the Riggs National Bank and ask him if he had heard that your columns were for sale to the highest bidder. I sort of think that would excite ol' C. Harry's journalistic curiosity, don't you, Roscoe?

"I'd tell ol' C. Harry I didn't believe for a second that the million dollars had come from Somalian pirates and/or Mexican drug lords, but you never know, and the IRS was going to find out. And suggest to him that if he found out where that money had come from before the IRS did, he'd have two scoops."

The President let that sink in a moment.

"'Don't make any hasty decisions' has always been my motto, Roscoe," the President went on. He turned to Supervisory Special

Agent Mulligan. "Get those two goons of yours to take Mr. Danton back to the Watergate. He's got some thinking to do."

He turned back to Roscoe Danton.

"Give me a call, Roscoe. Before five, and tell me what you've decided to do."

[THREE]
Lorimer Manor
7200 West Boulevard Drive
Alexandria, Virginia
1155 8 June 2007

If it had been anyone else but Miss Louise Chambers, the silver-haired septuagenarian who proposed the motto for Lorimer Manor and rammed it through the Management Committee and then insisted it be applied, there probably would have been no motto.

"Ask not what Lorimer Manor can do for you, but what you can do for Lorimer Manor" sounded socialist at best, the naysayers complained.

But Miss Chambers prevailed, in large part because she had early on enlisted the support of Mr. Edgar Delchamps. It was whispered about that she had plied him with most of a half-gallon of twenty-four-year-old Dewar's Scotch whisky before seeking his support, but however she got it, she had it.

And while the personal courage of the ladies and gentlemen of Lorimer Manor, all of whom were retired from the Clandestine Service of the CIA, could not be questioned, none of them was willing to take on the most carnivorous of all their fellow dinosaurs, as Miss Chambers and Mr. Delchamps were universally recognized to be.

What Edgar Delchamps decided he could do for Lorimer Manor was enlist the contribution of someone who was not a resident of Lorimer Manor, but who had laid his head on one of its pillows often in the past and was sure to do so again in the future.

He went to David W. Yung, Junior, and announced, "Louise Chambers tells me she has a hole in her schedule, noon on the first Friday of each month, so you're elected."

"Excuse me?"

"You know Louise is chairwoman of the Lorimer Education and Recreation Committee, right?"

"So what?"

"I told you: She has a hole in her schedule, which you're going to fill by either doing magic tricks—pulling a rabbit out of a hat, for example—or delivering some sort of educational lecture."

"Why should I do that? I don't live there."

"Because you're interested in the welfare and morale of the senior citizens, and also because if you don't, Louise will booby-trap your new electric automatic flushing toilet. She was very good at that sort of thing in her prime."

"As a matter of fact, there is something I could talk to the old folks about, but you'd have to help me."

"Help you how?" Delchamps inquired dubiously.

"Move charts onto the easel, that sort of thing."

"What the hell, Two-Gun, why not?"

Edgar Delchamps was arranging charts and diagrams on the easel and David W. Yung, Junior, Esquire, was standing at his lectern preparing to deliver this month's lecture, "How to Turn the Gaping

Gaps in the IRS Code to Your Advantage," to the ladies and gentlemen residing in Lorimer Manor when Miss Louise Chambers got quickly out of her La-Z-Boy recliner, walked to his lectern, and whispered in his ear.

"David, dear," the elegantly attired septuagenarian said, "I think you and Edgar should see to your journalist friend. It appears to me that something has him scared shitless."

Two-Gun looked at the door to the recreation room, saw Roscoe J. Danton's face, and immediately agreed with Miss Chambers's analysis of the situation.

"You'll have to excuse me a moment," he announced to his audience, and started toward the door. Miss Chambers and Mr. Delchamps followed him.

"What's up, Roscoe?" Two-Gun asked.

"You two bastards got me into this mess," Roscoe replied. "And you sonsofbitches are going to have to get me out of it!" He heard what he had said, and added, "Please excuse the language, ma'am."

"Hell, a man who doesn't swear is like a soldier who won't . . . you know what," Louise said. "And you know what Patton said about soldiers who won't you know what."

"Tell us exactly what's bothering you," Delchamps said.

"I was kidnapped," Roscoe announced.

"Who kidnapped you, dear?" Louise asked.

"The Secret Service," Roscoe announced.

"But you got away, obviously," Louise said. "Good for you!"

"Why did the Secret Service kidnap you?" Two-Gun asked.

"The President told them to."

"Cutting to the chase, Roscoe," Delchamps said, "why did the President tell the Secret Service to kidnap you?"

Roscoe told them.

"Frankly, Roscoe," Delchamps said, "I don't see that as much of a problem."

"Actually, I would suggest that it offers a number of interesting opportunities, scenario-wise," Louise said.

"That's because the President is not sending you two to Mogadishu," Roscoc said. "With the choice between lying to the President or having Castillo kill me for telling the truth."

"Well, I'll admit that Mogadishu isn't Paris," Louise said, "but the current scenario sees Charley going to Budapest before he goes to Mogadishu. I've always loved Budapest."

"Roscoe, you know that Charley's not going to kill you unless he has a good reason," Delchamps said. "But since you're concerned, what we'll do is see what our so-far-unindicted co-conspirators have to say."

He took his CaseyBerry from his pocket and punched the buttons that set up a conference call between the secretary of State, the director of the Central Intelligence Agency, and himself. He also activated the speakerphone function.

When green LEDs indicated the circuit was complete, he said, "Langley, Foggy Bottom, this is Mission Control. We may have a little problem."

Neither Secretary Cohen nor DCI Lammelle saw any great problems in Roscoe's situation. To the contrary, Mr. Lammelle saw it as a great opportunity to provide the President with disinformation.

"I don't see where Roscoe has any choice but to do what the President wants him to do," Secretary Cohen said.

"Except tell him what's really going on, of course," Lammelle said.

"Looking at Roscoe's face," Delchamps said, "I suspect he's considering another alternative. Like, for example, going to the President, telling him what's really going on, and placing himself, so to speak, at the mercy of the dingbat in the Oval Office."

Roscoe, who had in fact been considering that alternative, did not reply.

"You know what would happen in that happenstance, Roscoe?" Delchamps asked rhetorically. "Two things. One, the President would tell you to join Charley and do what he told you to do. Two, Sweaty would consider that what you had done had placed her Carlos in danger and she would come after you with her *otxokee mecto nanara*."

"With her what?"

"It means latrine shovel," Louise explained. "I don't know about you, dear, but I wouldn't want any woman, much less a former SVR *podpolkovnik* protecting her beloved, coming after me with an *otxokee mecto nanara*."

Thirty minutes later, after his third stiff drink of twelve-year-old Macallan single malt Scotch whisky, Roscoe called the White House, asked for and was connected with the President, and then read from the sheet of paper on which Edgar Delchamps had written his suggestions vis-à-vis what Roscoe should tell the Commander in Chief:

"Mr. President, sir, after serious consideration, I have decided to accept your kind offer to serve my Commander in Chief to the best of my ability."

He did not read the last four words Mr. Delchamps had suggested: "So help me God." That was just too much.

[FOUR]
Office of the First Director
The Sluzhba Vneshney Razvedki
Yasenevo II, Kolpachny
Moscow, Russia
1710 8 June 2007

General Sergei Murov had known when, in February, he had been relieved of his duties as cultural counselor of the embassy of the Russian Federation in Washington, D.C., and ordered home that he stood a very good chance of being summarily executed.

His family has been intelligence officers serving the motherland for more than three hundred years, starting with Ivan the Terrible's Special Section, and then in the Cheka, the OGPU, the NKVD, the KGB, and finally the SVR. He knew the price of failure, even when that failure was not due to something one did wrong.

It was presumed that if there was a failure, and if it wasn't due to someone doing something wrong, it was because someone had not done what should have been done.

General—then-Colonel—Murov's failure had nothing to do with culture. He had been the SVR's man, the *rezident*, in Washington. His cultural counselor title had been his cover. It had been no secret to the FBI or the CIA, or even to some members of the Washington Press Corps, that he been the ranking member of the SVR in the United States. A. Franklin Lammelle, then the deputy director for operations of the CIA, had met his Aeroflot flight from Moscow at Dulles, greeted him warmly, and told him he thought it appropriate he greet the new *rezident* in person, as they would be "working together."

Murov knew he was more than likely going to be held responsible for not doing what should have been done to prevent the failure of several of the most important kinds of operations, defined as those conceived and ordered executed by Vladimir Vladimirovich Putin himself.

Those operations had turned out disastrously. The first was intended to show the world, and, perhaps more importantly, the SVR itself, that Putin was back running the SVR and that the SVR was to be feared. It called for the assassination of people—a police official in Argentina; a CIA asset in Vienna; and a journalist in Germany—who had gotten in the way of the SVR in one way or another, followed by the assassinations of the publisher and the owner of the Tages Zeitung newspaper chain.

The latter was so important to Putin that he ordered the Berlin *rezident* to take personal control of the action.

Only the CIA asset and the journalist lost their lives. The Berlin *rezident* and his sister, who had been the Copenhagen *rezident*, not only defected but tipped off the Americans to a secret biological warfare operation run by the SVR in the Congo. The Americans promptly bombed the Congo operation into oblivion. The Vienna *rezident* responsible for the CIA asset elimination was found garroted to death outside the American embassy in Vienna.

In an attempt to double down, Putin then ordered General Vladimir Sirinov of the SVR to exchange a small quantity of the biological warfare substance, dubbed Congo-X, for the two *rezident*s who had defected, and the American intelligence officer who had aided their defection.

That, too, had turned out to be a disaster for him. The American intelligence officer who was supposed to have been kidnapped and taken to Russia, instead staged a raid on a Venezuelan island where Sirinov was waiting. He left the island in the highly secret Tupolev Tu-934A airplane Sirinov had flown from Russia, taking with him the Congo-X and Sirinov. On landing in Washington, General Sirinov, whom Putin expected to commit suicide under such conditions, instead placed himself under the protection of the CIA and began to sing, as the Americans so aptly put it, like a lovesick canary.

Colonel Sergei Murov was responsible for nothing that caused the multiple disasters. But he had done nothing, either, that might have caused the disasters *not* to happen.

That was enough, in his really solemn judgment, to earn him a bullet behind the ear in the basement of that infamous building on Lubyanka Square. Or at least an extended stay in Siberia cutting down trees and feasting on bean soup twice a day.

But that hadn't happened.

General Vladimir Sirinov's treason had been Murov's salvation. Vladimir Vladimirovich had sent for Murov the day after he returned to Moscow, greeted him like an old friend—which in fact he was—and told him that he was going to "have to pick up the pieces and get what has to be done finally done."

Murov was appointed to replace Sirinov as first director of the SVR, and his promotion to general came through the day he actually moved into Sirinov's old office.

Vladimir Vladimirovich didn't have to tell him specifically what he wanted; Murov knew. Vladimir Vladimirovich wanted former SVR Polkovnik Dmitri Berezovsky; his sister, former SVR Podpolkovnik Svetlana Alekseeva, and Lieutenant Colonel Carlos G. Castillo, USA, Retired, in one of the rooms in the basement of the building on Lubyanka Square. He would be barely satisfied to hear they were dead, even if they were disposed of with great imagination—for example, skinned alive and then roasted while hanging head down over a small fire.

Vladimir Vladimirovich wanted them alive.

Murov didn't think getting all three in the bag was going to be that difficult. He thought the negatives involved were outweighed by the positives.

The negatives were that none of the three were naïve about the SVR. They knew its capabilities and would be prepared for them. The "extended families"—Aleksandr Pevsner and Nicolai Tarasov in the case of Berezovsky and Alekseeva; Castillo's former associates in the American intelligence community—would have to be dealt with, of course. That wouldn't be easy. Both Pevsner and Tarasov were former colonels in the KGB, which had evolved into the SVR. Pevsner had what amounted not only to a private army but a private army of former KGB people and Spetsnaz officers and soldiers of unquestioned loyalty to him.

Murov not only had no one inside Pevsner's estate in Bariloche, his home outside Buenos Aires, or even in the Grand Cozumel Beach & Golf Resort in Mexico, or for that matter on any of the vessels of his fleet of cruise ships, he had little hope of getting someone inside Pevsner's organization. All attempts to get people inside, which dated from the earliest days, had resulted in dead operatives.

Only once, when a former FBI agent in Pevsner's employ had been turned by the offer of a great deal of money, had there been even a suggestion of success in that area. Pevsner's assassination had been set up but had failed when the American, Castillo, got wind of it and ambushed the ambushers. The former FBI agent had been slowly beaten to death, possibly by Aleksandr Pevsner himself, in the Conrad, a gambling resort in Punta del Este, Uruguay.

Getting at any of them when they were traveling was made next to impossible, as they traveled only by aircraft owned by Pevsner or Tarasov. Or, in the case of Castillo, on aircraft he owned or were owned by Panamanian Executive Aircraft, which he controlled, the crews of which were all former members of the USAF Special Operations Command—"Air Commandos"—or the U.S. Army's 160th Special Operations Aviation Regiment.

On the other hand, there were some things that almost certainly were going to make things easier. The most significant of these was the incredible stupidity of Lieutenant Colonel Castillo. He fancied himself to be in love with former SVR Podpolkovnik Alekseeva.

When he'd first heard that, Murov had had a hard time believing it. Getting emotionally involved with someone with whom one was professionally involved was something an intelligence officer—and giving the devil his due, Colonel Castillo was an extraordinarily good intelligence officer—simply did not do.

But it was true. The fool actually wanted to marry her. The proof was there. The Widow Alekseeva had gone to the head of the Orthodox Church Outside Russia and asked for permission to marry. He in turn had gone to the Patriarch of Moscow. Murov had people there, and Murov had learned of it immediately.

Very conscious that he himself had an emotional, as well as a professional, interest in the players involved—he had known Svetlana and Dmitri Berezovsky since childhood; had in fact had a schoolboy's crush on Svetlana when he was fourteen, and had been a guest at her wedding when she married Evgeny Alekseev, another childhood friend—Murov had proceeded very cautiously.

He had informed His Beatitude that the circumstances of the death of Evgeny Alekseev—which, of course, had made Svetlana the Widow Alekseeva and freed her to marry—were suspicious. That put the marriage on hold.

The bodies of Lavrenti Tarasov and Evgeny Alekseev had been found near the airport in Buenos Aires. Murov didn't know the facts. It was possible that they had been killed by the Argentine policeman Liam Duffy as revenge for the failed attempt to assassinate him and his family. Duffy was known to have terminated on the spot individuals he apprehended moving drugs through Argentina. That interference with the SVR operation that funded many operations in South America had been the reason Vladimir Vladimirovich had ordered his termination.

It was also possible that Svetlana or her brother had been involved in the death of her husband. They both knew that the only way Evgeny could have redeemed his own SVR career after her defection was to find and terminate her. The unwritten rule was that if an SVR officer could not control his own wife, how could he control others? So when he had appeared in Argentina, her brother had decided—or she had, or they had—that Evgeny had to go.

That was credible, but Murov thought the most likely scenario was that Colonel Castillo had taken out Evgeny. Doing so would not only have protected Svetlana from Evgeny but make her eligible as a widow to marry him in the church.

Whatever the actuality, Murov's whispered word in the ear of His Beatitude had resulted in a report from Murov's people at the wonderfully named Aeropuerto Internacional Teniente Luis Candelaria in Bariloche that His Eminence Archbishop Valentin, the head of ROCOR, and his deputy, the Archimandrite Boris, had flown in there, nonstop from Chicago, in a Gulfstream V aircraft belonging to Chilean Sea Foods, which Murov knew was yet another business formed by Aleksandr Pevsner from the profits of hiding the SVR's money.

Murov believed that His Eminence would decide there was nothing to the rumors that Svetlana had been involved in the termination of her husband, and the marriage could take place. For one thing, Aleksandr Pevsner's generosity to ROCOR was well known. For another, Colonel Castillo could credibly say that he had never had the privilege of the acquaintance of his fiancée's late husband. And if nothing else worked, Dmitri Berezovsky would confess that he had taken out Evgeny to protect his little sister.

All of these factors came together to convince General Murov that his best opportunity to deal with the problem was during the wedding.

It would not be easy, of course. He could not personally go to Bariloche, running the risk of being seen by any of the players, all of whom knew him.

And the team would have to be able to blend, so to speak, into the woodwork, which meant Spanish-speaking terminators would be needed. There were people available in Argentina, Paraguay, and Uruguay, but Liam Duffy would know who they were and have an eye on them.

That left Cuba and Venezuela. The successor to Hugo Chávez, whom Murov thought of privately as something of a joke, would be more than willing to do what he could for the SVR, but his people were, compared to the Cuban Dirección General de Inteligencia, bumbling amateurs.

Furthermore, earlier on Colonel Castillo had taken out Major Alejandro Vincenzo of the DGI in Uruguay. That was something the Cubans, in particular Fidel's little brother, Raúl—who before he took over from Fidel had run the DGI—had never forgotten and would love to avenge.

General Murov picked up his telephone and ordered that five seats on the next Aeroflot flight to Havana be reserved for him and his security detail.

He hung up and then picked up the telephone again.

"When you pack me for the Havana trip," he ordered, "put a case of Kubanskaya with my luggage."

Not only was Kubanskaya one of the better Russian vodkas—and ol' Raúl really liked a taste a couple times a day—but he liked to let visiting American progressives read the label and get the idea it was made right there in Cuba.

[FIVE]
The Oval Office
The White House
1600 Pennsylvania Avenue, N.W.
Washington, D.C.
2135 8 June 2007

"Mr. President," Supervisory Secret Service Agent Robert J. Mulligan announced, "the secretary of State and the DCI are here."

"Let them wait five minutes and then escort them in," President Clendennen ordered.

After consulting his watch, presidential spokesperson Robin Hoboken announced, "That will be at nine-forty, plus a few seconds, Agent Mulligan."

"Good evening, Mr. President," Secretary Cohen said, five minutes and seven seconds later.

"What's he doing here?" the President asked, indicating DCI Lammelle.

"The DCI was with me, Mr. President, when Lieutenant Colonel Naylor's message was delivered to me. I suggested he come with me in case he might be helpful."

"Let's see the message," the President said.

She handed it to him and he read it, and then passed it to Robin Hoboken.

TOP SECRET

URGENT

DUPLICATION FORBIDDEN

TO: POTUS

SUBJECT: CGC

VIA SECRETARY OF STATE

MAKE AVAILABLE (EYES ONLY) TO:

DIRECTOR, CIA

SECRETARY OF DEFENSE

DIRECTOR OF NATIONAL INTELLIGENCE

C IN C CENTRAL COMMAND

SITREP #2

US EMBASSY MONTEVIDEO 2230 ZULU 8 JUNE 2007

1-FACE-TO-FACE CONTACT ESTABLISHED WITH CGC 2010 ZULU 8 JUNE

2-CGC AMENABLE TO CALL TO EXTENDED HAZARDOUS DUTY UNDER FOLLOWING CONDITIONS:

A-PERIOD OF DUTY SHALL NOT EXCEED NINETY (90) DAYS.

B-POTUS WILL PROVIDE THE FOLLOWING SUPPORT

-1- A SUPPORT TEAM OF EIGHT TO TEN TECHNICIANS ON A CONTRACT BASIS FROM SPARKLING WATER DUE DILIGENCE, INC.

-2- A GULFSTREAM V AIRCRAFT WITH CREW FROM PANAMANIAN EXECUTIVE AIRCRAFT, INC., PANAMA CITY, PANAMA

-3- IN LIEU OF MILITARY PER DIEM, ALL ACTUAL LIVING COSTS WILL BE ON A REIMBURSABLE BASIS,

```
        TO BE PAID IN CASH, IT BEING UNDERSTOOD THAT
        ALL ACCOMMODATIONS FOR ALL CONCERNED WILL BE
        IN FIVE-STAR HOTELS, WHEN AVAILABLE.

    -4- REPORTING TO POTUS WILL BE ON AN IRREGULAR
        BASIS AS INTELLIGENCE IS DEVELOPED, BUT NOT
        LESS THAN ONCE EVERY TWO WEEKS.

  3-CGC REQUESTS ACCEPTANCE VIA UNDERSIGNED AT US
     EMBASSY, MONTEVIDEO, WITHIN TWENTY-FOUR (24)
     HOURS AS CGC MUST CANCEL GSTAAD, SWITZERLAND,
     SKI RESERVATIONS WITHIN FORTY-EIGHT (48) HOURS
     OR LOSE HIS DEPOSIT THEREON.

NAYLOR, LTC

TOP SECRET
```

"Who the hell does he think he is?" the President snapped. "Telling me his conditions?"

He looked at Robin Hoboken in expectation of an answer to his rhetorical question.

When none was forthcoming, the President asked, "What the hell is Sparkling Water?"

"It's what some people call soda water, Mr. President," Supervisory Secret Service Agent Mulligan replied. "You know, sir, like scotch and soda."

In the split second before he was to say something both unkind and rude, the President realized Mulligan had not seen the message.

He turned to DCI Lammelle and said, "You're the DCI, Lammelle. You're supposed to know everything. What the hell is Sparkling Water?"

"It's a contracting firm, sir, one of the better ones."

"It sounds as if Colonel Castillo wants to build a garage, or put in a swimming pool," Robin said thoughtfully, "and wants the U.S. government to pay for it. That's outrageous!"

"Mr. President," the secretary of State said, "as I'm sure you know, from time to time it is in the best interests of the government, for any number of reasons, not to use a governmental agency, or government employees, to accomplish a specific mission, but rather to turn to the private sector and contract for their services—"

"In other words," the President interrupted, "Sparkling Water is one of those Rent-a-Spook outfits, right?"

"Yes, sir. You could put it that way," the secretary said.

"Renting a spook, a good one, that's pretty expensive, right?" the President asked.

"You get what you pay for, sir," Lammelle said.

"And this airplane he wants us to rent for him in Panama, that's going to cost a bundle, too, am I right?"

"I'm afraid so, Mr. President," Lammelle said.

"And those five-star hotels he wants everybody to stay in," Robin Hoboken chimed in. "That's really going to cost a fortune, isn't it?"

"I wouldn't say a fortune," the secretary of State said. "But it will be very expensive."

"Not a problem," the President said. "Since this is an intelligence-gathering project, I'll send the bills to ol' Truman C. Ellsworth. The director of National Intelligence can figure out who's going to pay for it—the CIA, the DIA, the FBI, anybody just so it doesn't come out of the White House budget."

"Good thinking, Mr. President," Robin Hoboken said.

"But there are a couple of tiny tweaks to the deal I want to make. First, Colonel Castillo will send me a report not less than once every two *days*, not less than once every two *weeks*. And second, tell him he's going to have to find a seat on that expensive airplane ol' Truman's going to rent for him for ol' Roscoe J. Danton."

"Excuse me?" the secretary of State asked.

"Wither Castillo goeth, so goeth Roscoe," the President said. "I made a deal—the nature of which is none of your business—with Danton." He paused. "You can show these nice people out now, Mulligan."

[SIX]

Estancia Shangri-La
Tacuarembó Provincia
Republic Orientale de Uruguay
1015 9 June 2007

A Chrysler van, bearing diplomatic license plates, pulled up before the veranda of the big house, and C. Gregory Damon, who was the chief security officer of the United States embassy in Montevideo, got out. Mr. Damon, who was forty-four years old and a very black-skinned man of African heritage, stood six feet three inches tall and weighed 225 pounds.

He bounded agilely up the steps to the veranda and said, "Good morning, Mr. Ambassador."

"Damon," Ambassador Philippe Lorimer, Retired—a seventy-four-year-old very black-skinned man of African heritage who stood five feet four inches tall and weighed 135 pounds—replied. "It's always a pleasure to welcome you to Shangri-La."

Mr. Damon walked to Lieutenant Colonel Allan B. Naylor, Junior, said, "You must be Naylor. I know these other three clowns," and handed him a manila envelope.

The three clowns to whom he referred were Chief Warrant Officer Five Colin Leverette, USA, Retired, a forty-five-year-old, very black-skinned man of African heritage who stood six feet two inches tall and weighed 210 pounds; Major H. Richard Miller, Junior, USA, Retired, a thirty-six-year-old, six-foot-two, 220-pound, very dark-skinned man of African heritage; and Lieutenant Colonel Carlos G. Castillo, USA, Retired, who was not only not of African heritage but whose fair skin didn't even suggest he might be of Spanish heritage.

Colonel Naylor took the envelope, extracted a single sheet of paper from it, read it, and handed it to Colonel Castillo.

TOP SECRET

WASH DC 0010 9 JUN 2007

FROM SEC STATE

LT COL A.B. NAYLOR, JR

US EMBASSY MONTEVIDEO

REFERENCE YOUR SITREP #2

INFORM CGC POTUS AGREEABLE TO TERMS WITH FOLLOWING CAVEATS:

-1- REPORTS TO POTUS WILL BE ON A TWO-DAY REPEAT TWO-DAY BASIS NOT REPEAT NOT TWO-WEEK SCHEDULE

-2- DO NOT BEGIN ANY TRAVEL UNTIL MR. ROSCOE J. DANTON JOINS YOUR PARTY; HE WILL GO WHEREVER YOU GO

COHEN, SEC STATE

TOP SECRET

Castillo read the message and handed it to Mr. Leverette.

"Well, Uncle Remus, now we know what she told us on the CaseyBerry last night," he said. "But not what this business about Roscoe is all about."

"I'm sure he will tell us when he gets here," Leverette said.

"And I'm sure someone is going to tell me what this Southern Cone meeting of the NAACP is all about," C. Gregory Damon said.

"We really don't want that word to get out in the State Department, Greg," Castillo said. "And since you've put on those striped pants and thus abandoned your friends in the special ops community . . ."

"With all possible respect, Colonel, sir," Mr. Damon said, and gave Castillo the finger.

"We have returned to where it all began to start again," Castillo said, "for a period not to exceed ninety days. I'm on a recruiting mission. Are you interested?"

"Hell no, I'm not interested. You've recruited me before, and every time I went along, people tried to kill me. And what do you mean, 'where it all began'?"

"If I told you, Greg, I'd have to kill you," Castillo said. "You know about the rule."

Leverette shook his head.

"Remember," he said, "when Jack the Stack Masterson got kidnapped and then whacked?"

Damon nodded. "You and I were in Afghanistan."

"And Charley and Dick here had just left Afghanistan, Dick on a medical evacuation flight—he'd dumped his bird—and Charley under something of a cloud for stealing a bird and going to pick him up where he'd dumped the bird and after he'd been given a direct order not to try it."

"I heard about that," Damon said.

"McNab saved his ass by getting him assigned to the head of Homeland Security in Washington as an interpreter and canapé passer."

"I hadn't heard that."

"Did you know that Jack the Stack was Ambassador Lorimer's son-in-law?" Leverette asked.

"Secretary Cohen told me," Damon said. "Just before I came down here, when she called me in and told me that anything the ambassador wanted—"

"When the President—the last President, not the current loony-tune—heard that Masterson had been snatched," Leverette went on, "and didn't like what he heard the embassy in Buenos Aires was doing about it, he had an idea. Send somebody down here to find out what was going on, somebody who would . . ."

"Charley, you mean?" Damon asked, but it was a statement, not a question.

". . . know what to look for, and report to him."

"So this current idea of our Commander in Chief is not only nutty, but not original," Castillo said. "He stole it from his predecessor."

"You want to tell this story, or should I?" Leverette asked.

Castillo answered by continuing.

"So I was taken off the canapé circuit and sent down here. The day after they arrived, they found Mrs. Masterson . . ."

"My daughter," the ambassador said softly.

". . . drugged, sitting in a car down by the river, beside her husband, who had been assassinated in front of her. When the President heard this, he went ballistic. He got on the horn and told the ambassador he was putting me in charge of getting Mrs. Masterson and the kids safely out of Argentina and to the States, and that he was sending a Globemaster to do that.

"So, a couple of days later, I loaded everybody on the Globemaster and took off for Keesler Air Force Base in Biloxi. En route, Mrs. Masterson told me that the people who had kidnapped her and killed her husband wanted her to tell them how to find her brother. They told her that unless she told them, they would kill her children, and proved their sincerity by killing her husband while she watched."

"Who was her brother?"

"My son, Dr. Jean-Paul Lorimer, at the time was an official of the United Nations stationed in Paris," Ambassador Lorimer said.

"Where he was the bagman for that Iraqi Oil-for-Food scandal," Castillo amplified, "but I didn't know that until later. Mrs. Masterson said so far as she knew he was in Paris.

"Air Force One, the President, and Natalie Cohen were waiting at Keesler Air Force Base in Mississippi."

"As I was," Ambassador Lorimer added.

"Natalie Cohen handed me this even before I had a chance to tell her what Mrs. Masterson had told me," Castillo said.

Castillo appeared to be opening his laptop, from which he extracted and handed Damon two sheets of paper.

TOP SECRET—PRESIDENTIAL

THE WHITE HOUSE, WASHINGTON, D.C.

DUPLICATION FORBIDDEN

COPY 2 OF 3 (SECRETARY COHEN)

JULY 25, 2005.

PRESIDENTIAL FINDING.

IT HAS BEEN FOUND THAT THE ASSASSINATION OF J. WINSLOW MASTERSON, DEPUTY CHIEF OF MISSION OF THE UNITED STATES EMBASSY IN BUENOS AIRES, ARGENTINA; THE ABDUCTION OF MR. MASTERSON'S WIFE, MRS. ELIZABETH LORIMER MASTERSON; THE ASSASSINATION OF SERGEANT ROGER MARKHAM, USMC; AND THE ATTEMPTED ASSASSINATION OF SECRET SERVICE SPECIAL AGENT ELIZABETH T. SCHNEIDER INDICATES BEYOND ANY REASONABLE DOUBT THE EXISTENCE OF A CONTINUING PLOT OR PLOTS BY TERRORISTS, OR TERRORIST ORGANIZATIONS, TO CAUSE SERIOUS DAMAGE TO THE INTERESTS OF THE UNITED STATES, ITS DIPLOMATIC OFFICERS, AND ITS CITIZENS, AND THAT THIS SITUATION CANNOT BE TOLERATED.

IT IS FURTHER FOUND THAT THE EFFORTS AND ACTIONS TAKEN AND TO BE TAKEN BY THE SEVERAL BRANCHES OF

THE UNITED STATES GOVERNMENT TO DETECT AND APPREHEND THOSE INDIVIDUALS WHO COMMITTED THE TERRORIST ACTS PREVIOUSLY DESCRIBED, AND TO PREVENT SIMILAR SUCH ACTS IN THE FUTURE, ARE BEING AND WILL BE HAMPERED AND RENDERED LESS EFFECTIVE BY STRICT ADHERENCE TO APPLICABLE LAWS AND REGULATIONS.

IT IS THEREFORE FOUND THAT CLANDESTINE AND COVERT ACTION UNDER THE SOLE SUPERVISION OF THE PRESIDENT IS NECESSARY.

IT IS DIRECTED AND ORDERED THAT THERE IMMEDIATELY BE ESTABLISHED A CLANDESTINE AND COVERT ORGANIZATION WITH THE MISSION OF DETERMINING THE IDENTITY OF THE TERRORISTS INVOLVED IN THE ASSASSINATIONS, ABDUCTION, AND ATTEMPTED ASSASSINATION PREVIOUSLY DESCRIBED AND TO RENDER THEM HARMLESS. AND TO PERFORM SUCH OTHER COVERT AND CLANDESTINE ACTIVITIES AS THE PRESIDENT MAY ELECT TO ASSIGN.

FOR PURPOSES OF CONCEALMENT, THE AFOREMENTIONED CLANDESTINE AND COVERT ORGANIZATION WILL BE KNOWN AS THE OFFICE OF ORGANIZATIONAL ANALYSIS, WITHIN THE DEPARTMENT OF HOMELAND SECURITY. FUNDING WILL INITIALLY BE FROM DISCRETIONAL FUNDS OF THE OFFICE OF THE PRESIDENT. THE MANNING OF THE ORGANIZATION WILL BE DECIDED BY THE PRESIDENT ACTING ON THE ADVICE OF THE CHIEF, OFFICE OF ORGANIZATIONAL ANALYSIS.

MAJOR CARLOS G. CASTILLO, SPECIAL FORCES, U.S. ARMY, IS HEREWITH APPOINTED CHIEF, OFFICE OF ORGANIZATIONAL ANALYSIS, WITH IMMEDIATE EFFECT.

PRESIDENT OF THE UNITED STATES OF AMERICA

Natalie G. Cohen

SECRETARY OF STATE

TOP SECRET—PRESIDENTIAL

"You carry this around, Charley, in case the cops stop you for speeding, right?" Damon asked, as he handed it back.

"I've been carrying it around in the false cover of my laptop until I decide what to do with it," Castillo said, and then continued, "When I told the President what Mrs. Masterson had told me, he told me to find the brother and find out what was going on.

"Mrs. Masterson had told me he was living in Paris, so I went there. The CIA station chief was a guy named Edgar Delchamps, a dinosaur who knew so many embarrassing things about the Agency they were happy he was happy with the Paris assignment.

"He told me that it wouldn't surprise him if Dr. Lorimer had been cut in little pieces and tossed in the Seine River. He said the word he had was that Jean-Paul had been the bagman for the Oil-for-Food people, had gotten greedy and walked off with sixteen million dollars and was either in the Seine or somewhere in South America.

"So I went back to South America, specifically here. And got lucky. I asked one of the so-called 'legal attachés' in the embassy if he had ever heard of Jean-Paul, and showed him his picture. He said he knew who it was, an antiquities—not *antiques*—dealer named Jean-Paul Bertrand; he had been watching him launder money.

"The simplest way to have him properly interrogated, I decided, was to get him to the States and let the FBI or IRS have at him. It wouldn't be a problem, I thought. He was living here in the middle of nowhere. So I set up a quick, simple op to snatch him and get him on a C-37 I had waiting at Jorge Newbery.

"I stupidly decided I didn't need Delta or Gray Fox, since I had a team consisting of myself, a very good sergeant named Jack Kensington—"

"This is the quick, simple op in which Jack got blown away?" Damon asked.

"Unfortunately, and my fault. I really fucked up. I really thought I could do it with just Jack and me, and some amateurs.

"Like Alfredo Munz, the former head of SIDE; Alex Darby, the CIA guy in Buenos Aires; Tony Santini and Jack Britton, of the Secret Service in Buenos Aires; Dave Yung, the FBI money-laundering guy from the Montevideo embassy; and last and least, I thought, nineteen-year-old Corporal Lester Bradley of the Marine guard at the Buenos Aires embassy.

"In addition to the C-37, I borrowed a chopper—"

"'Borrowed,' Charley? Or stole?"

"Aleksandr Pevsner owed me a favor. He loaned me a Bell."

"Aleksandr Pevsner as in 'notorious arms dealer'? That Aleksandr Pevsner?"

"That one. Don't be so judgmental, Greg," Castillo said. "Remember what it says in the Good Book: 'Judge not . . .' "

"So, what the hell went wrong?"

"I flew the chopper here, and refueled it. Corporal Bradley had driven over with two fifty-five-gallon barrels in the back of a Yukon. Then I left Bradley with the bird and Jack Kensington's rifle, telling him to guard the bird.

"All Jack and I had to do then was get in the house under a simple pretense, bag Jean-Paul, and convince him to come home with us. The worst scenario was that he would be reluctant to do so, which would mean that Jack would have had to stick him with a needle. Then we would load him into the Bell, fly back across the River Plate to Jorge Newbery, and get wheels up in the C-37. A piece of cake.

"We got as far as introducing ourselves to Dr. Lorimer when there came—what did MacArthur call it?—'*the rattle of musketry.*' Some of it came from Corporal Bradley's musket but most of it came from the fully automatic weapons of eight guys in black coveralls aimed at us."

"Who were they?"

"At the time we didn't know, so we called them the Ninjas; they looked like characters in a comic book. Later we found out they were ex–Államvédelmi Hatóság being run by a major from the Cuban Dirección General de Inteligencia named Alejandro Vincenzo."

"And the kid from the Marines actually got in the firefight?"

"The kid from the Marines took out two of them with head shots fired offhand from at least a hundred yards. What the Ninjas were after was Dr. Lorimer dead and the sixteen million he'd stolen back. They got him, but we got the money. When we got back to the States, and I told the President about the money—actually, it was in bearer bonds—he told me I hadn't mentioned bearer bonds, but apropos of nothing at all, if I happened to find some, they would make a nice source of funding for OOA.

"He also gave me permission to keep Lester the Marine and Yung, the FBI's money-laundering expert—actually permission to recruit, draft, anybody I wanted."

"At this point the ambassador and I got in the picture," Leverette put in. "I was running Camp McCall, and all of a sudden this teenaged Marine showed up. Superb judge of military men that I am, I immediately decided that he was wholly unfit to be a Special Operator and put him to work on a computer ordering laundry supplies, and that sort of thing.

"Then McNab choppers into McCall with the announcement he's there to take Lester to Arlington for Jack Kensington's funeral, and that, since Jack and I had been around the block together on several occasions, I was welcome to come along if I wanted to.

"I was so shocked by this that I momentarily forgot my military courtesy and asked the general what the hell the boy Marine had to do with Jack and his funeral.

"'I can't imagine why nobody told you,' the general replied, 'that Corporal Bradley put a 7.62-millimeter slug in the ear of the bad guy who put Jack down and another in the back of the head of the bad guy who was shooting at Charley.'

"He went on to explain that Lester now worked for Charley, and that Charley had sent him to McCall—to me—so he could get a quick run-through of the Qualification Course. Just the highlights. None of the psychological harassment to give us an idea how he'd behave when someone was shooting at him. We already knew that.

"By the time we came back from Washington, I knew all about the OOA and by prostrating myself before McNab and weeping piteously, got him to let me go work for Charley."

"I put Dave Yung in charge of the money," Castillo said, "reasoning that if he was so good in finding out who was laundering money, he'd probably be just as good at hiding our sixteen million from prying eyes. And thus was born the Lorimer Charitable and Benevolent Fund."

"That's when I met Mr. Yung and Mr. Leverette," Ambassador Lorimer said. "They came to Louisiana, where Jack's father and mother had graciously taken me in after Hurricane Katrina had destroyed my home in New Orleans.

"Secretary Cohen knew what had happened here at Shangri-La, and of my son's shameful behavior. And she knew Mr. Yung, who had been working for her, sub rosa, in his money-laundering investigations in Uruguay before he had met Charley.

"She knew that Mr. Yung would be familiar with the Uruguayan inheritance laws, as indeed he was. I was now the owner of Estancia Shangri-La. Charley sent Mr. Leverette with him because he's a fellow New Orleanian, and also to tell me that he felt I was also entitled to the bearer bonds from my son's safe."

"The ambassador wanted neither," Leverette picked up the story. "It was only after Yung told him that he either took Shangri-La or it would wind up in the possession of some highly deserving Uruguayan politician that he agreed to take it. And he said he could think of no better use for the sixteen million than where it was, funding the OOA."

"Turning ill-gotten gains into something constructive, so to speak," Ambassador Lorimer clarified. "And I frankly had a second motive. If I came here to examine my inheritance, I would have an excuse to leave the Mastersons' home, where I strongly suspected my extended stay was beginning to strain even their extraordinarily gracious hospitality.

"So I came down here accompanied by Mr. Yung and the man I had by then become close enough to so as to have the privilege of addressing him as 'Uncle Remus' without, in his charming phraseology, 'being handed my ass on a pitchfork.'"

"Natalie Cohen is one of the ambassador's many admirers, Greg," Castillo said. "And as I am one of hers, when she said she was a little worried about his coming down here alone, I told Uncle Remus and Two-Gun to pack their bags."

"For me, it was love at first sight," Uncle Remus said.

"You've got a crush on Secretary Cohen?" Damon asked.

"Greg," Leverette said patiently, "try turning on your brain before you open your mouth. How many times have you heard one of us with a few belts aboard say, 'I've had enough of this Special Operations bullshit. What I'm going to do is retire and buy a chicken farm'?"

"Not more than two or three hundred times, now that you mention it," Damon said.

"I took one look at this place," Uncle Remus said, gesturing at the verdant pasturelands of Estancia Shangri-La and the cattle roaming them, "and said, 'Fuck the chickens; this is what I want when I retire.'

"So I struck a partner deal with the ambassador right then, Two-Gun drew it up, and got the LCBF to make me a little loan for my ante. And then when the President—the sane one, not Clendennen—pulled the plug on OOA, I retired and came down here."

"Good story, Uncle Remus," Damon said. "It almost, but not quite, makes me yearn for the good old days. But it doesn't answer my question, 'What's the reason for this Southern Cone meeting of the NAACP—plus two honkies, no offense, Colonels—all about?'"

"You tell him, Colonel Naylor," Castillo said. "If I tell him, I'd have to shoot him, and I really would hate to do that. Every time he gets shot, he sounds like Madonna having a baby."

Colonel Naylor explained what they were doing at Estancia Shangri-La.

"Even with your brain in neutral, Damon, you can see why Charley is recruiting those of African heritage, right?" Uncle Remus asked. "That he and Colonel Naylor would have just a little bit of trouble in Mogadishu trying to pass themselves off as native Somalians?"

"I don't know why," Damon said, "I know Charley speaks Af-Soomaali and Arabic . . . Oh!"

"Yeah."

"Well, count me in, Uncle Remus," Damon said.

"Count you in where?"

"If Charley's going to Mogadishu, I'm going."

"You weren't listening, Greg," Castillo said. "*I'm* not going to Mogadishu. *Uncle Remus* is going to Mogadishu with Dick and Master Sergeant Phineas DeWitt, Retired—and now gainfully employed by Sparkling Water Due Diligence, Inc.—and Jack Britton."

"Who?"

"He used to be an undercover cop in Philadelphia, specializing in infiltrating would-be rag-head terrorist groups," Castillo clarified. "He is also now associated with Sparkling Water."

"And what we are going to do in picturesque Mogadishu," Dick Miller said, "is take photographs of each other standing in front of easily recognizable landmarks—"

"Which I will send to POTUS as visual proof that we are carrying out his orders," Castillo said, finishing the sentence for him.

"Which are, specifically?" Damon asked.

"To assess the situation and make recommendations vis-à-vis the solution of the problems known as the Mexican drug cartels and Somalian pirates."

"What are you going to suggest?" Damon asked.

"Ambassador Lorimer suggests that following the motto of Special Forces—'*Kill Them All and Let God Sort It Out*'—would be one solution, but I don't think the President would go along with it. He doesn't stand a chance of reelection without the Somali-American vote."

"Charley," Ambassador Lorimer said, laughing, "that's not what I said and you know it. What I said was that President Clendennen is going to have a harder problem with the pirates than President Thomas Jefferson did. The law then—I said the law *then*, Charley—permitted Jefferson to hang pirates from the nearest yardarm. Now they have to be tried in a court of law."

"Well, maybe President Clendennen doesn't know that," Castillo said, "or I'll have to think of some other suggestion to make."

"And what are you going to be doing, Charley, while Uncle Remus is in picturesque Mogadishu, besides thinking of another suggestion to make to the President?" Damon asked.

"Hoping he has another nutty idea that will make him forget this one."

"And where are you going to do that?"

"We were discussing that when you drove up in that car with the *'I can park anywhere, I'm a diplomat'* license plates. There were two possibilities for a location for my command post. One was the Danubius Hotel Gellért in Budapest. The advantages of that would be that I could talk to my Uncle Billy Kocian . . ." He stopped, said, "I have now stopped pulling your chain, Greg," and then went on, "about the pirates. He has amazing contacts. And also it has a foreign-intrigue sound to it that I suspect will appeal to the President. The other option was the Grand Cozumel Beach and Golf Resort in Mexico. That would probably make the President think that we're all sunning ourselves on a beach while sucking on bottles of Dos Equis instead of investigating the bad guys. But I have a friend, a lifelong friend, a Mexican cop—an *honest* Mexican cop—who knows all about the cartels and will have some practical ideas about how to deal with them the President should hear."

"So, what did you decide?" Damon asked.

"My fiancée just told me we're going to Mexico first, and then Budapest."

"Your fiancée? You're back to pulling my leg?"

"Not at all."

"You have a fiancée?"

"Indeed, I do. You'll meet Sweaty on our way to Cozumel."

"On *our* way to Cozumel?"

"Sweaty said the smart way to do this is to go to Mexico, get organized there, see my cop friend Juan Carlos Pena, then go to Budapest, and then sneak you tourists into Mogadishu on Air Bulgaria. So that's what we're going to do."

"I'm going to have to come up with some story to tell the ambassador. I can't just disappear, Charley."

"When you get back to Montevideo," Uncle Remus said, "the ambassador will tell you he's just had a call from the secretary of State ordering you to Washington immediately for an indefinite period to assist her in some unspecified task."

"You can do that?"

"It's already done."

[ONE]
The Oval Office
The White House
1600 Pennsylvania Avenue, N.W.
Washington, D.C.
0905 10 June 2007

Supervisory Secret Service Agent Robert J. Mulligan held open the door to the Oval Office and Truman C. Ellsworth, the director of National Intelligence, and CIA Director A. Franklin Lammelle came through it.

"Good morning, Mr. President," Ellsworth said. He took from his briefcase a brown manila envelope and handed it to him.

"We have heard from Colonel Castillo, Mr. President," Ellsworth said.

President Joshua Ezekiel Clendennen quickly glanced at what it contained:

```
TOP SECRET

URGENT

DUPLICATION FORBIDDEN

TO: POTUS

SUBJECT: REPORT

VIA SECRETARY OF STATE

MAKE AVAILABLE (EYES ONLY) TO:

DIRECTOR, CIA

SECRETARY OF DEFENSE

DIRECTOR OF NATIONAL INTELLIGENCE

C IN C CENTRAL COMMAND

OOR SITREP #1
```

US EMBASSY BUENOS AIRES 2020 ZULU 9 JUNE 2007

1- WITHIN TWENTY-FOUR (24) HOURS AFTER ARRIVAL IN ARGENTINA OF MR. ROSCOE J. DANTON, OPERATION OBSERVE AND REPORT (OOR) WILL PROCEED TO AS YET UNDETERMINED LOCATION IN MEXICO FOR FOLLOWING PURPOSES:

A. ASSEMBLE OOR OPERATIONAL TEAM

B. WHEN A. ABOVE ACCOMPLISHED DETERMINING BEST METHOD OF MEETING REQUIREMENTS OOR AS ORDERED BY POTUS.

C. INITIAL CONTACT WITH MEXICAN POLICE AUTHORITIES.

2-TRAVEL WILL BE BY AIRCRAFT LEASED FROM PANAMANIAN EXECUTIVE AIRCRAFT AND BILLED TO CIA.

3-ROSTER OF PERSONNEL INVOLVED FOR DURATION OF POTUS MISSION:

A. CASTILLO, LTC C.G. RETD.

B. NAYLOR, LTC ALLAN B. USA

C. D'ALESSANDRO, MR. VICTOR DA CIV GS-15

D. CIVILIAN CONTRACT PERSONNEL OF PANAMANIAN EXECUTIVE AIRCRAFT:

(1) TORINE, JACOB (PILOT)

(2) MILLER, H. RICHARD, JR (CO-PILOT)

E. THE FOLLOWING PERSONNEL HAVE BEEN EMPLOYED ON A CONTRACT BASIS FROM SPARKLING WATER DUE DILIGENCE, INC., AND BILLED TO THE CIA. UNLESS ADVISED TO THE CONTRARY, POTUS MAY ASSUME THEY HAVE JOINED OOR AT THE TO-BE-DETERMINED LOCATION IN MEXICO. IT SHOULD BE NOTED THAT OTHER PERSONNEL, IN ADDITION TO THOSE LISTED HEREIN, MAY BE REQUIRED TO ACCOMPLISH THE MISSION OF OOR AS SPECIFIED BY POTUS.

(1) LEVERETTE, COLIN (TEAM CHIEF)

(2) BRADLEY, LESTER (SECURITY TECHNICIAN)

(3) LORIMER, EDMUND (COMMUNICATIONS TECHNICIAN)

(4) BRITTON, JOHN (SECURITY TECHNICIAN)

(5) BRITTON, DR. SANDRA (LINGUIST)

(6) SIENO, PAUL (INTELLIGENCE ANALYST)

(7) SIENO, SUSANA (INTELLIGENCE ANALYST)

(8) DAMON, C. GREGORY (DIPLOMATIC ANALYST)

RESPECTFULLY SUBMITTED.

CASTILLO, LTC RETD

TOP SECRET

The President handed the report to presidential spokesperson Robin Hoboken and then demanded, "Where's Cohen? Isn't she supposed to deliver this?"

"I have no idea where the secretary of State is, Mr. President," Hoboken said. "But I'm sure the Secret Service could find her for you."

The President looked as if he was going to reply to Hoboken, but didn't, instead shaking his head.

"The protocol, Mr. President," DCI Lammelle said, "provides that when the secretary is not available, the message goes to the next person on the list, in this case the DCI, me. When I got it, I immediately went to see Mr. Ellsworth and we came here together."

"That answers the second part of my question," the President said. "But not the first."

"To the best of my knowledge, sir, Secretary Cohen is in New York at the UN," Ellsworth said.

"Doing what?"

"As I understand the matter, sir, the French are experiencing beach erosion problems in Normandy."

"What the hell can that possibly have to do with us?"

"The French position, Mr. President," Lammelle said, "as I understand it, is the problem began in the spring of 1944, when we landed our invasion force there and tore them up—the beaches, I mean—in so doing. And that therefore we should pay for restoring their beaches to their pre–June sixth, 1944, condition."

"Well, I can understand that," Hoboken said.

"And how much is that going to cost the American taxpayer?" Truman Ellsworth asked innocently.

"I don't know," Lammelle said. "I understand the secretary is trying to get the French to charge the cost of restoring their beaches in Normandy against their debt to us. So far, they have been unwilling to do so."

"That's going to have to go on the back burner," the President said. "Tell Secretary Cohen not to give the Frogs a dime until she clears it with me."

"Yes, sir."

"First things first, I always say."

"Yes, sir."

"So explain this to me," the President said, waving Castillo's report.

"What is it you don't understand, Mr. President?"

"Practically none of it," the President admitted. "But let's start with all these Rent-a-Spooks he's hired from Sparkling Water Due Diligence, Inc. What the hell? Who exactly are these people and what are they going to do for me?"

"Several years ago, Mr. President, several companies were formed to furnish certain services to the intelligence community on a contract basis," Ellsworth answered. "What happened, Mr. President, is that the FBI, the DIA, and others realized that some of the best people, particularly those in the Clandestine Service—"

"Spooks."

"Yes, sir. Many of them had reached retirement age, or length of service—one can retire from the Clandestine Service after twenty years—and were not interested in continuing to serve beyond their twenty years because they could make a great deal more money working for industry and Wall Street.

"Eventually sort of an employment agency, which called itself 'Blackwater,' came into being to match the needs of Wall Street and industry with available personnel. That quickly evolved into Blackwater providing Wall Street and industry—who didn't want it to get out that they had spies on their payrolls—with the appropriate personnel on a contract basis.

"When the Agency began to miss the Clandestine Service personnel who had retired—they really needed them—it occurred to the Agency that if Wall Street could hire these ex-spies, so could they. And that's how it began, Mr. President. And I must say it's worked out well."

"You are using ex-spies from this Blackwater thing to do the CIA's spying—is that what you're telling me?"

"Since I took over as DCI, Mr. President, I have been moving more toward Sparkling Water and away from Blackwater."

"Why is that?"

"Blackwater kept raising its prices, Mr. President. Not only did Sparkling Water come to me and offer the same quality ex-spies for less money, but also the services of ex–Delta Force Special Operators and retired Secret Service personnel. The Delta Force people were unhappy performing services for Wall Street. So the Agency has just about moved to placing all its contract business with Sparkling Water."

"So you know who the people on here are?" the President asked, waving Castillo's report.

"Yes, sir, I do."

"And you're going to tell me about them, right?"

"Yes, sir. May I have a look at Colonel Castillo's report, sir?"

"Why don't you have your own copy?"

"Because it says 'Duplication Forbidden,' sir. Right at the top."

"Okay. Who are they?"

"Leverette and Gregory, Mr. President, are both Afro-Americans and retired from Delta Force," Lammelle began.

"What's Afro-American got to do with anything? Why did you have to bring that up? You know full well my administration is color blind."

"I think it probably has something to do with their being able to move inconspicuously around Somalia, Mr. President," Ellsworth said. "Most of the people in Somalia are Afro-Amer . . . African . . . of the Negro race."

"I don't think you're supposed to say that either," the President said.

"Mr. and Dr. Britton are also African-Americans," Lammelle said.

"Why does Castillo think he needs a doctor in Somalia?"

"She's a Ph.D., Mr. President, a philologist, not a physician."

"She's a stamp collector?" the President asked incredulously.

"Stamp collectors are *philatelists*, Mr. President. *Philologists* are language experts."

"Okay, so she speaks whatever gibberish they speak in Somalia. Why not say that, that she's an interpreter? I'm beginning to wonder if Castillo is purposely trying to confuse me."

"I don't know if Dr. Britton speaks Af-Soomaali or not, Mr. President," Ellsworth said.

"Speaks what?"

"Af-Soomaali, Mr. President, the language spoken in Somalia."

"Of course she does," the President said impatiently. "If she doesn't speak Af-soo . . . whatever you said . . . why would Castillo be taking her there? But find out for sure. If she doesn't, that would really sound fishy to me."

"Yes, sir, Mr. President." Ellsworth paused, then went on: "Mr. Britton is a former Secret Service agent, Mr. President. And before that he was an undercover detective in Philadelphia."

"Does he speak Af-soo whatever?"

"I just don't know, Mr. President," Ellsworth confessed.

"Mr. and Mrs. Sieno, Mr. President," Lammelle said quickly, "are both retired from the Clandestine Service of the Agency."

"*Both* of them are retired CIA spies?"

"We like to think of people like that as 'field officers,' Mr. President," Ellsworth said.

"Why can't you people call a spade a spade?" the President said.

"Many African-Americans find the term 'spade' offensive, Mr. President," Robin Hoboken said. "I for one would never think of calling CIA field officers 'spades.' "

The President glared at his spokesman.

"Actually, Mr. President, I'm not sure whether the Sienos are Italian-Americans or Latinos," Lammelle said.

"If you two are the best intelligence people we have," the President said, "the country's in deep trouble. Get the hell out of here!"

[TWO]
The Presidential Suite
The Meliá Cohiba Hotel
Verdado, Havana, Cuba
1425 10 June 2007

General Sergei Murov and his security detail had not gone to Havana openly. That would not be in the tradition of the Cheka and its successor organizations. Instead, their documents identified them all as members of the Greater Sverdlovsk Table Tennis Association and Mr. Murov as Grigori Slobozhanin, the chief coach thereof.

His true identity was known of course to General Jesus Manuel Cosada, who had replaced Raúl Castro as head of the Dirección General de Inteligencia, or DGI, when Señor Castro had replaced his brother, Fidel, as president of the Republic of Cuba.

General Cosada therefore ordered that the visiting Ping-Pongers be housed in the five-star high-rise Meliá Cohiba Hotel on Avenida de Maceo, more commonly known as the Malecón, the broad esplanade that stretches for four miles along the coast of Havana.

He did so for several reasons. He knew that General Murov and President Castro were close personal friends, for one thing, and for another that the Presidential Suite was equipped with state-of-the-art cameras and microphones—some of them literally as small as the head of a pin—with which the visit of General Murov could be recorded for posterity and other purposes.

General Cosada's expert in this type of equipment, Señor Kurt Hassburger, who had immigrated to Cuba from the former East Germany and really hated Russians, had also installed a microphone and transmitter in the lid of the cigar humidor Señor Castro would give—filled with Cohiba cigars—to General Murov as a little "Welcome Back to Cuba" memento.

When General Cosada and President Castro entered the Presidential Suite carrying the humidor of cigars, they were wearing the customary attire of senior officials of the Cuban government.

In the early days of the Cuban revolution, the Castro forces had raided a government warehouse and helped themselves to U.S. Army equipment the Yankee Imperialists had given to the Batista regime. This included U.S. Army "fatigue" uniforms and combat boots, which Fidel promptly adopted as the revolutionary uniform, primarily because they were far more suitable for waging revolution than the blue jeans, polo shirts, and tennis shoes he had been wearing.

When the revolution had been won, Fidel and Raúl and their subordinates had continued to wear the fatigues because—depending on who you were listening to—they represented solidarity with the peasants and workers or because they were much more comfortable in the muggy heat of Cuba than a suit and shirt and necktie would have been.

The fatigues President Castro and General Cosada were wearing today were of course not the ones liberated from Batista's warehouse—there was a tailor on the presidential staff who made theirs to order—but they looked like U.S. Army fatigues.

General Murov thought their uniforms made them look like aging San Francisco hippies. Or Wanna-Be-Warriors at a Soldiers of Fortune convention.

Murov was far more elegantly attired. When he had been the cultural attaché of the Russian embassy in Washington he had regularly watched J. Pastor Jones and C. Harry Whelan, Junior, on Wolf News to keep abreast of what the American reactionaries were up to.

Their programs were in part sponsored by Jos. A. Bank Clothiers and the Men's Wearhouse. Eventually, their advertisements got through to him and he investigated what he thought were their preposterous claims by visiting an emporium of each.

There he found that not only was the reasonably priced clothing they offered superior to that offered for sale in Moscow, but that they really would give you two suits—or an overcoat and a suit, or two overcoats, or a half dozen shirts and neckties and a sports coat and slacks—absolutely free if you bought one suit at the regular price.

He found this fascinating because recently, having nothing better to do, he had been flipping through the SVR manual on *rezident* operations and had come across an interesting item buried in the manual as a small-font footnote. It stated that anything purchased, including items of clothing, deemed by the *rezident* as necessary to carry out intelligence missions could be billed to the SVR's Bureau for the Provision of Non-Standard Equipment.

Murov had turned almost overnight into a fashion plate. And he was not only happy with the way he looked—as the spokesman for Men's Wearhouse said he would be—but convinced that the SVR man who had written the footnote was right on the money. How could one be a really good spy wearing clothing that made one look as if one was drawing unemployment?

This of course applied to the staff of the *rezident*, the junior spies, so to speak. They shouldn't look like they were drawing unemployment, either. He went to the management of both Men's Wearhouse and Jos. A. Bank and asked them if he could throw a little business their way, what could they do for him? Not in terms of free sports coats, but in cash?

A mutually agreed upon figure—5.5 percent of the total—was

reached, and Murov sent his staff to both establishments with orders to acquire a wardrobe in keeping with the high standards expected of SVR spies, and not to worry about what it cost, as the bill would be paid by the SVR's Bureau for the Provision of Non-Standard Equipment.

President Castro handed General Murov the humidor of Cohibas, and Murov handed General Cosada the case of Kubanskaya.

"Fidel sent these for you," Raúl said.

"How kind of him."

"I really appreciate the Kubanskaya, Sergei," Raúl said. "You can't get it in Cuba."

"I understand we're selling a lot of it to Venezuela," Sergei replied.

"Yeah, but between us, it's hard to get from there, too. Fidel is a little overenthusiastic about that 'Drink Cuban' program of his. It means we're supposed to drink rum and it's treasonous to the revolution to import spirits made anywhere else. So I have to remember to hide my Kubanskaya when he comes by the house. And whenever I take a chance and get the Bulgarians to slip me a case on the quiet through their embassy here, the sonofabitches are on the phone next day asking, 'So, what are you going to do for Bulgaria now?'"

"Bulgarians do tend to be a bit greedy, don't they?" Sergei asked rhetorically. "Did you ever see them eat?"

"I'd hate to tell you what Fidel calls them," Raúl said.

"How is Fidel?"

"He sends his regards along with the cigars."

"Well, thank him for the Cohibas when you see him."

"I will. You've heard he's stopped smoking himself?"

No, Murov thought, *but if I had to smoke these, I'd stop smoking myself.*

Among other intelligence Murov had acquired while he was the *rezident* in Washington was that all the good cigar makers had fled from Cuba immediately after the revolution. The really good ones had gone to the Canary Islands, where they continued to turn out Cohibas and other top-of-the-line cigars.

The Cuban Cohibas were not really Cuban Cohibas, in other words. When Murov saw the humidor of Cuban Cohibas, he had immediately decided to take it to Moscow, where he would give them to people he didn't like, and he hoped ol' Raúl wouldn't expect him to light up one of the ones he had given him.

"No, I hadn't," Murov said.

"He said he feels better now that he's stopped smoking."

"Well, I can understand that," Murov replied, and mentally added, *If he was smoking these steadily, I'm surprised they didn't kill him.*

"So tell me, Sergei," Raúl said, "what brings you to Havana?"

"I need about a dozen of your best DGI men," Murov replied. "For a month, maybe a little longer."

"To do what?" General Cosada asked.

"Vladimir Vladimirovich wants to entertain three people now in Argentina, and I need your people to assist them in getting on the plane to Moscow."

"What three people?" Raúl asked.

"Former SVR Polkovnik Dmitri Berezovsky, former SVR Podpolkovnik Svetlana Alekseeva, and Lieutenant Colonel C. G. Castillo, U.S. Army, Retired."

"Why don't you go to the Venezuelans?" General Cosada asked. "I know they don't like the American. For that matter any Americans."

"Have you already forgotten Major Alejandro Vincenzo, Raúl? *Sic transit gloria,* Major Alejandro Vincenzo?"

"I don't like to think about Alejandro," Castro said. "But no, I haven't forgotten the loss of my sister Gloria's second-oldest son. But it momentarily slipped my mind that that bastard Castillo was responsible for what happened to him."

"Raúl," Murov asked, "does the fact that that bastard Castillo killed your nephew in Uruguay change our conversation from *'What can the SVR do for the DGI?'* to *'What can the DGI do for the SVR?'*"

President Castro considered that a moment.

"No," he said finally. "It doesn't. Where we are now is *'What can the SVR do for the DGI, in exchange for what the SVR wants the DGI to do for the SVR?'*"

When Murov didn't immediately reply, Castro went on, "I wouldn't want this to get around, Sergei, but neither Fidel nor I ever really liked Vincenzo. But he was our sister's kid, and you know how that goes: We were stuck with him."

"And between you and me, Sergei," General Jesus Manuel Cosada said, "the sonofabitch was always sucking up to Fidel. He wanted my job."

"But then why did you send him to Uruguay?" Murov asked.

"Sending him there," Cosada said, "is not exactly the same thing as sending him there and hoping he got to come back."

"Jesus Christ, Jesus!" Raúl said. "If Gloria ever heard you say that, you'd be a dead man!"

"I asked why you sent him, feeling the way you apparently felt, to Uruguay," Murov said.

"Well, when the Iraqi Oil-for-Food people told us what they wanted . . ."

"Which was?" Murov asked.

"They wanted the UN guy, Lorimer, dead."

"Because he ripped them off for sixteen million dollars?"

"Well, once he'd done that, they knew he couldn't be trusted. And he knew too much, too many names. He had to be dead. They didn't seem to care too much about the money," Raúl said.

"Which got Raúl and me to thinking . . ." Cosada said.

"What would happen if we sent Alejandro down there with the Hungarians . . ." Raúl said.

"For which they were offering us a lot of money," Cosada picked up. "And they took out Dr. Lorimer . . ."

"But then we told them there was no sixteen million dollars in bearer bonds in his safe."

"And somebody tipped the Uruguayan cops to what the Hungarians had done, and where to find them."

"And Alejandro brought us the bearer bonds," Raúl said. "Getting the picture?"

"Brilliant!" General Murov said.

"The Oil-for-Food people were not about to make a stink. They would have gotten the important part of what they wanted—Lorimer dead—and the money wasn't that important to them. The money those rag-headed Iraqi bastards made from Oil-for-Food is unbelievable, except it's true."

"So that's what happened," Murov said.

"No, that's not what happened," Raúl said. "What happened was this goddamn Yankee Castillo killed Alejandro *and* killed the Hungarians *and* made off with our sixteen million dollars. The notion of that thieving Yankee sonofabitch sitting naked in a cell in Lubyanka getting sprayed with ice water—I presume that's what you have in mind for him—has a certain appeal. I don't like it when people steal sixteen million dollars from me. Tell me what you have in mind, Sergei."

"Well, so long as they were in Argentina—"

"'*Were* in Argentina'?" Cosada interrupted.

"Jesus Christ, Jesus, for Christ's sake stop interrupting my friend Sergei," Raúl snapped.

"As I was saying," Murov went on, "so long as the three of them, 'the Unholy Trio,' so to speak, are in Argentina, we can't get at them. Not only are they protected by Aleksandr Pevsner's private army, but that goddamn Irish cop Liam Duffy has my photograph on the wall of every immigration booth in the country."

"So what are you proposing?" Raúl asked.

"Just as I got on the plane to fly here—"

"Speaking of flying, Sergei," Raúl said, "we have to talk about the Tupolev Tu-934A."

"What do you mean, 'talk about it'?"

"Fidel wants one. He told me to tell you his feelings were hurt when you gave one to the late Fat Hugo . . ."

"I did not give one to Fat Hugo."

". . . and didn't give one to him," Raúl said. "And I can see his point."

"Read my lips, Raúl. I did not give a Tupolev Tu-934A to Fat Hugo."

"That's not what we heard," Cosada said.

"If you didn't give one to Fat Hugo, what was that airplane our friend Castillo stole from him? A Piper Cub?" Raúl challenged.

"What Castillo stole from Fat Hugo's island was General Vladimir Sirinov's Tupolev Tu-934A," Murov said.

"I don't think Fidel's going to believe that," Raúl said.

"Raúl, listen to me. I don't want this to get around, but we don't have that many Tupolev Tu-934As. We don't have enough for us. Do you think I would have come here on that Aeroflot Sukhoi Superjet 100-95 if I could have talked Vladimir Vladimirovich into letting me use a Tu-934A? That so-called Superjet is a disaster. I didn't uncross my fingers until we landed here, and I'm going home on Air Bulgaria. They're flying DC-9s that are as old as I am, but their engines don't fall off."

"Well, I'll tell Fidel what you said, but if I were you, I'd try real hard to get him a Tupolev."

"Can we get on with this?"

"You'd be in a better bargaining position, Sergei, if you got Fidel one of those Tupolevs, but go ahead."

"I thought you were the president now."

"I am, but Fidel is still Fidel. He just doesn't come to the office as often as he used to."

"I found out just before I got on the plane to come here that Castillo and his fiancée, the former Podpolkovnik Svetlana Alekseeva, and a couple of Castillo's people, the Merry Outlaws, just left Bariloche for Cozumel."

"Couple of questions, Sergei. Castillo's fiancée?"

"He's going to marry her. That's what 'fiancée' means."

"You're kidding, right?"

"No, I'm not."

"Unbelievable! He's not a bad-looking guy. And no offense, Sergei, but every female SVR *podpolkovnik* I've ever seen looks like a Green Bay Packers tackle in drag."

"This one doesn't. Believe it."

"Merry Outlaws?"

"That's what President Clendennen calls Castillo's people. If that's good enough for him . . ."

"What are they going to do in Cozumel?"

"I gave that a good deal of thought before I understood."

"Understood what?"

"What they're going to do in Cozumel. It's going to be a great big wedding. All the OOOR—and there's a hell of a lot of them."

"All the what?"

"Like ROCOR, which, as I'm sure you know, stands for Russian Orthodox Church Outside Russia."

"No, I didn't," Raúl confessed.

"Me, either," Cosada said. "What the hell is it?"

"We don't have time for that right now, maybe later. OOOR stands for Oprichnina Outside of Russia."

"And what the hell does Oprichnina mean?" Castro asked.

"I really don't have the time to get into that with you either, Raúl. But trust me, there's more of them than anybody suspects and they'll all want to come to the wedding. The Berezovsky family—and Svetlana was Svetlana Berezovsky before she married Evgeny Alekseev and became Svetlana Alekseeva—is one of the oldest, most prestigious families in the Oprichnina.

"If anybody in the OOOR gets invited to the wedding, and they all will, they'll go. Just the Oprichniks in Coney Island would fill a 747. And they'll all bring their security people, now that I think of it. So two 747s from Coney Island alone."

"Where the hell is Coney Island?" Cosada asked.

"In New York City. You know the place where they have—or had—the parachute tower? For ten dollars, you got to make sort of a parachute jump?"

"Oh, yeah," Cosada said. "I think the parachute tower is gone, but I know where you mean."

"Don't take offense, Sergei," Raúl said, "but I don't have any idea what you're talking about."

"Aleksandr Pevsner's La Casa en Bosque in Bariloche is big, but not big enough for all those Oprichnik wedding guests. And there's only a few hotels there. And Aeropuerto Internacional Teniente Luis Candelaria couldn't handle one 747, much less a bunch of them. So what are they going to do? A cruise ship—maybe two cruise ships—is what they're going to do. A cruise ship is sort of a floating hotel."

"Where are they going to get a cruise ship?"

"The last I heard, Pevsner owned twelve of them," Murov said. "Most of them are like floating prisons, but a couple of them, I understand, are very nice."

"I'm an old man, Sergei," Raúl said. "Not as swift as I used to be. You want to explain this to me in simple terms?"

"Aleksandr Pevsner owns the Grand Cozumel Beach and Golf Resort. Which—Cozumel—is also a stop for cruise ships. So they hold the wedding in the resort and put up the guests who won't fit in the resort in one of his cruise ships. Or two of them. That's what Castillo and Svetlana are going there for, to set this up.

"Dmitri Berezovsky didn't go along with them to Cozumel now, but he'll be there for the wedding. He'll probably give the bride away; he's her brother. So we go there now, and get set up ourselves. And when everybody is jamming the place, there's all the wedding excitement, we snatch the three of them, load them onto an Aeroflot airplane conveniently parked at Cozumel International—"

"For a nonstop flight to Moscow," Raúl finished.

"Where your boss will tie the Yankee sonofabitch who stole our sixteen million in bearer bonds to a chair in Lubyanka," Cosada furnished.

"And spray him with ice water," Raúl picked up.

"Until he is an ice sculpture," Cosada said.

"How many men are you asking for, Sergei?" Raúl asked.

"Ten or twelve should do it."

"General Cosada," Raúl said, "make twenty-four of your best men available to General Murov immediately."

"Yes, sir, Mr. President."

"As a matter of fact, Jesus, I think you better go with him," Raúl added.

[THREE]
The Imperial Penthouse Suite
The Grand Cozumel Beach & Golf Resort
Cozumel, Mexico
0945 11 June 2007

Castillo's CaseyBerry vibrated and rang—the ringtone actually a recording of a bugler playing "Charge!"

"And how may I help the comandante on this beautiful spring morning?" he answered it.

There was a reply from Comandante Juan Carlos Pena, *el Jefe* of the Policía Federal for the Province of Oaxaca, to which Castillo answered, "Your wish is my command, my Comandante," and then broke the connection.

Castillo then turned to the women taking the sun in lounge chairs beside the swimming pool. There were three of them: Svetlana Alekseeva; Susanna Sieno, a trim, pale-freckled-skin redhead; and Sandra Britton, a slim, tall, sharp-featured black-skinned woman.

"I'm afraid it's back to the village for you, ladies," Castillo said.

"What did you say?" Sweaty asked.

"El Comandante just told me to put my pants on and send the girls back to the village."

Sweaty threw a large, economy-size bottle of suntan lotion at him and said some very rude and obscene things in Russian.

Max leapt to his feet and caught the suntan lotion bottle in midair. But to do so he had to go airborne himself, which resulted in him dropping from about eight feet in the air into the pool. This caused the ladies to be twice drenched, first when he entered the water—a 120-pound Bouvier des Flandres makes quite a splash—and again when Max, triumphantly clutching the bottle in his teeth, climbed out of the pool and shook himself dry.

With a massive and barely successful effort, the men attached to the ladies—Castillo; Paul Sieno, an olive-skinned, dark-haired man in his early forties; and John M. "Jack" Britton, a trim thirty-eight-year-old black-skinned man—managed to control what would have been hysterical laughter.

"Over here, girls," Castillo said, as he went to the side of the penthouse and pointed downward, "you really should see this."

Curiosity overwhelmed feminine indignation and they went and looked twenty-four floors down. So did Jack Britton, Roscoe J. Danton, and Paul Sieno.

They saw four identical brown Suburbans, each roof festooned with a rack of what is known in the law enforcement community as "Bubble Gum Machines," approaching and then disappearing beneath the canopied entrance to the Grand Cozumel Beach & Golf Resort.

"American Express is here," Castillo said.

"What the hell does that mean?" Roscoe asked.

"Juan Carlos calls them that because he never leaves home without them," Castillo explained.

"Your friend has a CaseyBerry?" Britton asked.

"I could do no less for the only honest police officer in Mexico," Castillo said. He turned to former Marine Gunnery Sergeant Lester Bradley.

"Lester, stand by the door. Our guests are about to arrive. The rest of you are cautioned not to make any sudden moves when they arrive."

Three minutes later the doorbell chimes bonged pleasantly. Lester pulled the door open. Three burly police officers came through the door, each armed with an Uzi submachine gun. They quickly surveilled the room, and then one of them gestured for whoever was still outside that it was safe to enter.

Jack Britton was impressed. During his career with the Philadelphia Police Department, he had once served on the SWAT team. His professional assessment of these people was that they really knew "how to take a door."

A short, stocky, unkempt olive-skinned man in a baggy suit and two more uniformed officers carrying Uzis came through the door.

Max dropped the suntan lotion bottle, rushed toward the man, put his paws on his shoulders—which pinned him to the wall—and then enthusiastically lapped at his face.

"Carlitos, you sonofabitch, you taught him to do that to me!" Juan Carlos Pena said.

"No, it's the remnants of your breakfast on your unshaven face," Castillo said.

Pena pushed Max off him, and then he and Castillo approached each other and embraced.

When they broke apart, Pena asked, pointing to the Sienos, the Brittons, and Roscoe J. Danton, "Who are these people? Excuse me for asking, but I have learned to be very careful when I'm around you."

"Dr. Britton, Sandra, is a philologist," Castillo said. "Her husband, Jack, is not nearly so respectable. He used to be a cop. The Sienos, Susanna and Paul, have an even less respectable history, and Mr. Danton is a practitioner of a profession held in even lower prestige than being a congressman. He's a journalist."

Pena smiled.

"Well, he must like you. Carlito only insults his friends," he said. "Which means I can move on to Question Two: What brings you to beautiful Cozumel? White-sand beaches and the sun setting over the sparkling Caribbean will not be a satisfactory answer."

"We come to offer you a unique opportunity," Castillo said.

"I'm afraid to ask what that might be, but I suppose I don't have a choice, do I? Tell me about my unique opportunity."

"Very few men are ever offered, as you are about to be, the opportunity of advising the President of the United States, Joshua Ezekiel Clendennen, vis-à-vis how he should handle the Mexican drug cartels."

"You didn't have to come all the way down here—or *up* here; my guy at the airport said you came from Argentina—to ask me that. You already know the answer."

"And what would that be, Señor Pena?" Susanna Sieno asked, in Spanish.

"Get people in the U.S. to stop buying illegal drugs," Pena said.

"Ouch!" Castillo said.

"Carlitos, you know I'm right. If you Americans were not buying drugs, we Mexicans wouldn't be slaughtering each other for the profitable privilege of moving them through Mexico and then across the border."

"You're right, Juan Carlos, but that's not an answer the President will like."

"Why not?"

"Let me tell you what we're really doing here, Juan Carlos," Castillo said, and did so.

"You're telling me," Juan Carlos asked when Castillo had finished, "that the President of the United States is not playing with a full deck?"

"I wouldn't want this to get around," Castillo replied, "but I estimate there are no more than forty-two of the normal complement of fifty-two cards in his deck. He doesn't think he's Napoleon, and he doesn't, so far as we know, howl at the moon. But . . ."

"So why hasn't he been moved out of the Oval Office and into a padded cell?"

"We've already forced one President—Nixon—to resign or face impeachment, and actually tried to impeach one—Clinton—in the Senate. Both times, it nearly tore the country apart; we don't want to do that again."

" 'We'?" Pena asked softly.

"I meant 'we Americans,'" Castillo replied. "The decision to—how do I say this?—*live with* Clendennen and try to keep him from doing real harm was made primarily by the secretary of State, Natalie Cohen, Generals Naylor and McNab, and a few others in pay grades much higher than my own. I'm just a simple old soldier obeying orders."

"You didn't make that up," Pena said. "You stole it."

"What?"

"I saw that movie, Carlitos. George C. Scott, playing General Patton, was trying to lay some crap on Karl Malden, who was playing

General Omar Bradley, and when Bradley called him on it, Patton said, smiling, what you just said, 'I'm just a simple old soldier obeying orders,' and Malden/Bradley said, 'Bullshit.'"

"I can't imagine General Bradley saying 'bullshit' under any circumstances," Castillo said prissily. "General Bradley marched in the Long Gray Line and was an officer and a gentleman."

"Oh, God," Pena said, laughing. "What you are, Carlitos, is an idiot with a death wish. Only an idiot with, say, *twenty*-two cards in his deck would come back here the way you have."

"What's that supposed to mean? There's a big sign in the airport that says 'Welcome to Cozumel!' That didn't mean me?"

"Juan Carlos," Svetlana asked, "what do you mean 'death wish'?"

It took Pena a moment to frame his reply, and when he gave it, his tone was dead serious.

"About six weeks ago, Svetlana," he said, "specifically on April twenty-second, eleven men were shot to death at KM 125.5 on National Road 200. That's near Huixtla, in the state of Chiapas.

"One of the bodies remains unidentified, but there is reason to believe that it is that of a Russian, an agent of the SVR. Two bodies were identified as those of Enrico Saldivia and Juan Sánchez, both known to be members of the Venezuelan Dirección de los Servicios de Inteligencia y Prevención, commonly referred to by its acronym, DISIP. The remaining bodies were all Mexican nationals. Two of them belonged to the Zambada Cartel, which is run by Joaquín Archivaldo. These bodies were further identified to be former Special Forces soldiers—*Mexican* Special Forces, trained and equipped by American Special Forces—who changed sides.

"The other six men are known to have been members of the

Sinaloa Cartel, which is run by Joaquín Guzmán Loera and Ismael Zambada García.

"Those two cartels are normally at each other's throats, but in this case were working together. What they had done was kidnap an American Special Forces officer, Lieutenant Colonel James D. Ferris, with the idea of exchanging him for a man named Félix Abrego, who had been convicted in the U.S. of the murder of several American DEA agents. He had been sentenced to life imprisonment without the possibility of parole and was then confined at the Florence Maximum Security Prison in Colorado.

"The American President, Clendennen, elected to abrogate the long-standing U.S. policy of not negotiating in situations like this, and their plan had proceeded to the point where, on April twenty-second, they were transporting Colonel Ferris to the Oaxaca State Prison, where his exchange for Señor Abrego was to take place.

"En route, their convoy of vehicles was intercepted by parties unknown. Colonel Ferris was liberated and shortly thereafter was welcomed home by President Clendennen in Washington.

"Everyone in the convoy—Russian, Venezuelan, and Mexican—died. As each was shot at least two times in the head, it had the appearance of what is known in law enforcement circles as a 'professional hit.'

"The Zambada and Sinaloa cartels, the Venezuelan DISIP, and, I would suppose, the SVR, believe our Carlito was the parties unknown—the shooter, so to speak—and are very anxious to get suitable revenge for his assault on their prestige. I have heard that after he's tortured to death, they plan to decapitate his corpse and hang his head from a bridge over the highway in Acapulco, with his genitalia in his mouth."

Castillo opened his mouth to protest, but in the split second before the words *"Hey, I didn't shoot any of those bastards and you know it!"* were to come out of his mouth, Castillo closed it.

That's moot. While I didn't actually shoot anybody, rescuing Jim Ferris was my operation. I planned it and I ordered its execution. I had no idea Juan Carlos planned not only to have his men kill them all, but also to personally fire two coup de grâce rounds into their ears, and would have told him not to had I known. But that's also moot.

And it wouldn't have mattered if I had left all of them neatly trussed up, but alive, at the side of the road. They would still know I was responsible for grabbing Ferris and would still be planning to hang my head from an Acapulco bridge with my severed dick in my mouth.

"And that, Sweaty," Juan Carlos said, "is why our Carlito's presence here suggests he has a death wish."

"You're underestimating him again, Juan Carlos," Sweaty said calmly. "My Carlos is not a fool, and he certainly doesn't have a death wish."

I think that's what they call blind loyalty.

"You're underestimating these people, Sweaty," Pena said.

"I never underestimate my enemies," she replied.

"I gather these people aren't planning to hang your head from an Acapulco bridge?" Castillo said.

"Why should they?" Pena said.

"Do you really want me to answer that?"

Castillo looked at Roscoe J. Danton, who looked sick.

"You have a question, Roscoe?" Castillo asked.

"He's serious, isn't he?" Danton asked. "If they catch you, these cartel people are going to . . . do what he said?"

"That would seem to be Comandante Pena's professional opinion," Castillo said.

"I investigated the incident—" Pena began.

"Incident?" Danton blurted. "A massacre is what you just described."

". . . at KM 125.5," Pena went on ignoring him. "And I turned in my report to the procurador general de la república, who is something like the attorney general in the United States. My report stated that the murders had been committed by parties unknown, most probably in connection with the drug trade. I further stated that since my investigation had turned up no suspects, the crime would most probably go unsolved.

"Shortly afterward, Señor Pedro Dagada, an attorney who has several times represented members of both the Zambada and Sinaloa cartels in their brushes with the law, happened upon me while I was having lunch in the Diamond."

He paused and then went on, "For your general edification, Señor Danton, 'the Diamond' is what we call the five-star Camino Real Acapulco Diamante hotel in Acapulco. In English, that's the Royal Road Acapulco Diamond. Got it?"

Roscoe nodded uncomfortably.

"As I was saying, there I was in the Diamond, having lunch, when Señor Dagada appeared, greeted me warmly—which I found a little surprising, as I have sent a number of his clients to prison—and insisted on buying me a drink.

"Thirty minutes and three drinks later, Señor Dagada asked me, just between old pals, not to go any further, if I had any ideas about what had happened at KM 125.5 that I had not put in my report to the procurador general. He also confided in me that the procurador general, an old pal, had shown him my report.

"So I said, 'Pedro, I wouldn't tell even you this, old pal, if you hadn't told me the procurador general had shown you my report. Just between us, the procurador general knows as well as I do what really happened out there at KM 125.5.'

"To which he replied, 'Well, what was that?'

"To which I replied, 'The Americans sent us a message. *Don't kidnap our diplomats who are also Special Forces. Special Forces doesn't like that, and we can't control our Special Forces any more than you can control your cartels. They got their guy back and left the bodies on the road at KM 125.5 as a polite suggestion not to kidnap anybody from Special Forces again.*'

"And then Pedro asked, 'You got a name?'

"And I said, 'Well, there was a guy named Costello down here.'

"And then Pedro asked, 'Costello or Castillo?'

"And I said I didn't know for sure, but there was a guy down here named one or the other and I heard he was Special Forces looking for Ferris. He disappeared just about the time what happened at KM 125.5 happened—as did Ferris. 'So draw your own conclusions, Pedro.'"

"You gave him Charley's name?" Roscoe asked, horrified.

"You're not listening. He already had Charley's name. And I suspect he knew a good deal about Charley," Pena said drily. He turned to Castillo. "So, what's on your agenda now, John Wayne, in whatever little time you have left before they cut off—among other parts—your head?"

"I thought I'd take Roscoe here to Drug Cartel International Airport and let him take some pictures to show the President how hard we're working."

"I've already seen Drug Cartel International, thank you just the same," Danton said.

"But the President, Roscoe, knows very little about it," Castillo said. "And we want to keep him abreast of things, don't we?" He turned to Juan Carlos Pena. "Keep in mind the idea is to stall the President until he tires of this nutty idea and moves on to another. So, what we're going to do is take Roscoe with us to Drug Cartel International and then let him write his news story, together with pictures of the Outlaws suitably garbed and heavily armed, putting their lives on the line going about the President's business by going, so to speak, literally into the mouth of the Drug Cartel dragon.

"We will send Roscoe's story to the President with my report. My report won't say much except that we are gathering intelligence, and are about to go to Budapest, from where I will report again."

"What are you going to do in Budapest?" Juan Carlos asked.

"I haven't figured that out yet, but whatever it is, it will be something that will keep the Commander in Chief thinking I'm really working hard for him. Getting the picture?"

"Yeah," Pena said thoughtfully. "So, what do you want from me?"

"Can you cover my back when we go to Drug Cartel International?"

Pena visibly collected his thoughts before he replied.

"If you go there, the cartels will know about it within an hour." He paused to let that sink in, then went on: "I can cover your back. But I won't, Carlito, unless I have your word that you and Sweaty get on your airplane the minute we get back and get the hell out of here."

As visibly as Pena had, Castillo visibly framed his answer. Pena saw this and took advantage of it.

"I don't want to see your heads hanging side by side from that bridge I mentioned, Carlito."

"It's that bad, huh?" Castillo asked.

Pena nodded.

"My God!" Roscoe said.

"Your head hanging from the bridge, Roscoe, I could live with," Pena said. "But I have a soft spot in my heart for Romeo and Juliet."

"Okay," Castillo said.

"That's your word of honor, Carlito, right?"

Castillo nodded.

"Say it."

"Word of honor," Castillo said.

"Okay."

"Is there time to drive there and back today? I don't think flying in would be too smart."

"That would depend on what you were flying," Pena said. "If you had a Black Hawk helicopter, you could make it to Drug Cartel International and back before supper."

"Sorry, Juan Carlos, I don't even know where mine is. It's not where I left it after we grabbed Ferris, and the CIA's satellites can't find it."

"The CIA's satellites?" Danton and Pena repeated just about simultaneously.

"Natalie Cohen was afraid it would wind up in the wrong hands and asked Frank Lammelle, the DCI, to find it for her."

"It didn't wind up in the wrong hands, Carlito," Pena said. "You should listen to Sweaty and stop underestimating people."

"You've got it?" Castillo asked.

Pena nodded.

"I can have it on the roof here in fifteen minutes," Pena said. "Then we will go to Drug Cartel International, Roscoe can take your picture, and then we will come back here. Where, your luggage having been packed while you were gone, and loaded aboard your airplane, you can immediately take off for . . . Where did you say you were going? Budapest? Agreed?"

Castillo, after a moment, nodded.

"Only one thing I can think of," he said. He turned to the Sienos.

"Where do you want us to drop you off?" he asked.

"What?" Paul Sieno asked.

"You know, Miami? Tampa? Palm Beach?"

"What are we going to do in Palm Beach?" Susanna Sieno asked.

"Susanna, you heard what the man said about these people. Stalling Clendennen in Mexico is not going to be a vacation on the CIA's dime. They'd cut off your head, and Paul's, as quickly as they'd cut off mine."

"I was thinking about that," she said.

"Good," Juan Carlos said.

"Juan Carlos, could you pass off Paul and me as your cousins from, say, Colombia? Better yet, Havana?" she asked.

"What the hell, Charley," Paul chimed in. "Maybe we could learn something about these people that somebody on top could use."

"You understand," Juan Carlos said, "that if these people find out who you are—"

"We spent five years in Cuba," she said. "Brother Raúl is a lot smarter than these cartel people, and he and his DGI never got close to us."

"My cousins from Havana are obviously as crazy as you are, Carlito," Juan Carlos said. "But I like the idea of getting the straight story to people at the top. The reports of your DEA never seem to get there."

"You realize, of course, that if you stay, it's going to cost Those People in Las Vegas a lot of money."

"Screw those people in Las Vegas," Susanna said.

[FOUR]
The Cabinet Room
The White House
1600 Pennsylvania Avenue, N.W.
Washington, D.C.
0905 14 June 2007

The President of the United States was not in a good mood when Secretary of State Natalie Cohen, DCI A. Franklin Lammelle, General Allan B. Naylor, Senior, and Director of National Intelligence Truman C. Ellsworth filed into the Cabinet Room and stood waiting to be acknowledged.

The President had just been informed by Supervisory Special Agent Robert J. Mulligan that his mother-in-law, who had gone missing from Happy Haven, the Baptist assisted living facility in Pascagoula, Mississippi, several days before had been located.

The "First Mother-in-Law" was in the Biloxi, Mississippi, jail charged with public drunkenness and assault on a police officer. It appeared that she had overly availed herself of the free cocktails offered by the Biloxi Palace Casino to its gaming guests at the roulette tables.

Mulligan said he could probably spring her from *durance vile* by noon, but that wasn't going to solve much. The Reverend J. Finley Cushman, DD, who had taken her in after she had been asked to leave the Ocean Springs branch of the Baptist assisted living facility, had made it quite clear if she ever got loose again and brought shame upon Happy Haven by getting into the Devil's Brew, they would have to find some other haven for her.

Since she had been asked to leave just about every other facility in Mississippi, that posed problems. The prospect of having to face the First Mother-in-Law every morning at breakfast in the White House struck terror in the heart of Joshua Ezekiel Clendennen.

"Mr. President," Secretary Cohen said, "we have another report from Colonel Castillo."

The President was so upset that he momentarily couldn't remember who Castillo was, and thought she was referring to the head of the Mississippi State Police, who was also a colonel.

"Mulligan just told me," the President said, rather impatiently. And then he remembered.

"Give it to me," he said, and then, "Sit."

He read the report:

```
TOP SECRET

URGENT

DUPLICATION FORBIDDEN

TO: POTUS
```

SUBJECT: REPORT

VIA SECRETARY OF STATE

MAKE AVAILABLE (EYES ONLY) TO:

DIRECTOR, CIA

SECRETARY OF DEFENSE

DIRECTOR OF NATIONAL INTELLIGENCE

C IN C CENTRAL COMMAND

OOR SITREP #2

US EMBASSY MEXICO CITY 2300 ZULU 14 JUNE 2007

1-INASMUCH AS THE NEWS REPORT OF MR. ROSCOE J. DANTON (ATTACHED, SUITABLY REDACTED) COVERS THE ACTIVITIES OF THE UNDERSIGNED IN SOME DETAIL, THE UNDERSIGNED WILL NOT WASTE THE TIME OF POTUS BY REPEATING THEM HEREIN.

2-THE UNDERSIGNED IS PRESENTLY EN ROUTE TO BUDAPEST, HUNGARY, IN THE PANAMANIAN EXECUTIVE AIRCRAFT FLOWN BY COLONEL TORINE, RETD., AND MAJOR MILLER, RETD., AND ACCOMPANIED BY THE FOLLOWING PERSONNEL:

A. NAYLOR, LTC ALLAN B. USA

B. D'ALESSANDRO, MR. VICTOR DA CIV GS-15

C. LEVERETTE, COLIN

D. BRADLEY, LESTER

E. LORIMER, EDMUND

F. BRITTON, JOHN

G. BRITTON, DR. SANDRA

H. DAMON, C. GREGORY

I. BARLOW, SUSAN

J. DANTON, ROSCOE J.

3-ONCE IN BUDAPEST, THE UNDERSIGNED WILL DETERMINE THE BEST WAY TO INFILTRATE LEVERETTE, THE BRITTONS, AND DAMON INTO SOMALIA, TO DEVELOP OTHER INTELLIGENCE, AND TAKE WHATEVER OTHER APPROPRIATE ACTION IS DEEMED NECESSARY. A REPORT WILL BE FURNISHED.

RESPECTFULLY SUBMITTED.

CASTILLO, LTC, RETD.

TOP SECRET

"What the hell does 'suitably redacted' mean?" the President asked.

"'Redact,' Mr. President," Presidential Spokesperson Robin Hoboken said, "means to adapt by obscuring sensitive information. I would think then that 'suitably redact' means to do so suitably."

"And how would you do that?" the President asked.

"Give me just a minute to look that up, Mr. President," Hoboken said.

"How are we going to talk about this if you don't have copies of it before you?" the President inquired of the three senior officials.

"Mr. President," Truman Ellsworth said, "if you'll look toward the head of Colonel Castillo's report, it says 'Duplication Forbidden.'"

"Let me tell you something, Mr. Ellsworth," President Clendennen said. "I'm POTUS and Commander in Chief of the Armed Forces. No lousy little lieutenant colonel like this man Castillo is going to tell me I can't make copies of any damned piece of paper I want."

"Yes, sir."

"Hoboken," the President ordered, "make copies of this for everybody."

"Yes, sir, Mr. President. Before or after I look up 'suitably redacted'?"

"'Suitably redacted' can wait," the President said, "since we don't even know what that means."

Three minutes later, Robin Hoboken passed out copies of Danton's story.

He got through the first two paragraphs . . .

SLUG: OPERATION OUT OF THE BOX

TAKE ONE

BY ROSCOE J. DANTON

WASHINGTON TIMES-POST WRITERS SYNDICATE

DAY ONE—JUNE 11, 2007

BUENOS AIRES, ARGENTINA

THIS REPORTER FLEW OVERNIGHT FROM WASHINGTON TO "THE PARIS OF SOUTH AMERICA" CARRYING ORDERS FROM PRESIDENT JOSHUA EZEKIEL CLENDENNEN TO LIEUTENANT COLONEL █████ "EMBEDDING" ME WITH "OPERATION OUT OF THE BOX" FOR THE DURATION OF THE TOP SECRET OPERATION.

THE PRESIDENT DECIDED HE NEEDED A FRESH, AND VERY EXPERIENCED, EYE TO HAVE A LOOK AT TWO PROBLEMS:

> THE MEXICAN DRUG CARTELS AND THE SOMALI PIRATES. HE DECIDED THAT █████, A RETIRED LEGENDARY SPECIAL OPERATOR AND INTELLIGENCE OFFICER, WAS TO BE THAT EYE, REPORTING DIRECTLY AND ONLY TO HIM, AND RECALLED █████ TO ACTIVE DUTY. PRESIDENT CLENDENNEN ALSO DECIDED THAT EMBEDDING WHAT HE DESCRIBED AS "A WELL-KNOWN JOURNALIST OF UNQUESTIONED INTEGRITY" WITH COLONEL █████ WAS THE BEST WAY TO BRING, WHEN THE TIME CAME, THE FULL STORY OF OPERATION OUT OF THE BOX TO THE AMERICAN PEOPLE, AND HUMBLED THIS REPORTER BY SELECTING ME.

"What the hell are these black boxes all over this?" President Clendennen then demanded.

"Mr. President," Secretary Cohen explained, "those are redacting marks showing what has been redacted."

"I'll be damned. And you didn't know that, Hoboken?"

"I will from now on, Mr. President," Hoboken said firmly.

The President resumed reading:

> THE ONLY RESTRICTION ON THIS REPORTER'S REPORTING, THE PRESIDENT TOLD ME, WAS THAT MY STORIES WOULD HAVE TO UNDERGO VETTING BY INTELLIGENCE OFFICERS SO AS TO ENSURE OUR ENEMIES LEARNED NOTHING OF VALUE FROM THEM, AND THAT I WOULD PUBLISH NOTHING UNTIL OPERATION OUT OF THE BOX WAS CONCLUDED.

> ON THIS REPORTER'S ARRIVAL IN BUENOS AIRES, I WAS INFORMED THAT THE U.S. EMBASSY HAD NO IDEA OF COLONEL ████ LOCATION. THIS REPORTER PERSEVERED, HOWEVER, AND LEARNED THAT THE LEGENDARY INTELLIGENCE OFFICER WAS IN BARILOCHE – A SKI RESORT SOMETIMES CALLED "THE VAIL OF ARGENTINA" – AND GOT HIM ON THE TELEPHONE.
>
> COLONEL ████ WAS NOT AT ALL PLEASED TO LEARN OF MY MISSION, BUT HE IS A SOLDIER, AND JOSHUA EZEKIEL CLENDENNEN IS THE COMMANDER IN CHIEF, AND COLONEL ████ HAD NO CHOICE BUT TO OBEY HIS ORDERS.

"Goddamn right he didn't," the President said.

"Sir?" Truman Ellsworth asked.

"If that black redact-whatyoucallit stands for Castillo, as I strongly suspect it does, goddamn right he had no choice but to obey his orders. That's what I told you when you showed a certain lack of enthusiasm for Operation Out of the Box."

"Yes, sir, Mr. President," Ellsworth said.

The President resumed reading:

> AND I GOT MINE. I AM TO BE STANDING, WITH MY LUGGAGE, OUTSIDE MY HOTEL AT NINE TOMORROW MORNING. I ASKED WHERE WE WERE GOING AND WAS TOLD VATICAN CITY, BUT I DON'T BELIEVE THIS.

WE SHALL SEE.

DAY TWO—JUNE 12, 2007

BUENOS AIRES, ARGENTINA

AT EXACTLY NINE A.M., A MERCEDES SPORT-UTILITY VEHICLE WITH DARKENED WINDOWS PULLED INTO THE RECEPTION AREA OF THE ALVEAR PALACE HOTEL. TWO BURLY MEN GOT OUT. ONE TOOK MY ARM AND LOADED ME INTO THE REAR SEAT WHILE THE OTHER LOADED MY LUGGAGE INTO THE BACK.

HOW THEY KNEW WHO THIS REPORTER WAS, I DON'T KNOW, AND WHEN I ASKED WHERE WE WERE GOING, THEY PRETENDED NOT TO HEAR. I DID NOTICE THAT BOTH MEN WERE ARMED WITH UZI SUBMACHINE GUNS.

AFTER A FIFTEEN-MINUTE DRIVE THROUGH THE HEAVY EARLY MORNING BUENOS AIRES TRAFFIC, WE ARRIVED AT THE "BUSINESS SIDE" OF JORGE NEWBERY AIRFIELD, WHICH ABUTS THE RIVER PLATE.

THIS REPORTER WAS DRIVEN TO THE SIDE OF A GULFSTREAM V AIRCRAFT.

LIEUTENANT COLONEL █████, A TALL, GOOD-LOOKING MAN IN HIS LATE THIRTIES OR EARLY FORTIES, CAME DOWN THE STAIR-DOOR STEPS AND GAVE ME HIS HAND.

"HELLO, ROSCOE," HE SAID. "PLEASE GET ABOARD."

THIS REPORTER HAD MET COLONEL █████ BEFORE, WHEN HE HAD FLOWN INTO █████ AIR FORCE BASE AT THE CONTROLS OF A █████ AIRCRAFT. THE STORY GOING AROUND AND EMPHATICALLY DENIED BY THE CIA WAS THAT █████ HAD STOLEN THE SECRET RUSSIAN AIRPLANE IN █████ AND THAT THE CIA HAD PAID HIM ONE HUNDRED MILLION DOLLARS FOR IT WHEN HE DELIVERED IT TO THEM.

"What the hell is going on here?" the President said. "If that black box stands for Castillo, what the hell is this? 'He had flown into *Castillo* Air Force Base at the controls of a *Castillo* aircraft he had stolen in *Castillo*'? Tell me that makes sense!"

"Those redacting remarks, Mr. President," Secretary Cohen explained, "replace other words that have been obscured. A redacted block has no meaning in and of itself."

"I think I'm getting it. Bear with me," the President said, and resumed reading:

THE ENGINES OF THE GULFSTREAM V STARTED AS THE DOOR WAS CLOSING, AND TEN MINUTES LATER WE HAD TAKEN OFF.

> AS SOON AS WE REACHED CRUISING ALTITUDE, █████ INTRODUCED ME TO THE OTHERS ON BOARD, STARTING WITH HIS FIANCÉE █████ █████, A REDHEADED BEAUTY ALLEGED – SHE REFUSES TO CONFIRM OR DENY – TO HAVE EXTENSIVE INTELLIGENCE EXPERIENCE.

"I think I'm getting this," the President announced. "He crossed out the name of his girlfriend, the Russian spy, right?"

"'Redacted' it, sir," Robin Hoboken said.

"Why the hell can't we just say 'crossed out'?"

"If that is your pleasure, sir, we certainly will," Robin Hoboken said.

The President resumed reading, this time finishing the report before saying anything else.

> ALSO ABOARD THE AIRCRAFT WERE LIEUTENANT COLONEL █████, JR., WHOM THIS REPORTER KNEW TO BE THE SON OF GENERAL █████ █████, SR., WHOM THIS REPORTER HAS DESCRIBED AS THE "MOST IMPORTANT █████ IN THE U.S. ARMY"; █████ █████, A LEGENDARY SPECIAL OPERATOR RUMORED TO HEAD THE TOP SECRET DELTA FORCE UNIT IN FORT BRAGG, N.C.; FORMER MARINE GUNNERY SERGEANT █████ █████, A SNIPER WHO DOUBLES AS █████ BODYGUARD; CWO(5) █████ █████ AND COMMAND SERGEANT

MAJOR ████ ████, BOTH RETIRED MEMBERS OF DELTA FORCE; FIRST LIEUTENANT ████ ████, KNOWN AS "████" MAKING REFERENCE TO ██ ██ WHILE A GREEN BERET; ████ ████, FORMERLY OF THE SECRET SERVICE, AND HIS WIFE, DR. ████ ████, A PHILOLOGIST.

████, ████ AND THE ████ ARE AFRO-AMERICAN AND ████ EXPLAINED THEY WILL FUNCTION PRIMARILY IN SOMALIA, WHERE IT WOULD BE DIFFICULT FOR HIM AND THE OTHERS TO "BLEND INTO THE WOODWORK."

THE GULFSTREAM AIRCRAFT, CHARTERED WITH ITS CREW FROM PANAMANIAN EXECUTIVE AIRCRAFT IN PANAMA, WAS FLOWN BY COLONEL ████ ████, USAF, RETIRED, AND MAJOR ████ ████ JR., RETIRED. ████ HAD BEEN WITH ████ IN THE SEIZURE OF THE ████ AIRCRAFT, AND ████ HAD SERVED WITH THE 160TH SPECIAL OPERATIONS AVIATION REGIMENT, INCLUDING SERVICE IN SOMALIA. ████ IS AN AFRO-AMERICAN.

THIS WAS THE TEAM ████ HAD ASSEMBLED AT THE ORDERS OF PRESIDENT CLENDENNEN TO "PUT A FRESH AND KNOWLEDGEABLE EYE" ON THE MEXICAN DRUG CARTELS AND THE PIRATES OF SOMALIA.

████ TOLD THIS REPORTER WE WERE HEADED FOR MEXICO, AND WOULD THEN GO TO BUDAPEST, HUNGARY.

EIGHT HOURS AFTER TAKING OFF, WE LANDED IN COZUMEL, MEXICO, WHERE TWO GMC YUKONS WERE WAITING TO TRANSPORT US TO THE FIVE-STAR ██████ ██████ BEACH & GOLF RESORT, WHERE WE WERE INSTALLED IN THE 24TH FLOOR IMPERIAL PENTHOUSE SUITE.

AFTER A GRILLED SEAFOOD DINNER, ██████, USING A SHORTWAVE RADIO OF A TYPE THIS REPORTER HAD NEVER SEEN, CONTACTED ██████ ██████ ██████ ████, OF THE POLICIA FEDERAL, WHOM HE DESCRIBED AS THE "ONLY HONEST COP IN MEXICO." FOLLOWING A BRIEF CONVERSATION, ██████ SAID THAT ████ WOULD COME TO THE HOTEL FIRST THING TOMORROW MORNING.

DAY THREE—JUNE 13, 2007

COZUMEL, MEXICO

AT EXACTLY TEN A.M. THIS MORNING, A BLACK HAWK HELICOPTER BEARING THE IDENTIFICATION MARKINGS OF THE MEXICAN POLICIA FEDERAL FLUTTERED TO THE LANDING PAD ON THE ROOF OF THE ██████ ██████ BEACH & GOLF RESORT.

IN IT, ACCOMPANIED BY HEAVILY ARMED FEDERAL POLICEMEN, WAS ██████ ███ ████ ███.

COLONEL ██████, ███ AND ██████ ████, ████ ██████, ██████ ██████ AND THIS REPORTER CLIMBED ABOARD AND THE BLACK HAWK TOOK OFF.

OUR DESTINATION TURNED OUT TO BE A SECRET AIRFIELD KNOWN SARDONICALLY TO ██████'S MERRY OUTLAWS AS "DRUG CARTEL INTERNATIONAL." IT IS LOCATED IN THE ██ ██████ █ ████ IN COAHUILA STATE.

(SEE PHOTOGRAPHS)

██████ TOLD THIS REPORTER THE AIRFIELD WAS USED TO TAKE SUITCASES FULL OF DRUG PROFIT MONEY OUT OF MEXICO AND TO BRING IN COCAINE FROM COLOMBIA, VENEZUELA, AND OTHER PLACES FOR TRANS-SHIPMENT OVER THE BORDER INTO THE UNITED STATES.

WHEN THIS REPORTER ASKED HOW THE AIRCRAFT INVOLVED COULD AVOID BEING DETECTED ON RADAR BY MEXICAN AUTHORITIES, ██████ ███ ████ ████ REPLIED THAT RADAR OPERATORS WERE GIVEN THE CHOICE OF NOT DETECTING THE ILLEGAL FLIGHTS, WHEREUPON THEY WOULD RECEIVE A STACK OF U.S. CURRENCY, OR DETECTING THEM AND REPORTING THEM TO THE POLICIA FEDERAL, WHEREUPON THEIR MOTHERS, WIVES, AND DAUGHTERS WOULD BE RAPED AND/OR MURDERED.

█████ TOLD THIS REPORTER THAT IF SOME WAY COULD BE FOUND TO SHUT DOWN "DRUG CARTEL INTERNATIONAL," IT WOULD PUT A "SERIOUS CRIMP" IN DRUG CARTEL ACTIVITIES AND THAT HE WAS WORKING WITH ██ ON A PLAN TO DO SO, WHICH HE WOULD FORWARD TO THE PRESIDENT.

AFTER NO MORE THAN AN HOUR AT THE AIRFIELD, WE REBOARDED THE BLACK HAWK HELICOPTER AND FLEW BACK TO COZUMEL AND BOARDED THE GULFSTREAM, LEAVING BEHIND ██ AND █████ ████, AND TOOK OFF FOR BUDAPEST. THE ████ WILL UNDERTAKE MISSIONS FOR █████ THAT HE WAS UNWILLING TO SHARE WITH THIS REPORTER.

MORE TO FOLLOW

"Okay, I got it. Castillo *redacted* all those things so in case this fell into the wrong hands, nobody would know who Roscoe J. Danton was talking about. Am I right?"

"Yes, sir, Mr. President," Truman Ellsworth said. "That is correct."

"Couple of questions," the President said. "General Naylor, Danton said you were the most important *what* in the Army?"

"I believe, Mr. President," Secretary Cohen said, "that Mr. Danton believes General Naylor is the most important general in the Army."

"Where did he get a nutty idea like that? Everybody knows the chief of staff is the most important general in the Army."

"I don't know where he got a nutty idea like that, Mr. President," Robin Hoboken said, "but I'll get on it right away and let you know as soon as I find out."

"Lammelle, I want you to get together with Ellsworth and come up with a plan to shut down this drug dealers' airfield. I don't want to do anything until I hear more from Castillo, but I want to be ready."

"Yes, sir," Lammelle said.

"This out-of-the box idea of mine is working out better than I thought. I wonder why I didn't think of it earlier."

"Well, you had a lot on your mind, Mr. President," Robin Hoboken said. "That probably had something to do with it."

VII

[ONE]
The Portico
The White House
1600 Pennsylvania Avenue, N.W.
Washington, D.C.
0935 14 June 2007

"Well," Truman Ellsworth said to Natalie Cohen as they and General Naylor and DCI Lammelle waited for their various vehicles to pull up, "on balance, I'd say that went well."

"I'm not so sure," she replied.

"And what do you think, General?" Ellsworth inquired of Naylor.

"I am very uncomfortable with the entire situation," Naylor replied. "I suspect that what Mr. Ellsworth means—"

"You can call me Truman," Ellsworth interrupted. "We are all in this together. Succeeding together, I would suggest."

"Forgive me, Mr. Ellsworth," Naylor said, "for not sharing your pleasure in our successfully deceiving the President."

"What would you have us do?" Lammelle asked. "Go to the Vice President and the Cabinet and ask them to bring on the men in the white coats and the straitjacket?"

"This is going to end badly," General Naylor said.

"Possibly," Lammelle said. "Everybody knows that. But the operative word is 'possibly.' It is also possible that we'll get away with it."

"Possible, but unlikely," Secretary Cohen said. "He told you and Truman to come up with a plan to shut down that Mexican airfield. What are you going to do about that?"

"Take a long time coming up with a plan," Lammelle said. "Hoping that he'll forget he told me that."

"And if he doesn't forget?" General Naylor asked.

"Then I will stall him, using Castillo, for as long as I can."

"And what if that doesn't work?" Naylor asked. "What if he says, 'Shut down that Mexican airfield now'?"

"Correct me if I'm wrong, General," Truman Ellsworth said, "but wasn't General Patton quoted as saying . . . something along this line—'Don't take counsel of your fears'?"

"That's your recommended course of action?" Naylor demanded tartly. "'Don't worry about it!'"

Just as tartly, Ellsworth replied, "General, our course of action, repeat, *our* course of action, mutually agreed between the four of us, is to indulge the President as long as we can do that without putting the country at serious risk. I don't see any greater risk to the country coming out of that meeting than I did going in. If you do, please share what you saw with us."

"The President told you and Lammelle to prepare a plan to shut down that airfield," Naylor said.

"And I just told you, General," Lammelle said, "that we will do so very, very slowly. If he persists in this notion to the point where I think it's necessary—let me rephrase, to the point where the four of us, repeat, the four of us, think it's necessary—we will have Natalie explain to him that shutting down that airfield would be an act of war. If he still insists, then, presuming we four are then in agreement, the four of us will go to the Cabinet and tell them he's out of control. Do you agree with that, or not?"

Naylor did not reply directly. Instead, he said, "I don't think any of us should forget that the President, under the War Powers Act, has the authority to order troops into action for thirty days wherever and whenever he thinks that's necessary. During those thirty days, if he tells me to shut down that airfield, I'll have to shut down that airfield."

"I think, General, that each of us is aware of the War Powers Act," Secretary Cohen said. "We'll have to deal with that if it comes up."

"Relax, Allan," Lammelle said. "Three will get you five that the Sage of Biloxi has already forgotten that notion and is now devoting all of his attention to getting the First Mother-in-Law out of jail."

Ellsworth chuckled. Secretary Cohen smiled.

"And there's one more thing, General," Ellsworth said. "Have you noticed that Hackensack—"

"I think you mean Hoboken, Truman," the secretary of State corrected him gently.

"Right. *Hoboken.* Have you noticed what a splendid job *Hoboken* does with what are known, I believe, as 'Presidential Photo-Ops'?"

Cohen, Lammelle, and Naylor all shrugged, suggesting, in the cases of Cohen and Naylor, that they were not aware of the splendid job Presidential Spokesperson Hoboken was doing with Presidential Photo-Ops. Lammelle's shrug asked, so to speak, "So what?"

"Every time a dozen Rotarians," Ellsworth clarified, "or for that matter eight Boy Scouts, come to Washington, they can count on getting their picture taken with the President."

"And Special Agent Mulligan," the secretary of State said. "He's usually in the picture."

"At the risk of repeating my shrug," Lammelle said, "so what?"

"When they are recording themselves for posterity, Frank," Ellsworth explained, "they won't have time to worry about seizing a Mexican airfield. It's a matter of priority. Getting your picture in the paper with the Rotarians or the Boy Scouts helps your reelection chances. Thanks to Mulligan and Hoboken, I don't think we really have to worry about getting ordered to seize the Mexican airfield."

"You may have something there, Truman," Lammelle said.

The conversation was interrupted by the arrival of their vehicles. Following the protocol of rank, Secretary Cohen's Yukon arrived first. Charlene Stevens jumped out and opened the right rear door for her, and Cohen got in without saying anything else and drove off. Then Ellsworth's Jaguar Vanden Plas pulled up and he got in it, and it drove off. Lammelle's Yukon was next, and he got in and drove off. Finally General Naylor's Suburban pulled up, a sergeant jumped out of the front seat and removed the covers from the four-star plates, and then held the right rear door open for the general.

[TWO]
The Cabinet Room
The White House
1600 Pennsylvania Avenue, N.W.
Washington, D.C.
0935 14 June 2007

"Mr. President," Presidential Spokesperson Robin Hoboken had asked the moment the door closed on Secretary Cohen and the others, "did you mean what you said about wanting to shut down that Mexican airfield, the one Castillo calls 'Drug Cartel International'?"

"By now, Robin, you should know that—unlike some other politicians I can name—I always mean what I say."

"Mr. President, I have an idea—"

"Oh, for Christ's sake, Hackensack," Supervisory Secret Service Agent Mulligan said, "not again! Every time you have one of your ideas, you get the Commander in Chief in trouble."

"What did you say?" the presidential spokesman demanded angrily.

"I said, Hoboken, that every time you get one of your ideas, you get the President in trouble."

"No, you didn't. You called me Hackensack and you know you did."

"You'll have to admit, Hackensack, that Mulligan is right," the President said. "Sometimes your ideas, while well intentioned, are really off the wall."

"Now you've got the Commander in Chief doing it!" Robin fumed.

"Doing what?" Clendennen asked.

"Calling me Hackensack!"

"Why would I call you Hackensack, Hoboken?" the President asked.

"Probably because Mulligan did, Mr. President," Robin replied.

"If I called you Hackensack, Hoboken, it was a slip of the tongue," Mulligan said.

"Hah!" Robin snorted.

"What's the big difference?" the President asked.

"I would say population, Mr. President," Robin said. "Hoboken is right at fifty thousand and Hackensack right at forty."

"There's only forty people in Hackensack?" Mulligan asked. "I would have thought there were more than that."

"Forty *thousand* people, you cretin!" Robin flared.

"Are you going to let him call me that, Mr. President?" Mulligan asked.

"You called him Hackensack, which he doesn't like, so he called you cretin. I'm not sure what that is, but what's grease for the goose, so to speak. Say, 'Yes, sir.' "

"Yes, sir, Mr. President," both said in unison.

"Well, Robin, let's hear this nutty idea of yours and get it out of the way."

"Mr. President, I'm sure you share my confidence that Operation Out of the Box will be successful; after all, it is your idea."

"That's true," President Clendennen admitted. "It's obviously one of my better ideas."

"And it would be a genuine shame if when Operation Out of the Box is successful that you didn't get all the credit you so richly deserve for it."

"Well, as my predecessor, Harry S Truman, said, 'You can get a lot done if you don't look for credit.'"

"President Truman didn't say that, Mr. President," Mulligan said. "President Truman said, 'The buck stops here.' That movie-star president . . . What's his name?"

"Ronald Something," Robin Hoboken said.

"Not 'Something,' Robin," the President said. "His name was President *Reagan*."

"His *name* was Ronald Reagan," Mulligan said. "He *was* the President. He was the one who said you can get a lot done on credit."

"Belinda-Sue says too much credit is what's ruining the country," the President said. "And, for once, she may be right."

"I'm not talking about that kind of credit, Mr. President," Robin Hoboken said.

"I wasn't aware there was more than one kind," the President said. "The kind I know is where you charge something, pay for it, and then can buy something else because your credit is good."

"The kind I'm talking about, Mr. President," Robin Hoboken said, "is where people *recognize* that you've done something good."

"Like what, for example?"

"For example, coming up with an idea like Operation Out of the Box."

"And how could I make that happen?" the President asked.

"What I was going to suggest, Mr. President, is that we take a photographer down to Fort Bragg and have him shoot you planning the operation to seize Drug Cartel International Airfield."

"Try saying 'take your picture,' Robin," the President said. "Having a photographer 'shoot me' makes me uncomfortable."

"Yes, sir. Sorry, sir."

"Why would I do that?"

"So that after Castillo and his Merry Outlaws seize Drug Cartel International, your political enemies—C. Harry Whelan, Junior, of Wolf News, for example—couldn't say you were taking credit for something you had very little, if anything, to do with."

"Stop calling them 'Merry Outlaws,' Robin," the President said, then cleared his throat dramatically. "Start calling them 'Clendennen's Commandos.'"

"Sir?"

"You heard me. Clendennen's Commandos!"

"Yes, sir."

"That has a nice ring to it, Mr. President," Mulligan said.

"Yes, it does," the President agreed. And then his face clouded.

"I see a couple of problems with this, Hoboken," he said. "Like, for example, if I go to Fort Bragg, everybody will know."

"Not if we sneak down there, Mr. President," Hoboken replied. "Use a little-bitty airplane, a Gulfstream Five, instead of that great big 747."

"That'd work," the President said, after a moment's thought.

"And it wouldn't really be a secret that we're going there, Mr. President. What you'd be doing there would be the secret. C. Harry Whelan would know you're going down there, have been there, et cetera, but he wouldn't know why—"

"Until Clendennen's Commandos have seized Drug Cartel International?"

"Yes, Mr. President. That's the idea."

"How would C. Harry Whelan know I'm going to Fort Bragg?"

"We'd leak it to him. We leak things all the time."

"Just one more itsy-bitsy problem, Robin. What if Castillo gets his ass kicked when he tries to seize Drug Cartel International?"

"Then we deny knowing anything about him or any of this."

"Can we get away with that?"

"Not a problem, Mr. President. I lie successfully to the press on a daily basis."

"Set it up, Robin. I want to leave first thing in the morning."

"Mr. President," Mulligan said, "if you'd like, we could stop in Biloxi and see about getting the First Mother-in-Law out of jail."

"Screw her," the President said. "I can't let the old bag keep me from carrying out my duties as President."

[THREE]
The Old Ebbitt Grill
675 Fifteenth Street, N.W.
Washington, D.C.
1155 14 June 2007

C. Harry Whelan, who had not seen Roscoe J. Danton around town for several days and thus wondered what the miserable sonofabitch was now up to in his perpetual quest to upstage him on Wolf News, telephoned Danton's unlisted number.

Danton had an automated telephone system. Ordinarily it worked like most of them. In other words, Roscoe J. Danton's recorded voice would announce that he was sorry he couldn't take the call right now, but if the caller would kindly leave his name and number after hearing the beep, he would get back to them as soon as he possibly could.

But that was before Mr. Edgar Delchamps reasoned that Roscoe's callers would be curious if, after leaving their names and numbers, Roscoe didn't get back to them at all. And he didn't want to change the message to "I'll be out of town for a few days and will get back to you just as soon as I return," as that would make people even more curious. So he explained the problem to Dr. Aloysius Casey, and they came up with a solution.

The result of this was that when C. Harry dialed Roscoe's number, he got a recorded voice that said with a heavy Slavic accent, "Embassy of the Bulgarian People's Republic. Press one for Bulgarian, two for Russian, or three . . ."

C. Harry, concluding he had misdialed, broke the connection and carefully punched in Roscoe's number again.

And got the same Bulgarian message. This time he listened to the message all the way through. When he'd heard it all, he pressed five, which the Bulgarian said was for English.

This time he got a crisp American voice: "FBI Embassy surveillance, Agent Jasper speaking. Be advised this call will be recorded under the Provisions of the Patriot Act as amended. Anything you say may be used against you in a court of law."

C. Harry broke the connection with such force that he knocked his BlackBerry out of his hand.

Jesus Christ, he thought, *if they trace that call, I'll be on the FBI's list of known Bulgarian sympathizers!*

Determined to find Roscoe J. Danton and learn what the sonofabitch was up to, C. Harry entered the Old Ebbitt, where he knew Roscoe habitually went for a pre-luncheon Bloody Mary.

Roscoe was not at his usual place at the bar. But five stools down the bar was a familiar face, that of Sean O'Grogarty, a large redheaded young man of Irish heritage wearing an almost black suit of the kind favored by Secret Service agents.

Roscoe happily thought: *O'Grogarty just might know where Roscoe is!*

C. Harry took the empty stool beside O'Grogarty but did not speak to him at first. Neither did O'Grogarty acknowledge C. Harry. C. Harry thought of Sean as his "mole in the motor pool," and neither wished to have people know they knew one another.

Mr. O'Grogarty was a member of the uniformed division of the Secret Service, but he didn't wear a uniform on duty. He was out of uniform, so to speak, because he was a driver of one of the White House's fleet of two-year-old Yukons, in which members of President Clendennen's lesser staff were chauffeured hither and yon.

A delegation of lesser staff personnel had gone to Supervisory Secret Service Agent Mulligan—who was in charge of everything the Secret Service did in and around the White House—and complained that having uniformed officers drive the vehicles and usher them into the backseats thereof gave the impression they were being arrested.

Mrs. Florence Horter had been chosen as the delegation's spokesperson not only because she looked like Whistler's mother but also because she suffered from an ocular malady that caused her eyes to water copiously whenever she squinted.

She borrowed a wheelchair, had herself wheeled into Mulligan's office, and, squinting, asked, "Please, Mr. Mulligan, sir, could the drivers be put into civilian clothing? I don't want to have my grandchildren think I'm being busted."

Mulligan knew the real reason the lesser staff people wanted the drivers in mufti was because they wanted people to think they were upper-level staff people. Upper-level members of the President's staff had, of course, their own brand-new Yukons, which were driven by Secret Service agents.

Mulligan granted the request, however, as he knew doing so would place the lower-level staff people in his debt. One day, inevitably, he would need a favor from them, and they would owe him one.

Mulligan had not come to this plan of action on his own, but rather had learned it from Mr. Francis Ford Coppola's three-part masterpiece titled *The Godfather.* Every time he watched it—and he watched at least one of the three parts once a week, usually on Sunday, when he came home from Mass—Mulligan was deeply impressed by how easily the moral lessons of the Mafia saga could be applied to the White House and to official Washington in general.

For a long time now, whenever he had a problem, he had asked himself how Marlon Brando would deal with it.

At the bar, C. Harry Whelan ordered a Johnnie Walker Black on the rocks. When it was served, he picked it up and took a long look down the bar toward the Fifteenth Street entrance, and with the glass still at his mouth, he softly inquired, "Got something for me?"

When he saw in the mirrors behind the rows of whisky bottles that O'Grogarty had nodded, C. Harry laid a fifty-dollar bill on the bar.

"It better be good, O'Grogarty."

"So good it's worth two of these bills," O'Grogarty replied.

C. Harry considered that for a long moment before adding two twenties and a ten on the bar.

"He whose name we dare not speak is going to Fort Bragg," O'Grogarty said sotto voce.

C. Harry's hand slammed down on the money.

"That's not worth a hundred bucks," C. Harry declared.

"He's going there secretly," O'Grogarty amplified. "First thing tomorrow morning. And not in Air Force One."

"What do you mean, not in Air Force One?"

"They laid on a Gulfstream. You know, that little airplane?"

"I know what a Gulfstream is. No limousine?"

"Just him and Robin Hoboken, Mulligan, a photographer, and a couple of Protection Detail guys."

"What are they going to do at Fort Bragg?"

"If I knew that, C. Harry, it would cost you a lot more than a hundred bucks."

"If you can find out, it would be worth more—a *little* more—than a hundred."

C. Harry lifted his hand off the bills on the bar. O'Grogarty pocketed them, and then pushed away from the bar and walked quickly out of the Old Ebbitt.

[FOUR]
The Office of the Presidential Spokesperson
The White House
1600 Pennsylvania Avenue, N.W.
Washington, D.C.
1210 14 June 2007

Presidential Spokesperson Robin Hoboken looked at the caller ID window of his desk telephone, and then picked up the receiver.

"How may I be of assistance to the preeminent journalist of Wolf News?" he inquired of C. Harry Whelan.

"By telling me why I've been dropped from the pool."

The pool to which Mr. Whelan referred was the small group of journalists who accompanied the President when he went anywhere and then made their reporting of presidential activities available to those members of the White House Press Corps who were not privileged to accompany the President.

The journalists who received the "pool" matériel then wrote their reports of the President's travel and activities in a manner that suggested—but did not say so directly—that they had been along on the trip. This was known as "journalistic license."

"C. Harry, old buddy, you have not been dropped from the pool. Trust me, the next time President Clendennen goes anywhere, you'll be among the first to be invited to go along."

"Like when he goes to Fort Bragg, for example?"

"When he goes anywhere, Harry."

"There's a story going around that he's going to Fort Bragg tomorrow morning."

"Where did you hear something like that?"

"Telling you where and from whom I learned this would betray my source. And I never do that. Suffice it to say that he is close to the center of things in the White House."

"I think this fellow is pulling your chain, Harry."

"I think you're being less than honest with me, Robin Redbreast, my fine-feathered friend."

"Harry, you know I don't like it when you call me that."

"I know. That's why I do it. You leave me no choice but to go on the air tonight—probably on *Wolf News at Five O'clock with J. Pastor Jones*, or on Andy McClarren's *As the World Spins* at seven, or maybe, probably both, with the story that President Clendennen is about to make a secret trip that Presidential Spokesman—"

"That's Spokes*person*, Harry," Presidential Spokesman Hoboken interrupted. "Spokes*person*. There is absolutely no sexism in the Clendennen White House."

". . . refuses to talk about."

"Can we go off the record here, Harry?" Hoboken asked.

"What would be in that for me?"

"The gratitude of the President."

"Gratitude for what?"

"Are we off the record?"

"Momentarily."

"Gratitude for understanding a certain problem he and the First Lady are having."

"That wouldn't have anything to do with the First Mother-in-Law being a world-class boozer, would it?"

"Hypothetically speaking, Harry—"

"We're back on the record, Robin Redbreast," C. Harry said. "The last time you sucker punched me with that hypothetical business, I swore I'd never let you do it again."

"Very well. Then hypothetically speaking on the record: What if a member of the President's family was in the hospital in Mississippi and the President wanted to visit her without attracting the attention of the White House Press Corps—"

"And having it come out she's a boozer, you mean?"

"If an allegation was made that that fine old lady had a drinking problem—"

"The voters may not like it?"

". . . that the President and the First Lady were doing their best to cope with—"

"With a remarkable lack of success—"

". . . and that, despite being fully aware of the pain it would cause to not only that poor, sick old lady, but to the First Lady and the President himself, a certain journalist wrote the story anyway—"

"News is news, Robin," C. Harry said.

". . . because he believes news is news, and to hell with compassion—"

"Nice try, Robin," C. Harry said.

". . . and this story would get out—about this hypothetical journalist, I mean—because other members of the White House Press Corps, jealous of our hypothetical journalist's scoop, would fall all over themselves to paint our hypothetical journalist as cold-hearted and unfeeling. They might even go so far as to suggest that it wasn't really a scoop."

"Meaning what?" C. Harry demanded.

"That our hypothetical journalist had paid for his information, bribed some underpaid White House staffer for it. If that hypothetical happened, of course, the Secret Service would have to investigate. Paying government employees to give you information they're not supposed to give you, as I'm sure you know, Harry, is a Class A felony."

C. Harry considered everything for a long moment, and then asked, "Is that what it is, he's going to Mississippi to see the First Mother-in-Law?"

"I regret," Hoboken said formally, "that there is nothing vis-à-vis the President's travel plans that I can tell you at this time, Mr. Whelan."

"Screw you, Robin Redbreast," Mr. Whelan said, and hung up.

[FIVE]

The Portico
The White House
1600 Pennsylvania Avenue, N.W.
Washington, D.C.
1215 14 June 2007

When he walked back to the White House from the Old Ebbitt, Sean O'Grogarty was quickly passed onto the White House grounds by the uniformed Secret Service guards. Not only did they know him but he had the proper identification tag hanging around his neck.

As he was walking up the curving drive to the portico, intending to go to "the shed"—where Yukon drivers on call waited—a Secret Service agent of the presidential security detail intercepted him.

He signaled with an index finger for O'Grogarty to follow him, and led him to a men's room just inside the building.

"Wait here," he said. "Someone wants to see you."

Supervisory Secret Service Agent Robert J. Mulligan appeared five minutes later, checked to see that they were alone in the room, and then leaned his considerable bulk against the door to ensure they were left that way.

"How did it go, Sean?" Mulligan asked.

"I was in the Old Ebbitt about twenty minutes," O'Grogarty replied. "C. Harry came in, asked if I had anything—"

"Nobody saw the two of you together, right? I told you that was important."

O'Grogarty shrugged. "I don't think so, but we were at the bar. He asked if I had anything—"

"Anybody hear him ask?"

O'Grogarty shook his head.

"When I nodded, he put a fifty on the bar. Nobody saw him do it. Then I told him what I had was worth more than fifty bucks, and he put another fifty on the bar. Two twenties and a ten. Then I told him about the President going to Fort Bragg tomorrow. And that nobody was to know."

"He believed you?"

O'Grogarty nodded.

"He said if I could find out why, there'd be more money in it for me."

"Good man!"

"Thank you, sir."

"Speaking of money . . ." Mulligan said.

"Yes, sir," O'Grogarty replied, and took the one hundred dollars C. Harry had given him from his pocket. He gave the fifty-dollar bill to Mulligan.

"The President calls this 'redistribution of the wealth,'" Mulligan said. "It's something he really believes in."

"You mean he gets the fifty dollars?"

"No, of course not. The President says he's worked too hard for his money to redistribute any of it. What it means is you had to give me half of what C. Harry gave you, and I'll have to give half of that to Mr. Hoboken. That's fair. You wouldn't have C. Harry's fifty unless he bribed you, and the leak to C. Harry was Hoboken's idea."

"Yes, sir."

"I probably shouldn't tell you this, Sean, but I see a good future for you in the Secret Service. Keep up the good work!"

"I'll try, sir."

Mulligan patted O'Grogarty on the shoulder, pushed himself off the men's room door, and left.

[SIX]
Quarters #3
Yadkin and Reilly Road
Fort Bragg, North Carolina
0605 15 June 2007

Colonel Max Caruthers, who was six feet three and weighed 225 pounds, and Captain Albert H. Walsh, who was even larger, were in the foyer of Quarters #3. The cordless telephone on the sideboard rang. Caruthers was closer to it, and answered it.

"General McNab's quarters."

"Who is this?" the caller demanded sharply.

There was an implication in the question that the telephone had been answered incorrectly. As, indeed, it had. What the protocol called for was for Colonel Caruthers to have answered the telephone by saying, "Sir, General McNab's quarters. Colonel Caruthers speaking, sir."

He had not done so for several reasons. Among them were that he was not only a colonel, but a colonel/brigadier general designate, which meant that when the chair warmers in the Pentagon finally finished doing their bureaucratic thing, he would swap the silver eagles of a colonel for the star of a brigadier general. That, in turn, meant that there were very few people around Fort Bragg in a position to remonstrate with him for answering the telephone in an incorrect manner.

But the primary reason he had failed to follow the protocol properly was that his ass was dragging. He had three minutes before he was finished accompanying General McNab on his ritual five-mile morning run around Smoke Bomb Hill and other Fort Bragg scenic attractions. This was understandably somewhat more difficult for someone weighing 225 pounds than it was for someone weighing 135 pounds, as did Lieutenant General Bruce J. McNab.

When they arrived at Quarters #3, and General McNab had announced his intention to grab a quick shower, Colonel Caruthers had collapsed into the chair in the foyer before the general had made it to the second floor.

"Who's calling?" Colonel Caruthers demanded, not very pleasantly.

"This is Colonel J. Charles DuBois, the Pope FOD."

FOD stood for field officer of the day, in other words the senior officer representing the commanding general that day. "Pope" made reference to the Air Force base abutting Fort Bragg, not to the head of the Roman Catholic Church.

"Charley, this is Max," Colonel Caruthers said. "What the hell does the Air Force want this time of the morning?"

"I have to speak to General McNab."

"Why?"

"He's the senior officer present on either Bragg or Pope. The other general officers are off somewhere."

"I meant about what, Charley," Caruthers said, impatiently.

"We have a Level One Situation, Max. The protocol states that the senior general officer present will be informed without delay."

"What kind of a Level One Situation?"

"The protocol states the senior general officer present gets informed, Max, not his senior aide-de-camp."

There were five Situation Levels, ranging in importance up from One—in layman's terms, *Peace & Tranquillity*—to Five, which implied something like *The War Is About to Begin.*

Colonel Caruthers erupted from his chair with an agility remarkable for someone of his bulk and, cordless phone in hand, took the stairs to the second floor three at a time. He bounded down the corridor and—knowing that Mrs. McNab was in the kitchen preparing coffee—burst into the master bedroom.

The commanding general, United States Special Operation Command, was sitting, in his birthday suit, at his wife's mirrored vanity, which reflected his face in three views as he trimmed and waxed his mustache.

He turned to Colonel Caruthers and calmly inquired, "Something on your mind, Max?"

"A Level One Situation, General," Caruthers said, as he thrust the telephone at him.

General McNab rose to his feet as he took it.

Naked, holding the telephone in one hand and his mustache comb in the other, he did not look much like a recruiting poster for Special Forces.

"McNab," he said calmly.

He listened to what Colonel J. Charles DuBois had to say.

"I'm on my way, Colonel," he said. "If this is an example of Air

Force humor, I suggest that you and anyone else involved in this commit hara-kiri before I get there."

He handed back the telephone to Caruthers.

"Tell Bobby to have the engine running and the door open when I get there. I will be down directly."

Bobby was Staff Sergeant Robert Nellis, the driver of General McNab's Chrysler Town & Country minivan.

Colonel Caruthers said, "Yes, sir," and bounded down the hall and stairs as quickly as he had come up them.

Three minutes and some seconds after he had ordered Colonel Caruthers to tell his driver to have the engine running and the door open, Lieutenant General Bruce J. McNab came out the front door of his quarters.

He now looked like a recruiting poster for Special Forces—for that matter, like a recruiting poster for the entire United States Army. He was wearing his dress blue uniform. It was said, more or less accurately, that he had more medals than General Patton, and today he was wearing them all.

General McNab jumped in the front seat of the Town & Country and ordered, "Pope! We need to be there yesterday!"

Sergeant Bobby Nellis started off with smoking tires.

"Sir, are you going to tell me what the Situation Five is?" Colonel Caruthers inquired.

"Would you believe me, Colonel, if I were to tell you the President of the United States and Commander in Chief of its armed forces is about to land at Pope?"

"Sir, I would have difficulty believing that."

"Why?"

"He's been here before, sir. The Secret Service and the press always start arriving three days before him. And there has been no 'heads-up' that I've heard."

"My thinking exactly. Have you ever heard, Max, that great minds follow the same path?"

"No, sir. But I will write that down so that I won't forget it."

[SEVEN]
Base Operations
Pope Air Force Base, North Carolina
0625 15 June 2007

Sergeant Nellis slammed on the brakes, threw the gearshift in park, then erupted from the Town & Country and raced around the front of it to open the door for General McNab.

He didn't make it. McNab was already out of the van.

"A little slow, weren't you, Bobby?" General McNab inquired.

Colonel J. Charles DuBois, USAF, rushed to the van, saluted, and said, "You just made it, General. There it is!"

He pointed to an aircraft just about to touch down.

"That's not Air Force One," General McNab replied. "That's a C-37A."

"Sir," Sergeant Nellis said, "any aircraft with the President aboard is designated Air Force One."

McNab turned and glowered at him.

"Sorry, sir," Nellis said, deeply chagrined.

"Sorry won't cut it, Sergeant. I've told you and told you and told you: Sergeants don't correct generals even when generals say something stupid!"

"Sir, it just slipped out!"

"You've got to learn not to let corrections of general officers just slip out. Colonel Caruthers, just as soon as we get to the bottom of what's going on here, cut the orders! It's Officer Candidate School for the loudmouth here."

"Yes, sir," Caruthers said.

"And just to cut off the Avenue of Escape and Evasion Sergeant Loudmouth is thinking of—flunking out of OCS and going back to an A-Team—call Fort Benning and tell them if he flunks out, he's to be sent to the Adjutant General's Corps!"

"Yes, sir," Colonel Caruthers said.

"Not the Adjutant General's Corps, sir, please!" Sergeant Nellis begged.

"Why not? They're always trying to correct honest soldiers. You'd be right at home with those paper pushers. Say, 'Yes, sir.'"

"Yes, sir," Sergeant Nellis said. He seemed on the brink of tears.

The C-37A turned off the runway and taxied to the base operations building, where it stopped.

The stair door unfolded.

Supervisory Secret Service Agent Robert J. Mulligan came down the stairs, followed by Sean O'Grogarty, who Mulligan at the last minute had decided to bring along, thinking he might be useful. Technically, O'Grogarty was undergoing "on-the-job training."

Next to come down the stairs was an Army officer, a full colonel in Battle Dress Uniform that also bore insignia identifying him as a member of the Adjutant General's Corps.

Colonel Caruthers, at the sight of the apparition, momentarily lost control and blurted, "Who the fuck are you?"

The AGC colonel answered the question by marching up to General McNab, saluting crisply, and announcing, "Sir, Colonel R. James Scott, deputy chief, Office of Heraldry, Office of the Adjutant General, reporting VOPOTUS to the C in C Special Operations Command for indefinite temporary duty, sir!"

McNab returned the salute in a Pavlovian reaction and was about to ask several questions when three more men came down the stair door and forestalled this intention. Two of the men were festooned with an assortment of still and motion picture cameras. The third was Presidential Spokesperson Robin Hoboken.

"Quick," Mr. Hoboken ordered the photographers, "before the President gets in the doorway of Air Force One, get a shot of General Whatshisname, the one in the fancy uniform, welcoming Colonel Whatsisname to Fort Bragg."

The photographers rushed to comply. As they did so, they trotted past Sergeant Nellis. Somehow, one of Sergeant Nellis's highly polished "jump boots"—the left one—became entangled with the ankle of the still photographer. Sergeant Nellis of course reached out to catch him as he stumbled. He not only failed to do so, but his right jump boot became simultaneously entangled with the ankle of the motion picture photographer, who then fell on top of the still photographer.

Sergeant Nellis rushed to help them to their feet, and Colonel Caruthers rushed to assist Sergeant Nellis.

By the time both photographers had been pulled to their feet and brushed off, Joshua Ezekiel Clendennen, President of the United States and Commander in Chief of its armed forces, was standing in the door of the Gulfstream.

But it was too late. The opportunity to record General McNab welcoming Colonel R. James Scott to Fort Bragg for posterity was lost forever.

The photographers rushed to record for posterity President Clendennen waving from the door and then as he descended the stair door.

General McNab was waiting for him there, and this time he got the protocol perfect.

He popped to rigid attention, saluted, and barked, "Sir, Lieutenant General Bruce J. McNab reports to the Commander in Chief!"

President Clendennen returned the salute, which annoyed General McNab more than a little, since he believed a salute was something warriors exchanged, and he knew the President had never worn a uniform and that the closest he had come to combat was dodging Mason jars of white lightning thrown at him by the First Mother-in-Law.

But General McNab said nothing through the entire five minutes Robin Hoboken spent posing him and the President for more photographs.

But finally his opportunity came. He came to attention again.

"Sir, how may the general be of service to the President?"

President Clendennen considered the question a moment, and then replied, "General, ask not what you can do for your President, but what your President can do for you."

"Yes, sir," General McNab said.

"Make sure you get this," Robin Hoboken said to the photographers. "It's important."

The photographers aimed their cameras.

"Okay, General," Robin said. "Ask."

"I beg your pardon?"

"Ask the President what he can do for you. He's waiting."

"Mr. President, what can you do for me?" General McNab inquired.

"I am here, General, to help you plan the assault on Drug Cartel International Airfield," President Clendennen said.

"Shit, that sounds bad," Robin Hoboken said. "We're going to have to do that again."

Hoboken waited until the motion picture photographer signaled he was ready to proceed, then called, "Quiet on the set! Rolling! Action! Go ahead, General, ask."

"Mr. President," General McNab asked again, "what can you do for me?"

"I am here, General, to help you plan the assault by Clendennen's Commandos on Drug Cartel International Airfield. I want to be on that Out of the Box Operation from the get-go."

The President paused, then turned to Robin Hoboken.

"Better?" he asked.

"Much better, Mr. President," Hoboken said. "I'm glad you remembered Clendennen's Commandos."

"Robin, how could I forget my boys?" the President asked chidingly. "They're like family to me."

"Excuse me, Mr. President, sir," General McNab said. "Who are Clendennen's Commandos?"

"You used to call them Delta Force and Black Coyote," the President replied. "Robin, who's really good at this sort of thing, suggested we needed something with more zing to it."

"No offense, General," Hoboken said, "but you military people really dropped the ball naming these people—"

"Actually, it's Black Fox, not Black Coyote," General McNab said.

"Fox, coyote, what's the difference?" the President asked.

"Coyotes and foxes are both members of the *Canis latrans* order of Mammalia, Mr. President," Robin Hoboken explained. "Coyotes are larger—"

"I meant," the President said, "that 'fox' and 'coyote' are really lousy names—not as bad as what they call those sailor boys, of course. Calling them 'Seals' make it sound as if they go into battle making funny noises and with fishes in their mouths—but bad enough."

"Yes, sir, Mr. President," Hoboken said. "That's why you wisely decided to rename them."

"Well, where are my boys, General?" the President asked. "Hard at work preparing things to seize Drug Cartel International as the first operation of Operation Out of the Box?"

"Sir, I only learned of your plans to seize Drug Cartel International yesterday. I don't even know where it is."

"It's in Mexico," the President said.

"Permit me to rephrase, sir. I don't even know precisely where *in Mexico* it is. We can't plan an operation until we have an exact location."

"Ask Colonel Castillo. He must know where it is."

"Sir, I don't know where Colonel Castillo is, except in the most general terms."

"What does that mean?"

"The last I heard, sir, he was in Europe, planning the infiltration of his intelligence people into Somalia."

"Well, tell him to put those goddamn pirates on the back burner; that'll have to wait."

"Yes, sir."

"I'm really disappointed in you, General," the President said. "I came all the way down here to see Clendennen's Commandos getting ready to seize Drug Cartel International, and here you are telling me you don't even know where it is."

"Sir, what we really came down here for was to record for history you and Clendennen's Commandos preparing to seize Drug Cartel International."

"That's what I just said," the President said unpleasantly.

"Mr. President, I'm sure General Naylor here—"

"This isn't General Naylor, for God's sake," the President snapped. "Naylor's the *big* general with four stars. General O'Nab is the *little* general with three stars. Maybe you'd better write that down."

"My name is McNab, sir."

"Whatever."

"What I was going to suggest, Mr. President," Hoboken said, "is that General *McNab* probably has some of his people preparing to seize something as we speak. That's what they do, seize things. Either that, or blow them up. Anyway, you could have your picture taken with them. Nobody would know the difference."

"That's true, but would that be honest?"

"Trust me, Mr. President, I do things like that all the time."

The President considered that option for a moment, and then said, "Okay, we'll do it. But let's make it quick. Before we go back to Washington, I've got to go to Biloxi and get Belinda-Sue's mother out of ja . . . where she is and back in the Baptist assisted living place."

[EIGHT]
Base Operations
Pope Air Force Base, North Carolina
1005 15 June 2007

"Get a couple more shots of General Whatsisname saluting the President farewell, and then we can get out of here," Presidential Spokesperson Robin Hoboken ordered the photographers.

General McNab saluted the President farewell for the third time and then asked, "Is there anything else I can do for you, Mr. President?"

"You're really a slow learner, aren't you, General?" President Clendennen replied. "We've already been down that street twice."

"Excuse me, sir," McNab said. "Is there anything else the President can do for the general?"

"The President—presuming the general can get Clendennen's Commandos up and running and seizing Drug Cartel International smoothly—can get the general another star. How does that sound?"

"Just as soon as I can get the precise locality of the airfield, sir, I'll get right on it."

"And that process would be speeded up if you could get a little more enthusiasm for getting Clendennen's Commandos into Clan Clendennen kilts, General."

"I'll do what I can, Mr. President," General McNab said.

"Get Colonel Whatsisname, the Heraldry guy, to give your people a little historical background on kilts in warfare."

"Yes, sir, I'll do that."

"As far as I'm concerned, those green berets you people wear make me think of wimpy Frenchmen. Who else wears a beret? Kilts, on the other hand, make me think of great big muscular, redheaded Scotchmen—like my ancestors in Clan Clendennen—waving great big swords."

"I'll keep that in mind, Mr. President," General McNab said, evenly.

The President went up the stair door. Robin Hoboken and then the photographers and Supervisory Special Agent Mulligan followed him.

Sean O'Grogarty remained on the tarmac.

"Excuse me, sir," General McNab said, "I think you're about to get left behind."

"That's the idea," Sean replied. "Special Agent Mulligan said I was to stick around and let him know how you're doing."

"Wonderful!" General McNab said, sharply sarcastic. "This just gets better by the moment."

The stair door closed as the engines started. Sixty seconds later, the C-37A, call sign "Air Force One," lifted off.

General McNab watched until the departing aircraft had vanished from sight, and then he walked away from the base operations building down a taxiway. When he was halfway to the runway and had looked around to make sure he was out of earshot, he took his CaseyBerry from his pocket and punched an autodial button.

"Good morning, Bruce," Secretary of State Natalie Cohen said thirty seconds later.

"Madam Secretary, I believe it would be best if no one but you was in a position to hear any part of this conversation."

"All right," she said, and he heard her announce to someone, somewhat curtly, "You'll have to excuse me while I take this call."

Thirty seconds after that, she said, "I get the feeling this call is important."

"The President just took off from here, back to Washington, via Biloxi."

"What in the world was he doing at Fort Bragg?"

"He wanted to have his picture taken with Clendennen's Commandos before they go to Mexico to seize Drug Cartel International Airport."

"'Clendennen's Commandos'?"

"He has renamed Delta Force and Black Fox."

"My God!"

"And he wants them to start wearing the kilts of Clan Clendennen."

"Unbelievable!"

"I respectfully suggest, Madam Secretary, that you convene a conference of the senior officials aware of the problem to discuss bringing the matter to the Vice President and the Cabinet."

"It looks as if we're going to have to do that. Is that what you're saying, Bruce?"

"Yes, Madam Secretary, it is."

"Your formality is making me nervous, frankly."

"I beg your pardon, if that is the case."

"There's a problem with convening something like that. Who are you thinking of?"

"Mr. Ellsworth, Mr. Lammelle, General Naylor, Attorney General Palmer, and FBI Director Schmidt, Madam Secretary."

"Not the Vice President?"

"Vice President Montvale, Madam Secretary, came to me privately and said that if the situation ever came to this, he wished not to be involved, so that later there could be no accusations that he had led a coup."

"He came to me saying the same thing. And he's right. But if the President learns, as I am very afraid he will, that I have convened these people, he's going to cry coup. What are we going to do about that?"

"Hold the meeting in secret, Madam Secretary."

"That would be just about impossible, Bruce, and you know it."

"Madam Secretary, I suggest we could hold the meeting in secret if we went to Greek Island."

It took her a moment to reply.

"If we're talking about the same Greek Island, Bruce, that was shut down shortly after the Berlin Wall came down."

"It's still there, Madam Secretary. No longer controlled by the government, but still there."

"Are you suggesting we go to West Virginia, to the Greenbrier Hotel, and reopen Greek Island? For one thing, how could we get in? If they haven't bricked up the opening, then they have gutted it."

"No, ma'am," McNab said. "When there was no longer a need for a place for Congress to go in case of a nuclear attack, the government stripped the place and turned it back over to its owner."

"So?"

"The owner is one of Those People in Las Vegas."

"And?"

"Frank, who was then working in Covert Operations at the Company, and had already started a relationship with Those People, went to them and told Hotelier he could put the place to good use, but it had to be kept quiet."

"I think I know where you're going," Secretary Cohen said.

"It's an ideal place to conduct interrogations of people we don't want anybody to know we're talking to. And to store things the Agency needs."

"The Agency and Special Operations Command, you mean?"

"Yes, ma'am."

"And by people you don't want anyone to know you're talking to, you mean people who didn't want to talk to you in the first place, right? People who didn't volunteer to come to the United States?"

McNab didn't answer.

"Sometimes, Bruce, I think that you and Frank Lammelle are as dangerous as President Clendennen."

"Well, just forget . . . please . . . that I even mentioned the hotel."

"Is that what you call it, 'the hotel'? Well, that sounds innocent enough, doesn't it?"

Again McNab didn't reply.

"The Lindbergh Act doesn't give either you or Frank an exemption from anti-kidnapping laws. I presume both of you loose cannons know that."

"Yes, ma'am. We're aware of that."

"Well, let's hear your plan, Bruce."

"Excuse me?"

"How are we going to get all these people to the hotel without letting anyone—especially the President—know?"

"May I infer, Madam Secretary . . ."

"Desperate times call for desperate measures. You may want to write that down."

"Yes, ma'am."

"Damn it, Bruce, now that we're—at least so far—unindicted co-conspirators, the least you can do is stop calling me 'ma'am.'"

"Yes, ma'am," he said automatically.

They laughed.

"One more uncomfortable question, Bruce. What are you going to do about the others? If they go to your hotel, they will know about your hotel."

"They don't want to know about the hotel. General Naylor's the only problem I see about that."

"In other words, everybody knows—or at least suspects—about the hotel except General Naylor, right?"

"Now that you know, he's the only one who doesn't."

"So, what are you going to do about him?"

"Pray that he doesn't want to see the rest of us go to jail. As you just said, desperate times call for desperate measures."

"Let's hear the plan."

"Frank brings the attorney general, the secretary of Defense, and the FBI director with him from Washington in his Gulfstream. You pick up General Naylor in yours, and then stop here and pick me up."

After a moment, the secretary of State said, "Okay, General, I'll see you soon. Should I bring my golf clubs to the Greenbrier?"

VIII

[ONE]

Saint Johan's Cemetery
Bad Hersfeld, Kreis Hersfeld-Rotenburg
Hesse, Germany
1605 15 June 2007

"It's over there," Charley said to Sweaty, pointing to the Gossinger plot in the cemetery.

Sweaty headed toward the plot, which Charley had always thought was sort of a cemetery within the cemetery. The whole thing was fenced in by a waist-high barrier of bronze poles between granite posts. In the center was an enormous pillar, topped by a statue of a weeping saint.

He had no idea how many graves were within the barrier, but there were at least fifty. The one they were looking for was near the pillar, under a gnarled thirty-foot tree.

"Over there, under the tree," Charley said, again pointing.

Sweaty followed his directions and found what they were looking for. A row of granite markers, into one of which was chiseled:

ERIKA VON UND ZU GOSSINGER
7 MAI 1952 – 13 JULI 1982

Sweaty dropped to her knees, bowed her head, and held her palms together.

Charley thought, and almost said, *You can knock that off; the chauffeur can't see you.*

And then the epiphany.

Jesus Christ, she's actually praying!

This was closely followed by the deeply shaming realization that, ever since they had arrived in Hersfeld a half hour before, he had really been a callous, unfeeling bastard, and that it had only been dumb luck that had kept Sweaty from seeing this.

Otto Göerner, the managing director of Gossinger Beteiligungsgesellschaft, G.m.b.H., had met them at the Das Haus im Wald airfield, after they had flown from Budapest. At that point, Charley had been greatly concerned about what Otto's reaction to Sweaty was going to be; they had never met.

The only reason Otto had not become Charley's stepfather when Charley was an infant, as his grandfather, the late Oberst Wilhelm von und zu Gossinger, and his late uncle Hermann Wilhelm von und zu Gossinger, had desperately hoped he would was because—despite enormous pressure from her father and her brother—Charley's mother had refused to marry Otto.

Otto still retained fatherly feelings for Charley. He had functioned as a de facto stepfather to him until, shortly before his mother's death, Karl Wilhelm von und zu Gossinger had been taken to the United States to become Carlos Guillermo Castillo.

And Otto didn't like Russians generally and hated the Sluzhba Vneshney Razvedki with a cold passion. Charley had dropped that nugget of information—that Sweaty had been an SVR lieutenant colonel—into his announcement of his pending marriage, deciding that getting that out in the open sooner was better than later.

The term "SVR *podpolkovnik*" had produced in Otto's mind the stereotype of a short-haired female with stainless steel teeth who looked like a weight lifter. When Sweaty came down the aircraft door stairs his face had shown his surprise at what he was getting—a spectacularly beautiful redhead—instead of what he had expected.

His biggest surprise, however, was to come shortly after they were loaded into Otto's Jaguar Vanden Plas, when, with visible effort, Otto produced a smile and inquired, "My dear, now that you're here in Hersfeld, what would you like to do?"

"Aside from going to the cemetery, which of course my Carlos wants to do before anything else, we're completely in your hands, Herr Göerner."

Charley was shamed to painfully remember his reaction to that had been thinking, *What the hell is Sweaty talking about?*

"Karl wants to go to the cemetery?" Otto had asked incredulously.

"He's told me what a saint, a truly godly woman, his mother was," Sweaty went on. "I want to be there when he asks her blessing on our marriage."

"Karl's mother was truly a saint," Otto agreed.

Charley was even more ashamed to remember his reaction to that, his thinking: *Jesus Christ, she's amazing. She hasn't been in his car thirty seconds and she's put ol' Otto in her pocket. Well, you don't get to be an SVR* podpolkovnik *without being able to manipulate people.*

Proof that Otto was in Sweaty's pocket had come almost immediately. As soon as they got to the house—several minutes later—Otto turned from the front seat and announced, "There's no sense in you two going into the house. I'll have someone take care of your luggage and then Kurt can take you to the cemetery."

The only reason, Charley remembered with chagrin, that he hadn't congratulated Sweaty on her manipulation of Otto on the way to the cemetery was because the chauffeur would have heard him.

Sweaty looked up at Charley.

"Aren't you going to pray?" she asked.

"I'm an Episcopalian," he said. "We pray standing up."

That's bullshit and I know it is. What it is is yet another proof that I'm a shameless liar. I wasn't praying.

And don't try to wiggle out of the shameless liar business by saying that you're a professional intelligence officer trained to instantly respond to a challenge by saying whatever necessary to get yourself off the hook.

Sweaty stood, took his hand, and kissed him tenderly on the cheek.

"I'm glad we came here," she said.

They started back to the car.

"What exactly did you pray for?" Charley asked.

"That's between God, your mother, and me."

"Okay."

"Okay," Sweaty said, obviously changing her mind. "I asked God to reward your mother for being such a good mother to you, and to give her everlasting peace now that I've taken over for her. And I asked your mother to pray to the Holy Virgin that I will be as good a mother to our baby as she was to you. And you?"

The reflexes of a professional intelligence officer trained to instantly respond to a challenge by saying whatever necessary to get himself off the hook kicked in automatically.

"I asked God to give my mother peace, and prayed for you and our baby," he heard himself say.

Where the hell did that come from?

It doesn't matter. If I didn't actually do that, I should have.

God, if there are really no secrets from You, You know that.

And by the way, thank You for Sweaty and the baby she's carrying.

When they got back in the car, Sweaty asked, in Russian, "Kurt, do you speak Russian?"

When it became evident that Kurt did not speak Russian, Sweaty said, in German, "I was just curious."

Then she switched back to Russian.

"Well, what do you think is going to happen tonight? Do we get to fool around in your childhood bed, or is Otto the Pure going to put us in separate rooms at opposite ends of that factory you call a house?"

"Sweaty, I just don't know."

God, if You didn't hear me the first time, thank You for this woman.

[TWO]

When they got to Das Haus im Wald they found the Merry Outlaws, less Master Sergeant C. Gregory Damon, Retired, John and Sandra Britton, and Vic D'Alessandro—whom they had left behind in Budapest to deal with the logistical and other problems of getting into Somalia on some credible excuse—sitting in an assortment of chairs and couches in the top-floor living room of the House in the Woods snacking on a massive display of cold cuts. Castillo saw that Peg-Leg Lorimer was working at his laptop.

Floor-to-ceiling plate-glass windows showed fields green with new growth and what at first glance appeared to be an airfield. The Gulfstream V on which they had flown first from Cozumel to Budapest and then here was parked near a runway beside a Cessna Mustang, the smaller jet bearing German markings. There was also what looked like a deserted control tower, a four-story structure built of concrete blocks, the top floor of which was windowed on all sides.

It was not a deserted aviation control tower, however. It had been built by the hated East German Volkspolizei after the Berlin Wall had gone up to keep an eye on the fence that then had separated East from West Germany, and had run through the Gossinger property.

When the Berlin Wall—and the fence—came down, Castillo, who had been born and spent the first twelve years of his life in Das Haus im Wald as Karl Wilhelm von und zu Gossinger, and now owned the property, ordered that the guard tower be left in place as a monument to the Cold War.

Castillo went to see how Peg-Leg was coming with his SitRep, saw that he was nearly finished, and then inquired, "What time is it in Washington?"

"Peg-Leg's finished?" Lieutenant Colonel Allan B. Naylor asked.

"How does that translate to hours and minutes?" Castillo asked.

Allan gave Charley the finger, then said, "Five minutes after ten in the morning."

Peg-Leg pressed a button, and a printer began to whine, purr, and ultimately began to spit out printed pages.

He handed them to Castillo, who read them, then handed them to Naylor.

"Nice job, Peg-Leg," he said.

"What happens now?" Lorimer asked.

"You get to ride to Berlin in the Mustang, where you will take these magnificent documents to the embassy for transmission. Meanwhile, Colonel Naylor and I will take Sweaty and whoever else wants to go on a tour of where we were innocent children together.

"Tomorrow, presuming the Somali experts finally get here, we will drive to Cologne, where we will board *Die Stadt Köln*, a five-star river cruiser which we have chartered to ensure our conversations will not be overheard by the forces of evil, and sail up and down the Rhine River for four days."

"Wait until Lammelle gets the bill for that," Dick Miller said.

Naylor said, "Charley, I think it would be better if I went to Berlin with Peg-Leg."

Castillo considered that a moment, and then said, "Yeah. That's not a shot at you, Peg-Leg. What I'm thinking is that an active duty light colonel from Central Command is liable to get more cooperation from the military attaché than some retired warrior such as you and me. And I don't want that stuff delayed."

[THREE]
Office of the Secretary of State
The Harry S Truman Building
2201 C Street, N.W.
Washington, D.C.
1125 15 June 2007

The secretary of State, on occasions like this, was extremely jealous of both Truman C. Ellsworth, the director of National Intelligence, and A. Franklin Lammelle, the director of the Central Intelligence Agency. It had to do with their freedom of schedule and of travel.

If they wanted to go somewhere, they got in their airplanes and went. With the exception of the President, no one had the authority to ask them where they were going or why. No one had that authority vis-à-vis the secretary of State, either, but the secretary of State was a public figure, and by definition the DCI and the DNI were the opposite. No one was supposed to know what they were doing.

For most of her life, until she had become secretary of State, Natalie Cohen had really believed that lying and deception had been not only wrong but counterproductive. She had learned that from her father, an investment banker. It had attracted her to Mortimer Cohen, also the son of an investment banker, whom she had married three months after graduating from Vassar.

Two sons had quickly followed, and she had tried—and thought she had succeeded in—instilling in them the high moral principles of her father and their father. She had been, she believed, a good Jewish mother to her boys, devoting her life to them until the youngest had gone off to preparatory school. The question then became what to do with the rest of her life.

She was well schooled in economics—it had been her major in college—and she had learned a good deal more about finance, in particular international finance, from both her father and her husband.

But neither, for reasons she understood, was happy with the prospect of her leaving her empty nest to join either of their firms. She was determined, however, to leave that empty nest, and the first thing she did was volunteer her services to various charitable organizations, including, for example, the United Jewish Appeal.

She immediately proved herself to be very good at two things: the raising of money, and the straightening out of the often out-of-kilter administration of such organizations. She moved from good works to the State Department when the U.S. ambassador to the United Nations, a Princeton classmate of Mortimer's, asked her to join his staff as financial adviser.

She moved from the UN to the State Department itself, where she was appointed deputy assistant secretary of State and given responsibility for doling out the taxpayers' money to various foreign governments for various reasons. She held that position until there was a change of administration. She resigned when it became apparent to her that the new President posed a real threat to the United States, and she could not in good conscience work for him.

She devoted the next three years and some months raising money for the campaign of the man who was to become Joshua Ezekiel Clendennen's predecessor. During that period, she got to know him well, and Mortimer joked that when he gave speeches on international monetary and economic problems and their solutions, the candidate sounded like Natalie.

As it became increasingly apparent that her guy was going to move into the White House, Natalie, who by then was familiar with the way Washington worked, knew that there was going to be some sort of reward for all the millions she had raised.

And that worried her because the most likely reward was for her to be appointed the President's ambassador extraordinary and plenipotentiary to the State of Israel. Considering, as she did, Israel as her spiritual homeland was not the same thing as being overjoyed at the prospect of moving there for four years.

She had been to Tel Aviv often enough to know that it was hot, muggy, noisy, and crowded. Furthermore, the ultraorthodox Jews who had so much power in Israel made her uncomfortable. Finally, the ambassador's residence there was not nearly as comfortable as either their house in Washington or their apartment in New York. And equally important, she was about to become a Jewish grandmother, and eagerly looking forward to that.

The man-who-was-to-be-President elected to learn the election results in the Plaza Hotel in New York. Before going there, there was a really small dinner—designed primarily to give him a little rest so that he would be better prepared for whatever happened—at the Cohens' apartment two blocks away on Fifth Avenue.

Natalie and Mortimer had seriously considered not going to the Plaza at all. Watching the returns on Wolf News in their living room with their feet on the coffee table held far more appeal than did the Plaza. But the candidate insisted.

"I need you around me, Natalie," he said.

So they went with him.

And thirty seconds after Andy McClarren of Wolf News called the election, the President-elect said, "Natalie, my first appointment will be my secretary of State. Guess who?"

"I have no idea, Mr. President-elect."

"I'll give you a hint. She just fed me dinner."

That marked, she often thought, the end of her innocence. She had quickly learned that while lying and deception were still wrong, she could not honestly argue that they were counterproductive. The exact opposite now seemed inarguably to be the case.

Some of the proofs of this were major, and some relatively minor, as her current problem showed.

The basic, major problem was that Joshua Ezekiel Clendennen

was as mad as a March hare. There was no question in Secretary Cohen's mind about either that, or that he posed a genuine threat to the security of the United States.

The law provided a solution to that problem. But it was very complicated. The Cabinet and certain other officers, in a meeting presided over by the secretary of State, would hear the evidence in the matter. Presuming they agreed that the President's mental state was such that he could not perform the duties of his office, that committee would inform the Vice President and speaker of the House of their judgment, and that the Vice President—who was also president of the Senate—now was in charge, pending action by Congress.

So many things could go terribly wrong, producing chaos in the country even exceeding the chaos and paralysis of the government the impeachment proceedings of President Nixon had caused, that Secretary Cohen had decided it would be undertaken only as the absolute last resort.

And she was very much, even painfully, aware that the decision whether or not to remove President Clendennen was hers alone. The makeup of the "committee" that she chaired under the law was not precisely defined in the law.

Frederick P. Palmer, the attorney general, had told her—unofficially—that it *could be* interpreted to mean that her authority to convene the committee carried with it the authority to decide which senior officials should be on it.

She had run with this. The committee she was about to convene now included Palmer, Secretary of Defense Frederick K. Beiderman, DNI Ellsworth, DCI Lammelle, FBI Director Mark Schmidt, and two men who she realized had no right to be on the committee except for her decision to include them. They were General Allan B. Naylor and Lieutenant General Bruce J. McNab.

McNab had insisted the meeting be held. President Clendennen's appearance at Fort Bragg convinced him the Chief Executive was over the edge and had to go.

Cohen had included Naylor because she concurred that he was, as Wolf News' Andy McClarren had dubbed him, "the most important American general." If the absolute worst scenario—civil insurrection—happened, he would be the man best able to apply martial law and—equally important—to end it when that became possible.

When she telephoned Naylor to tell him they needed to meet, she had to be evasive to the point of not telling him that they were going to the Greenbrier. Frank Lammelle had told her that even encrypted conversations over the White House circuits were intercepted and decrypted by the NSA at Fort Meade, and that an astonishing number of people in many intelligence agencies had access to the intercepts—including outside contractors on occasion.

The one thing that absolutely could not be allowed to happen was for President Clendennen to learn of the meeting.

She had had the same problem when she spoke with the FBI director, the secretary of Defense, and the attorney general. But not when she talked to Lammelle or McNab. Charley Castillo had equipped the latter, as he had Cohen, with CaseyBerry telephones. The interception equipment at Fort Meade had been designed and installed and was maintained by Aloysius Casey, Ph.D., and his design of the CaseyBerry ensured that the computers at Meade could not decrypt anything sent over the CaseyBerry network.

The secretary had just finished her last call—with Defense Secretary Beiderman—setting up the travel arrangements for the meeting at the Greenbrier when the Communications Center duty officer appeared at her door.

"Madam Secretary, there is a message from Lieutenant Colonel Naylor."

"Thank you, Martha."

The duty officer laid the messages on Cohen's desk and she read them:

```
TOP SECRET

URGENT

DUPLICATION FORBIDDEN

TO: POTUS

SUBJECT: CGC

VIA SECRETARY OF STATE

MAKE AVAILABLE (EYES ONLY) TO:

DIRECTOR, CIA

SECRETARY OF DEFENSE
```

DIRECTOR OF NATIONAL INTELLIGENCE

C IN C CENTRAL COMMAND

SITREP #3

US EMBASSY BERLIN 1900 ZULU 15 JUNE 2007

1-FOLLOWING FLIGHT TO BUDAPEST, MR. D'ALESSANDRO, THE BRITTONS, AND DAMON WERE PUT IN CONTACT WITH PERSONNEL WHO WILL ARRANGE THEIR INFILTRATION INTO SOMALIA AND THEIR EXTRACTION THEREFROM.

2-REMAINING PERSONNEL OF OPERATION OUT OF THE BOX THEN FLEW TO HERSFELD, GERMANY, WHERE THEY WILL CONFER WITH CERTAIN JOURNALISTS KNOWN TO BE EXPERT REGARDING THE SOMALI PIRATE SITUATION.

3-MR. DANTON'S REDACTED NEWS STORY ATTACHED WILL PROVIDE OTHER DETAILS. AS OF THIS TIME LTC CASTILLO STATES HE CANNOT ESTIMATE DATE OF SOMALIA INSERTION WITH MORE PRECISION THAN "WITHIN THE NEXT WEEK OR TEN DAYS."

RESPECTFULLY SUBMITTED.

NAYLOR, LTC

TOP SECRET

SLUG: OPERATION OUT OF THE BOX

TAKE TWO

BY ROSCOE J. DANTON

WASHINGTON TIMES-POST WRITERS SYNDICATE

DAY FIVE—JUNE 14, 2007

BUDAPEST, HUNGARY

THIS REPORTER FLEW OVERNIGHT IN A CHARTERED GULFSTREAM V JET AIRCRAFT FROM COZUMEL, MEXICO, TO BUDAPEST, HUNGARY, WITH LIEUTENANT COLONEL ███ ██████ AND MEMBERS OF HIS TEAM, KNOWN AS "THE MERRY OUTLAWS," CARRYING OUT PRESIDENT CLENDENNEN'S ORDERS TO INVESTIGATE THE SOMALIA PIRACY SITUATION AND MAKE RECOMMENDATIONS AS TO THE SOLUTION OF THE PROBLEM.

WE WERE MET AT FERIHEGY INTERNATIONAL AIRPORT BY ███ █████, EDITOR IN CHIEF OF THE ██████ ████ ████ ████ NEWSPAPER AND ██████ ███, CHIEF OF SECURITY OF THE NEWSPAPER, AND TAKEN TO THE HOTEL GELLERT ON THE BANKS OF THE DANUBE RIVER, WHERE, AFTER

DINNER, CASTILLO CONFERRED ON SOMALIA GENERALLY WITH THESE MEN.

OBVIOUSLY, THIS REPORTER CANNOT DIVULGE THE DETAILS OF ANYTHING DISCUSSED AT THAT MEETING, EXCEPT TO SAY THAT █████ ARRANGED FOR █████ TO MEET WITH JOURNALISTS KNOWN TO BE EXPERT ON SOMALIA TOMORROW IN █████, GERMANY.

WE WILL BE FLYING THERE TOMORROW.

DAY SIX—JUNE 15, 2007

LEAVING █████ THE ████ AND █████ BEHIND IN BUDAPEST TO ARRANGE THEIR SURREPTITIOUS ENTRY INTO SOMALIA, THIS REPORTER FLEW THIS MORNING WITH LIEUTENANT COLONEL █████ AND THE MERRY OUTLAWS ON THE GULFSTREAM V TO A PRIVATE AIRFIELD NEAR █████, GERMANY.

THERE WE WERE MET BY ████ █████ MANAGING DIRECTOR OF █████ ██████████████, G.M.B.H., WHICH OWNS THE ████ █████ NEWSPAPER CHAIN. HE IS A HESSIAN, BUT HE LOOKED LIKE A POSTCARD BAVARIAN. HE IS A TALL, HEAVYSET, RUDDY-FACED MAN.

█████ TOLD █████ THE ████ █████ CORRESPONDENTS HE HAD ORDERED TO COME FROM MOGADISHU TO █████

```
HAD BEEN DELAYED IN ██████, ██████ AND HAD NOT YET
ARRIVED. THEY ARE EXPECTED TOMORROW OR THE NEXT
DAY. IN THE MEANTIME, ██████ AND HIS TEAM HAVE
BEEN GIVEN ACCESS TO THE FILES OF THE NEWSPAPER
CHAIN.

MORE TO FOLLOW
```

"Will there be a reply, Madam Secretary?"

"Martha, we've known each other ever since the UN, and you can't bring yourself to call me Natalie, even when we're alone?"

"Oh, I couldn't do that, Madam Secretary."

"There won't be a reply right now, Martha, thank you. If Charlene is out there, would you ask her to come in, please?"

Charlene Stevens, the former Secret Service agent who headed Secretary Cohen's security detail, came into the office and announced, "Anytime you're ready, boss."

"We can't leave until I deliver this to the President," Cohen said, holding up the messages.

"I'll tell them to stand down," Charlene said. "Any guess as to when we can go?"

"Let's find out," Cohen said, and pressed the buttons on her red White House switchboard telephone that would connect her with the President and put the conversation on loudspeaker.

A male voice was on the line in less than ten seconds.

"The President's line. May I ask who's calling?"

"Secretary Cohen."

"Madam Secretary, the President is not available at the moment, and has asked not to be disturbed in less than a Category Two Situation. Would you like me to put you through to the President?"

"No, thank you. Please tell the President I have information for him and that I would like to see him at his earliest convenience."

"Yes, ma'am. I will pass on to the President that you would like to see him at his earliest convenience."

"Thank you," Secretary Cohen said, and broke the connection.

"Well, while obviously important," Charlene said, "whatever that message says, it doesn't pose as much of a threat to the nation's security as getting the First Mother-in-Law back in the loony bin does."

Natalie shook her head, but didn't reply.

"You knew he wasn't there, right?" Charlene asked. "That he's in Biloxi?"

"I didn't tell you that."

"Some of my boys were talking."

"See if you can get some of your boys to let you know when they have an ETA for him at Andrews. I'd like to be at the White House when he gets back."

"Done. Anything else?"

"Not unless you want to sit here and listen to me tell *my* boys that our golf at the Greenbrier will have to be delayed for a while."

"I'll pass, thank you," Charlene said.

[FOUR]
The Oval Office
The White House
1600 Pennsylvania Avenue, N.W.
Washington, D.C.
1805 15 June 2007

"Thank you for seeing me on such short notice, Mr. President," Secretary Cohen said. "But you said you wanted to see Colonel Naylor's reports as soon as they arrived."

"Actually, Madam Secretary," Robin Hoboken said, "what the President said was that he wanted to see Colonel *Castillo's* reports as soon as they arrived."

"I stand corrected," Cohen said.

"How'd you know I'd be here?" President Clendennen asked. "I just got back three minutes ago."

"When I called earlier, when I first received these messages, Mr. President, I was told you were unavailable, not that you had gone somewhere."

"Belinda-Sue's mother, that saintly old woman," the President said, "is very ill. She wanted to see me. I could not, of course, turn her down. God alone knows how long she'll be with us. But I could not in good conscience ask the American taxpayer to pay the enormous expense of my going down to Biloxi in the 747 on a personal matter. So I went, very quietly, in a Gulfstream, taking only Robin and Mulligan with me."

"How is the First Mother-in-Law?" Natalie asked.

"Not well, but with prayer there's always hope," the President said. "Now let me see Colonel Castillo's report."

"She doesn't have Colonel Castillo's report, Mr. President," Robin Hoboken said. "She said she had Colonel Naylor's report."

"And Mr. Whelan's redacted news story," Cohen said.

The President read both.

"Well," he said, "to judge from this, and other information I have, I think it would be fair to assume my Out of the Box Operation is starting to take shape. Wouldn't you agree, Madam Secretary?"

"'Other information,' Mr. President?"

"Natalie," he said condescendingly, "I learned a long time ago that the more people who know a secret, the less chance there is that it will remain a secret. Right now, you don't have the Need to Know about my other information."

"May I ask, sir, if your other information might result in something that would require my services in the next twenty-four hours?"

"The President just told you, Madam Secretary, that you don't have the Need to Know," Robin Hoboken said.

"Why do you ask, Madam Secretary?" the President asked.

"I'd like to run down to the Greenbrier and play a little golf, Mr. President."

"For how long?"

"I would be back tomorrow afternoon no later than five, sir."

"Sure, go ahead. All work and no play makes Jack . . . in this case, Natalie, of course . . . the dull girl, as I always say."

"Thank you, Mr. President."

"Did you know, Natalie, that during the Cold War, they had a great big underground place at the Greenbrier where Congress could meet in case the Russians nuked Washington?"

"I've heard that, Mr. President."

"Robin here told me that only last week. Which made me wonder what else is going on around here that I don't know about."

"Mr. President," Natalie said, "I would suggest that with Hoboken and Mulligan looking after you, there's very little of that sort of thing."

"You're right," the President said. "I only wish I was as sure of the loyalty of other people around here as I am of theirs."

Then he added: "Have a good time playing golf at the Greenbrier, Natalie."

[FIVE]
In the Secretary of State's Yukon
Approaching Joint Base Andrews, Maryland
1835 15 June 2007

One of the three cellular telephones Charlene Stevens always carried with her rang—giving off a sound like that of a feline in heat—and she quickly put it to her ear.

She listened and then said, "Thanks. You are now forgiven for not putting out the garbage."

She turned from the front passenger seat to address Secretary Cohen.

"That was my Lord and Master, boss."

Secretary Cohen understood Charlene was referring to her husband, Arthur, who was known as "King Kong" to his fellow Secret

Service agents, possibly because he stood five feet five inches tall and weighed 135 pounds.

"Arthur said," Charlene reported, "that Mulligan just called the Presidential Flight Detachment and told them to get a chopper ready for a flight to carry two agents to the Greenbrier Valley Airport."

"Damn!" Natalie Cohen said.

"And when the Air Force guy said you were getting ready to go there and were usually willing to carry people with you, Mulligan not only cut him off but said he didn't even want you to know he was sending agents there."

"Pull off somewhere, please, Tom," Secretary Cohen ordered the Yukon's driver as she searched in her purse for her CaseyBerry.

She pushed one autodial button and five seconds later A. Franklin Lammelle came over the phone's loudspeaker.

"And how may the CIA be of service to the secretary of State?"

"Get on the phone and tell everybody the Greenbrier's off," she said.

"What happened?"

She told him.

"Do you think he figured this out himself, or was Mulligan involved?"

"I think he was suspicious—he's paranoid about a coup—and Mulligan poured gasoline on those embers."

"So no meeting?"

"Unless we can find someplace else to hold it, I really don't know what to do."

"Someplace else isn't that much of a problem. I've got a safe house outside Harrisburg that isn't in use at the moment."

"Harrisburg, Pennsylvania?" she asked incredulously.

"Harrisburg, Pennsylvania," Lammelle confirmed. "And everybody but McNab and Naylor could drive there. And you could tell Naylor to visit the Indiantown Gap Military Reservation, using his airplane and taking McNab with him."

She considered that a moment. "This safe house of yours is really safe?"

"Who's going to think there'd be a CIA safe house in Harrisburg, Pennsylvania?"

"Make the calls, please, Frank, and get everybody there after eight o'clock tomorrow night."

"And what about you, Madam Secretary, as the senior government official?"

"I'll get back to Washington at five or a little after, let the President know I'm back—"

"Back from where?"

"Playing golf at the Greenbrier," she replied, "and then I'll drive up there. How do I find it?"

"I suppose Brünnhilde the Bodyguard is with you?"

"Up yours, Frank," Charlene said.

"I'll see that Art has a map by the time you need it," Lammelle said.

"Fine," Charlene said.

"You're really going down there and play golf?"

"That's what I told the President I was going to do. How could I not go? Call me and let me know what's going on."

"Yes, ma'am, Madam Secretary," Lammelle said.

Cohen broke the connection.

"Agent Stevens, I wasn't aware that you and Director Lammelle were so intimately acquainted," she said.

"He and Art went through the FBI Academy together," Charlene said. "They decided that they didn't want to spend their lives investigating white-collar crimes, so Art went into the Secret Service, and Frank into the Agency. Frank was Art's best man when we got married, and I held Frank's hand through both of his divorces."

"You never said anything."

"Yeah, well," Charlene said. "That doesn't mean we don't talk about you."

"What does that mean?"

"It means that Frank thinks you're the cat's pajamas, boss."

Natalie shook her head, then pressed another autodial button and then shut off the loudspeaker function. Charlene heard only one side of the conversation:

"I hope you didn't have big plans for tomorrow, sweetheart . . .

"Put enough clothes in your bag for a fancy dinner tonight, and then take your golf clubs and get in a cab and go out to Teterboro. I'm about ten minutes from taking off from Andrews for Teterboro . . .

"Because we're going to the Greenbrier to play golf . . .

"Of course you can make time for something like that. Your call, sweetheart. Would you rather have a romantic dinner with me tonight, and eighteen holes tomorrow, or the next time your Aunt Rebecca wants me to talk to the girls at the Beth Sinai Home have me tell her to go suck on a lemon . . . ?

"That's what *my* mother said about you, too, darling. That I would regret marrying you. See you at Teterboro . . ."

[SIX]
Aboard *Der Stadt Köln*
The River Rhine
Koblenz, Germany
1125 16 June 2007

Charley Castillo's CaseyBerry sounded "Charge!" and he picked it up, saw who was calling, and put it to his ear.

"Hey, Paul."

"Charley, are you really in the middle of the Rhine River, or did you tell Aloysius to send out spurious GPS data again?" Paul Sieno asked.

"Not exactly in the middle; we're about to tie up in Koblenz. How are things in sunny Cozumel?"

"Getting interesting, which is why I called."

"How so?"

"You'll never guess who's here."

"But you are going to tell me, right? I'm so exhausted from my labors that I'm not up to playing guessing games."

"Grigori Slobozhanin."

"Who the hell is he?"

"He's the chief coach of the Greater Sverdlovsk Table Tennis Association, and he brought a half-dozen of his better Ping-Pong players here with him. Plus a couple of dozen Cuban Ping-Pongers."

"Okay, Paul, I give up."

"Before he took up table tennis, he was known as General Sergei Murov."

Castillo was suddenly very serious.

"Paul, get with Juan Carlos Pena as soon as you can—"

"Way ahead of you, Charley," Sieno interrupted.

"I know Juan Carlos doesn't exactly look like that suave Mexican actor," Castillo went on, stopping when he couldn't recall the actor's name, and then, when he had partial recall, continuing, "Antonio Bandana, or whatever the hell his name is, but he's not only one damned smart cop but one of my oldest friends."

"Gringo, if I can have 'one damned smart cop' in writing, I'll pretend I didn't hear your unflattering comparison of me to Antonio Whatsisname," Juan Carlos Pena said.

"How are you, Juan Carlos?" Castillo asked.

"I hope we interrupted something important," Pena said.

"You did. I was sitting here in a deck chair drinking wine and watching Sweaty sunbathe in a bikini."

"You both better stay there," Pena said. "Why don't you go to Las Vegas and get married in the Elvis Presley Wedding Chapel, like normal people?"

"Instead of Cozumel, you mean?"

"I have enough trouble in Cozumel already. I don't need another river of blood scaring the tourists away because the Cuban DGI doesn't like you."

"What makes you think the Cuban DGI doesn't like me?"

"When Paul told me that General Sergei Murov was here with his Ping-Pong players, and General Jesus Manuel Cosada was here with a dozen of his Ping-Pong players—"

"Who?"

"I can hear your *abuela* saying, 'Carlos, you have to learn not to interrupt your betters when they're talking, otherwise people won't like you.'"

"My *abuela* was talking about adults, Juan Carlos, and if you recall, I'm three weeks older than you are."

"As I was saying, when I heard General Jesus Manuel Cosada, who became DGI after Raúl moved up to be president when ol' Fidel retired from public life, was here, the really wild thought that it might be connected with you just sort of popped into my mind.

"Then, when Paul told me he'd seen several DGI heavyweights in addition to the general, and happened to mention you were planning to tie the knot here, things that were happening began to make sense."

"What sort of things were happening?"

"Well, the DGI guys immediately began finding employment at the Cruise Ship Terminal and several of the hotels, including the Grand Cozumel Beach and Golf Resort, which seemed a little odd."

"The Grand Cozumel hired some of them?"

"The Grand Cozumel hired seven Cubans and the Terminal six."

"That's surprising."

"Why?"

"I don't know who runs the Terminal for Aleksandr Pevsner, but Sweaty told me that the guy who runs the Grand Cozumel learned the hotel trade running the SVR dachas in Sochi."

"The what, where?"

"Sochi, on the Black Sea, is sort of the Mexican Cozumel. I don't know about the czars, but important Russians from Stalin down—"

"It goes back to the later czars," Sweaty said. Charley looked at her and saw she had her CaseyBerry to her ear.

Where the hell did she have that phone? There's not enough material in her bikini to safely blow her nose!

"Starting in the 1860s," Sweaty went on, "they started developing it as a place for sanatoriums; tuberculosis was a big problem then."

"Hey, Red, how are you?" Juan Carlos inquired.

"I'm well and my Carlito's right, Juan Carlos," Sweaty said. "Pietr Urbanovsky, the general manager of the Grand Cozumel, is ex-SVR. He's going to be—or should be—very careful about who he hires."

"Let me tell you how I think that could have happened, Red," Juan Carlos said. "The Cubans are tight with the drug cartels. So some cartel people went to the barrio where, for example, the people who pick up trash on the beach, polish the marble in the lobby, work in the laundry, people like that, live. They said, 'Hey, Jose. You've been working too hard. Take a vacation. Go to your village. Stay there for a month. Here's three months' pay and a bus ticket.' Then if Jose or Pedro says, 'Thank you very much, but I like my job and don't want to risk losing it by not showing up for work,' Pasquale, the cartel guy, says, 'Pedro, you either accept our generosity, or we'll cut your head off and hang it from a bridge over the highway. And then we'll go to your village and rape your wife, mother, and any daughters you happen to have.' Then when Pedro and Jose and everybody else doesn't show up for work, no problem for your pal . . . What did you say his name was?"

"Pietr Urbanovsky," Sweaty furnished.

"Your pal Pietr had no trouble filling his vacancies because the Cubans—who probably said they were Mexican—were looking for employment. Getting the picture, Red?"

"I don't think you're getting the picture, Pancho Villa," Sweaty said sweetly. "My Carlito told you Pietr is not stupid."

"I didn't say he was, Red. I didn't mean to imply that he was taken in. What I think your pal Pietr will do is watch the Cubans closely as they pick trash off the beach, polish the marble, et cetera—which of course gets those necessary tasks accomplished—while he looks into his new employees and what happened to the ones who didn't show up for work.

"Sooner or later, most likely sooner, he will know all. And then he will get rid of his new employees the way he gets rid of employees foolish enough to think they can take home hams and roasts of beef and things they have stolen from the rooms of Grand Cozumel guests by dropping them into garbage cans."

"How does he do that, Juan Carlos?" Charley asked.

"The rumor going around is that he retrieves the hams and roasts and whatever from the garbage cans and then puts the thieves in them. Then they are loaded aboard one of Señor Pevsner's cruise ships for disposal with the other garbage on the high seas."

"Does the Service Employees International Union know about this?" Charley asked.

"The rumor going around is that the union organizers they sent down here also went for a cruise in garbage cans," Juan Carlos said.

"The reason we called, Charley," Paul Sieno said, "was to ask whether we should just let things take their natural course, or whether you want to tell Señor Urbanovsky not to put the Cubans in garbage cans right away, so we can keep an eye on them."

"Keep them alive," Sweaty answered for him.

"Yeah," Castillo agreed thoughtfully, after a moment.

"And I called, as I said before, to beg you to join yourselves in holy matrimony in the Elvis Presley Wedding Chapel in Vegas," Juan Carlos said. "If you try to get married here, there will be bodies and rivers of blood all over the streets, which will greatly distress the Greater Cozumel Area Chamber of Tourism."

Again, Sweaty answered for Castillo: "We can't get married until this nonsense with President Clendennen is over. But when it is, I intend to be married in the Grand Ballroom of the Grand Cozumel by His Eminence Archbishop Valentin, assisted by Archimandrite Boris. I don't think His Eminence would be willing to conduct the service in the Elvis Presley Wedding Chapel."

"I don't see it as a problem," Charley said. "I don't know how long it will take to dissuade President Clendennen of his notions I should get rid of the Somali pirates *and* seize Drug Cartel International, but it's not going to be anytime soon. Another month or six weeks at a minimum, during which I have no intention of going anywhere near the North American continent."

"I hear and obey, Master," Paul Sieno said.

"Pancho," Sweaty said, "as soon as we get off the line, I'll call my brother and tell him to call Pietr and explain the situation to him."

"Take care, Red," Juan Carlos said, and the green LEDs on their CaseyBerrys stopped glowing.

[SEVEN]
Green Acres Farm
Near Hershey, Pennsylvania
0830 17 June 2007

"Nice breakfast, Frank," FBI Director Mark Schmidt said to DCI Lammelle. "Really nice ham!"

"We do it all here on the farm," Lammelle replied. "Breed the pigs, slaughter them, and cure the hams and bacon in our own smokehouse. We had a Russian—an SVR biological warfare chemist we turned in

Africa—in here a couple of years ago who showed us how to do that. Before him, we used to sell the live pigs to an Amish farmer."

"May I suggest we get started?" General Allan B. Naylor asked, with an unmistakable tone of annoyance in his voice.

As someone once suggested, the best-laid plans of mice and men "gang aft agley," which meant they often don't come to pass. In this case, not everyone who was to participate in what Secretary Cohen was diplomatically calling "the conversation" was able to make it to Green Acres Farm as early as Secretary Cohen had hoped.

The first delayed arrival, that of DCI Lammelle, had been caused by the motion picture star Shawn Ohio, whose portrayal of CIA agent Dirk Eastwood in a series of films had made him the thirty-fourth-highest-paid actor in Hollywood. In his private life Mr. Ohio was somewhat to the left of his screen persona. He was a great admirer of Hugo Chávez, and deeply convinced that Mr. Chávez had been grossly wronged by the CIA.

To bring this outrage to the attention of the American people, Mr. Ohio, wearing a T-shirt, the back of which was emblazoned with the legend GET THE CIA OUT OF VENEZUELA AND GIVE HUGO HIS TUPOLEV BACK!! had covered his hands with Magic Glue and attached himself to the plate-glass doors leading to the foyer of CIA headquarters in Langley, Virginia.

It had taken some time to get Mr. Ohio out of sight of the members of the media—including Mr. C. Harry Whelan of Wolf News—he had brought with him, and into the hands of the Virginia State Police, as it proved to be extremely difficult to separate Magic Glue–covered hands from plate glass. Mr. Ohio, who was really not nearly as stupid as some of his right-wing critics alleged, had learned this technique after he had handcuffed himself to the fence around the

White House on two previous occasions of protest. Then it had taken only seconds to detach him with bolt cutters.

His demonstration this time had caused DCI Lammelle to delay his departure for Pennsylvania by nearly two hours. Lammelle did not feel comfortable in leaving until Mr. Ohio was firmly—and safely—in the hands of the state police, as he feared the CIA security officers might not enthusiastically obey his admonition not to hurt the sonofabitch. If that should happen, Mr. Lammelle knew, Mr. Whelan would bring it to the world's attention on Wolf News, as would the other media members via their respective outlets. The world would love to see and hear the real CIA clubbing a fictional CIA hero into unconsciousness while he was glued to their front door, and the media knew it.

And then Director of National Intelligence Truman Ellsworth had telephoned at nine p.m. to say he was lost somewhere in the vicinity of Intercourse, Pennsylvania, and God only knew when he would be at Green Acres. Secretary Cohen had then decided they would hold off starting the meeting until after breakfast the next morning, when everybody would be there and fresh to deal with the problem.

Gathered around the picnic table set up for breakfast on the veranda of the farmhouse were Attorney General Palmer, Defense Secretary Beiderman, DNI Ellsworth, DCI Lammelle, FBI Director Schmidt, and Generals Naylor and McNab.

Secretary Cohen began the conversation by saying, "General McNab, you have the floor."

"The President arrived at Fort Bragg unannounced," General McNab began simply, "and in a C-37A, not in his 737."

"What's a C-37A?" FBI Director Schmidt asked.

"A Gulfstream," DCI Lammelle answered for him, adding, "Mark, for Christ's sake, if you keep interrupting, we'll be here all day."

Schmidt was unrepentant.

"I want to get the facts straight. This is important business we're undertaking."

"Please continue, General McNab," Secretary Cohen said.

"Yes, ma'am," McNab went on. "With him, the President had . . ."

Five minutes later, McNab concluded with: "As he left the President implied that I might be promoted if the seizure of the airfield by Clendennen's Commandos went smoothly, and that my promotion might be further speeded if I showed more enthusiasm for getting Clendennen's Commandos to wear Clan Clendennen kilts. After the President left, I called Secretary Cohen and reported his visit."

"He's bonkers, absolutely bonkers," Lammelle said.

"You're speaking of the President of the United States, Mr. Lammelle," Secretary Beiderman said.

"Unfortunately," Lammelle said.

"Who, to judge by his sending the Secret Service to the Greenbrier to see if Natalie was really there to play golf, believes there is a plot to remove him from office," the attorney general said.

"Isn't there?" Beiderman challenged.

"Let's talk about seizing the airfield," Truman Ellsworth said, ignoring the question. "First of all, where is it?"

"It's in, or on, a dry lake in the middle of Mexico," Lammelle answered.

"And how difficult would it be to seize, General McNab?"

"I would not accept an order to seize it," McNab replied.

"But if you were?" Ellsworth pursued.

"Ordered to seize it, you mean?"

"Yes."

"I would refuse the order."

"And he would be in his rights to do so," the attorney general said. "It is not unlawful to refuse to obey an unlawful order."

"Splitting legal hairs, as we were both taught to do at our beloved Yale School of Law, Freddie," Ellsworth went on, "that is not precisely the case. Under the War Powers Act—and please correct me if I err—the President can order military action for a period not to exceed thirty days anywhere in the world he feels the need."

"Point well taken, Ellsworth. I clearly remember Professor Hathaway's brilliant—"

"Good ol' Oona," Ellsworth interjected. "A giant in the law!"

". . . lectures on the subject," the attorney general went on. "I believe that would be '*giantess* of the law,' Ellsworth."

"Right you are! I stand corrected!"

"Let me ask a question," FBI Director Schmidt asked.

"Certainly," Ellsworth and Palmer said over one another.

"If the President ordered Secretary Beiderman to seize this airfield, and Beiderman ordered General Naylor to carry it out, and then General Naylor ordered General McNab to conduct the operation, and General McNab refused, then what?"

"In that circumstance, I would resign," Secretary Cohen said.

"With all possible respect, Madam Secretary," Schmidt said, "that question was addressed to Secretary Beiderman and General Naylor. What would you do, General Naylor, if you issued an order and General McNab, in effect, said go piss up a rope? Excuse the language, Madam Secretary."

"If General McNab refused the order—"

"Presumably you think it would be a lawful order?" Ellsworth asked.

"Yes, sir. I believe the President has the authority to issue such an order."

"And if General McNab refused to accept it?"

"Then I would have no alternative but to relieve him of his command and place him under arrest."

"And then what?"

"What do you mean, 'and then what'?"

"What does it sound like, General?"

"Well, charges would be drawn up, and then—"

"I meant to the order to seize the airfield."

"Oh, I see what you mean. Well, sir, on General McNab's relief, command would pass to his deputy—"

"Enough!" Natalie Cohen said softly, but with such great intensity that every head around the table turned to her.

"General McNab is not going to be relieved," she said. "Aside from Frank Lammelle, he's the only one of you who seems to both comprehend the situation and know what he's doing.

"Now, I'm going to go around the table and see if there is at least one thing on which we all agree. The question is, 'Do you believe that the President's mental state poses a genuine threat to the United States?' Just that, and I want a simple 'yes' or 'no,' not a learned, legal hairsplitting. Mr. Attorney General . . ."

Attorney General Palmer met her eyes for a long moment and then said, "Yes."

So, one by one, did everyone around the picnic table.

When the last man, General McNab, had spoken, she nodded

and said, "Thank you. Now in the same manner, I'm going to ask another question and again want a yes or no answer. The second question is, 'Do you have a specific course of action you would take if you were in my position, that is, as secretary of State, to keep the President from proceeding with his plan to seize the airfield, which would be an act of war?' Understand that I am not asking for your opinion about what we should do about the President, just about stopping him from executing his seize-the-airfield plans. And again I'll start with the attorney general. Mr. Palmer?"

When everyone had answered in the negative, she said, "Thank you," again, and added, "I am left with no choice but to take whatever action, or actions, I feel are necessary to keep this situation from getting any further out of control. I will accept full responsibility for so doing. The flip side of that coin is that I am not going to ask permission, either individually or as a result of a vote, for what I will do. If this is unsatisfactory to any of you, I will return to Washington and place my resignation on President Clendennen's desk today. If I hear no objections, I will assume I have your permission to proceed."

Although several of the men around the picnic table seemed on the verge of objecting, none did.

Director of National Intelligence Ellsworth, however, asked, "May I ask what you plan to do, Madam Secretary?"

She chuckled.

"I'm going to do what President Clendennen said he was going to do. Put the problem before someone who thinks out of the box and see what he has to say."

"I don't think I follow you, Madam Secretary," Ellsworth said.

She didn't reply, instead taking her CaseyBerry from her attaché case and punching autodial and the loudspeaker button.

"Yes, ma'am, Madam Secretary," Castillo's voice came over the line. "And how are you?"

"Colonel, I need you here," she said.

"Is she talking to Castillo?" FBI Director Schmidt asked incredulously.

"No, ma'am," Castillo said. "Sorry. The deal I made was I stall You Know Who for as long as it takes, meanwhile staying out of sight, and more importantly out of reach of any claws You Know Who might want to extend toward me."

"Colonel, I realize that I have no authority to order you to do anything. But if I had that authority, I would."

"I knew this call would be a disaster when you called me 'Colonel,'" Castillo said. "What's happened?"

"If you're not coming, there's no point in telling you."

There was a ten-second—which seemed much longer—pause.

"I'm floating down the Rhine. . . ."

"So the CaseyBerry tells me."

"It'll take me three hours, maybe a little more, to get to the airplane. Andrews?"

"Fort Bragg would be better."

"Does General McNab know I'm—"

"We're," a sultry voice injected.

". . . know *we're* coming?"

"General McNab is with me now. So is Frank."

"I knew I shouldn't have answered the damn phone," Castillo said, and the green LEDs on Secretary Cohen's phone died.

"And who was the woman who chimed in?" FBI Director Schmidt asked.

"She's the colonel's fiancée, Mark," Lammelle said. "Stunning redhead. In a previous life, she was an SVR lieutenant colonel."

"You look very thoughtful, General," Cohen said to McNab. "Is there something you want to say?"

"I was thinking, Madam Secretary, that you and Charley's *abuela* are the only people in the world who could get him to come to the States."

"No, I'm sure he would come if you asked," she said.

"Not for me?" Lammelle asked.

"Not for you or anyone else," she said.

She immediately regretted the comment when she saw General Naylor's face, but it was too late to take the words back, or even try to lamely include Naylor.

And I'm supposed to be a diplomat.

IX

[ONE]
Office of the Secretary of State
The Harry S Truman Building
2201 C Street, N.W.
Washington, D.C.
1425 17 June 2007

When her CaseyBerry vibrated and she looked at it and saw that Charley Castillo was calling, Secretary Cohen's first reactions were relief and pleasure.

He's calling to tell me he's on his way to Fort Bragg.

But even as she pushed the TALK button and put the cellular to her ear, she had second, worrisome thoughts.

If there is one absolutely predictable facet of dealing with Lieutenant Colonel Castillo it is that he is absolutely unpredictable.

"Hello, Charley. I gather you got off all right?"

"Goddamn it, Max! Give Sweaty her shoe back!"

"And that Miss Alekseeva and your adorable dog are with you," Secretary Cohen added.

"Technically, that's Mrs. Alekseeva, Madam Secretary. Or the Widow Alekseeva."

"Yes, of course. Where are you, Charley?"

"According to the Garmin GPS monitor on the wall, thirty-five thousand feet over Aberdeen, Scotland, making nearly seven hundred and fifty knots."

"And when do you think you'll be at Fort Bragg?"

"That's what I called to talk to you about, ma'am."

I knew it. I knew it. I knew it.

"What's on your mind, Charley?"

"Well, in the car on the way to Hersfeld, I called General McNab . . ."

I should have known he would do that.

". . . and he told me about You Know Who's Commandos, and the kilts and so on. And he also said that since You Know Who's visit is now known all over Bragg and Pope, my going there is not likely to pass unnoticed. If we land the Gulfstream at Pope, the Air Force band there will be ready to play 'Hail to the Chief' as I come down the door stairs."

Why do I know this is going to get worse?

"So where do you think you should go?"

"Sweaty also picked up on what you said to Frank and the others about you doing what You Know Who wants to do himself."

"What was that, Charley?"

"Getting somebody else who will be thinking out of the box to evaluate the problem."

"And who would that be, Charley?"

"And, no offense, Madam Secretary, but Sweaty also picked up on what you said about you having no authority to order me to do anything."

I am not surprised.

"All of which means what, Charley?"

"I'm not going to Fort Bragg—"

"*We're* not going to Fort Bragg," the Widow Alekseeva's voice came over the connection.

"Sweaty had some thoughts about that, too, Madam Secretary. She said, and I think we have to agree with her, that if you don't know where we'll be, you won't have to lie to You Know Who if he asks where we are."

"So you're not going to tell me where you're going or what you're going to do when you get there?"

"That about sums it up, Madam Secretary. As soon as I have anything, I will of course let you know."

Presuming, of course, that your beloved red-haired beauty thinks that's the thing to do. You're putty in her hands, Charley.

Probably not as much as Mortimer is in mine, but putty nonetheless.

Why couldn't you, Widow Alekseeva, be ugly with stainless steel teeth?

"In that case, there's not much point in further conversation, is there?"

"I suppose not. Wait! Sweaty wants to know if you saw Shawn Ohio glued to the CIA's door. We saw it on *Wolf World Wide News.* Sweaty said it was the funniest thing she's seen since Vladimir Vladimirovich Putin took off his shirt and showed the world his biceps."

"I saw it," the secretary said. "But speaking of Wolf News: May I ask if Mr. Danton is with you?"

"Yes, of course you may, Madam Secretary," Castillo said, and the green LEDs on the secretary's CaseyBerry ceased to glow.

[TWO]

Wolf News World Headquarters
The Wolf News Building
Avenue of the Americas and Forty-third Street
New York City, New York
0001 18 June 2007

It was said, probably accurately, that there were more television monitors in the Wolf News newsroom than there were in the Sony and Sanyo warehouses combined. It was here that Wolf News not only maintained contact with its journalists worldwide but kept its eye on what the competition was up to.

This latter task was normally assigned to the most junior of the newsroom staff, the reason offered being that watching the competition broadened their journalistic horizons. Cynics said it was because somebody had to do it, and better that someone on the payroll who couldn't find his or her buttocks with either or both hands do it than someone who could be put to laboring on more useful tasks.

And so it was that Miss Sarah Ward, who was twenty-two, a year out of Vassar, and the niece of the Wolf News Corporation's senior vice president–real estate, was charged to see what the Continental Broadcasting Corporation was up to at midnight.

Specifically, she was tasked to watch Continental's midnight news telecast, which was called *Hockey Puck with Matthew Christian*.

The show opened, as it always did, with a hockey player taking a healthy swipe at a hockey puck. The camera followed the puck down the ice as the puck went airborne and then struck a goalkeeper right in his mask, which knocked him off his feet and onto his rear end.

A basso profundo voice, while this was going on, solemnly announced, "It's midnight, and time for *Hockey Puck with Matthew Christian*. Let the puck strike where it may!"

The camera then closed in on Mr. Christian, who his detractors said looked like a middle-aged chubby choirboy, sitting behind a desk.

"Good evening," Mr. Christian said. "Welcome to *Hockey Puck*!

"My friends, I confess I don't know what I'm talking about here. You watch, you decide!

"This just in from Sin City, otherwise known as Las Vegas, Nevada."

The camera showed a crowd of journalists watching a Gulfstream V taxi to the tarmac before a hangar.

"Las Vegas is hosting the fifteenth annual award ceremonies of the adult motion picture business," Mr. Christian said. "And the word going around is that Red Ravisher is the leading candidate for the best actress award. That much we know. And here she is arriving in Las Vegas in her private jet."

The camera showed the stair door of the airplane rotating downward as it opened. A huge dog came down the stairs, and then a man started down the steps. The video image went into "freeze-frame mode" and a superimposed flashing arrow pointed to the man.

"Now, and I'm willing to stake my reputation on this," Mr. Christian said. "That is Roscoe J. Danton, the syndicated columnist who is also employed by another, here unnamed, television news organization. One understandably wonders what Mr. Danton is doing on Red Ravisher's private jet, but one also recalls that other networks boast that they will go anywhere and do anything to get a story."

The video image began moving again and the camera followed

the man on the stairs to the ground and then as he went to the crowd of journalists. Then the camera went back to the door of the Gulfstream.

"And here is Red Ravisher," Mr. Christian announced. "One cannot help but note that magnificent head of red hair and . . . other physical attributes . . . that make her, so to speak, the Ethel Barrymore of the adult film industry."

The camera closed in on the redhead's physical attributes, and then went into freeze-frame mode again.

"Now watch this carefully," Mr. Christian said, "for we're about to lose the picture!"

The camera now showed the redhead walking up to a photographer, exchanging a few words with him, and then punching him so hard he fell down. The redhead then kicked him in what sometimes were referred to as a man's "private parts," and then picked him up. Next, Mr. Christian's viewers saw him flying through the air toward the camera.

And then the picture was lost.

Miss Sarah Ward said, "Oh, my!"

And then she saved a digital file of the story to a portable hard drive and took it across the room to the desk of the senior producer.

"What have you got, honey?" he asked.

"Red Ravisher, the porn star, and Roscoe J. Danton," Miss Ward said. "Miss Ravisher threw a photographer at Mr. Danton."

[THREE]
The Niccolò Machiavelli Penthouse
The Venetian Hotel, Resort & Casino
Las Vegas, Nevada
0830 18 June 2007

When the elevator door opened and Hotelier, Annapolis, and Radio & TV Stations walked off onto the upper-foyer level of the duplex penthouse suite, Max, who had been sampling the steak and eggs of the breakfast buffet on the lower floor, took the stairs of the curved staircase three at a time, put his paws on Radio & TV Stations' shoulders—standing on his hind paws, Max was taller than Radio & TV Stations—and affectionately licked his face.

Radio & TV Stations didn't look very happy about it, but Charley Castillo was delighted.

If that's any indication, coming here was one of my very few good ideas. Max is an excellent judge of character.

Hotelier and Annapolis, and finally Radio & TV Stations and Max, came down the stairs.

"Thanks for meeting with us on such short notice," Charley said, as he offered his hand to Annapolis.

"You said it was important, Colonel," Annapolis said.

Castillo turned to Hotelier.

"Good to see you," he said. "And before I forget it, make sure I get the bill for all this." He gestured around the suite, which he had been reliably informed was available only to those who could afford fifteen thousand dollars a night or who had been unlucky enough to lose five hundred thousand or more playing blackjack or some other innocent game of chance.

"I told you, Colonel, your money's no good in Las Vegas," Hotelier said.

"How about the CIA's money?" Castillo asked. "I am about the Commander in Chief's business, and on the CIA's dime."

"If that's the case, I'll have the fellow who owns this place get me a bill, and forward it to you."

"Thanks."

"How'd things go at the airport?" Radio & TV Stations asked. "Any problems? The cars I sent were waiting for you when you got there?"

"Your cars and . . . some other cars," Castillo said, and visibly fought laughter.

"What other cars?"

"You had better be very careful, my darling, when you answer that question," the Widow Alekseeva said.

"Something happen at the airport?"

"Yes, you could say that, I suppose," Castillo said.

"What?" Radio & TV Stations asked.

"You have been warned, my darling," Sweaty said menacingly.

"Sweetheart, I have to tell them. I'll be as discreet as I can."

"You had better be," she said, "or the problems I will cause you will make the problems your demented President is causing you seem less than insignificant."

"Our demented President is causing you more problems, Charley?" Hotelier asked.

"Yes, he is. That's why we're here."

"What happened at the airport?"

"As well as I have been able to put this all together," Charley said, "Las Vegas is hosting some sort of award ceremonies dealing with the adult motion picture business."

"The fifteenth annual Hard-On Awards," Hotelier said. "At the Streets of San Francisco Hotel, Resort and Casino."

"What do they call them?" the Widow Alekseeva asked.

"The Hard-On Awards, Svetlana," Hotelier said. "You know, like the Oscars? The winners get golden—or at least gold-plated—little statues, called Hard-Ons."

"What's a hard-on?" the Widow Alekseeva asked.

"Moving right along," Castillo said quickly. "Apparently one of the contenders for the . . . top award . . . is a lady professionally known as 'Red Ravisher.'"

"Yeah, she won last year, too," Hotelier said. "I think she's got five, maybe six, Hard-Ons total."

"I asked what a hard-on is," the Widow Alekseeva pursued.

Charley went on: ". . . and the, what do you call those photographers who chase celebrities around?"

"Paparazzi," Annapolis furnished.

"Right. *Paparazzi.* Well, the paparazzi apparently heard Miss Red Ravisher was flying into Vegas in her personal Gulfstream . . ."

"I hear there's almost no limit to how much money those people with Hard-Ons can make," Radio & TV Stations said.

". . . so when we landed and taxied to the Casey hangars in our Gulfstream," Castillo went on, "the paparazzi apparently decided that it was Miss Red Ravisher, and that she was trying to escape their attentions."

"Some of the really big Hard-On stars are like that," Hotelier said. "They forget their humble beginnings."

"In any event, when we got to the Casey hangars on the far side of the field, all we knew when we looked out the window was that there were three lines of limousines, and maybe fifty paparazzi waiting for us."

"Three lines of limousines?" Annapolis asked.

"I didn't know Hotelier was going to send limos," Aloysius Casey, Ph.D., said. "So I sent five of ours. Then there was Hotelier's line, and then the line that the dirty movie awards people sent."

"They were spectacular," Castillo said. "All white, and with lines of flashing lights around the doors and windows."

"They call that 'the Bride's Carriage Model,'" Hotelier explained. "The Elvis Presley Wedding Chapel and Casino Incorporated has a fleet of them. They charge fifty dollars extra for turning on the flashing lights around the windows."

"I don't want to hear anything about the Elvis Presley Wedding Chapel, thank you very much," the Widow Alekseeva said. "I've gone through enough tonight."

"Aloysius," Hotelier said, "the adult film industry people don't like the term 'dirty movies.' They would prefer for you to call them 'adult films.'"

"You ever heard that 'once a Green Beret, always a Green Beret'?" Dr. Casey asked.

"What's that got to do with anything?"

"Well, I'm a Green Beret and I know a dirty movie when I see one. An adult movie is one like that *Anna Karen*—whatever, where the Russian broad jumps under a train at the end. That adult movie made me cry."

"I cried, too, Aloysius," the Widow Alekseeva said. "That's very sweet of you to admit it. My Carlito said she was a damned fool."

"Don't mention it, Sweaty," Dr. Casey said.

"Well, when we saw all this activity," Charley went on, "and knew it couldn't possibly be for us, I sent Roscoe J. Danton down the stairs to find out what was going on. One journalist to other journalists, so to speak. Then Sweaty—"

"I'll take it from here, my darling, if you don't mind," the Widow Alekseeva interrupted. "I thought perhaps I would have a chance to see a movie star, maybe Antonio Bandana, or Clint Eastwood, so I followed Roscoe out the door. Actually, Roscoe and I followed Max out the door. Max always gets out first to attend to his calls of nature.

"I didn't get halfway down the stairs when this despicable little pervert started aiming his camera at me and screaming vulgar things. I'm sure he was French; they always have their minds in the gutter."

"I have to ask this, Mrs. Alekseeva," Annapolis said. "What exactly did he scream at you?"

The Widow Alekseeva blushed.

"Go on, Sweaty, you started the story, now you have to finish it," Charley said.

She looked at him for a moment, and then said, "If you insist. What this miserable French pervert screamed at me—"

"In the belief, of course, that Sweaty was Miss Red Ravisher," Castillo injected.

". . . was 'Show us your teats, Red!'" the Widow Alekseeva furnished.

"How awful for you," Annapolis said. "May I ask what happened then?"

"I asked him what he had said, and he repeated it, adding, 'I don't have all night, and you came here prepared to show the whole world your' . . . you know whats . . . 'so out with your boobs, baby!'"

"And then what happened?"

"I demonstrated with him."

"Sweetheart, I think you mean 'remonstrated,'" Charley said.

"What she did," Dr. Casey furnished, "was coldcock this clown with a one-two jab, and then when he went down, she kicked him in the . . . you can guess, and then she picked him up and threw him into the other bums, taking out four of them. Actually, three of them and Roscoe, who was standing there with them."

"And then Max got into the act," Castillo said. "Max loves Sweaty, and it is not wise to threaten anyone a Bouvier des Flandres is fond of."

"And then my Carlito came to my defense," the Widow Alekseeva said. "My knight in shining armor."

"And then Lester and Peg-Leg came to help," Castillo said. "Peg-Leg hopped around on his good leg and used his titanium one like a club."

"By the time the cops stopped it—" Dr. Casey said.

"And you, too, Aloysius," the Widow Alekseeva said. "You were just as quick to rush to my side as the others were."

". . . there were a lot fewer paparazzi standing up than there were before," Dr. Casey concluded.

"Aloysius," Annapolis asked, "you said the police stopped it. Are there going to be any problems in that area, with the law?"

"I don't think so," Dr. Casey replied. "Terence McGonagall?"

"Captain Terry McGonagall, chief of the Las Vegas Police Department's Celebrity Affairs Bureau?"

"Yeah. Well, when we got to the jail, Terry was there to see who got out of the paddy wagon."

"I don't think you're supposed to use the term 'paddy wagon,'

Aloysius," Annapolis said. "It's considered offensive to those of Irish heritage."

"I'm a Boston Irishman, Swab Jockey," Dr. Casey replied, somewhat impatiently. "And I've been in paddy wagons often enough to know a paddy wagon when I'm in one. As I was saying, when we got out of the police prisoner transport vehicle, Terry was there and he talked to the cops who had busted us, and eventually they let us go."

"And why did they do that?"

"Well, Terry—he and I are fellow Grand Exalted Oracles in the Knights of Columbus—pointed out that if they charged Sweaty and us with assault and battery and destruction of property, such as their movie cameras, I could charge them with criminal trespass. Charley's airplane was parked on my property. And so far as the camera guy Sweaty took out with a right cross, Terry asked him what judge was going to believe a good-looking redheaded lady weighing maybe a hundred and twenty pounds soaking wet had broken the nose of a six-foot-five two-hundred-and-fifty-pound male. So it turned out to be a wash."

"All's well that ends well, as they say," Annapolis said.

"That's what I just said," Dr. Casey said.

"So tell me, Colonel," Annapolis said. "What brings you to Las Vegas? How may we be of assistance to the Merry Outlaws?"

"Well, we are having a small problem with the Commander in Chief," Castillo said.

"Tell us about it."

Castillo did.

"Interesting," Annapolis said. "Why don't you start by telling us the major problem vis-à-vis the Somalia pirates?"

"Insurance companies," Castillo said.

"Insurance companies?" Annapolis parroted incredulously. "I happen to own a couple of them, and I find that hard to understand."

"I just spent a couple days floating down the Rhine talking to a group of journalists very familiar with the situation. That's what they told me."

"No offense, Colonel," Annapolis said, "but two things occur to me. One, we all know how far we can trust journalists, and two, why should they confide in you?"

"My Carlito owns the newspaper chain they work for," Sweaty said, "and then I dropped into the conversation that I was formerly associated with the SVR."

"I'm sure they were telling us the truth," Castillo said.

"Under those circumstances, I'm sure they were," Annapolis said. "So, what exactly did they have to say?"

"The way I understand the situation," Castillo replied, "is that the shipowners take out insurance on their vessels operating in those waters, on the ships themselves, and the cargoes."

"As well they should," Annapolis said, more than a little piously. "Insurance is the sturdy fence protecting industry from the hazards of a very dangerous world."

"I don't know what a supertanker loaded to the gills with crude oil is worth, but a bundle, since oil has been averaging about one hundred dollars a barrel. And then there's the replacement cost of the ship itself, another—"

"I saw some figures," Annapolis said. "For the sake of this discussion, why not work with fifty million?"

"The figure I got was close to one hundred million," Charley said. "Maybe you're thinking of what insurance companies are willing to pay out on a hundred mil policy."

"Far be it from me to argue," Annapolis said, ignoring the shot. "Work with one hundred million dollars."

"So," Castillo then said, "the shipowners take out insurance for the ship and her cargo. They don't really care what the insurance costs, because they just add that cost to what they charge for moving the oil."

"Standard business practice," Annapolis said.

"So it adds about a nickel to a gallon of gas at the pump," Charley said. "So what?"

"So what indeed. The owners are protected. The oil flows. Or is transported. In any event, the gasoline is there at the pump when you fill up."

"And then the Somali pirates seize the tanker. My sources told me, incidentally, that the typical pirate is illiterate and eighteen years old.

"Then, I was told, the insurance companies send an adjuster to Somalia, where he establishes contact with these eighteen-year-old illiterate pirates and negotiates with them. For example, the pirates start out asking for five million dollars for the tanker. The adjuster tries—and usually succeeds—in negotiating them down to two million. Or even less, if he throws in a Mercedes convertible and a Sony DVD player and a dozen triple-X adult DVDs starring the Red Ravisher."

"Watch it, my darling," the Widow Alekseeva hissed warningly.

"That's what adjusters are paid to do, Colonel," Annapolis said.

"And the insurance company, with a smile, hands over a briefcase full of money—cashier's checks have yet to become known in Somalia—to the pirates, and a smaller check to the ship's owner for the additional expenses incurred while the ship has been in the hands of the pirates. Say for half a million."

"That's the proud tradition of the insurance industry," Annapolis said, "handing the check over with a smile."

"I understand," Castillo said, "that they are smiling from ear to ear and meaning it when they finally write the check."

"Well, I'm not sure how much they mean it," Annapolis said. "I mean, the smile is sort of public relations."

"Here, it's a smile of intense personal pleasure," Castillo said.

"What's your point, Charley?" Radio & TV Stations asked.

"Take a wild guess, Chopper Jockey, what the premium is to insure a one-hundred-million-dollar supertanker loaded with two million barrels of oil at a hundred dollars a barrel."

"I can't do numbers that big in my head," Radio & TV Stations admitted.

"Based on my experience in the insurance industry, I would estimate twenty-five million," Annapolis said pontifically.

"Well, you're the expert, you should know. So twenty-five million it is. Now, take two million, plus the price of a Mercedes convertible, a dozen dirty movies, and a Sony DVD player from that twenty-five million and what would you say is left?"

"Oh, those goddamn Swedes," Annapolis said after a moment, his voice heavy with admiration. "They're worse than even the goddamn Dutchmen and the goddamn Swiss! Why didn't I think of this?"

"What have the goddamn Swedes, Dutchmen, and Swiss got to do with anything?" Hotelier asked.

"Ninety-point-seven percent of maritime insurance like this is underwritten by those clever sonsofbitches," Annapolis said.

"And everybody is happy," Castillo said. "The pirates, they have their ransom and the Mercedes and the dirty movies; the shipowners, who have their tanker back, and, of course, the smiling maritime insurance companies of whatever nationality who have a profit of, say, twenty-two million."

"Pure genius!" Annapolis said. "My hat's off to them."

"Is there no way to stop the piracy, Charley?" Radio & TV Stations asked.

"President Clendennen could send Delta Force teams into Somalia with orders to shoot every illiterate eighteen-year-old," Castillo said. "That'd stop it."

"Do you think he'd do that, Colonel?" Annapolis said, worry evident in his tone.

"I think he might order it," Castillo said. "But I don't think Delta Force would go. I don't know anyone in Delta who likes shooting illiterate eighteen-year-olds. Unless they shoot first."

"If he did and they did," Radio & TV Stations said, "he'd have a hell of a public relations problem with his legacy."

"With his what?" the Widow Alekseeva inquired.

"Let's move to the airfield, Drug Cartel International," Annapolis said. "How about that, Charley? How difficult would that be to seize?"

"Not hard at all," Castillo said. "The only problem would be keeping all the Delta Force guys who wanted to go off the C-130."

"Delta Force would want to go, is that what you're saying?" Radio & TV Stations asked.

"That's what I'm saying. They're still smarting after the drug cartel guys whacked Danny Salazar. They'd all love to go to Mexico and whack as many drug guys as they could find."

"You mean as vigilantes?" Radio & TV Stations asked.

"No. If Clendennen sends them down there, the people they would whack would be whacked as they carry out their official duties. They would have a license to whack, in other words." He paused, chuckled, and added, "I think most of them would even wear the kilts of Clan Clendennen if that's what they had to do."

"And Clendennen doesn't know this? Or at least suspect it?" Radio & TV Stations asked.

"I don't think he would care if he did."

"That's surprising. I would have thought—he's big in the ego department—that he'd really be concerned with his legacy."

"There's that word again," the Widow Alekseeva said. "What are you talking about?"

"You used the word, Chopper Jockey, you explain it to the lady," Charley said, chuckling.

"The way that works, Mrs. Alekseeva—"

"My Carlito likes you," she interrupted. "You may call me Sweaty."

"The way that works, *Sweaty*," Radio & TV Stations said, "is that the minute someone gets elected President—and I mean someone of whatever political party and sexual preference—he starts thinking of how he'll be remembered twenty, fifty, a hundred years from now. He starts thinking of his legacy."

"I don't think I understand," Sweaty admitted.

"Let me have another shot at it. I guess it started with Roosevelt, Franklin D. What they do is have a presidential library. Roosevelt's was built in Hyde Park, New York, where he's buried. Ronald Reagan's is in California. So is the Richard Nixon library. And they're buried at their libraries."

"They're buried in their libraries?" the Widow Alekseeva asked incredulously.

"Usually, my darling, in sort of a garden just outside their libraries," Charley qualified.

"Even Jimmy Carter has a presidential library," Radio & TV Stations said. "With, I suppose, a lot of empty shelves."

Charley and Hotelier chuckled.

"That's unkind," Annapolis said.

"You're only saying that because you both went to that school for sailors," Castillo said. "You'll have to admit that Carter's library has to have a lot of empty shelves."

"The Harry S Truman Library is in Missouri," Radio & TV Stations said. "One of the better libraries, really."

"They all have libraries?" the Widow Alekseeva asked. "What's that about?"

"Their legacies, Sweaty," Radio & TV Stations explained. "They appoint some guy to run their libraries, and he spends his time filling them with books and newspaper stories and other material proving their guy was the best President since George Washington."

"And collecting and then burning books and newspaper stories and other material proving their guy was the worst President since Millard G. Fillmore," Charley contributed.

This time all of them chuckled.

"Either that," Annapolis chimed in, "or they send the non-flattering stuff to the Library of Congress."

"Where it will be misfiled," Radio & TV Stations said.

"And absolutely will never again be read by anyone," Charley concluded for him.

All the men were now chuckling, visibly pleased with their own humor.

"Before you all grow hysterical and incoherent," the Widow Alekseeva said, "tell me where President Clendennen has his legacy library."

"He doesn't have one yet," Charley said. "But he'll get around to preserving his legacy, Sweaty, sooner or later. His ego—and Belinda-Sue's ego—will demand it."

"Not later, my darling," the Widow Alekseeva said. "Sooner. Now."

"Excuse me?"

"Now. Right now," she said.

"I don't understand," Charley confessed.

"I'm not surprised. Tell me, my darling, what do you think just might take President Clendennen's mind off putting your beloved Delta Force into Clan Clendennen kilts?"

There was silence.

All the men shrugged.

"I will be damned," Radio & TV Stations said finally.

"She's a genius!" Hotelier said.

"Supervising the design and construction of the Clendennen presidential library," Aloysius Casey said.

"The Joshua Ezekiel and Belinda-Sue Clendennen Presidential Library and Last Resting Place," Annapolis corrected him.

"Sweaty, I love you," Charley said.

"I figure we start off with initial anonymous contributions of ten million dollars," Casey said.

"Where are you going to get ten million dollars?" Annapolis said.

"Well, I'll throw in a million," Casey said. "It's worth that much to me to keep Delta Force from having to wear skirts. The rest we get a million a pop from other public-minded citizens like an insurance tycoon I know."

"I'm in," Radio & TV Stations said.

"Me, too," Hotelier said.

"The other people in Las Vegas will, I'm sure, be willing to contribute to such a noble cause," Annapolis said. "But I have to ask, isn't the President going to be suspicious that this suddenly popped up? You said he was paranoid, that he even suspected Secretary Cohen wasn't really playing golf when she went to the Greenbrier."

Castillo took out his CaseyBerry and punched the ON button. When the green LEDs glowed, he punched the loudspeaker and one of the autodial buttons.

"Charley, thank God!" Secretary Cohen's voice bounced back from space.

"Good morning, Madam Secretary."

"I've been trying to get you for hours!"

"Sorry. My CaseyBerry was turned off. I just turned it on a moment ago."

"Why did you turn it off?"

"Truth to tell, I didn't. I guess one of the jailers turned it off when they took my personal property from me."

"*Jailers?* What jailers?"

"The ones at the Clark County Detention Center."

"Clark County, *Nevada*?"

"Yes, ma'am."

"So you are in Las Vegas with Roscoe J. Danton?"

"Who told you I was?"

"What were you doing in the Las Vegas jail?"

"It was a misunderstanding. We were released two hours ago." He paused and then asked, "Who told you I was out here?"

"President Clendennen told me. The First Lady told the President and he told me."

"How did she find out?"

"Does it matter?"

"I'm a little curious, that's all."

"The First Lady was watching television with the First Mother-in-Law, watching *Hockey Puck with Matthew Christian*, and there was Roscoe in a brawl with a porn queen."

"Actually, it wasn't a porn queen in that brawl. It was my fiancée, Mrs. Alekseeva, not Red Ravisher."

"And it wasn't a brawl," the Widow Alekseeva objected. "My Carlito and the others were defending my honor."

"Excuse me?"

"What would you do, Madam Secretary," the Widow Alekseeva demanded, "if some pimply-faced French pervert pointed his television camera at you and demanded that you show him your . . . you-know-whats? Wouldn't you expect Mr. Cohen to defend your honor?"

The secretary of State considered the question for a long moment, and then, in the finest traditions of diplomacy, decided a reply could be put off until there was more time for consideration of the question and all its ramifications.

"Let me put a question to you," she said instead. "The last time I spoke with the President, just a few moments ago, in a conference call in which DCI Lammelle, Generals Naylor and McNab, and DNI Ellsworth participated, the President had some interesting things to say. I recorded the conversation. Listen to it, please, Charley, and then tell me what you think I should do."

"Yes, ma'am."

President Clendennen's voice came over the loudspeaker:

"I told you all last night, after Belinda-Sue told me she and the First Mother-in-Law saw Roscoe J. Danton on *Hockey Puck* cavorting with a porn queen in Las Vegas, and I'm telling you for the last time now. Danton is supposed to be with Castillo and Castillo is supposed to be in Hungary getting ready to go to Somalia. I want to know where they are and what they're doing and I want to know now. Unless I get a satisfactory answer within the hour, I shall have to presume what I have suspected all along, that there is a coup to drive me from office under way, and I will take appropriate action. By that I mean I will have you all arrested pending trial for high treason."

Castillo didn't say anything.

"Well, Charley?" Secretary Cohen asked finally.

"He does sound a little annoyed, doesn't he? Not to mention paranoid?"

"He's not kidding, Charley," Cohen said. "There are four Secret Service agents in my outer office waiting for the order to arrest me."

"Don't worry, Charley," another female voice bounced back from space. "Nobody's going to arrest the secretary on my watch."

"Hey, Brünnhilde," Castillo replied. "How goes it? We could have used you here last night."

"Why am I not surprised that you two are pals?" Secretary Cohen mused aloud.

"You didn't need me," Charlene Stevens replied. "Whoever that redhead was, she knows what she's doing. I don't think I could have thrown that clown so far myself."

"She's my fiancée, Charlene. Her name is Sweaty."

"Actually, since I met my Carlito I've gotten a little out of shape," the Widow Alekseeva said. "In my prime, I could have thrown that French pervert a lot farther."

"Frank said you were a real looker," Charlene said. "But he says that about everything in a skirt. I can't wait to meet you."

"You'll have to come to our wedding," Sweaty said.

"When and where?"

"There are four Secret Service agents in my outer office," Secretary Cohen repeated. "What do I do about them?"

"Unless you've got a better idea, Charley," Charlene said, "what I'm going to do is pepper-spray them, then drag them into the ladies' room, strip them down to their undershorts, and then handcuff them to that automatic flush sensor thing on the toilets. That should hold them until Frank can get You Know Who into a straitjacket and over to the Washington Psychiatric Institute."

"Oh, my God!" Secretary Cohen moaned.

"That'd work, Charlene," Charley said, "but before you do that, let's see if the Joshua Ezekiel and Belinda-Sue Clendennen Presidential Library and Last Resting Place doesn't take the Commander in Chief's mind off throwing the secretary of State into the slam."

"What?" Charlene asked, obviously confused.

"Now what the hell are you talking about, Charley?" Secretary Cohen asked.

Her use of the word "hell" was the third time in two years that she had used a term that could possibly be interpreted to be profane, vulgar, or indecent.

"Sweaty came up with this," Charley said. "Everyone agrees it's brilliant."

And then he explained the Joshua Ezekiel and Belinda-Sue Clendennen Presidential Library and Last Resting Place to her.

"That's what you were really doing at the Greenbrier, Madam Secretary, meeting with the public-spirited citizens who are going to fund the library. And what Roscoe was doing here was getting the story for his millions of readers and of course Wolf News."

"And that's why your fiancée threw the French gentleman at him, right? President Clendennen isn't going to believe this, Charley."

"He will when Dr. Aloysius Casey shows him the cashier's check for ten million dollars."

Dr. Casey said, "I'll throw in a million, two million if I have to, but I'm not going anywhere near that craz—the President. No way, Charley."

"You have been running at the mouth, Aloysius, about once a Green Beret, always a Green Beret," Castillo said. "Now it's time to put up. This Green Beanie needs your help."

"Well, if you put it that way," Dr. Casey said reluctantly. "I guess I do hear the bugler sounding 'Boots and Saddles.'"

"Into the valley of madness, so to speak," Annapolis said, chuckling, "rides the Merry Irish Outlaw."

"One more word out of you, Admiral, and you'll be on Aloysius's Gulfstream with him," Castillo said.

"My lips are sealed," Annapolis said.

"And where do you plan to be, Charley," Secretary Cohen asked, "when all this is going on?"

"I haven't quite decided that yet—"

"Cozumel," the Widow Alekseeva furnished.

"Suffice it to say, a considerable distance from our nation's capital and the Commander in Chief."

"Arranging the wedding details," the Widow Alekseeva concluded. "You're invited, too, of course, Madam Secretary. You and your husband, even if you're not sure he'd defend your honor if some French pervert shouted at you to show him—"

"If You Know Who is really curious, Madam Secretary," Castillo interrupted, "tell him that I'm somewhere in the Western Hemisphere training SEALs to defend our merchant ships from the Barbary—excuse me, *Somalian* pirates."

"What SEALs?"

"The ones I'm going to tell General Naylor you said it's all right to send to me in Mexico. I think you'd have to agree that hearing I'm training SEALs would please You Know Who more than hearing I'm going to Mexico to get married. I'm going to call General Naylor just as soon as we get off our CaseyBerrys."

"You're insane. This whole thing is insane," Secretary Cohen said. "I refuse to have anything to do with it."

"Yes, ma'am," Castillo said. "In that event, I'm all ears to hear your solution to the problem."

There was a long, long pause, finally broken by Secretary Cohen.

"How long do you think it will take for Dr. Casey to come to Washington?" she asked.

"Flight time in his Gulfstream, plus however long it takes for him to go by the bank to pick up the check and get to the airport."

"Please have him call me when he's an hour out of Reagan National."

"Yes, ma'am."

The green LEDs on the CaseyBerrys faded after the secretary of State broke the connection.

"May I ask, Colonel, how you plan to use the SEALs?" Annapolis asked.

"Of course you may," Castillo replied. "I fully understand why a former naval person such as yourself would be curious."

This was followed by sixty seconds of silence, following which Annapolis asked, "Well, are you going to tell me?"

"Frankly, I'm still considering my options," Castillo admitted.

"In other words, you don't know."

"Don't be cruel, Admiral. You know that in time I'll think of something."

"The *Czarina of the Gulf*," the Widow Alekseeva said.

"Isn't it amazing how great minds march down similar paths?" Castillo asked. "I was just thinking of her."

"Our marriage will be much happier, my darling," the Widow Alekseeva said, "if you remember I always know when you're lying to me."

"Female intuition?"

"Actually, I think it's more a course I took—Advanced Interrogation Techniques 204/2—at the SVR Staff College."

"Who the hell is the Czarina of the Gulf?" Annapolis inquired.

"Not a 'who,' Admiral. A 'she.' The *Czarina of the Gulf* is the flagship of the Imperial Cruise Lines, Incorporated."

"My darling," the Widow Alekseeva interrupted, "get it right. That's the Imperial Cruise Lines *and Floating Casinos*, Incorporated."

"And a great operation that is," Hotelier said admiringly. "They pack more people per square foot onto their vessels than any other cruise ship line and their food cost per passenger is the lowest in the industry. And from what I hear, their take from their casinos is just as good as mine, maybe a little better."

"My cousin Aleksandr tells me the way he does that is to give his passengers all the free vodka they can drink," the Widow Alekseeva explained. "Starting with a shot in their breakfast orange juice. That way they're not as hungry or as particular when the food is served, and they tend to take greater chances at the crap tables."

"Whatever he's doing, Sweaty, he's doing it right," Hotelier said.

"Which vessel has been taken temporarily out of service so she may be used to accommodate the guests at our wedding," Castillo went on. "Which frees her for use in the 'C. G. Castillo Pirated Ship Recovery Training Program.'"

"How does that involve the SEALs?" Annapolis asked.

"What we're going to do is have a couple of Delta Force A Teams simulate seizing the *Czarina of the Gulf*, and then the SEALs will try to take it back. All of this, of course, will be captured on motion cameras, so that we can send the video to President Clendennen to show him how hard we're working."

"How are you going to keep the SEALs and the Delta Force people from killing each other?" Radio & TV Stations asked.

"I'm still working on that," Castillo replied. "The first thing that pops into my mind is taking their knives and other lethal weapons away from them and giving them paintball guns."

[FOUR]
The Oval Office
The White House
1600 Pennsylvania Avenue, N.W.
Washington, D.C.
1645 18 June 2007

"I thought I made it perfectly clear, Madam Secretary," the President said, not at all pleasantly, "that I wanted to see Colonel Castillo and Roscoe J. Danton so they can explain to me what they were doing with the porn queen in Las Vegas."

"You certainly made that perfectly clear, Mr. President," Robin Hoboken said. "Didn't you think he made that perfectly clear, Supervisory Special Agent Mulligan?"

"It was perfectly clear to me," Mulligan said.

"And this fat Irishman doesn't look like either of them," the President said.

"Mr. President," Secretary Cohen said, "this is Dr. Aloysius Casey."

"If he's a doctor, where's his white coat and that thing that goes in his ears that every doctor I've ever seen has hanging around his neck?"

"Good question, Mr. President," Robin Hoboken said. "How can he possibly be a doctor without that thing that goes in his ears?"

"I'm not a medical doctor, Mr. President," Aloysius said.

"Then why did she say you were?"

"What I am, Mr. President," Aloysius announced, "is temporary chairman of the Citizens Committee to Build the Joshua Ezekiel and Belinda-Sue Clendennen Presidential Library and Last Resting Place."

"Watch it, Mr. President," Mulligan said. "That sounds pretty fishy to me."

"And I have with me a cashier's check in the amount of ten million dollars to get things rolling," Aloysius said.

He handed the check to the President.

"That's hard to believe," Robin Hoboken said.

The President examined the check and then said, "Shut up, Hackensack, I want to hear what ideas Dr. Casey has for my library and last resting place."

[FIVE]

1500, 1600, 1700 18 June 2007

The screens of television sets tuned to Wolf News were, accompanied by a trumpet blast, suddenly filled with the Arabic numbers 3, 4, and 5 swirling around the globe like satellites.

"Hello there, again," the voice of Andy McClarren boomed, as his image appeared in a corner of the screen. "This is Andy McClarren, and it's five o'clock in New York."

"And this is C. Harry Whelan," Mr. Whelan intoned, "and it's four o'clock in Chicago."

His image, standing on a Chicago street, came onto the screen.

"And this is Bridget O'Shaugnessy," Miss O'Shaugnessy proclaimed, "and it's three o'clock in Sin City."

Her image, showing her sitting with a good deal of shapely thigh showing on the fender of a shiny black Bentley, came onto the screen. The Bentley was parked on the street outside the Elvis Presley Wedding Chapel and Casino, Incorporated.

"And it's time for *Three, Four, and Five,*" Mr. McClarren announced. "The big story today is the fifty-million-dollar defamation of character suit filed against Continental Broadcasting and Matthew Christian by adult film star Red Ravisher for this sequence on *Hockey Puck*. Roll the tape!"

Mr. Christian's show of very early that morning was replayed for the edification of Wolf News viewers worldwide.

"Now, what's wrong with that?" Andy asked. "Can you tell us, Bridget? Over to you in Sin City!"

"Why don't I let Miss Ravisher herself explain that to you, Andy?"

Miss O'Shaugnessy replied. "She's right here with me. Welcome to *Three, Four, and Five*, Miss Ravisher."

Miss Ravisher appeared wearing a dress the side slits of which exposed even more thigh than Miss O'Shaugnessy was displaying.

"Thank you for having me."

"And exactly what is it, Miss Ravisher, about that video recording showing you punching the paparazzo and then throwing him at Wolf News's distinguished correspondent Roscoe J. Danton that you find offensive? That you think defames your character?"

"There are those kind enough to refer to me as the Ethel Barrymore of the adult film industry. I have been honored with five Hard-Ons, plus the Lifelong Hard-On Achievement Award. I'm proud of that."

"Perhaps you should have thought of that before you punched that paparazzo gentleman and threw him at Mr. Danton. You should have known that might, as indeed it happened, see you arrested and taken to jail."

"That wasn't me, you stupid [*BLEEEEP*]ing broad! I never met Mr. Danton, and I never threw anybody at him."

"That wasn't you?"

"You're [*BLEEP BLEEP*]ed right it wasn't. I wasn't anywhere near the [*BLEEP*]ing airport last night."

"Then how do you explain what happened?"

"I guess that [*BLEEP*]ing Matthew Christian was into the sauce again. Like he was when he said just looking at the First Lady made him tingle all over."

"So what do you think happened at the airport?"

"I'll be [*BLEEP BLEEP*]ed if I know. All I know is that if I get my hands on that [*BLEEP*]ing Matthew Christian, I'm going to [*BLEE—*]"

"Over to you, Andy," Miss O'Shaugnessy said.

"Thank you, Bridget," Andy McClarren said. "C. Harry, can you shed any light on this?"

"I've checked into this, and my sources tell me that Roscoe J. Danton is in Europe on a story for Wolf News."

"Well, there was an airplane at the airfield out there, and someone who looks something like Miss Ravisher threw a cameraman at someone who looks something like Roscoe. How do you explain that?"

"Well, it could be a publicity stunt to gain attention for the Hard-On Awards. That's possible. So far as the airplane is concerned, I checked into that and learned it belongs to a charter operation in Panama City, Panama. I also learned that it left American airspace sometime this afternoon. When I called the charter company in Panama City, I couldn't get anyone on the line who spoke English."

"Well, that's not surprising in that part of the world. Have you ever tried to call Miami International and been able to get someone on the phone who speaks English? And now for a word from our sponsors."

[SIX]
Penthouse B
The Royal Aztec Table Tennis and
Golf Resort and Casino
Cozumel, Mexico
0900 19 June 2007

When General Jesus Manuel Cosada of the Cuban DGI walked onto the balcony of the suite in which General Sergei Murov of the

SVR had installed himself, he found the general in shorts and a T-shirt sitting in a lounge chair. Murov was sipping at a cup of clear liquid.

"Good morning, General," Cosada said.

Murov raised somewhat glazed eyes to him and replied, in a cloud of *essence d'alcool*, "Jesus, Jesus, try to remember my cover. I'm supposed to be Grigori Slobozhanin of the Greater Sverdlovsk Table Tennis Association."

"Why couldn't you have picked a cover name people can pronounce?"

General Murov gave General Cosada the finger.

"Isn't it a little early for that?" General Cosada inquired, pointing to the nearly empty liter bottle of Stolichnaya vodka sitting on the Ping-Pong table beside the general.

"It's always too early for that stupid game. As far as I'm concerned, whoever invented Ping-Pong should be shot in the kneecaps."

"I was referring to the vodka."

"The last thing Vladimir Vladimirovich said to me before I left the Kremlin was, 'Remember, my dear Sergei, when you get to Mexico, whatever you do, don't drink the water.'"

"Sergei—excuse me, *Grigori*—what I came here to tell you is that we have a problem, a morale problem."

"I don't want to hear about it," Murov said. "The next to last thing Vladimir Vladimirovich said to me before I left the Kremlin was, 'I don't want to hear about any of your problems, Sergei. The only thing I want to hear from you is when the Aeroflot airplane with Berezovsky, Alekseeva, and Castillo neatly trussed up in the baggage compartment is going to land at Domodedovo.'"

"Where's that? I thought he wanted them taken to Moscow."

"Jesus Christ, Jesus! How did you get to be a general? Domodedovo is the Moscow airport."

"There are some dissidents and counterrevolutionaries who say I got promoted because my mother is Fidel's and Raúl's first cousin once removed, but I think that's just jealousy, so I don't pay attention to it."

"Tell me about this morale problem. What's that all about?"

"I guess you could say it's a family problem."

"What is?"

"You remember when we left Havana, it was in sort of a hurry?"

"I remember. The ride to the airport in that 1958 Studebaker Hawk of yours was terrifying. It's just too old to drive it at more than forty m.p.h., which you were dumb enough to try to do."

"And do you remember Raúl ordering me to give you twenty-four of our best DGI people to help you get these people on the Aeroflot plane to Moscow?"

"Jesus, Jesus! To *Domodedovo.* Moscow is the city. Domodedovo is the airport. Why don't you write that down?"

"Well, when we had to push my Hawk to get it to start, Raúl was looking out the window and saw us. So he decided to be helpful and called the DGI personnel officer himself and told him to get twenty-four of our best DGI agents out to the airport."

"So?"

"The thing is, Grigori, although the People's Democratic Republic of Cuba has absolutely done away with class distinctions, the truth is that there are two kinds of 'best DGI agents.'"

"I have no idea what you're talking about."

"One group of 'best DGI agents' are the ones who have worked their way from the bottom."

"And the other kind?"

"The other kind are the ones whose fathers, or uncles, are high-ranking officials of the government of the People's Democratic Republic."

"I think I know what's coming," General Murov said.

"So what the DGI personnel officer did was assume, since Raúl himself had called, that he was talking about that second group. So he took one of those buses we swapped rum for from the Bulgarians and went out to the Workers and Peasants Golf and Tennis Club and loaded twenty-four of them onto the bus and took them out to the airport."

"They didn't complain?"

"Not then. When I saw who they were, I told them we were going to the Cuban Mission to the UN in New York. They all knew, of course, that meant they would have diplomatic immunity so they could get in a UN stretch limousine, head for Park Avenue, find a fire hydrant, park next to it, and when the cops show up, open the sunroof and moon the cops to show their disdain for capitalist imperialism and its minions."

"Well, I can understand that," General Murov said. "But what happened when the plane landed here?"

"I lied to them again. I told them that before they went to New York they would have to prove they had been paying attention in Spy School, and the way they were going to do that was to pass themselves off as poor Mexicans and find menial employment at either the Grand Cozumel Beach and Golf Resort or with Imperial Cruise Lines, Incorporated. Those who did so successfully, I told them, got to go to New York. Those who didn't would get sent back to Havana."

"And this worked? Jesus, Jesus, I seem to have underestimated you."

"Well, I was, you should know, trained in Moscow."

"That would explain it, wouldn't it?" Murov asked rhetorically. "So, what's the problem?"

"The *Czarina of the Gulf* docked here this morning. I told you Aleksandr Pevsner is going to use her to house guests at the Castillo–Alekseeva nuptials."

"No, Jesus, I told you that," Murov said. "Is that how you got to be a general? Taking credit for intelligence developed by other people?"

"And I suppose you told me Castillo and his fiancée flew in here late yesterday?"

"No, I didn't know that. Are you sure?"

"Would I tell you if I wasn't sure?"

"You just told me Aleksandr Pevsner is going to use the *Czarina of the Gulf* to house wedding guests. If you lied about that, why wouldn't you lie about this?"

"You'll just have to trust me that I'm not. Do you want to hear about the *Czarina of the Gulf* or not?"

"If you promise on your mother's grave to tell the truth."

"My mother's still alive, so that wouldn't work. How about on my honor as a graduate of the SVR Academy for Peace, International Cooperation, and Espionage?"

"That'll do it."

"Consider it given. The people we infiltrated into both the Grand Cozumel Beach and Golf Resort and Imperial Cruise Lines, Incorporated, have been told there is an emergency situation aboard the

Czarina of the Gulf and they are going to have to work around the clock until it is cleared up."

"What kind of an emergency situation?"

"I spent a lot of time and money developing this intel, Grigori, so pay attention."

"I'm all ears."

"Somehow—and I don't know how; I'm still working on it—Aleksandr Pevsner has really pissed off some Mexican Indian witch doctors. So they put a curse on the *Czarina of the Gulf.*"

"What do you mean, a curse?"

"They call it 'Montezuma's revenge.'"

"What does it do?"

"I'm still working on that, too, but what I have learned is the toilets have stopped working, and when the ship unloaded its passengers, a bunch of them had to be carried off on stretchers, and the rest, who had medical masks over their mouths, had to be helped off and into the buses waiting for them."

"What's the problem? Isn't that good for us?"

"Quite the opposite. Our people have heard about it—actually they smelled it—and are terrified. They sent a workers' delegation to see me, and they said everybody wants to go back to Havana now, even if that means they can't go to New York and moon the cops from the roof window of a UN limousine. That's what I meant when I said we have a morale problem."

"Jesus, Jesus, don't panic," General Murov said. "Let me think about this. Hand me the bottle, please. We Russians always think better with a little boost from our friend Stoli."

[ONE]

Hacienda Santa Maria
Oaxaca Province, Mexico
1001 19 June 2007

"Don Fernando's House," as the main residence of Hacienda Santa Maria was known, was a sprawling, red-tile-roofed house with a wide shaded veranda all around it sitting on a bluff overlooking the Pacific Ocean.

"I hate to mention this, Gringo," Don Fernando Lopez, great-grandson of the man for whom the house was named, a heavyset, almost massive olive-skinned man in his late thirties, said from the wicker lounge on which he was sprawled on the veranda, "but the magic moment of ten hundred has come and gone."

His cousin, Carlos Guillermo Castillo, gave him the finger.

"Fernando," their grandmother, Doña Alicia Castillo, a trim woman who appeared to be in her fifties but was actually the far side of seventy, said, "don't call Carlos 'Gringo.'" And then she said, in awe, "Oh, my God!" and pointed out to sea.

Juan Carlos Pena, who was seated between Castillo and Doña Alicia, said, "I'll be a sonofabitch!"

Doña Alicia said, "Watch your mouth, Juan Carlos. I haven't forgotten how to wash your mouth out!"

"Sorry, Abuela," Pena said, genuinely contrite.

"Great big son of a b— gun, isn't she?" Castillo inquired admiringly.

The nuclear attack submarine USS *San Juan* (SSN-751) had just surfaced a thousand yards offshore. As the national colors were hoisted from her conning tower, hatches on her forward deck opened and lines of men in black rubber suits emerged. A davit then winched up black semi-rigid-hulled inflatable boats, which were quickly put over the side. The men in black rubber suits leapt into the sea and then climbed into the rubber boats. The hatches closed, the national colors were lowered, and the USS *San Juan* started to sink below the surface as the outboard-engine-powered rubber boats raced for the beach. The whole process had taken no more than four minutes.

"Fernando," Castillo said, "I think that cheap watch of yours is running a little fast. Why don't you get a real watch?"

Then he turned to Gunnery Sergeant Lester Bradley, USMC, and said, "Bradley, as the senior naval person on my staff—once a Marine, always a Marine—why don't you go with Comandante Pena's men to welcome our naval guests ashore?"

"Aye, aye, sir!"

"Carry on, Gunnery Sergeant," Castillo ordered.

About five minutes later, a very large man in a rubber suit and carrying a CAR-4 got out of one of the Policía Federal Suburbans and, looking more than a little uncomfortable, walked onto the veranda.

"Welcome to Hacienda Santa Maria," Doña Alicia said.

"Yes, ma'am. Thank you, ma'am. I'm looking for Colonel C. G. Castillo."

"Congratulations, you have found *Lieutenant* Colonel C. G. Castillo, Retired. And you are?"

The man in the black rubber suit came to attention and saluted.

"Sir, Lieutenant Commander Edwin Bitter, SEAL Team Five, reporting as ordered to the colonel for hazardous duty."

"Hello, Eddie," Major H. Richard Miller, Junior, said. "Long time no see. How are you?"

"I will be goddamned!" Commander Bitter said.

"Probably," Castillo said. "I have heard some really terrible things about you SEALs. But I must warn you, if you keep talking like that, my grandmother will wash your mouth out with soap."

"And I know who you are, too!" Commander Bitter said excitedly.

"Indeed?"

"When Dick Miller dumped his Black Hawk in Afghanistan, with me and some other SEALs on it, you're the crazy sonofabitch who stole another Black Hawk and came and got us off that mountain in the middle of a blizzard. The last I heard they were either going to court-martial you or give you the Medal of Honor."

"In the end, wiser heads prevailed and they did neither," Castillo said.

Sweaty came onto the veranda.

Commander Bitter's face showed great surprise.

"Good morning," Sweaty said, and offered Bitter her hand.

He took it and said, "A great honor, Miss Ravisher. I'm one of your biggest fans!"

Commander Bitter suddenly found himself flying through the air.

Castillo walked to the edge of the veranda and looked down at

Bitter, who was now lying on his back on the hood of one of the Policía Federal Suburbans with his feet on the roof.

"If you think you can ever get off there, and make it back up here, Commander," Castillo said, "and apologize nicely, I will ask the Widow Alekseeva to give you back your CAR-4, and then I will attempt to answer any questions you might have."

"What he didn't tell you, Commander," Juan Carlos Pena said ten minutes later when Castillo had finished explaining the problem and what the role of the SEALs was to be in dealing with it, "is what at least three of the drug cartels want to do with him."

"Which is?"

Pena looked uncomfortably at Doña Alicia.

"How do I say this delicately?" he asked.

"What they have announced they are going to do to Carlos, Commander," Doña Alicia said, "is behead him, and then hang his head from a bridge over the highway in Acapulco."

Juan Carlos Pena nodded. "They seem to feel Carlos had something to do with the untimely deaths of about a dozen of the drug cartel people who murdered—"

"Danny Salazar?" Bitter interrupted, and when Pena nodded again, said, "We heard about that."

"He also didn't tell you we are going to be married in Cozumel," Sweaty said. "We would be pleased if you and your men were to come."

"Excuse me, ma'am," Bitter said very respectfully, "but neither you nor this lady seem to be very concerned with this threat to Colonel Castillo."

"You've heard of Pancho Villa, Commander?" Doña Alicia asked. "The famous Mexican bandito?"

"Yes, ma'am."

"Villa announced to the world that after he cut the throat of Carlos's great-grandfather Marcos Castillo—who was, of course, also Fernando's great-grand-uncle Marcos—he intended to drag his corpse through the streets of Tampico behind his horse until there was nothing left but the rope."

"Why did he want to do that, ma'am?" Bitter asked.

"In those days, this was a cattle ranch. Now we grow grapefruit, but in those days we raised cattle. Well, Señor Villa decided he needed some of our cattle, and helped himself. Great-grandfather Marcos did the only thing he could—he applied Texas law."

"Which was?"

"He hung twenty-seven of Señor Villa's banditos," she said. "So, Señor Villa—he was something of a blowhard, truth to tell—announced he was going to drag Great-grandfather Marcos behind his horse. That didn't happen. But it was necessary for Great-grandfather Marcos to hang another thirty-four banditos before Señor Villa understood that those sorts of threats were unacceptable.

"And when, in 1923, Señor Villa met his untimely death, in a manner similar to the deaths of those drug people near here—that is to say, he was shot multiple times while riding in his automobile—the same sort of scurrilous allegations were made that Great-grandfather Marcos was responsible. Until his death, at ninety-two, he refused to comment publicly on them."

"My Carlito's beloved ancestor, Commander," Sweaty said, "was—as my Carlito is—what they call a Texican. That means an American of Mexican blood. There's a phrase, 'Don't mess with a Texican.' You might want to write that down."

"Yes, ma'am," Commander Bitter said. "And may I take the liberty of saying, ma'am, that I think I understand why you and Colonel Castillo were attracted to one another?"

"Yes, you may," Sweaty said. "Actually, it was love at first sight."

"Oh, really? Where did you meet?"

"In the charming ancient university town of Marburg an der Lahn in Germany. Vladimir Vladimirovich Putin had sent my brother and me there—we were at the time SVR officers—to whack him. Circumstances didn't permit that to happen. And the next day, we met for the first time. One glance and—well, here we are."

[TWO]

The Dignitary's Exhibition Area
The Pots of Gold Grand Theater and Slots Arena
The Streets of San Francisco Hotel, Resort and Casino
Las Vegas, Nevada
2159:55 19 June 2007

The producer held up his hand with four fingers extended and began to count downward, "Five, four, three . . ."

Where he would have said "two" he balled his fist, extended his index finger upward, and, where he would have said "one," pointed it toward Pastor Jones, who was wearing a wing-collared boiled shirt and a tuxedo.

"Good evening, it's twelve o'clock in Montpelier and nine o'clock here in Sin City, and this is Pastor Jones."

He stopped suddenly and put his finger on what looked like a hearing aid. His face showed either chagrin or annoyance and then he went on. "Excuse me, I've just been informed it's *ten* o'clock here in Sin City, where we have *Wolf News World Wide* cameras set up at the fabled Streets of San Francisco Hotel, Resort and Casino, where Miss Red Ravisher just moments ago won the distinguished actress award in the fifteenth annual Climax Awards of the Adult Motion Picture Industry Association.

"And that means, Mommies and Daddies across the world, that it's time to send the wee ones off to bed, as we expect Miss Ravisher to be with us momentarily, and if we're lucky, we hope to have a clip from her epic film *Catherine and the Household Cavalry.*

"And here she is," Pastor Jones said, as Red Ravisher walked up to him. She was wearing a gold lamé frock that clung closely to her body and carrying against her bosom the gold—probably gold-plated—sculpture the AMPIA had just awarded her.

"Thank you for finding time for us," Pastor Jones said.

"My pleasure, Reverend."

"I'm not a reverend. Pastor is my first name."

"How odd!"

"Red isn't exactly an ordinary name, if I may say so."

"Red Ravisher is my professional name," she said. "My birth certificate says 'Agrafina Bogdanovich.' Agrafina means 'born feet first.' What's your real name?"

"Pastor Jones is my real name."

"How odd! Have you ever thought of taking a professional name? If you did, you wouldn't be mistaken for a man of the cloth."

"Your name sounds Russian," Pastor said.

"I am of Russian heritage."

"Well, let me congratulate you on your award. There aren't very many women who have earned so many Hard-Ons as you have. How many is it that you have?"

"I have six Best Actress Hard-Ons, plus this one, which is for best film of the year. I wrote, produced, and directed *Catherine and the Household Cavalry*. That's seven, altogether."

"So tell me, who is Catherine?"

"You're kidding, right? You don't know who Catherine was?"

"You tell me."

"She was Empress of Russia."

"And she liked the cavalry, I take it."

"She liked cavalrymen. I make adult films, not documentaries."

"And you played Catherine?"

"No. I played one of the horses. Are you for real?"

"So tell me, Miss Bog— Bogdo—"

"Bogdanovich. Agrafina Bogdanovich."

"Now that you've walked off the stage with a Hard-On—"

"*Two* Hard-Ons. For a total of seven. I just told you that."

"What are your plans?"

"A little vacation. In Mexico. To get away from my fans, to tell you the truth."

"Where in Mexico?"

"If I told you where in Mexico, then my fans would know where to find me, wouldn't they?"

"Well, can you tell me why you're going to this place you won't tell me where it is?"

Red Ravisher shook her head, but answered the question.

"Two reasons. They make great borscht."

"That's unusual for Mexico, isn't it?"

"Well, the resort makes it for the security staff, all of whom are Russian émigrés. They're all ex-Spetsnaz, which is like our Special

Forces, but Russian. There's nobody better at security, except maybe our Special Forces or SEALs, than ex-Spetsnaz."

"So you're going to this place so these Russian ex-Spetsnaz émigrés can protect you from the attention of your millions of fans?"

"Not exactly. The last time I was there, they said if I ever came back, they would show me how to slowly and painfully kill people by breaking their bones one at a time."

"You want to break the bones of your fans?"

"Not of my fans, stupid. I want to break Matthew Christian's bones. If I ever run into that miserable twerp, I intend to be ready for him."

[THREE]
The Lady Bird Johnson VIP Guest Room
The White House
1600 Pennsylvania Avenue, N.W.
Washington, D.C.
2205 19 June 2007

The President of the United States knocked softly on the door and politely inquired, "May I—or more specifically, may I and Robin Hoboken—intrude?"

When there was no reply, President Clendennen slowly and carefully opened the door.

The First Lady and the First Mother-in-Law were seated on identical red-leather-upholstered reclining armchairs, which were in the reclined position, watching a wall-mounted flat-screen television.

"Mommy, dearest," the First Lady inquired, "what do they call that gold-plated thing Miss Ravisher is cradling so lovingly in her arms?"

"I don't know what they call it, Belinda-Sue," the First Mother-in-Law replied, her voice coarsened by cigarettes from what once had been a three-pack-a-day habit, "and as a Southern lady, I'm certainly not going to say what it looks like."

"Getting settled in comfortably, are you, Mother Krauthammer?" President Clendennen inquired politely.

"Shut up, Joshua," the First Mother-in-Law snapped. "Can't you see that Belinda-Sue and I are watching Pastor Jones interview Red Ravisher live from the Climax Awards at the Streets of San Francisco in Las Vegas?"

"Mommy, dearest," the First Lady inquired, "what's 'borscht'?"

"I think that's what the Russians call grits, darling."

"Actually, Madam First Mother-in-Law," Robin Hoboken offered, "borscht is a soup made with fresh red beets, beef shank, onions, carrots, potatoes, cabbage, dill, and sour cream."

"Belinda-Sue, darling," Mother Krauthammer said, "guess who Whatsisname has with him? The talking encyclopedia."

"Is there any chance, girls," the President asked, "that you'd be willing to turn Wolf News off for a minute or two—"

"Not a chance in hell until Pastor Jones is finished interviewing Red Ravisher," Mother Krauthammer said.

"I gather you're a fan of Miss Ravisher, Madam First Mother-in-Law?" Robin Hoboken asked.

"Yes, I am. On several levels. I was deeply touched by her portrayal of Catherine the Great. It brought on a flood of memories of my time as the Magnolia Queen of the University of Mississippi. The

Ole Miss Rebels weren't cavalry, of course, they were football players, but they sure knew how to ride, so to speak.

"And then I certainly admire her for throwing that French pervert at the other one. I refer, of course, Joshua, to your dear friend Roscoe J. Danton."

"Actually, Madam First Mother-in-Law," Robin Hoboken said, "that might be a slight mischaracterization vis-à-vis Mr. Danton's relationship with the nation's Commander in Chief and that incident in general as reported by Mr. Matthew Christian."

"Joshua, do you have any idea what the hell he's talking about?" Mother Krauthammer asked.

"Miss Ravisher," the First Lady said, "just said she wants to break Mr. Christian's bones."

"I'd like to break his bones," the President said. "Roscoe J. Danton's bones, I mean. He's supposed to be in Europe trying to get into Somalia, not in Las Vegas having French perverts thrown at him by the Ethel Barrymore of the dirty movie business."

"People who keep a box full of adult films in the James Earl Carter historical presidential desk in the Oval Office are in no position—"

"What Robin and I were hoping to talk to you and Belinda-Sue about, Mother Krauthammer," the President said, "is my library . . . actually Belinda-Sue's and my library and last resting place."

"And the necessity for you, Madam First Mother-in-Law," Robin Hoboken amplified, "to make a real effort, as we start to raise money for the foregoing, to avoid as much as possible doing anything, such as your recent difficulties with the Public Drunkenness Squad of the Pascagoula Police Department, that might be in the newspapers or, God forbid, on Wolf News, as that might impede our fund-raising efforts."

"This I have to hear," Mother Krauthammer said. "But make it quick. Belinda-Sue and I want to watch the rerun of the Pastor Jones show."

[FOUR]
The Ivan the Terrible Penthouse Suite
The Grand Cozumel Beach & Golf Resort
Cozumel, Mexico
0915 20 June 2007

"Good morning, Alek," Charley Castillo called cheerfully as he got off the elevator. "Tom and I understand you need a little cheering up."

He pointed to Tom Barlow, formerly Colonel Dmitri Berezovsky of the SVR, who had followed him off the elevator. Both Dmitri and Charley, who looked so much alike they could have been mistaken for brothers, were wearing polo shirts and tennis shorts and carrying rackets and cans of balls.

Aleksandr Pevsner, attired in a terry-cloth bathrobe, darted his large, blue, and extraordinarily bright eyes coldly at them but didn't reply.

"So, what's bothering you on this sunny morning in sunny Cozumel?" Castillo pursued.

Again Pevsner didn't reply. But the look in his eyes, which previously had been chilly, changed to one that would have frozen Mount Vesuvius.

"I guess he didn't see that sign in the lobby, Tom," Castillo said.

"What sign in the lobby?" Barlow asked.

"The one that says, 'Abandon Despair, All Ye Who Enter Here! Welcome to the Grand Cozumel Beach and Golf Resort!'"

"I guess not," Tom agreed.

"Tell us why you haven't abandoned despair, Alek," Castillo said. "Perhaps we can help."

"I knew I should have killed you on the Cobenzl," Pevsner said.

The Battle of Vienna in 1693, which saw the troops of the Ottoman Empire flee the battlefield leaving only bags of coffee beans behind, was directed from the Cobenzl, a high point in the fabled Vienna Woods.

Castillo had first met Pevsner there after Pevsner had had him abducted at pistol point from the men's room of the Sacher Hotel.

"You told us God stayed your murderous intentions," Castillo said. "You remember him saying that, Tom, right?"

"I remember him saying just that," Barlow replied. "'I was just about to kill Charley when God stayed my hand' is exactly what he said."

"Well, that wasn't the first mistake God's made," Pevsner said. "Staying my hand like that."

"We're back to what's troubling you, Alek," Castillo said. "You can tell us. Tom is family, and I soon will be. What's bothering you?"

"Do you have any idea how much money that stupid sonofabitch has cost me?"

"It would help, Cousin Alek, if you told us to which stupid sonofabitch you're referring. Then we could guess."

"Nicolai Nicolaiovitch Putin."

"Nicolai Nicolaiovitch Putin? Vladimir Vladimirovich Putin's cousin?" Tom Barlow asked. "I thought he'd joined the Bolshoi Corps de Ballet after they threw him and his boyfriend out of the Navy."

"No, stupid. Not that stupid Nicolai Nicolaiovitch Putin. The other one. The one who's captain of the *Czarina of the Gulf* and before that captain of the atomic submarine *Blue September.* The submarine the Americans stole. No wonder we lost the Cold War."

"So, what has Captain Putin done to so annoy you, Alek?" Castillo asked.

"He's cost me a fortune, that's what he's done. And ruined the reputation of Imperial Cruise Lines, Incorporated. People will now be laughing at Imperial, instead of at Cavalcade Cruise Lines."

"Refresh my memory, Cousin Alek," Tom Barlow said. "Why were people laughing at Cavalcade Cruise Lines?"

"Some people thought it was amusing when the helmsman of the *Cavalcade Carnival* became distracted by the sight of bare-breasted maidens in grass skirts and ran the ship aground on the island of Bali."

"I remember now," Castillo said. "It turned over and they had to cut holes in her bottom to get the passengers off. So what has Captain Putin done that's worse than that?"

"When I gave him command of the *Czarina of the Gulf,* Charley," Pevsner said, suddenly far more calm than he had been just moments before, "I counseled him. I'm sure both you and Dmitri—excuse me, *Tom*—have yourselves counseled your subordinates before giving them an important command, so you'll understand what I'm saying here, right?"

Both Tom and Charley nodded.

"What I said was, 'Nicolai Nicolaiovitch, you are an experienced officer and seaman. You're an honors graduate of the Potemkin Naval Academy. In the glorious days of Communism, you rose to command the nuclear-powered submarine *Blue September,* in which you prowled under the seas for years trying to scare the Americans. I wouldn't dream of telling someone of your experience and reputation how to command the *Czarina of the Gulf.* But, as I'm sure you know, there is always an exception to every rule. And here's that exception: The *Czarina of the Gulf* will be calling at ports in Mexico. When that happens, whatever you do, don't take on any water. Not for the boilers. Not for the water system. Not even water in plastic bottles.'

"That's what I told Captain Putin. So I ask you, does that order seem clear enough?"

"Sounds clear enough to me," Tom Barlow said.

"Maybe you should have added, 'under any circumstances,'" Castillo said. "That would have cleared up any possible misunderstanding."

"Maybe I could have, but I didn't," Pevsner said. "I thought I was making myself perfectly clear."

"I gather Captain Putin didn't obey your order," Barlow said.

"Let me tell you what that sonofabitch did," Pevsner said. "He sailed from Miami on schedule. The *Czarina of the Gulf* had the AEA Single Women's Sabbatical Educational Tour aboard. Sixteen hundred and six of them. It should have been a pleasant voyage for him and his officers, and a really profitable voyage for Imperial Cruise Lines, Incorporated."

"And who are they?"

"Schoolteachers from Alabama. Single women schoolteachers, either ones who never got married or are divorced. When school is out, they get a vacation—that's what 'sabbatical' means—paid for by the taxpayers. It's supposed to broaden their horizons. Anyway, since they do this every year, we know how to handle them. They get on the *Czarina of the Gulf* in Miami. There's a captain's dinner with free champagne to get things started, and they start either romancing the ship's officers—those schoolteachers really go for those blue uniforms with all the gold braid—or they head for the slot machines or the blackjack tables.

"The next day, when they wake up about noon, they're in the middle of the Gulf of Mexico. There's a captain's luncheon, with more free champagne and more romancing of the officers, presuming the officers have any strength left. Some of the schoolteachers, especially some of the divorcées, are surprisingly . . . how do I say this? . . ."

"Frisky?" Castillo proposed.

"I was going to say 'insatiable,' but okay, 'frisky.' And then back to the casino as the *Czarina of the Gulf* makes for Tampico. They dock there and spend the night. Some of the teachers actually get off the ship to mail postcards home, things like that, but most of them stay aboard sucking up the free champagne and fooling around with the officers.

"In the morning, the *Czarina of the Gulf* heads here to Cozumel. Another captain's brunch, more free champagne . . . getting the picture?"

"Getting it," Castillo and Barlow chorused.

"And they finally dock here in Cozumel. They disembark, get on the buses waiting for them, drive to Cozumel International, get on the planes waiting for them, and two hours later they're back in Mobile, Alabama, wearing smiles."

"So what went wrong?" Barlow asked.

"When the *Czarina of the Gulf* docked at Tampico, Captain Putin went to bed in his cabin. He says alone, but I'm not sure I believe that. It doesn't matter. He went to bed, and in the morning, when he didn't answer a knock at his cabin door, the *Czarina of the Gulf*'s first mate took her to sea."

"What's wrong with that?" Castillo asked.

"While they were tied up, and while Captain Putin was asleep, supplies were taken aboard. The officer who was supposed to be watching wasn't. He was tied up with an English teacher from Decatur. Or maybe the English teacher had *him* tied up.

"Anyway, he wasn't where he was supposed to be, doing what he was supposed to be doing, so Mexican water was taken aboard. Some went into the ship's tanks, some went to the boilers, and there were five hundred cases of Mexican water, in twelve-ounce bottles, twenty-four bottles to the case. They call it 'Aqua Mexicana,' whatever the hell that means. It's got a picture of a cactus on the label."

"So what happened?" Barlow asked.

"About four hours out of Tampico, in other words about ten a.m., the air-conditioning went out. Now, I'm willing to accept some small responsibility for that—"

"You got here last night, right?" Barlow interrupted.

"Correct."

"Which means before that, you were in Argentina, right?"

"Correct."

"So how could you be responsible for an air-conditioning system failing in the middle of the Gulf of Mexico?"

"Because, when I was in Korea having them build the *Czarina of the Gulf* I naively believed a Korean swindler when he told me his Korean Karrier air conditioners were just as good as American Carrier air conditioners and he could let me have them for half of what Carrier was asking. Okay? Curiosity satisfied?"

"You say the air conditioners went out?" Castillo asked. "So what?"

"So it gets pretty warm in the middle of the Gulf of Mexico on a sunny day."

"So you open the portholes," Charley said. "And let the cool sea air breezes in."

"Unfortunately, that is not possible on the *Czarina of the Gulf,*" Pevsner said.

"You can't open the portholes on the *Czarina of the Gulf*?"

"The way that miserable Korean con man sold me his Korean Karrier air conditioners was to tell me that since I would have air-conditioning I wouldn't have to open any portholes; that I could save all the money it would have cost me to install all those fancy and expensive brass porthole hinges and locks. And that the money I was going to save by not installing openable portholes was going to just about pay for his Korean Karrier air-conditioning. At the time, I considered it a cogent argument. So there you are."

"Well, what happened when the air-conditioning went out in the middle of the Gulf of Mexico?" Barlow asked.

"Well, the Alabama schoolteachers, most of whom were a little hungover anyway, naturally got pretty thirsty and started drinking that goddamned bottled Aqua Mexicana. And thirty minutes after they did—whammo!"

"Montezuma's revenge," Castillo said sympathetically.

"In spades," Pevsner said. "In spades!"

"What does that mean?" Barlow asked.

"Try to picture this, Dmitri," Pevsner said. "Try to imagine sixteen hundred and six hungover schoolteachers afflicted with Montezuma's revenge—"

"What's Montezuma's revenge?" Barlow asked.

"Think urgent needs, Tom," Castillo explained.

"Oh!"

". . . all trying to get into the *Czarina of the Gulf*'s four hundred ladies' restrooms at the same time. That averages out to four schoolteachers per restroom. It was chaos, absolute chaos, and that's an understatement if there ever was one."

"What finally happened?" Barlow asked.

"Well, and I'll admit that at this point Captain Putin had no choice, he managed to get most of the crew into the engine room."

"Why did he do that?" Barlow asked.

"Unless he had there would have been a massacre. The schoolteachers were roaming the ship with fire axes they were going to use to behead—or maybe castrate—the crew. Captain Putin had to use fire hoses to restrain them. And when he finally got everybody he could into the engine room—the Karrier a/c shorted out the engines—he battened the hatches and sent out an SOS. And the rest is history."

"What do you mean by that?"

"The Mexican Coast Guard sent a tugboat out to the *Czarina of the Gulf* and towed her here. Where the world's press was waiting. The whole world saw Captain Putin being taken off in chains to face charges of crimes against humanity. The Mexicans had a hard time protecting him from the schoolteachers and their union representatives."

"And the schoolteachers will sue for damages," Barlow said. "That's really going to cost you a fortune, Alek."

"Actually, no," Pevsner said.

"No?" Castillo said. "You underestimate tort attorneys."

"You underestimate me," Pevsner retorted. "Of course I thought of those miserable parasites. I hired the best one I could find. Which of course cost me a small fortune."

"Whatever it cost," Castillo said, "it was money well spent to have the best of the parasites defending you in court."

"What my legal counsel did, Friend Charley," Pevsner said, "was compose the small print on the back of the tickets. When my passengers sign the back of their tickets, acknowledging receipt of same, they also acknowledge the hazards of the sea, and agree that if something unpleasant happens, a one-time payment of seven dollars and fifty cents will provide full and adequate compensation for any and all inconveniences they may have experienced."

"You're an evil man, Alek," Castillo said.

"No more or less than any other cruise ship operator," Pevsner said.

"I guess the *Czarina of the Gulf* will be out of service for some time," Castillo said.

"I'll have it cleaned up by the time your wedding guests arrive, if that's what you mean."

"No, it's not. Before I heard what had happened to it, I was hoping I could charter her for twenty-four hours."

"Why on earth would you want to do that?"

"So that I can run the C. G. Castillo Pirated Ship Recovery Training Program on her."

"And what in hell is that?"

Castillo told him, concluding, "My plan was that cameras would be rolling as the SEALs take the ship back from Delta Force. I would then have loaded Roscoe J. Danton into my birthday present and Dick Miller would have flown him to Washington, where he would have shown the video to the President, which would have convinced ol' Joshua Ezekiel Clendennen I'm working hard to carry out his orders."

"Several questions, Charley," Pevsner said. "Starting with what birthday present?"

"The Cessna Mustang Sweaty gave me for my birthday."

"I'd momentarily—probably due to the disaster on the *Czarina of the Gulf*—forgotten that," Pevsner said. "But now that it's come up—if you don't mind a little advice. Once you marry Svetlana, Charley, you're going to have to get her spending under control. That's the key to a happy marriage. That and never saying 'yes' or even 'maybe' to your wife when she asks you if you don't agree she's putting on a little weight where she sits."

"I'll keep that in mind," Castillo said. "What other questions did you have?"

"How much of the ship will you require for your movie for President Clendennen?"

"Enough cabins for the Delta Force people and the SEALs. About twenty of the former, and a few more than that many SEALs. Plus the photographers and some of my people. Not much, on a ship that large."

"And when is this going to happen?"

"As soon as possible after Delta and the SEALs get here. The SEALs are coming, bringing their boats and telephone poles, by bus from my grapefruit farm in Oaxaca Province. The Delta people will be flying in here this afternoon. They're coming as the Fayetteville Blood Alley Ping-Pong Wizards."

"As the what?"

"The Fayetteville Blood Alley Ping-Pong Wizards. While they're here, they hope to challenge the Greater Sverdlovsk Table Tennis Association to a demonstration match."

"Sorry to rain on your parade, Charley, but I don't think those Russians know how to play Ping-Pong," Pevsner said.

"I thought that might be the case," Castillo said. "Roscoe J. Danton is arranging for the match to be televised on the Wolf Sports International channel."

"You're an evil man, Charley Castillo," Pevsner said.

"No more or less than any other former Delta Force operator," Castillo said. "Endeavoring to win the hearts and minds of people by whatever non-lethal means one has available."

"What were the SEALs doing at your grapefruit farm in wherever you said?"

"They were aboard the nuclear submarine USS *San Juan* returning to California from Venezuela when General Naylor ordered them to report to me for hazardous duty. Because I was at the grapefruit farm, that's where they went. When they got there, the sub surfaced, they loaded their telephone poles into their rubber boats, and headed for shore. You should have been there, Alek. The sight of twenty-four large SEALs and six telephone poles jammed into two small rubber boats racing across the waves is one I won't soon forget."

"A couple of questions, Charley. What's with the telephone poles? And what was the nuclear submarine doing off the coast of Venezuela?"

"So far as the telephone poles are concerned—the SEALs are touchy on the subject—the best I've been able to figure out is that the SEALs train with them. Like when I went through the Q course—"

"The what?"

"Q for Special Forces qualification. When I went through the Q course at Camp Mackall, they issued us a rifle, a pistol, and a knife. We had to keep all three with us around the clock. I don't know that

I buy it, but I've been told that the SEALs do the same thing with telephone poles. Makes one think about it. Did you ever see a picture of SEALs training without a telephone pole in it?"

"Now that you mention it, no."

"So, what was suggested to me is they become emotionally involved with their telephone poles. They become, so to speak, their security blankets. They just don't feel comfortable unless they have a telephone pole—the bigger the better, I was told—around."

"Makes sense," Pevsner said. "And what was the sub doing off the coast of Venezuela?"

"Just between us? I wouldn't want this to get around."

"My lips are sealed."

"Well, you remember when the Venezuelans nationalized the American oil companies, seizing them, so to speak, for the workers and peasants?"

"Indeed, I do. And I confess that I was surprised when you didn't send your Marines to take them back from the workers and peasants. That's what we would have done. In the bad old days, I mean."

"We've learned subtlety, Alek," Castillo said. "What we did was refuse to sell them any more parts for the oil well drilling equipment and refineries they seized."

"Whereupon we—I mean the Russian Federation—leapt to their aid in the interest of internal peace and cooperation, and sent them the parts they needed."

"Which you—I mean the Russian Federation—since they don't make those parts themselves, bought from us, doubled the price, and then sold to the Venezuelans. Correct?"

"You're not saying there's anything wrong with turning a little profit on a business deal, are you?"

"Absolutely not! So when we found out what the Russians were doing, we had several options. We could stop selling the parts to the Russians, which would have meant our parts people wouldn't have made their normal profit. That was unacceptable, of course."

"Of course."

"Or we could have sunk the Russian Federation ships either as they were leaving the U.S. or—after the parts had been put ashore in Russia, where they were reloaded into crates marked 'More Fine Products of Russian Federation Craftsmen'—when the ships carrying the parts were en route to Venezuela. That would have been an act of war, so we didn't do that, either."

"So, what did you do?"

"We made some parts that wouldn't quite fit, or would wear out in a week or so, or would cause the drilling strings to break, or all three, and put them into crates marked 'More Fine Products of Russian Federation Craftsmen.' Then we loaded them and some SEALs onto nuclear submarines."

"I know what's coming," Pevsner said. "Genius! No wonder we—I mean the USSR—lost the Cold War!"

"When the crates were off-loaded from the Russian ships onto docks in Venezuela, that same night the SEALs exchanged our crates for their crates. The parts the Russians bought from us were taken back to the U.S., put on shelves, and sold. They're good parts. The—excuse the expression—bad parts no doubt now are installed in Venezuelan drilling rigs and refinery equipment. It's only a matter of time before that equipment promptly breaks down or blows up—or both. The Venezuelans then will say unkind things to the Russians, and the Russians, who know they haven't done anything wrong, will say unkind things to the Venezuelans."

"When I changed sides, I knew it was time for us to change sides," Pevsner said. "Didn't I say that, Dmitri?"

"I remember you saying exactly that," Tom Barlow said. "And you were right."

"I'm always right. Or almost always. I have to admit that I did place my trust in that Korean sonofabitch who sold me those lousy air conditioners."

He turned to Castillo.

"So when are you going to start the C. G. Castillo Pirated Ship Recovery Training Program?"

"After what you've just told me, how can I?" Castillo asked. "Won't it take days to . . . how do I say this delicately? . . . restore the ladies' rooms to their normal pristine and functioning condition?"

"This is another of those times when I wonder both how you got to be an intelligence officer and whether or not you're intelligent enough to be let into the family. The last I heard there are zero females in your Delta Force and zero in your SEALs. That suggests there will not be a requirement for ladies' restrooms, whether functioning and pristine or not."

"You have a point," Castillo admitted. "Does that mean I can charter the *Czarina of the Gulf*?"

"Absolutely!"

[FIVE]

Aboard Cessna Mustang "Happy 38th Birthday"
31,000 feet above Petersburg, Virginia
1015 21 June 2007

"Roscoe," Major Dick Miller, USA, Retired, said to Roscoe J. Danton, who was sitting beside him in the co-pilot's seat of the aircraft, "I'm about to begin our descent into John Foster Dulles International Airport. Should I call ahead and get a limousine for you?"

"You mean a limousine for us?"

"No, I mean a limousine for you."

"You're not going to the White House with me?"

"What I'm going to do is drop you off and then fly to Chicago to pick up Archbishop Valentin and Archimandrite Boris and take them to Cozumel."

"Who the hell are they?"

"The clergymen who are going to unite Sweaty and Charley in holy matrimony."

After a moment's thought, Roscoe said, "Thank you, Dick, but no. I'll just get a taxi."

"Why not a limousine? We're living high on the CIA's dime. If Charley can charter a Gulfstream Five, the Rhine River cruiser *Die Stadt Köln*, and now the two-thousand-plus-passenger *Czarina of the Gulf*, why can't you ride to the White House in a limousine?"

"Frankly, Dick, I'm shocked at the suggestion. Here you are marching along in the Great Gray Line of West Pointers and suggesting that I waste the taxpayers' hard-earned money by taking a limousine."

"And now that I think of it, Charley's going to bill the CIA five thousand dollars an hour for flying you here in his thirty-eighth birthday present."

"Be that as it may, I will take a cab."

"Suit yourself. And that's the *Long* Gray Line of West Pointers, not the *Great* Gray Line."

"Thank you. I'll make a note of that. As a journalist I pride myself on making accurate statements."

"If that's the case, since my leg is still pretty well fucked up, you should have said, 'Here you are *limping* along in the *Long* Gray Line.'"

"I'll make a note of that, too. Accuracy and truth in all things has long been the creed of Roscoe J. Danton."

The truth of the matter here was that Mr. Danton not only did not wish to go to the White House in a limousine, he had no intention of going to the White House at all.

He had made that decision while Castillo was still on his Casey-Berry speaking with Secretary of State Cohen and DCI Lammelle. She had called to say that the First Lady wanted Danton's version—in person—of why Red Ravisher had thrown the paparazzo at him, and the President wanted to hear—in person—what he was doing in Las Vegas with Miss Ravisher when he was supposed to be in Budapest trying to sneak into Somalia.

The moment Castillo had said, "Well, okay. If you two are agreed it's that important, I'll have Dick Miller fly him up there in the morning," Roscoe had had an epiphany, the first he could ever recall having, and which he had previously believed was a religious holiday, falling somewhere during Lent.

I'm not going, his epiphany had told him. *I don't know how I'm not going, but I am not going to try to explain to the President or the First Lady what happened at the airport in Las Vegas. Cohen and Lammelle and Castillo want to throw me at them—like a chunk of raw meat thrown to a starving tiger—to get the pressure off themselves, and I am just not going to permit that to happen.*

He had had no idea how he was just not going to permit that to happen until Miller had brought up the subject of a limousine to take him from Dulles to the White House. Then, in an instant, he had another epiphany: He would get in a taxi, go directly to Union Station, take the train to New York, and seek asylum in the embassy of the People's Democratic Republic of Burundi.

Several months before, while driving home from a party at the Peruvian embassy, he had come across a sea of flashing lights on patrol cars and police prisoner transport vehicles, and stopped to investigate. He had quickly learned what was going on.

The police were in the process of raiding the K Street Stress Relief Center, as the stress relief techniques offered apparently violated the District's ordinances vis-à-vis the operation of what were known as disorderly houses.

Roscoe, in the hope that he would see, which seemed to be a distinct possibility, in the lines of now stress-free customers being led in handcuffs to the police prisoner transport vehicles, one or more distinguished members of Congress, had gotten out of his car for a better look.

Surprising him, he hadn't seen any congressmen, but he had recognized someone who had been at the Peruvian embassy party. He recognized him because he was about seven feet tall and weighed probably 350 pounds, and wore a zebra-striped robe and an alligator-tooth necklace.

He saw, too, that the Burundian ambassador had recognized him.

He hadn't written anything about the incident for a number of reasons. For one thing, diplomats being hauled off by the cops from establishments like the K Street Stress Relief Center was hardly news. For another, the ambassador had a name that could be pronounced and spelled only by fellow Burundians.

Roscoe had not been surprised to see the ambassador's photo in the society section of the next day's edition of the *Washington Times-Post.* He was pictured with his wife, who was even larger and more formidable-appearing than he. That explained why he had sought stress relief.

But he was surprised when that same afternoon a messenger delivered a burlap bag containing twenty-five pounds of Burundian coffee beans and a note from the ambassador, in which the ambassador expressed his profound gratitude for Roscoe's discretion when they had met the previous evening. Roscoe correctly interpreted that to mean the ambassador was grateful his picture had appeared in the society section only.

The ambassador's note had gone on to say that if there was any way, any way at all, that he could be of service to Roscoe, all Roscoe had to do was ask.

Under these circumstances, Roscoe decided, the ambassador would be happy to conceal him for a few days, a week, however long it took until the situation was resolved. And he doubted very much that the President would look for him in the Burundian embassy.

Roscoe's good feelings lasted until he came out of Immigration into the Arriving Passengers area of the airport.

"Welcome to our nation's capital, Roscoe," David W. Yung greeted him. "Let me help you with your bag."

"You look a little green around the gills, Roscoe, if you don't mind my saying so," Edgar Delchamps said. "Would you like to stop at the Old Ebbitt Grill for a Bloody Mary, or would you prefer to go directly to the White House?"

[SIX]
The Reception Area
The Grand Cozumel Beach & Golf Resort
Cozumel, Mexico
1020 21 June 2007

"Words cannot express my chagrin and remorse, Miss Bogdanovich," the general manager of the Grand Cozumel said.

"There's some sort of problem?"

"Indeed there is," he said. "I'm afraid there is no room at this inn."

"Why not?"

"The owner's cousin is to be married here. The entire establishment will be required to accommodate the guests."

"But you told me I would always be welcome here."

"And you always will be, except, of course, when the owner's cousin is to be married, which unfortunately changes things."

"But what am I to do? I was so looking forward to a huge bowl of your marvelous borscht whilst looking down from a penthouse at the white sands of the beach."

"Let me tell you what we're going to do. I can only hope it meets your approval."

"It better."

"Not far down the beach is a splendid establishment—not as

splendid as this, of course, but splendid—the Royal Aztec Table Tennis and Golf Resort and Casino. The manager is a personal friend of mine. When I saw your reservation, I explained this unfortunate happenstance to him, and he has arranged an exquisite penthouse suite for you overlooking the white sands of the beach."

"A penthouse suite seems nice, but what about the borscht?"

"As we speak, Miss Bogdanovich, two of our chefs are in the kitchen of the Royal Aztec preparing borscht—as only they can—for you."

"That's all very nice, but what about security? I don't want any of my fans, and certainly no paparazzi, butting into my personal life while I'm resting to recover from an unfortunate incident in Las Vegas that I'd rather not talk about."

"Not a problem, Miss Bogdanovich. We have trained the security staff of the Royal Aztec. You may rest assured on that score. And did I mention that the Grand Cozumel is going to pick up your bill at the Royal Aztec to make up a little for any inconvenience we may have caused?"

"How kind of you!"

[SEVEN]
Penthouse A
The Royal Aztec Table Tennis and Golf Resort and Casino
Cozumel, Mexico
1130 21 June 2007

When she had looked around Penthouse A, which occupied half of the twenty-second floor of the Royal Aztec, and found it satisfactory,

Agrafina Bogdanovich thanked the Royal Aztec's general manager and sent him on his way.

Then she unpacked, took a shower, and put on what she thought of as her itsy-bitsy tiny polka-dot bikini and her sunglasses and went onto the balcony of the suite. She saw that a steam table had been set up, and resting above the bubbling waters thereof was a silver bowl. She lifted the lid, sniffed appreciatively of the borscht it contained, replaced the lid, and started to pull a chair up to the table.

She was in the act of opening a bottle of Dos Equis *cerveza* when she sensed eyes on her. She looked and saw a head looking at her over the colored-glass partition that separated the balcony of Penthouse A from that of Penthouse B.

"That's borscht I smell, isn't it?" the man inquired.

"It's none of your goddamned business what it is, you goddamned perverted Peeping Tom," Agrafina said, and threw the bottle of Dos Equis at him.

She missed, the bottle striking the glass partition instead. It shattered. The Peeping Tom fled his balcony.

Ten minutes later, her door chime went off. The general manager stood there. So did three bellmen. One of them held two dozen long-stemmed roses. A second held a silver dish with a pound of caviar in it, resting on a bed of ice. The third held an ice-filled bucket and a two-liter bottle of Stolichnaya vodka.

"Miss Bogdanovich, I come bearing these small gifts from your neighbor . . ."

"Señor Peeping Tom, you mean? I was led to believe I would be left alone to recover from the unfortunate incident in Las Vegas—"

"What unfortunate incident was that, my dear Miss Bogdanovich?"

"I'd rather not talk about it. And I barely had time to settle myself when this Mexican Peeping Tom intrudes on my privacy—"

"Actually, he's Russian, not Mexican, Miss Bogdanovich."

"Okay. *Russian* Peeping Tom. What do you mean, he's Russian?"

"He's from Greater Sverdlovsk—"

"That's just Sverdlovsk, not Greater Sverdlovsk," Peeping Tom said from behind the bellman with the long-stemmed roses. "And I'm actually from Kiev, not Greater Sverdlovsk."

"And did you have a mother in Kiev?"

"Of course I had a mother in Kiev. May she rest in peace."

"And she didn't teach you not to leer at strange women in itsy-bitsy tiny polka-dot bikinis while they are trying to recover from certain unpleasant things that happened to them in Las Vegas?"

"It was my nose that got me in trouble," Peeping Tom said.

"You weren't leering at me with your nose!"

"Your borscht smelled just like the borscht my sainted mother, may she rest in peace, used to make for me in Kiev. I got carried away."

"It's pretty good borscht, I'll admit that. What did you say your name was?"

"Grigori Slobozhanin," he said, and then: "To hell with it! My real name is Sergei Murov."

"You're in the theater?"

"Why do you ask that?"

"Well, I'm in the theater myself, so to speak. I know about stage names. My name as it appears in the credits is Red Ravisher. Agrafina Bogdanovich is my real, off-camera name."

"A beautiful name for a beautiful lady," Murov said. "It sounds Russian."

"I am of Russian heritage."

"So here we are, two Russians far from the motherland—"

"Actually, I'm from Cleveland, Ohio."

"How about 'two Russians in a strange land'?"

"It's a strange land, all right, but I just told you, Grigori, that I'm an American."

"The sound of my name coming from your lips is like heavenly music."

"Thank you. I did study elocution, of course."

"That's obvious."

"And you're in the theater, too, I gather, Grigori?"

"There it is again! You don't perhaps hear softly playing violins, my dear Agrafina?"

"What I hear actually sounds like a mariachi band. I asked if you, too, are a thespian."

"Well, let's say I'm playing a role."

"All the world's a stage, as they say."

"Indeed it is. May I make a somewhat intimate suggestion, my dear Agrafina?"

"I sort of like the way Agrafina rolls off your lips, too, Grigori. Yes, you may, with the understanding that if I were to take offense at your somewhat intimate suggestion, I will break your legs."

"What I was going to suggest is since you have that absolutely marvelous borscht, the kind my mother, may she rest in peace, used to make, and I have two liters of Stolichnaya and a pound of caviar, we merge our assets."

Agrafina turned to the general manager of the Royal Aztec and the bellmen.

"After you put my roses in water," she said, "our caviar on the table on the balcony, and hand me our Stolichnaya, you may leave me alone with this silver-tongued devil."

[ONE]
The Old Ebbitt Grill
675 Fifteenth Street, N.W.
Washington, D.C.
1245 21 June 2007

When he had time, later, to reconstruct the disaster at the Old Ebbitt, Edgar Delchamps was forced to conclude that he was at least partially responsible for it.

There had been no question in his mind when he met Roscoe J. Danton at Dulles International that the journalist needed a little—more than a little—liquid courage before going to the White House to explain what he was doing in Las Vegas when he was supposed to be in Budapest.

Especially since the story Charley Castillo had come up with to explain Danton's presence there seemed to stretch credibility. When Castillo had called to tell him that he wanted Delchamps and Two-Gun to meet Danton and see (a) that he got to the White House, and

(b) that he had his story for the President right, he had both explained his concern that Roscoe might be considering desertion from the Merry Outlaws and related the story he had given Roscoe to explain his presence in Las Vegas.

Danton was to tell the President that when he had heard from various sources, whose identity he was honor-bound as a journalist to not make public, the rumors about the formation of the committee to build the President Joshua Ezekiel and Mrs. Belinda-Sue Clendennen Presidential Library and Last Resting Place, he had prevailed upon Castillo to make a quick stop in Las Vegas en route to Cozumel so that he could check out the rumors.

As a manifestation of his great admiration for the President and the First Lady, Danton was to tell the President, he wanted to be the one to break the story to his millions of readers in his syndicated column and to the millions more who couldn't or wouldn't read but who watched him on Wolf News.

Roscoe was to tell the President that no sooner had he gotten off Castillo's Gulfstream than another identical Gulfstream had appeared. A large crowd of journalists was on hand to meet the second airplane and, his journalist's curiosity naturally aroused, he had stood with them to see which famous person was arriving.

What had happened next, Roscoe was to tell the President, was that a porn star named Red Ravisher, whom Roscoe recognized even though he had never met her in his life, got off the airplane, apparently in her cups, picked a fight with a French cameraman, and then threw him at the crowd of journalists in which he was innocently standing. A riot had then ensued.

Aware that the President's political foes might attempt to somehow connect this shameful event to the President Joshua Ezekiel and

Mrs. Belinda-Sue Clendennen Presidential Library and Last Resting Place, and determined that that should not be permitted to happen, Roscoe had immediately gotten back on Castillo's Gulfstream and they had instantly taken off and flown on to Cozumel, where Castillo was going to train SEALs and members of the Delta Force to take back pirated ships from their Somalian captors.

Delchamps thought the story smelled worse than a twenty-five-pound catfish left to rot in the Mississippi sun for ten days. But on the other hand, he thought that if President Clendennen believed that public-spirited citizens had donated ten million dollars to his library because of their admiration for him, he was likely to believe anything, up to and including this cockamamy yarn Roscoe was going to try to feed him.

The other mistake he had made, Delchamps was forced to admit later, was taking Roscoe to the Old Ebbitt, instead of, for example, to the Round Robin Bar in the Willard Hotel, which was right around the corner.

He had taken Roscoe to the Old Ebbitt because he knew Roscoe was an habitué of the establishment, and also because he and Two-Gun Yung, too, were fond of the Old Ebbitt's version of the Bloody Mary.

He completely forgot that others knew that Roscoe was an habitué of the establishment—especially before and at lunchtime—and that one or more of these people might go there looking for Roscoe, which might complicate things.

As it turned out, three such people were there when they led Roscoe in and ordered double Bloody Marys for the three of them.

He didn't see any of them at first. This was because two of them—C. Harry Whelan and Matthew "Hockey Puck" Christian—

had immediately hidden behind their copies of the enormous Old Ebbitt's menu cards so as not to be seen by Delchamps, Yung, and Danton when they saw them come in.

Delchamps, who was, after all, as a result of his long service with the Clandestine Service of the CIA, skilled in deducing things, had deduced that both journalists had come—independently—to the Old Ebbitt hoping to see Roscoe. If he showed up, Mr. Whelan intended to corner Roscoe to demand to know what "out of the box" story vis-à-vis President Clendennen he was chasing.

Mr. Christian intended to corner Roscoe to learn the identity of the woman whom he had seen throwing the French paparazzo at Danton. Christian knew that it wasn't Miss Red Ravisher, as her attorneys were suing him and Continental Broadcasting for misidentifying her as the thrower. He didn't think they would be seeking fifty million dollars in slander damages if there was any chance at all she had indeed been the thrower.

The third person to have come to the Old Ebbitt in the hope of encountering Mr. Danton was Miss Eleanor Dillworth, who at one time—before she had been, in her judgment, unfairly terminated by the CIA—had been the CIA station chief in Vienna, Austria.

Miss Dillworth planned to share with Mr. Danton—and through him with his millions of readers and viewers—some little jewels of CIA mistakes and blunders that, when Mr. Danton made them public, would make those miserable bastards in Langley really rue the day when they had messed with Miss Eleanor Dillworth.

Everything at first had gone smoothly. As they appreciatively imbibed their first two double Bloody Marys, Edgar and Two-Gun had rehearsed Roscoe over and over until they were satisfied he had his cockamamy story for President Clendennen down pat.

That accomplished, a celebratory third double Bloody Mary was certainly called for. Edgar had just taken his first sip when he was assaulted by Miss Dillworth.

One moment he was patting Roscoe on the shoulder, telling him not to worry, and the next he was on his back on the floor with a more than Rubenesque fiftyish blonde lady—Miss Dillworth—sitting on his chest, and choking him.

"At first I couldn't believe my eyes," she screamed. "But then I knew it was you, you sonofabitch!"

"And which sonofabitch, madam, is it that you mistakenly believe I am?" Edgar courteously inquired in sort of a whisper. Miss Dillworth's hands on his throat were surprisingly strong for someone of her years.

"The sonofabitch who garroted the Russian *rezident* in Vienna and left his pop-eyed corpse with my calling card on his chest in a taxicab outside the embassy, thus ruining my CIA career," she replied.

Edgar's own CIA training and experience produced a Pavlovian reaction to his predicament.

"Get Roscoe over to the White House, Two-Gun! Forget about me!" he cried nobly.

Before the lights went out, so to speak, Edgar saw Two-Gun hustling Roscoe out of the Old Ebbitt. And then he saw C. Harry Whelan following them. And then he saw Matthew "Hockey Puck" Christian following C. Harry.

And finally he saw the polished brass spittoon Miss Dillworth was directing toward his head with both her hands.

The next thing Edgar Delchamps saw was the ruddy face of a policeman looking down at him.

"You'll be all right, pal," the policeman said. "The ambulance is on the way. It took two bartenders and three cocktail waitresses to do it, but they finally pulled her off of you."

"Blessed are the lifesavers, for they shall inherit the earth," Edgar said.

"What did you say to the lady that so pissed her off?"

"I said nothing to her. I've never seen her before in my life."

"She says you're a CIA assassin who's left bodies all over the world, including one in a taxicab outside the U.S. embassy in Vienna."

"Poor thing," Edgar said. "She's obviously bereft of her senses. In my work as a shepherd of souls I have learned that often happens to ugly old women who have finally given up all hope of finding a mate with whom to walk down life's path."

"If you're not a CIA assassin, who are you? Got any identification?"

"My card, sir," Edgar said, taking one from his wallet. "As you can see, I am the Reverend Edgar Delchamps, religious director of the American Association of Motorized Wheelchair Manufacturers."

"Well, Reverend," the cop said, handing the card back, "just as soon as the ambulance gets here, we'll get you to the hospital. You can sign the charges there."

"You mean the Old Ebbitt is giving me a bill after I have been criminally assaulted by a crazy woman on their premises?"

"No. I mean you sign the charges against the crazy woman who thinks you're an assassin and did this to you."

"Heavens, no! To err is human, to forgive divine," Edgar said. "That poor crazy woman has enough problems without my adding to them. Just make sure she's given a thorough psychological examination before she's released."

"You're a kind man, Reverend."

"So I have been told. God bless you, my son."

[TWO]

The Presidential Apartments

The White House

1600 Pennsylvania Avenue, N.W.

Washington, D.C.

1320 21 June 2007

"I'm very sorry to interrupt you, the First Lady, and the First Mother-in-Law at lunch, Mr. President," Robin Hoboken said.

"What is it, Hoboken?"

"Mr. Danton is here."

"About damned time."

"He was just dropped off at the gate, Mr. President. Drunk."

"What do you mean, dropped off drunk?"

"Someone the Secret Service described as an individual with Asian characteristics dropped him—actually pushed him out of a Yukon—at the gate and then drove rapidly away. Drunk means intoxicated with alcoholic spirits to the point of impairment of physical and mental faculties."

"Plastered or not, I want to see him," the First Mother-in-Law said. "Bring him up, Hackensack."

"Mommy dearest, why do you want to see him if he's in his cups?" the First Lady asked.

"Because I want to hear what happened in Las Vegas."

"Mother Krauthammer," the President said, "I'm not sure that's a good idea."

"You wouldn't know a good idea if I hit you over the head with one," the First Mother-in-Law said. "Go get him, Hackensack."

"I personally hope Red Ravisher takes that miserable pervert to the cleaners," the First Mother-in-Law said, when Roscoe J. Danton had reported his version of what had transpired, "but I can't see how she hopes to collect if she did throw the Frenchman at you."

"What miserable pervert?" the President asked.

"Who said that just looking at your wife made him tinkle down his leg? Santa Claus? No, Ol' Hockey Puck Christian. *That* miserable pervert."

"Mommy dearest, what Mr. Christian said was that looking at me made him *tingle* down his leg. Not *tinkle*."

"What's the difference?" the First Mother-in-Law asked.

"To tingle," Robin Hoboken said, "is to feel a ringing, stinging, prickling, or thrilling sensation. Tinkle is what small children say when they have to urinate."

"Either way, it's perverted. But anyway it's moot."

"What's moot, Mother Krauthammer?" the President inquired.

"Whether that miserable pervert pisses down his leg when he sees Belinda-Sue here, or just prickles. As a Southern lady, I don't even want to think about Matthew Christian prickling. But I know perversion, whether it's tinkle, tingle, or prickle, when I hear it. But that's not your problem, Joshua. That's what's called moot."

"What is my problem, Mother Krauthammer? If I may ask."

"If it ever gets out what you're planning to have this Colonel Castillo of yours do to those poor illiterate teenagers with your Delta Force and your SEALs, you can rename this new library of yours."

"What do you mean rename it?"

"The President Joshua 'Child Murderer' Ezekiel and Mrs. Belinda-Sue Clendennen Presidential Library and Last Resting Place of the

Monster comes quickly to mind. 'Here Lies the Murderous Bastard' also comes to mind."

"I have no idea what you're talking about!" the President said.

"If I may hazard a guess, Mr. President," Robin Hoboken said, "I suspect that the First Mother-in-Law is alluding to Somalian teenagers."

"What about Somalian teenagers?"

"God, he doesn't know, does he?" Mother Krauthammer said.

"I don't know what?"

"Demographically speaking, Joshua," the First Mother-in-Law said, "your typical Somalian pirate is between fifteen and nineteen years of age, and a kindergarten dropout. In other words, he can't read or write."

"I can't believe that!"

"Believe it, Joshua. I got it from the Vienna *Tages Zeitung*."

"From the what?"

"It's a newspaper. I suppose if my name was O'Hara, I'd be reading the *Dublin Daily* to get the news I can't get here, but my late husband, Otto, may he rest in peace, was a Krauthammer and of Viennese ancestry, and he taught me to get it from the online edition of the Vienna *Tages Zeitung*."

"Hackensack, you know about this newspaper?"

"That's Hoboken, Mr. President," Robin replied. "Yes, sir. It's a daily, three hundred and sixty-five thousand circulation, four hundred and forty-five thousand on Sunday. It is a member of the Tages Zeitung chain, which is a wholly owned subsidiary of Gossinger Beteiligungsgesellschaft, G.m.b.H. It has a very good reputation."

"And this newspaper says the Somalian pirates are illiterate teenagers?"

"So they do," Mother Krauthammer said. "And they suggest that one of the reasons the piracy can't be stopped is that so far no one has been heartless enough to start shooting illiterate teenagers."

"My God, I'd be known as the Heartless Butcher of Somalia!" the President said. "Every Somalian-American in the country would vote for my opponent! I'd never get reelected! Is there nothing I can do?"

"One wild thought running through my mind," Mother Krauthammer offered, "is that you turn this Colonel Castillo of yours to other things."

"Hoboken—" the President began.

"Thank you, Mr. President," Robin interrupted.

"For what?"

"Getting my name right."

"Right. You're welcome. What I want you to do, Hackensack, is get DCI Lammelle on the phone."

"Yes, sir, Mr. President. May I ask why?"

"Because I told you to, you moron. By now you should understand that I'm the President and you're the flunky, and that means I give the orders and you obey them. Got it?"

"Yes, Mr. President."

"When you finally get around to obeying your orders and get Lammelle on the phone, I'm going to order him . . . which I can do because I'm the President and he's another flunky . . . to immediately get on his airplane and fly to Cozumel, where he will order Colonel Castillo to immediately cease and desist any outrageous plans he may have in mind to slaughter innocent and illiterate Somalian teenagers."

[THREE]
Penthouse A
The Royal Aztec Table Tennis and Golf Resort and Casino
Cozumel, Mexico
1030 21 June 2007

"Well, we seem to have been swept away on Cupid's wings, don't we, my dear Agrafina?" General Sergei Murov said as he reached for the bottle of Stolichnaya on the bedside table.

"Either on Cupid's wings, or on a wave of lust," she replied. "Stolichnaya tends to arouse that in me."

"In that regard, my darling, vis-à-vis lust, I have a confession to make."

"If you're about to confess it was the smell of the borscht, I would advise you not to."

"I won't deny the smell of the borscht had something to do with what happened just now . . ."

"Careful, my love!"

"What the smell of the borscht did was first make me think of my mother, may she rest in peace, and then of my first love. Her name was Svetlana."

"And this Svetlana smelled of borscht?"

"Sometimes. But what I was trying to say was that the smell of the borscht reminded me of my lost love, Svetlana. At that point, I lost control, moved the mirrored vanity onto my patio, climbed up on it, and looked over the glass barrier."

"Now that this has happened to us, I'm glad I missed with the bottle of Dos Equis I threw at you."

"And what I saw made my heart beat even faster. For a moment, I thought I was going to faint."

"When you peeped over the glass barrier, I was modestly clothed in my itsy-bitsy tiny polka-dot bikini. If seeing me in that almost made you faint, how come you didn't faint later after you ripped it off me?"

"What made me nearly faint was seeing you, seeing the remarkable resemblance you bear, my darling, to my lost love Svetlana."

"Really? I gather you saw this Svetlana dame when she was not wearing her whatever they call itsy-bitsy tiny polka-dot bikinis in Russia?"

"No. Our love was not only one-sided—she never really liked me—but pure. I never saw her less than fully clothed."

"And that's why you didn't marry this broad? She didn't like you and wouldn't take her clothes off?"

"I am sure that my beloved Svetlana never took her clothing off in the presence of any man—with the possible exception, of course, of her gynecologist—until she went to her marriage bed."

"What did the guy she married have that you didn't?"

"Evgeny Alekseev was an SVR *polkovnik*."

"A what?"

"A colonel in the SVR, which is sort of like your Department of Homeland Security."

"I know what the SVR is," Agrafina said. "So you're confessing that you're not really the coach of the Greater Sverdlovsk Table Tennis Association?"

"I was going to get to that, my precious," Murov said. "I want no secrets between us. I am General Sergei Murov of the SVR. At the time my beloved Svetlana married Evgeny Alekseev, I was a junior captain. He was a colonel, and she was a lieutenant colonel, so what chance did a lowly junior captain have?"

"Wait just a minute! I find this insulting, Sergei. You're telling me I bear a remarkable resemblance to some short-haired two-hundred-and-fifty-pound female with stainless steel teeth?"

"I'm saying you bear a remarkable resemblance to an astonishingly beautiful female."

"I thought you said she was an SVR lieutenant colonel?"

"She is. Or was when she married Evgeny. Oh, I see where you're coming from. Let us say that my beloved Svetlana is the rare exception to that rule vis-à-vis female SVR lieutenant colonels."

"Well, if you put it that way, Sergei, darling. So, what happened to her after she married Colonel Whatsisname?"

"The marriage didn't last long, and then she defected. Evgeny chased her to Argentina, where he got himself whacked by some Irish cop."

"So she's a widow?"

"Yes, she is. The Widow Alekseeva. That's what I'm really doing here, my love. I'm supposed to get my darling Svetlana, her brother, former SVR Polkovnik Dmitri Berezovsky, and this goddamned American, Colonel C. G. Castillo, onto an airplane and fly them to Moscow."

"I have to tell you, my darling, that I'm tempted to break both your legs for profanely referring to an American officer like that, but my female curiosity seems to have overwhelmed me. Why do you want to take these people to Moscow?"

"Well, I think Vladimir Vladimirovich Putin wants to start by turning them into ice statues."

"You want to help Putin turn them into ice statues? How's he going to do that?"

General Murov explained the process to her.

"I'm shocked," Agrafina said, "as I got the distinct impression you still have feelings about this lady."

"Yes, my love, I do. Not as much, of course, as I did before you came into my life, my precious. But I will love her to my dying day—or hers, whichever comes first—and the thought of turning her into an ice statue, immediately before—or immediately after, whichever comes first—she marries is giving me a good deal of personal pain."

"Who is she going to marry?"

"The godd— the American gentleman."

"At the Grand Cozumel Beach and Golf Resort, down the beach?"

"Yes. But how could you possibly know that?"

"They told me when I was there earlier."

She handed him the liter bottle of Stolichnaya.

"Tell me, Sergei, are we to be just two ships that passed in the night, or would you like to see how this relationship develops?"

"I realized about an hour or so ago, my precious, that I want to spend the rest of my life with you."

"Well, there are several problems that I can see with that. Starting with I have my career to think of."

"I can understand that."

"Which means I cannot move to Russia."

"I can understand that, too."

"When you said you want to spend the rest of your life with me, did you mean it? Was that a proposal of marriage, or did you mean you would like to continue to take sexual advantage of my naiveté and innocence?"

General Murov got off the bed and onto his knees.

"My darling Agrafina Bogdanovich, will you do me the great honor of becoming my bride?"

"Before I answer that, darling Sergei, I have a little confession of my own to make."

"Which is?"

"My latest film, *Catherine and the Household Cavalry*, to which I referred is not actually a documentary."

"I know, I know. I've watched it a hundred times. Another reason, my precious, that my heart was beating so wildly when I first saw you in the flesh."

Thirty minutes later:

"Well, that's the end of the Stolichnaya, my darling, and almost the end of me," General Murov said somewhat breathlessly. "What should we do now?"

"Actually, I've been giving that some serious thought, my precious."

"What occurred to me was getting into the Jacuzzi—they say that restores vigor—and then ordering up another bottle of the Stolichnaya and a couple dozen oysters. How does that sound?"

"I was thinking of our future. Since you agree that your only option is to defect and become—once you're finished with the CIA debriefing—chairman of the board of Red Ravisher Films, Inc."

"I look forward to that. I've always had a secret yearning to be a capitalist."

"And you told me, right, that to defect and not find yourself playing soccer with a bunch of crazy Arabs in Guantánamo, you'll have to defect through the director of the CIA, A. Franklin Lampoon."

"That's *Lammelle*, my darling, A. Franklin *Lammelle*. Frank and I, professional differences aside, of course, always got along very well."

"And you said that getting in touch with him might be difficult—"

"What I said, my precious, is that if I just called the CIA in Langley and asked to speak with him, they would ask who was calling, and if I replied I was General Sergei Murov of the SVR, they would laugh hysterically and hang up on me."

"I think I see a way around that, my darling. You also said that Mr. Lammelle and the officer who is about to marry your beloved Svetlana are friends."

"They're as tight as ticks," Murov said.

"I've always wondered what that means. It brings to my mind an image of intoxicated insects."

"Well, that's what people are always saying."

"What I think we should do, my darling, striking while the iron is hot, so to speak, is go over to the Grand Cozumel and speak with Colonel Costello—"

"That's Castillo, my precious."

"And ask him to get Mr. Lammelle on the line for you."

"Darling, I don't know—"

"Going to the Grand Cozumel, my darling, would also give you the opportunity to not only see your beloved Svetlana but to offer her your best wishes on her upcoming nuptials."

"My precious, I don't think—"

"Not closing the door on your relationship with your beloved Svetlana would be a deal breaker, my darling, on our own upcoming nuptials."

"Well, viewed from that perspective, the idea of going over to the Grand Cozumel does have great appeal."

"Well then, my precious, put your trousers on. The last time I saw them they were hanging from the chandelier."

"There's something I didn't tell you about Colonel Castillo, my precious."

"Which is?"

"There are twenty-four members of the Cuban DGI—the Cuban version of the SVR—here in Cozumel under orders to whack Castillo."

"And these people are likely to be at the Grand Cozumel? Is that what you're saying?"

"At the moment, they're engaged in cleaning the ladies' rooms on the *Czarina of the Gulf*, the cruise ship. But they should be about finished, and when they are, they'll go looking for Castillo."

"We'll cross that bridge when we come to it, my darling. Now go put your pants on while I repair my makeup."

"You're going with me to the Grand Cozumel?"

"I want to be there, my precious, when you finally close the door on your Svetlana. To be sure there's no mistake, no misunderstanding."

[FOUR]
The Grand Lobby and Reception Hall
The Grand Cozumel Beach & Golf Resort
Cozumel, Mexico
2110 21 June 2007

Hiding behind two of the larger potted palms in the lobby when the Archbishop Valentin and the Archimandrite Boris made their spectacular—one might even say regal—entrance were Mr. C. Harry Whelan and Mr. Matthew "Hockey Puck" Christian.

They had been traveling together since they had met at the White House gate earlier in the day, immediately after Mr. Roscoe J. Danton had been pushed out of the Yukon in which he had traveled from the Old Ebbitt to meet with President Clendennen.

Although they normally loathed one another, the situation here dictated a truce between them. C. Harry was determined to find out, and damn the cost of finding out, what Roscoe was doing with the President and the reason behind the porn queen throwing the French paparazzo at Danton in Las Vegas.

Mr. Christian had been told by his superiors at the Continental Broadcasting Corporation that unless he got them out from under the fifty-million-dollar libel suit brought by Miss Red Ravisher for mis-identifying Miss Ravisher as the person who had thrown the French paparazzo at Mr. Danton, he could not only expect to lose the *Hockey Puck* show, but would work out the balance of his contract doing the midnight weather broadcast over the Continental station in Dry River, North Dakota, where he would have to write his own copy, do without the company-furnished chauffeur-driven Mercedes he had grown used to, and learn to live without an expense account.

C. Harry and Hockey Puck quickly agreed to share whatever information they acquired from their highly placed confidential sources within the White House, no matter how many folded hundred-dollar bills they would have to pass out to these people.

Their plan succeeded. A third assistant botanical superintendent, who was bitter at his low pay of only $96,500 per annum, and happy to get the tax-free C-note, informed C. Harry that while he had been rearranging the white roses on the dining room table in the Very, Very Important Person guest room, he had accidentally happened to overhear the President's conversation with DCI Lammelle.

He reported that the President had ordered DCI Lammelle to immediately get his ass out to Andrews and get his airplane warmed up. As soon as he could get Roscoe J. Danton sobered up and out there they were to get their asses on the DCI's airplane and fly to the Grand Cozumel Beach and Golf Resort in Cozumel, Mexico, where they were to make it perfectly clear to Colonel Castillo that the Clendennen administration was not in the business of slaughtering innocent and illiterate Somali teenagers and that he was to immediately cease and desist carrying out any nefarious and criminal plans he had made to do so.

On hearing this, C. Harry told Hockey Puck that he had a line on a Learjet at Baltimore International and was going to fly to Cozumel. He asked Hockey Puck if he wanted to share the ride and the cost.

"Absolutely," Hockey Puck had immediately replied. "Just make sure you get two original copies of the bill, so that we can both get our respective employers to reimburse us."

When they got to the Cozumel Beach & Golf Resort, they were told there were no rooms at the inn, unfortunately, as all accommodations were reserved for the upcoming nuptials of the owner's cousin.

At first this was disappointing, but then they saw a silver lining in the black cloud. For one thing, they were going to have to hang around the lobby anyway as the only thing they could see in their rooms was Mexican television, and for another, another folded C-note got them spurious bills for deluxe suites so they might be later reimbursed by their respective employers.

They took up positions behind potted palms.

The first thing they saw was truly shocking. Both deeply regretted not having charged their cell phones in order to have cameras to record it.

DCI Lammelle came into the lobby, followed by two burly CIA operatives supporting Roscoe J. Danton between them.

Then Lieutenant Colonel C. G. Castillo appeared, accompanied by a spectacular redheaded female.

There was an excited conversation between the two men. Seated as far away as they were behind the potted palms, they could only hear parts of the conversation. But they did hear that the President was ordering Castillo to immediately cancel any plans he had with Somalian teenagers, including slaughtering them.

Castillo then asked, "And he has no other nutty orders for me?"

"Just that you are to fall off the edge of the earth again, and never be seen by anyone."

Castillo had then grabbed DCI Lammelle and kissed him wetly on both cheeks. And then the spectacular redhead had grabbed Lammelle and kissed him. Wetly. On the mouth.

"I love you, Frank," she cried. "I don't care what everyone says about you!"

Both men, fully aware of the news value of films of CIA directors being kissed by females to whom they were not married, not to mention their being bussed by men, groaned with the regret that this kissing session was lost to posterity.

They had then disappeared, only to appear fifteen minutes later with large numbers of other people dressed to the nines.

It was at this point that the Archbishop Valentin and the Archimandrite Boris marched into the lobby attired in their finest vestments.

A man whom neither Hockey Puck nor C. Harry recognized—Aleksandr Pevsner—then advanced on the clergymen, dropped to his knees, and kissed their rings.

Then Castillo and the spectacular redhead did the same.

"That redhead looks somehow familiar," Hockey Puck whispered to C. Harry.

"What the hell are you doing here?" A. Franklin Lammelle demanded to know.

"We're here to unite Carlos and Svetlana in holy matrimony," Archbishop Valentin said.

"Not you, Your Grace," Lammelle said. "Him."

He pointed to General Sergei Murov, who, with Agrafina Bogdanovich, had just come through the revolving door into the lobby.

"Actually, Frank, old buddy, this is a delightful surprise. I want to defect."

"My God, there's two of them!" Hockey Puck cried loudly, as he came out from behind his potted palm to demand, "Which one of you redheads threw the Frenchman at Roscoe J. Danton and ruined my television career?"

"I don't know who that is," Aleksandr Pevsner ordered. "But grab him."

Two burly ex-Spetsnaz instantly complied. And then two more went after C. Harry Whelan.

"I know who that ugly man is, Sergei, my precious," Agrafina said. "He's the pervert who made all those awful allegations about me!"

"I hate to say this with these distinguished Russian Orthodox clergymen standing here," Murov said, "but you're a dead man, sir. No one insults the woman General Sergei Murov loves. Not and lives."

"As a distinguished Russian Orthodox clergyman, my son, I must forbid you from killing anyone."

"Excuse me, miss," Svetlana said. "Did Sergei say he loves you?"

"That's what he says, Svetlana," Agrafina said.

"Your Grace," Murov asked, "if you say I can't, I won't kill the pervert. But how does Your Grace feel about me sending him to Moscow and turning him into an ice sculpture?"

"I have a confession to make," Svetlana said. "It was I who threw the French pervert into the paparazzi. I wasn't aiming at Roscoe; he was just collateral damage. And this lady was in no way involved."

"Why, my daughter, would you do something like that?" the archbishop asked.

"Can I whisper why in your ear?"

"Of course."

She did so.

"I understand your anger, my daughter," the archbishop said. "But that doesn't excuse the violence."

"I guess that means I can't turn the pervert into an ice sculpture, either," Murov said.

"No, you can't," the archbishop said.

"Your Grace," Agrafina said, "I confess that I am a FAMOTORC—"

"What the hell is that?" Castillo asked.

"Fallen Away Member of the Orthodox Russian Church," Sweaty

said. "Now shut up, my beloved heathen, while we Christians deal with this."

"But I seem to recall, Your Grace, that bearing false witness is a sin," Agrafina went on.

"Yes, my daughter, it is."

"Well, that sonofabitch certainly bore—beared?—false witness against me. I just have to swallow that?"

"What would you suggest, my daughter? Since I'm not going to permit you, no matter how far you've fallen from Holy Mother Church, to either kill him or turn him into an ice sculpture."

"I have a suggestion," Aleksandr Pevsner said. "First thing in the morning, I'll take him out on the *Czarina of the Gulf* and put him with the Cubans."

"What Cubans are those, my son?" the archbishop asked.

"The ones the Cuban DGI doesn't know that I know they sneaked onto my ship."

"I don't understand, my son," the archbishop said.

"What I plan to do, Your Grace," Pevsner said, "when we're five or ten miles offshore, and they have finished restoring the ladies' restrooms to a suitably pristine condition, is gather the Cubans on the fantail, tell them I know who they are, and ask them how well they can swim."

"That's okay with me insofar as ol' Hockey Puck is concerned," Agrafina said. "But it seems a little tough on the Cubans."

"Not to worry, my daughter," the archbishop said, "I am not going to permit my son Aleksandr to drown twenty-four Cubans."

"What if I put them in lifeboats, give them plenty of Aqua Mexicana to drink, and make them row back here?"

The archbishop considered that thoughtfully for a moment, and then said, "That'd work for me."

"Thank you, Your Grace," Pevsner said. "Take both those clowns down to the *Czarina of the Gulf*."

"You're an evil man, Aleksandr Pevsner," Charley Castillo said.

"Thank you. I like to think so," Pevsner replied.

AFTERWORD

For those who may be wondering why this story sounds like *M*A*S*H*, an explanation:

Years ago, when I was writing the dozen sequels to *M*A*S*H* by "Richard Hooker"—the pen name for the distinguished surgeon H. Richard Hornberger, M.D., F.A.C.S.—I got to know Dick well enough to ask why he wrote the original book.

In essence, he said that humor can wash out bad memories. And that he wasn't trying to remember our time in Korea—he was trying to forget it.

I had just begun this book when my son and I went to the annual OSS Society dinner at which former CIA director Robert Gates—whom I regard as a great patriot—was given the William J. Donovan Award.

Also at the banquet were a number of old pals who I also regard as great patriots. Some of them were general officers and some were the spook business equivalent of junior officers and PFCs.

And also at the banquet was a former general officer and soon-to-be former DCI, who attended with his girlfriend, a fellow alumnus of West Point.

So much for Duty, Honor and Country, I thought. Not to mention how not to keep a sweetie on the side a secret.

I suddenly understood why I was having a hard time writing this book about current spooks and Commanders in Chief and DCIs. And, conversely, why I was having such a good time writing "Death of Innocence," a story about another era—one of magnificent OSS directors, DCIs, spooks, and a superb Commander in Chief named Harry S Truman.

So I figured that if *Hazardous Duty* were written as a sort of *M*A*S*H Goes to the White House and Langley*, maybe readers could appreciate it for that—maybe even get a chuckle, helping them to forget for a minute or so the mess we have in Washington, D.C.

W.E.B. Griffin